Hi everyone!

Just a note to say **THANKS SO MUCH** for choosing to read *Summer Daydreams*. There are so many demands on your hard-earned cash these days, that I really appreciate it. I hope that you're managing to take a break from the daily grind this summer to kick back with family and friends.

I love it when readers write to me and tell me where they're taking me on holiday! I have been halfway round the world and back in someone's luggage or backpack. Even better, sometimes readers send me photographs of my books up the top of mountains or on cruise ships or even on sunloungers by the pool. It's lovely to know that you're sharing that time with me.

Whether you take me somewhere exotic or whether you're in the back garden with me, I really hope that you can just take some time to sit back in the sunshine, relax, have a lovely read with maybe a glass of something chilled and recharge your batteries.

Wishing everyone a lovely summer!

Love Carole ☺ xx

P.S. Wear sunscreen!

Carole Matthews

Summer Daydreams

sphere

SPHERE

First published in Great Britain in 2012 by Sphere
This paperback edition published in 2012 by Sphere
Reprinted 2012

A CIP catalogue record for this book
is available from the British Library.

ISBN 978-0-7515-4543-2

Typeset in Sabon by M Rules
Printed and bound in Great Britain by
Clays Ltd, St Ives plc

Papers used by Sphere are from well-managed forests
and other responsible sources.

 MIX
Paper from
responsible sources
FSC
www.fsc.org FSC® C104740

Sphere
An imprint of
Little, Brown Book Group
100 Victoria Embankment
London EC4Y 0DY

An Hachette UK Company
www.hachette.co.uk

www.littlebrown.co.uk

To my dear friend and long-time hairdresser, Sue,
who has gone far, far too soon.
You'll be missed more than words can say, lovely lady.

Susan Margaret MacGregor Perry
27 March 1955 – 20 July 2011

Chapter 1

'Two cod and chips?' I look up from the counter.

'Yes please, love.' The man gives me a welcome smile.

It's lunchtime, Friday, and we should be busier than this. Much busier. There's been a steady trickle, but the usual queue at Live and Let Fry has been noticeably missing for some weeks now, maybe even months. I dish out the chips, golden and hot, and top them with two cod, freshly cooked, with crisp batter sizzling.

'Salt? Vinegar?'

'Just as they are,' the customer says. He's licking his lips already. It's certainly not Phil's fish and chips that are putting off the customers.

Wrapping them in white paper, I hand over his package and with a spring in his step, the customer leaves.

Phil Preston, my boss and fish-fryer extraordinaire, looks at his watch. 'How many have been in today, Nell?'

'Not many.' I give a sympathetic grimace. A handful at best.

'The cold weather normally brings in people in droves.' Phil rubs his hands together even though it's as warm as always in here.

As well as the takeaway counter, we also have a small eat-in café too, which is normally very popular. Today, there are just two people enjoying their lunch. Jenny, my co-worker, who is the waitress today, has spent most of her time flicking through *Heat* magazine.

'I could stand outside and waft some chips about,' Jenny offers helpfully as she drags her attention away from the latest celebrity dramas.

'It's going to take a bit more than that.' Phil shakes his head. 'We can't keep blaming everything on the credit crunch.'

'What about up-selling?' Jen continues. 'Like they do in coffee shops. Do you want a pie with that? Mushy peas? Pickled egg? Gherkin?'

We all laugh.

'You have that down to a fine art, Jen,' I tell her.

'I'm going to try it tonight,' she insists. 'You watch me.'

Pinching a chip from the warmer, I nibble it absently. I've worked at the chippy now for well over a year. I do shifts at lunchtime – twelve until two – and then I'm back again in the evening – six through to ten. It means that my boyfriend, Olly, and I can share childcare for our daughter, Petal. I'm not saying it's easy – we could probably both get jobs in the circus with the amount of juggling we have to do to get through the week – but needs must. We're not alone in having to keep a lot of plates in the air these days. Everyone has to do it. Right? Petal's just four years old and as much as I don't want to wish her life away, I can't wait for her to start school. I'm hoping that once she does, life won't be quite as frantic as it is now.

'What am I going to do?' Phil asks, running his hand through his hair. 'This is getting dire.'

The unspoken thought is that if it goes on like this then he won't need to keep on so many staff. It's probably only because Jenny, our other colleague, Constance, and I have been here for so long and the fact that we all get on so well that Phil hasn't let one or more of us go before now. It's a worrying time.

I look round at the café. The tables are glossy orange pine, the walls are painted peach and there's a flowery border at waist-height that's curling up in more places than it's stuck to the wall. 'It does look a bit tired in here, Phil,' I venture. 'If you don't mind me saying.'

'You think so?'

'You're a bloke,' I remind him. 'You never notice these things.'

'It is a bit of an eighties throwback look,' Jenny adds.

'Really?' Phil looks round as if he's seeing the café with new eyes. 'I'm useless with a paintbrush. I could get a decorator in to give us a quote if you think it needs a spruce up.'

'They call it a makeover these days, Phil. It probably wouldn't hurt,' I say. It's fair to say that it's been a long time since Phil spent any money on the interior of this place.

Phil tuts. 'What do reckon it would cost? Cash is the one thing I haven't got to splash about.'

'Give me some money,' I say before my brain has fully engaged. 'I'll do it for you.'

Phil laughs.

'You said yourself that you can't afford to bring in the pros. I could do it a lot cheaper. We can all muck in to help. After all, it's our jobs that are on the line if this place sinks.'

'Yes, but—'

'I'm a great decorator,' I protest before he lays out his objections. 'You've been to my house.'

'I know. It's ... what's the word?'

'Unique,' I supply, 'and fun. And all my own work.' My living room has pink candy-stripe wallpaper with matching spotty chairs. I sanded and stained the floorboards myself and whizzed up some cushions that look like big cupcakes. 'We could do something like that here. Jazz the place up.'

Phil brightens. 'You think so?'

I shrug. 'Why not? I'll make a mood board tonight.'

'Mood board?' Jenny and Phil exchange a puzzled look.

'I can start tomorrow after we close up.'

Now Phil looks surprised – and not a little terrified. 'Tomorrow?'

'No time like the present.'

'I'm not doing anything tomorrow night – more's the pity,' Jenny offers.

She is currently man-free – a fairly rare occurrence. My friend is a curvy brunette with ample comely charms and, as such, is a big hit with the gentlemen. Though cads and bounders feature heavily on the menu and none of them ever stay around for long.

'I'm not exactly a dab hand with a paintbrush,' she admits, 'but I can do labouring and make tea.'

'Sounds good to me,' I say.

We both look at Phil expectantly.

'I'm not doing anything either,' he confesses with a shrug.

Phil is in his early sixties, I would think, and his wife left him about five years ago for a younger man who's been giving her the runaround ever since. He doesn't get out much unless we drag him to the pub or for a pizza. Live and Let Fry is pretty much his life. But he looks good for his age. Dapper, you could say. He's a bit portly due to his largely chip-based diet, and we all tease him about his hair being a bit thin on top. But bald isn't a bad thing now, is it? Jenny is always trying to fix him up with sundry women, but he doesn't seem very interested. I think secretly he's probably worried that he'd end up with someone just like Jenny. And she's way too much woman for him to handle.

Phil purses his lips in thought. 'How much do you think it would cost?'

'No idea.' I normally have to beg, steal or borrow paint if the decorating urge comes upon me, so I'm somewhat out of touch with B&Q's current price list. Most of our house is painted with leftover half-tins purloined from my parents' garage and all mixed together. I'm thinking that Phil might want a slightly more upmarket approach than this. 'But say you stump up three hundred pounds and see what we can get with that?' I know that paint's expensive now – what isn't? – but the café is only small. 'If we start on Saturday night, we could work all day Sunday and be open for business again on Monday.'

Phil looks a bit teary. 'Did anyone ever tell you that you're a little treasure, Nell McNamara?'

'All the time,' I say, lightly batting the compliment away before Phil gets into full blub-mode and starts me off too.

'You lot might get on my nerves most of the time,' he jokes, 'but you're all like family to me. I don't know what I'd do without you.'

'If we don't get some more customers through the doors you might well be finding out,' I remind him. And I, for one, need this job. So if it means spending my precious weekend slapping a bit of paint on, then that works for me.

Chapter 2

As always when we shut up the chippy, I take great pleasure in liberating my long blonde bob from beneath my utilitarian cap, and then I always steal ten minutes for myself and walk a circuitous route home, passing my favourite shop. Today, the crackle of autumn is in the air and I enjoy being outside, breathing in the scent of coffee that drifts from a dozen different cafés that I pass.

We live in the small market town of Hitchin, in the heart of the beautiful county of Hertfordshire. It's a nice enough place to live, though I'm sure some of its charms have been lost on me after living here for so many years. You take things like that for granted, don't you? I think if you came here as a visitor you'd love it, but for me, well, it's just where I live. You don't really stop to look around and think how fab it is.

My love, Olly Meyers, and I were both born and brought up here and sometimes I think we should move somewhere more obviously cool, more creative, like Brighton or ... well, wherever else is more happening. Petal would like it by the sea too. Though this place isn't exactly a cultural desert when it comes to style. There are some trendy independent boutiques selling weird, wacky and wonderful stuff which I love. Olly and I are both mad keen fans of the sixties – music, films, clothes – and one thing I can say about Hitchin is that we're well served here when it comes to our passion.

There's a great market that has been here since time began. I get a lot of clothes cheaply from the vintage stall that's always there, and the rest I run up on my trusty sewing machine. There are also a couple of fantastic haberdashery stalls that are brilliant for picking up cheap ribbons, buttons and the like. Olly's favourite pit stop is the second-hand record stall and we have a mountain of vinyl in our spare room. There's a scooter shop run by one of Olly's mates – my dearly beloved's other obsession – and a couple of great retro lifestyle shops that keep us supplied with cheap furnishings.

The chippy is located in one of the small shopping arcades that radiate off from the Market Place. It might be Victorian – I have no idea – but it's decorated with pretty ironwork and has an arched glass roof. Marvellous for pigeons to settle in, but it's quaint and full of character. The place isn't without its fair share of the unsightly 1960s carbuncles that most English towns now harbour, but there's actually a lot of the centre that's managed to survive untrammelled by council insanity.

I wander away from the Market Place, turning from the rash of chain stores and down through the old part of town where the shops are in small alleys, still packed tightly together in quaint, timbered buildings, all higgledy-piggledy. This is where my favourite shop is tucked away. Betty the Bag

Lady is an oasis for me. When people are stressed they might go to yoga classes or take a swim or down a good glass of Pinot Grigio. Me, I head for Betty the Bag Lady.

The Betty in question isn't an ageing lady with a blue rinse as her name might suggest. This Betty is young and trendy. She's even smaller than me and I'm not exactly an Amazonian woman. My mum bought me a school blazer with 'room to grow' when I was eleven and it was still way too big for me when I hit sixteen. My mother was clearly overly optimistic about the size I would eventually attain. Betty has her immaculately straightened hair dyed white, whereas mine is a golden blonde and is often tied up so someone doesn't enjoy a portion of it with their chips. Betty is probably about twenty-five, I'm fast approaching thirty: it's fair to say that I'm hideously jealous of her. Fancy having your own shop! Oh, I'd think I'd died and gone to heaven.

Clearly Betty paid attention at school and did her homework and went on to do 'good things'. I stared out of the window and daydreamed and wondered how much better our uniform would have been if it wasn't fashioned from nylon and had been in luscious shades of pink instead of bottle-green. I lost my homework on the way home, hung round with boys in the park and, so, never amounted to much. I wanted to learn – I really did – I just didn't want to learn about Pythagoras's Theorem or Ox-bow lakes or the Tolpuddle Martyrs. I wanted to learn about 'interesting' things, even though I had no clue what they might be. I just know that I felt like a very square peg in a very round hole. So I left school at sixteen, ignoring my parents' despairing pleas and cries of 'university!', and drifted. I worked in Tesco and a shoe shop and a dozen other dead-end jobs before I rocked up at Live and Let Fry. Some days I wish I'd tried harder. Some days I love my work. Let's face it, how many jobs come with free chips?

Betty also runs with the London crowd, whereas I met Olly and settled down. She 'knows' people in the 'know'. I know no one. If I get another turn at life, I think I'd like to come back as Betty.

This afternoon, Betty the Bag Lady is open for business. The shop has been here for about a year and in my humble opinion, it's a welcome addition to the Hitchin shopping experience. At night, when I've finished my shift and the shop is closed, I actually press my nose against the window and dream of things that might have been.

Betty's handbags are not mere bags but are veritable works of art and, as such, are completely beyond my price range. I might be a regular visitor here but I'm not a very good customer. I'm purely a window-shopper, but Betty doesn't seem to mind too much. I come in to coo and purr at the bags, but I always have to put them back on the shelf.

'Hi, Nell,' Betty says as I push through the door. 'All right?'

'Fine.' The shop is a calm oasis. If I could ever have my own shop one day, this is the atmosphere I'd like to create. It's done out like someone's living room and I can feel myself unwind as soon as I'm over the threshold. The only thing that I'm conscious of is that until I've been in the shower, I bring with me the lingering odour of cod and chips. 'What's new?'

'Get a load of these,' she moons as she strokes a bag I've

not seen before. 'New in today. Bought them from a designer up in Manchester.'

The bags are all handmade in felt, vintage-style, and smothered in buttons of all different shapes, sizes and colours. They are luscious and I'm instantly in love. I pick up an oversized one in differing, shimmering rainbow tones – red, yellow, green, blue, orange, purple – and hook it over my arm. It's mesmerising. And it fits me perfectly.

Ever since I was a child, I've loved handbags. My earliest memory is taking my mother's out of her cupboard and parading round the house with each of them in turn. Looks like I inherited the handbag-fiend gene from her. I am hoping to pass it on to my own daughter, too.

My mum's responsible for my interest in fashion – compared to my friends' parents, mine were a tiny bit bohemian and fun. Every Saturday when I was growing up, we'd go into town and look at what was new in the shops. Even if we couldn't buy anything, we'd spend hours trying stuff on. She often made my clothes for me so I didn't look like all the other kids and she taught me how to sew and knit, do patchwork and crochet. We'd spend hours together painting in our old, lean-to conservatory – something I'd like to do with Petal if she didn't have the patience of Attila the Hun. It's a shame that I hardly see my mum now that I'm older and she's moved away. Retirement to a small town in Norfolk was something that I hadn't seen on the cards for her, but she loves it.

My own extensive collection of handbags is in a wardrobe in our spare room, which drives Olly mad as he'd like to take over the entire space for his precious collection of vinyl records. Sometimes I take all the bags out just to look at them. Occasionally I let Petal play with them, just as my mum did with me. Men just don't get the whole handbag thing, do they? Though they come in surprisingly useful when they want us to carry all their stuff in them. Right? All my handbags are in their own dust bags, each one with happy memories attached. A woman can never have too many handbags.

'I love it,' I breathe, admiring myself this way and that in the full-length mirror.

'Suits you,' Betty agrees.

'I can't even bring myself to ask how much.'

'A hundred,' she says. Then, at my sharp intake of breath, 'I could do you a discount. As a regular.'

I don't point out that I'm a regular who buys nothing.

'Even with a discount, I can't consider it,' I say reluctantly. Even though it's much cheaper than many of her bags, Betty might as well have asked me for a million quid. 'Olly would kill me.' In a particularly painful manner.

My handbag-buying has been severely curtailed in recent years. Frankly, I can't even think of the last time I bought one. But I can all too easily bring to mind the mountain of bills sitting on our sideboard: gas, electricity, council tax. The rent is due and as always, Petal needs more shoes. The very last thing on earth that I can afford to splash money on is a fancy handbag.

'Want me to put it to one side for you?' Betty cajoles. 'I could keep it for a couple of weeks if you put a small deposit on it. A tenner would do it.'

I can feel myself weakening. In my purse is a tenner. My last one. In my wardrobe there is the perfect outfit to go with this bag. If there's a greater temptation than the perfect handbag, then I certainly can't think of it. Running my fingers over the buttons, I chew at my lip. Surely my child wouldn't mind wearing scuffed shoes for a while longer for the greater good?

Then I come to my senses. 'I can't, Betty. Much as I'd love to.' Taking the handbag off my shoulder, I reluctantly hand it back to her.

'Another time,' she says.

'Yeah.' I leave the shop, crestfallen. Another time. Another life.

Chapter 3

When I finally get home, Olly is playing tea party with Petal. They're both sitting on the lounge floor, picnic rug spread out, surrounded by dolls. Petal is pouring pretend tea out of an orange plastic teapot and Olly is humouring her by eating a Jammie Dodger in the style of the Queen from a child-size plate. Even our dog, Dude – the least walked dog on the planet – is in tea party mood, with a checked napkin tied round his neck. He is looking longingly at the biscuits.

'Daddy, share your biscuit with Dude,' Petal instructs as I come through the door.

Olly does as he is told and Dude whines with relief. He's very fond of food, our dog, and treats every meal as his last after having been dumped at a rescue centre, half-starved. The kennel girl described him to us as 'the most minging dog she'd ever seen'. Of course, that made us fall in love with him instantly. He's a black something or other with a white patch on his chest and a face that looks like it has seen the hard side of life. Happily, those sad days are behind him and apart from in the walkies department, he lives a life of comfort, ease, regular meals and occasional Jammie Dodgers.

'Hey,' I say. 'The worker returns.'

'I was just about to call,' Olly says when he sees me. 'Thought you'd got lost, hun.'

'Needed a bit of therapy,' I tell him.

'Ah, Betty's handbag emporium.'

I throw myself onto a beanbag. 'Yes.' Said with a yearning sigh.

'Petal and I had pasta and pesto for lunch,' he tells me. 'I've left a bowl for you to put in the microwave later.'

'Daddy's cooking is nicer than yours,' Petal tells me.

That is because everything I give her to eat comes out of a packet. 'That's why I'm very kind and let Daddy do it so much.'

'Thanks,' Olly says. 'You're all heart.' We both laugh and, although we've been together now for over ten years, I never tire of the sound of it. 'I'm just going to finish this *delicious* Jammie Dodger that Petal has prepared for me and then I've got to see a man about a disco.'

'Don't forget I'm back on at six.'

'Eat a biscuit, Mummy.' Petal presses one on me. 'They're good for you.'

I do hope she hasn't gleaned this slightly flawed nutritional titbit from me.

'I won't,' Olly says. 'I'll be back in time. There might be a new residency at a punk bar that's opening.'

'In Hitchin?'

'Don't knock it. We're a very diverse community.'

'Isn't it a little bit late for punk?'

'I'm told there's a resurgence.' Olly shrugs his bewilderment at the ways of the world. But then, to be fair, we do still have an unhealthy attachment to all things sixties. I guess some people have never been able to throw away their dog collars and bondage trousers.

'Do you actually know anything about punk music?' I take in Olly's crisp white button-down shirt and cords.

'Sex Pistols. Clash. Buzzcocks. Er . . .'

'Bob the Builder,' Petal chimes in.

'Bob the Builder,' Olly agrees. 'That well-known pogoer.'

'What's a pogoer, Daddy?'

'It's someone who jumps up and down a lot.'

So, of course, my daughter has to try it. As does the dog.

'I'm outta here,' Olly says.

'Sure,' I say. 'Thanks for leaving me with an overexcited child and dog. Go and knock them dead with your extensive knowledge of punk.'

'We need the money, Nell. If that means I have to become a latter-day expert on punk rock, then so be it.'

'I know. I'm only teasing.' I lean over and kiss Olly. 'You're wonderful. Are you on shift tonight?'

'Yeah. I'll be ready to leave as soon as you get home.'

And that sums up our life really. Ships that pass in the night, handing over our child as we do. I know that money isn't everything, but life is certainly a lot harder if you don't have any.

Olly works the night shift in a pizza factory, which fits in with him looking after Petal and shoehorns round my shifts too, though it means his sleep is generally random and insufficient. It pays the bills but it's not exactly living the life. Like my job, it does come with free food. There is, however, only so much pizza one can eat in a lifetime.

Olly picks up Petal – which does momentarily stop her from bouncing, although Dude does it more to compensate – and squeezes her. 'Be good for Mummy.'

She looks at him as if that's never in any doubt.

'Come and give me a cuddle,' I say, and my wriggly daughter joins me on the beanbag. As does the dog.

Petal's hair smells of strawberry shampoo – Olly must have washed it for her today – and I kiss it softly. My baby looks just like her dad. Dark unruly hair, chocolate brown eyes, rugby player's legs. 'Do you know that you're the best little girl in the whole wide world?'

'Yes,' Petal says. 'Can I have another Jammie Dodger?'

Might as well try to push it while you're in favour, I think.

'Yes. Then you can help Mummy to do a mood board. She's going to decorate Uncle Phil's chip shop.' I remember that I've completely forgotten to mention this to Olly or the fact that he will, as a result, be in charge of childcare for the whole weekend. I hope he's not arranged extra work as he quite often does.

'Pink,' Petal suggests. 'Do the chip shop pink.'

And do you know, I might well do.

Chapter 4

I'm never happier than when I'm doing stuff like this. The living room floor is covered with scraps of fabric, trimmings, beads and buttons that I've collected over the years from goodness knows where.

'Cut out this one for me please,' I say to my small assistant.

Petal has her tiny pink tongue out in concentration and is snipping pictures from my collection of old, battered magazines with her plastic, kiddy scissors and meticulous care. I'm sticking and pasting like a thing possessed and my ideas for the big Live and Let Fry makeover are crystallising nicely.

The door opens and Olly pops his head round. 'I suppose my lady would like a cup of tea before she goes to work?'

'Work?' I glance at my watch. 'Omigod, is that the time?' Hours have passed. I haven't showered, eaten, troubled myself with housework. All I've done this afternoon is fiddle with this mood board. 'I've got to fly.'

'What are you doing?'

'I forgot to tell you that I've volunteered to decorate Phil's place this weekend. We're really struggling for business, Olly. I felt it was the least I could do.'

'Cool.'

'That means you're on parenting duty again.'

He shrugs. 'When am I ever *not* on parenting duty?'

'Soon she'll be twenty-two and we can have a day off,' I promise him.

'I'll look forward to it.'

'How did the meeting go?'

'Good,' he says with a self-satisfied smile. 'Between now and Wednesday I need to become Hitchin's answer to the Malcolm McLaren I managed to convince them that I am.'

I get up and give him a hug. 'You've got such a very clever daddy, Petal.'

'Whatever,' our child says. She even does the 'W' with her hands. I don't know who has taught her this.

'I've checked with Stu Stapleton. He's got a loft full of punk vinyl that I can borrow.'

'That's nice. Didn't know Stu was a closet punk rocker.'

'We all have our dark secrets,' Olly says. 'Now,' he smacks me soundly on the bottom, 'go and get yourself showered while I make some tea and ping this pasta for you.'

'I can get some chips at the shop.'

'You can't live on chips, woman,' he says. 'If you're giving up your entire weekend for Phil, surely he won't mind if you're ten minutes late.'

Phil, bless him, never minds what we do. I don't think that

anyone has ever told him that sometimes bosses can actually be in control of their staff. I hope no one ever does either as we love him just as he is.

'I'll come and give a hand, too.'

'What about Petal?'

'She's not too young to learn about the working end of a paintbrush.'

'She's four.' Going on thirty-four.

'Once upon a time she would have been up a chimney at her age.'

'Knowing our daughter, she would have enjoyed it.'

'I know that you're talking about me,' Petal says without looking up.

Olly and I smile at each other. God help us when she's sixteen.

My lover pulls me into the hallway and winds his arms round me. 'You smell of chips.'

'Sorry,' I say. 'I got so caught up in myself, I haven't even showered yet.'

'I find it quite a turn-on,' he whispers in my ear.

'Oh, really?'

'Hmm. When exactly did you and I last have a night of passion?'

'Er? When was Petal conceived?'

'Ah, yes,' he says. 'I remember it well.'

But, joking aside, it has been some considerable time since our bodies were horizontal without having a small child wedged between them.

'I promise I will rectify that very soon.'

'Oh, yes?' His beautiful brown eyes glint with mischief. 'I'll hold you to that.'

Clearly it won't be this weekend as the only stripping off I have in mind is Phil's 1980s border from his scruffy chip shop walls.

Chapter 5

'This is it?' Phil's eyes widen at the sight of my colourful mood board. 'Are you sure?'

'Trust me,' I say. 'It will look fabulous.'

'What's that?' He points to one of the cuttings.

'A little twiddle,' I inform him. 'Nothing to worry about.'

'Twiddle,' he mutters under his breath. 'Since when does a chip shop have twiddles?'

'Take a chill pill, Phil,' Jenny throws in. 'Nell knows what she's doing.' Then to me, 'You do, don't you?'

I do a theatrical sigh. 'Oh, ye of little faith.'

This morning I went out and bought the paint before my lunchtime shift, having cajoled the promised three hundred pounds out of my boss. I also got us brushes, trays, white spirit and all the other guff you need for decorating. At least I hope I got everything. Now, at ten o'clock, the shop is shut up for the night an hour earlier than usual and Phil's small but perfectly formed army of willing workers is about to get cracking.

I'm so thankful that Jenny has turned up because if she'd

had a better offer from a hot, or even slightly lukewarm, bloke it could have gone either way.

Our co-worker, Constance, is also here. She's quite a bit older than Jen and me, late fifties probably, and has been with Phil since he first opened the shop which must be more than twenty years ago. She has a great figure, unnaturally red hair and a penchant for leopard print leggings, tight sweaters and hooker heels, which is, indeed, the outfit she has turned up to paint in. Foreseeing this and, in the interest of protecting her clothing, I bought us all white paper overalls in Poundland. Now we've pulled them on, we look like some sort of crack team of forensic investigators instead of hapless amateur decorators.

Phil levers the lid off the first tin of paint and turns pale. It's the lightest shade of pink I could find. Think the inside of a shell, sugared almonds, a ballet tutu.

'Pink?'

'Don't question,' I tell him. 'Just paint.'

Constance has inch-long fingernails, manicured in the brightest of reds, but that doesn't stop her from picking up a scraper and setting about the skanky border with vigour. Within seconds, scraps of it are lying at her high-heeled feet.

'If you wash down the walls first with sugar soap and then we'll set to on the painting,' I tell Phil and Jenny. 'OK?'

They both shrug their acquiescence and pick up the cheap buckets and sponges I bought and start to wash down the walls. We've already covered the black and white tiled floors with newspaper and grouped the furniture in the middle of the room. While they scrub away, I start to strip the varnish from the glossy, orange pine tables and chairs, which is going to be a long and messy job.

Constance pauses from her scraping to turn up the stereo. Disco classics pump out. 'We're going to need something to keep us going,' she says. So we all sing along to 'Saturday Night Fever'. We even throw some moves with our sponges.

As we happily clean and scrub and strip, the occasional drunk, seeing all the lights still on, bangs on the door in search of chips, only to be disappointed.

It's pushing midnight before Phil dips his brush in the paint for the first time. He closes his eyes momentarily, fresh, shiny pink poised over the ancient, skanky peach. 'For better, for worse,' he says.

'Go on with you,' I chide. 'It will look marvellous.'

'Pink,' he mutters under his breath. 'Pink.'

I don't confide in him that my four-year-old was my style advisor.

'I'm done,' Constance says. She stands back and admires her handiwork. The entire curled-up border has gone and the remnants of it have been sanded from the walls. 'And I haven't even chipped a nail.'

'You're a star.'

My mobile rings and I'm so pleased to see that it's Olly on the line. 'Hey,' I say. 'Missing me?'

'As always. How's it going?'

'Constance is our star turn and Phil is about to start painting. I've done nothing but strip all night.'

'Now I'm interested,' Olly says. 'I wish I could come over.'

'I know.' I thought Olly and Petal could come down here

24

for an hour or two tomorrow, but it's too chaotic already to accommodate Petal and she'd probably be bored within ten minutes. Besides, I'm missing Olly now. 'How's Petal?'

'Fast asleep since eight.'

'Are you tired?'

'Not especially. I managed a doze earlier.'

My dearly beloved's ability to exist only on regular catnaps constantly amazes me. He has, through force of necessity, learned to grab forty winks whenever he can – sometimes while standing up, quite frequently in the middle of a conversation.

'I can go and take over from Olly if he wants to come down here for a couple of hours,' Constance suggests. 'I'm happy stretched out on your sofa as I am anywhere.'

Not that we get a great deal of nights out but when we do, Constance is always willing to lend a hand. She lives on her own and has no pressing commitments and she absolutely adores Petal and vice versa, so she's become a surrogate nan to my daughter. Unfortunately, we've no family that live close to help us out. Olly's dad died over ten years ago, not that long before we got together, and his mum now lives out in Spain. My dear old dad took early retirement and, as I said before, he and mum moved to Norfolk years ago now. Great for holidays but not a lot else. So we do lean heavily on Constance when the cracks start to show in our compli-cated domestic arrangements. Jenny, too, has been known to step into the breach when we've needed an extra pair of hands.

'Want to come down and give us the benefit of your expertise with a paintbrush?' I ask Olly. 'Constance will come to the house.'

'Sure.'

I turn to Constance. 'He says yes.'

'I'll be there in five.' The unflattering overalls are already being peeled off.

Half an hour later and Olly joins us and just the energy that he brings when he turns up lifts us all and we keep painting and sanding late into the night. He works with Jenny, doing the bits she can't reach and it's good to hear them laughing together. They've always got on like a house on fire.

It's three o'clock before I look at my watch again. Then I notice that Phil is flagging. 'Come on,' I say. 'Get that overall off and get yourself home.'

'I am a bit tired,' he admits wearily and I could kick myself that I've let him stay here so long. I'd clean forgotten that he's done a full day at work already. 'Are you going to pack it in, too?'

'We might just stay a bit longer. What do you say, Olly?'

'Plenty of life in me yet.' My other half stifles a fake yawn.

'Go home,' I say to Phil. 'We've cracked the back of it now. Get a few hours sleep and come back tomorrow, refreshed and raring to go.'

'My bed *is* calling.'

'So is mine,' Jenny says.

'Go. Both of you. See you tomorrow?'

'Unless Robert Pattinson phones and wants to bite me,' Jen says.

'Are you sure you're OK on your own?' Phil asks one more time.

'Yes!' Olly and I chorus.

He holds up his hands. 'I'm gone. I'm gone.'

Minutes later, Olly and I are on our own. I turn off the disco music and put on some of the sixties soul music I insist on listening to in the shop. A CD of slowies. The mellow sounds of Marvin Gaye and 'I Heard It Through the Grapevine' fill the shop. I make a cup of tea in the kitchen, stick a couple of sugars in it for some energy and take it back through to Olly who is still painting. He stops and we sit on the floor together. As Smokey Robinson sings 'The Tracks of My Tears', he wraps an arm round my shoulder and I lean into him. We let the soft music flow over us.

'This is almost like a date,' I say to him.

'It's the closest we've had to one in a long time.'

'I do love you,' I tell him. 'Even though we have no money and no time and no sex.'

'I love you, too.' Olly kisses me and for a moment, I forget all about the painting or that I'm sitting on the floor of a chip shop.

Chapter 6

On Monday morning, I'm at my sewing machine, foot to the pedal, whizzing frantically through the fabric. I'm due at work in an hour and I want to get down there early to see Phil's face when he opens up.

'Nearly done?' Olly asks.

'Last bit.' I whip the fabric out of the machine and check my handiwork.

'Phil will be blown away.'

'I hope so.' I'm up and packing my final surprise into a carrier bag. 'You'll be all right holding the fort until I come back?'

'Petal and I are going to see the ducks in the town. Aren't we, Petalmeister?'

'Yay!' my daughter cries and I kiss her.

'I love you both so much,' I say, and then I'm out of the door running towards Live and Let Fry.

Last night I herded everyone out of the café at about seven o'clock. But what I didn't tell Phil was that I was sneaking back during the hours of darkness to add a few finishing touches. I've been up most of the night, painting and planning, sewing and swearing, and now I'm giddy with a heady mix of extreme tiredness and excitement.

When I get to the chippy, Jenny and Constance are already waiting for me and rush to hug me. 'We can't believe what you've done with the place!'

The walls are fresh, the palest of pinks. The once glossy, orange furniture is now pared down and paint-washed with a distressed white finish. At the head of each table where they butt with the wall, I've painted candelabra in fine black paint complete with bright pink candles. The wall by the door is painted with an ornate fireplace with a clock on top, again in black with highlights of bright pink. I've put some more twiddles round the coat rack. On the front of the counter, there are three busy waitresses painted in French 50s style – capturing Constance, Jenny and me for time immemorial. Or, at least until the next refit. At their feet, Dude sits expectantly, a ruff round his neck. Phil has been transformed into a large-tummied proprietor with a middle parting and a comedy-villain moustache.

'You can't have done this all last night?'

'I finished at four this morning,' I confess. At the very thought of my all-night marathon, weariness washes over me. 'You like it?'

'It looks sensational,' they say in unison.

'You think Phil will like it?'

'He'll love it,' they reassure me.

'One more surprise.' Out of my carrier bag, I whip the fruits of my labour.

'Omigod,' Jenny says. 'They're fab. You really made these?'

'Quick, quick, put them on. Phil will be here any second.' We all help each other to tie on the pink-and-white frilly gingham aprons and hats that I've spent all night working on. As instructed, we're all wearing white blouses and black pencil skirts. The aprons and hats are edged with some lace that I've had lying around for ages. I bought the gingham fabric cheaply from the market to run up a new duvet cover for Petal, but I've just never got round to it. It would be really great if I could make some café-style curtains in the same fabric for the windows, but that would mean tapping up Phil for some more cash as the three hundred quid is all gone.

'Get an eyeful of us,' Constance says, admiring her apron. Now we look exactly like the ladies in my illustration. 'Who will be able to resist chips from girls as hot as this?'

'Let's hope it works.' I take a steadying breath. 'Otherwise we'll all be signing on in a few weeks.'

'He's here! He's here!' Jen shouts as Phil's car pulls into the small car park opposite.

All three of us bounce nervously as we watch him cross the road. I can't help notice how tired and worn my boss looks as he comes towards us. Hopefully this will put the smile back on his face.

He opens the door and the bell chimes.

'What are you lot doing in so early?' Then he stops in his tracks and looks round. 'Bloody hell,' Phil says. 'Bloody, bloody hell.' Tears spring to his eyes and, of course, we all follow suit. 'Look at you,' he adds, finally noticing our new outfits. He turns round and round, unable to take it all in. He points at the painting on the front of the counter and his mouth gapes open. 'I hardly recognise the place. This is fantastic.'

He stands, speechless, staring at his transformed chippy, until Constance says, 'Come here, you silly old fool.'

He comes to hug us all. 'Thank you,' he says, choked. 'Thank you so much.'

'It's Nell you've got to thank,' Jenny says. 'We just did a bit of donkey work.'

Phil stands in front of me. 'What can I say?'

'Let's see if it pulls in the customers.'

'How could it not?' My boss grabs me in a bear hug. 'You're one in a million, Nell McNamara. One in a million.'

'Well,' I say. 'It wasn't just me.'

'Constance! Nip to the supermarket, love. We have to have a toast,' Phil says. 'We need champagne!'

Champagne, indeed! As if I'm going to argue with that.

Chapter 7

Within a week, there are queues down the street outside Live and Let Fry. Word of our new look has clearly spread and the café is permanently full. So much so, that we're turning people away at closing time. Phil is saying that from next week, we'll be open all afternoon. Frankly, I've never seen him grin so much. Constance is doing nothing but complain about how much her feet are hurting and that only serves to make Phil grin more. They're bad enough that she's even thinking of swapping her trademark stilettos for flatties.

Phil is so pleased with the makeover that he's already given me the money for some matching gingham curtains and I'm going to run those up this weekend. He's also talking about splashing out on a fancy black chandelier for the café to complement my painted ones and I think that would look great.

At close of business, I've lost count of how many portions of fish and chips I've doled out. It's not only Constance's feet that are hurting. I think all the excitement is catching up with me and I wonder if I can persuade Petal that she'd like an afternoon nap today so we can snuggle up together for an hour. Hopefully, Olly will have done something with her to have worn her out. I'm just folding my pretty, gingham apron when Phil takes my arm and pulls me into the kitchen.

'I've got something for you,' he says, suddenly bashful and from behind his back, he pulls out a familiar, upmarket carrier.

'Betty's?'

Phil smiles softly. 'I've seen you looking in that window week in, week out, Nell.'

'You have?'

'I do notice some things,' he chides. 'Even though I'm a bloke.' He holds out the bag. 'Just a little gift. To say thank you. For everything.'

'It's too much,' I tell him.

'You haven't seen what it is yet.'

Taking the posh paper carrier, I peep inside.

'Betty said it was the one you liked.'

I pull out the handbag. It's the felt one, covered in gorgeous rainbow-coloured buttons. The one I have coveted from afar. 'It is,' I breathe. My fingers trace over the buttons. 'It's beautiful. But I can't accept this. All I did was splash a bit of paint around.'

'Nell, you've doubled my takings in a week. I was having sleepless nights wondering how I was going to pay the bills. You've turned it all around. It's up to me now to keep it going.'

'But—'

'I want you to take the bag, Nell. Take it and enjoy it. You deserve it.'

'It's lovely, Phil,' I say. 'I didn't expect this.'

'Can I offer you something else, Nell?' he says. 'A piece of advice?'

I shrug.

'Don't stay here.' His voice cracks with emotion. 'I don't want to lose you, but you've got so much more to offer than serving fish and chips. Look at what you've done. *Really* look at it. It's amazing.'

Now I'm blushing.

'You've got to find a way to use that creativity. Don't waste your talent. Go to art college or something. I don't know. But you have to do something with your life, Nell. Promise me that.'

'OK,' I say.

But what? What can I do? Phil has said out loud what has, for some time, been silently tiptoeing through my brain. I would love to do something more creative. Be someone special. But how? Where would I even start? I've got commitments. To Olly, to Petal. To add to that, we're flat broke. How can I possibly be selfish and do something for myself?

Chapter 8

Tonight is a rare occasion. Olly and I are in bed together – alone. Petal is fast asleep in the next room for once, and even the dog has stayed in his bed.

We only rent this small, two-up, two-down, terraced house, but we've done our best to make it home. The landlord is very tolerant of our somewhat eclectic decorating style. All he says when he sees yet more of our handiwork is 'just make sure it's all magnolia when you leave.' Can't say fairer than that.

On the downside, the house is on a busy main road so all our conversation has a backdrop of thundering traffic. On the upside, it's just a short walk into the town centre – ten minutes max, which is just as well as neither Olly or I drive. Olly has actually passed his test whereas I haven't. Sometimes he does a bit of van driving for friends for some extra cash, but we can't really afford to run a car. We own a slightly battered but much loved Vespa scooter as our sole mode of transport. It's not exactly practical now that we've got Petal – we can't exactly put a toddler on the back of a scooter – but Olly has owned it since he was nineteen and I think he'd rather saw off one of his arms than part with it. He insists that it was his impressive skills on his scooter that made me fall in love with him. Even now, he and Petal sit and polish it together for hours on end. I snuggle down next to Olly. My shiny new handbag sits on the dressing table and I'm admiring it by the light of the moon, watching the myriad colours as they glimmer.

'Phil said I should do something more with my life,' I tell him.

'Like what?'

'He said maybe art college.'

Olly makes a 'hmm' noise in the dark. Is it a yes 'hmm' or a no 'hmm'? Can't be sure.

'Soooo, I took Petal into the college this afternoon,' I continue. 'Just to see what they had on offer.'

I feel Olly sit up slightly. 'You're seriously thinking about it?'

'I really don't know,' I admit. 'But it got me wondering. Maybe I shouldn't spend my life in a chip shop.'

'But you love it.'

'I do,' I agree. 'But perhaps I could love something else more.' I can't even begin to express how proud I am of the makeover at the chippy. It turned out so much better than I'd expected. If I can do something like that in a weekend on a tiny budget, what else could I achieve if I really put my mind to it? I hoped Olly would understand that. 'Perhaps I should try to achieve something, be a better role model for Petal.'

'Hmm.' That noise again.

'We should both try to do more. Build a better life.'

'We're doing OK.'

'We're not,' I remind him. 'Not really. We can barely make ends meet.' There's certainly nothing left over for luxuries. 'You can't want to spend the rest of your life in a pizza factory?'

'I haven't actually thought about it,' Olly admits.

'Well, I have and I want to do something about it. The college have got an art and design foundation course starting in a couple of weeks. I've already spoken to the admissions staff and they've got a few places left.'

Olly sits bolt upright now and switches on the bedside light. 'You're kidding me?'

'No.'

'How much is it?'

Now the hard part. Gulp. 'The best part of two and a half grand including materials and exam fees.'

'Wow.'

Wow, indeed. Like the price of the handbag, I might as well have said a million pounds. Now it's out, I rush on. 'It covers fine art, fashion, textiles, photography and print techniques.'

I confess that I haven't been able to stop pouring over the brochure since I picked it up.

'What do you get at the end of it? Can you walk straight into a job?'

'I don't know.'

'Two and half grand is a heck of a lot of money for an "I don't know".'

That I *do* know.

Olly sighs. 'We simply don't have that kind of money, Nell. How would we manage? Would you have to give up your job?'

'I might still be able to do some shifts. I'm sure Phil would help me out as much as he could. After all it was him that put this idea in my head.' Or, more accurately, gave it a voice.

'Wow,' Olly says again and runs his hands through his hair. 'You have been giving this a lot of thought.'

'Yes,' I admit. 'I have.'

He puts his arm round me and pulls me close. 'Perhaps next year,' he says. 'We can save up. I can do some extra work.'

I gaze up at him. 'You mean it?'

'If it's what you want to do. There's no way we can possibly raise the cash in the next few weeks, but we should be able to do it in a year.'

I ignore the nagging little voice in my head that says 'how?' We've never had enough spare money to be able to save any. What's going to be different from now on? Instead of questioning it further, I kiss him soundly. He likes the idea of me doing this course and that's enough for now. 'I love you.'

'Mmm,' he murmurs and leans over me. 'Just how much do you love me?'

'Very, very much,' I say in my best seductive voice as I ease myself beneath him.

My lover plants soft kisses along my throat.

Then our bedroom door bangs open. 'I can't sleep,' Petal announces.

'Not now, Petalmeister!' Olly cries.

Unperturbed about interrupting her parents' futile attempts at romance, our child stomps in.

'There's a monster in my wardrobe and he's eating crisps. Loudly.'

Olly sighs, rolls off me and flops back on the bed while I stifle a giggle. Any passion that had been rising ebbs away.

'I need to get in bed with you. Now.' Petal bounces onto the bed and pushes her way between us. When she's barged us both out of the way, she settles down in the middle. For a small person, she takes up an awful lot of room.

The dog, clearly feeling left out, has broken free from the bounds of the kitchen and pelts up the stairs and leaps onto the bed too.

'Oh, Dude!'

Petal is never likely to have a baby brother or sister if things carry on this way.

In a weary tone, Olly asks, 'Think you could cope with studying *and* a job and *this*?'

As I try to ease Petal's elbow out of my ribs and move my leg so the dog doesn't give it pins and needles, I think I could. If I wanted it enough.

Chapter 9

I work solidly for four hours in Live and Let Fry. The queue is never less than ten deep. I am a lean, mean, chip-dishing-out machine.

Frankly, I'm lucky my eyes have stayed open. Petal has to be the wriggliest child in Christendom. I don't think either Olly or I got more than a couple of hours of kip. She's got sharp elbows and sharp knees and uses them to good effect to get more room. Oh, the joys of parenthood. The only good thing is that she doesn't fart quite so much as the dog.

At the chippy, we close the doors at four – our new regime until Phil can find an extra member of staff to take us right through until six when the evening shift normally starts.

Sitting at one of the newly painted tables, I have a much needed cup of tea and a small helping of chips. Phil comes and sits opposite me with the same.

'I still can't believe how fantastic it looks in here,' he says. 'Thanks, Nell.'

'Don't start that again,' I tease. 'You'll be making me so big-headed I won't want to work here.'

He stirs a couple of spoonfuls of sugar into his tea, despite the fact that Constance is always nagging him to cut down.

'Did you think about what I said?' he asks with an over-casual air. 'About art college or something?'

'I did.' That makes him sit up in surprise. 'I took myself down to the college and got a brochure on their art courses.'

'Yeah?' Phil now looks quite pleased with himself. 'Anything interesting?'

I take the brochure out of my pocket, open it at the well-thumbed page and push it towards him.

'I'd like to do an art and design foundation course,' I confide. 'I had a word with Olly and he thinks we'd be able to afford it. Not this year, obviously, but maybe next.'

At that, Phil frowns.

'It's two and a half grand, Phil. We don't have that kind of cash lying around.' In all honesty, we don't even have two and a half quid lying around. 'This year's course starts in two weeks, which is way too soon. But now that I've got a plan, we can start saving towards it.'

'Let me lend you the money.'

'No.' I dismiss the suggestion with a wave of my hand. 'You can't possibly do that.'

'I can.' Phil puts his hand over mine.

'How would you get the money?'

'Look at this place,' he says. 'The takings are going up every week. I can manage it.'

I chew anxiously on my fingernails.

'Don't waste another year, Nell. Do it now while you're fired up. Wait a year and there'll be all kinds of reasons why you can't do it. Bite the bullet. Now.'

'They only had two places left when I spoke to them. They might have already gone.'

Constance and Jenny come and sit down with us. Constance sighs and kicks off her shoes with a grateful sigh. 'I bet even Ronald bloody McDonald isn't as busy as this.'

Phil grins. 'I'm just telling Nell that she should go to art college.'

'Wow, Nell,' Jenny says. 'That'd be cool.'

'It's a scary amount of money,' I point out.

'But it would get you out of here. No offence, Phil,' she adds hastily.

Phil rolls his eyes. 'None taken.'

'You deserve to do well, girl,' Constance offers. 'Look at this place, at what you can do. You can hardly call it a dump, Jen. It's like a palace.' My friend pinches one of the boss's chips. 'He's right, love. You've got a real talent. Don't waste it here.'

Now I'm racked with indecision. I'd agreed with Olly that I'd wait, but something inside of me has started to burn and I want to break out now while I have the chance. For the first time in my life, I feel passionate about doing something. It thrills me and it frightens me. Could this be how ambition feels? I suck in a wobbly breath. 'I don't know.'

'Phone the college,' Phil insists. 'See if they've got a place left. If they have, then it's fate or whatever that stuff is that you women know all about.'

A frisson of excitement sweeps over me. 'Shall I?'

'Go on,' Phil urges. 'What have you got to lose?'

'Just do it. Just do it. Do it, do it, do it!' Jen sings in the style of The Black Eyed Peas.

Constance gives me a nudge. 'Go on, Nell. I wish I'd had the chance when I was your age.'

And do you know, that's what does it. As much as I love Constance, would I want to be in her shoes? Do I still want to be working in a chip shop when I'm coming up to retirement? I'm thirty next year. That's not getting any younger in anyone's book and maybe I should be getting a move on.

Mind made up, I take my mobile out of my pocket. Phil reads out the number from the brochure as I punch it in with trembling fingers. They answer within seconds, instead of it going to voicemail or something, and I should take that as a sign too. I speak to the woman on the other end realising that I'm babbling. Moments later I hang up. Phil, Jenny and Constance all stare at me, holding their breath with anticipation.

'They had one place left,' I say. 'I'm in.'

They go crazy and cheer and kiss me and hug me. Phil hugs me the hardest. Our eyes meet. 'Thanks,' I say to him. 'Thanks so much. You don't know what this means.'

'I do,' he assures me. 'Just make me proud, Nell. That's all I ask.'

I'm in. My head's spinning. In two weeks I start my new Art and Design foundation course. In two weeks I start my new life.

Chapter 10

Olly stares at me open-mouthed. 'I thought we agreed that we'd wait until next year?'

'But Phil offered to lend me the money,' I remind him. 'I can do it now.'

We're sitting on the steps by the duck pond opposite St Mary's Church. We're enjoying some quality time together as a family – grabbing a guilty hour before I'm back on shift again at six. The intended visit to Mount Ironalot will have to wait. Crumpled clothes will be *de rigour* again for the week.

It's a beautiful, sunny day in downtown Hitchin. The sky is blue and cloud free. But the air is cool today and I pull my cardigan around me. Normally, Olly would put his arm round my shoulders, but he doesn't.

Petal is busy bossing the poor, unfortunate ducks about and doling out bread to those she thinks are well behaved enough to deserve it. Even the dog is out with us and is trying to pretend he's cool about the ducks, but I know that he's secretly longing to give one just a little chew.

'What's the rush?' Olly asks.

'Why wait?'

We descend into silence.

'Stay away from the edge,' Olly warns our daughter as she waddles after a duck. 'I just thought we'd make such a big decision together, as partners. I can't help feeling hurt that Phil, Jenny and Constance seem to take precedence.'

'It was a spur of the moment thing. I got caught up in their enthusiasm,' I confess. 'It felt nice to have them cheering me on.'

'Are you saying I don't?'

'Why are we arguing about this? I feel really lucky to have got the last place, really lucky to have friends who care enough to want a better life for me, for us.'

'You're right,' Olly concedes. 'Of course, you're right. I just feel a bit excluded.'

I lean against him and, finally, his arms slip round my waist. 'It wasn't intentional. It was simply how it happened.'

Olly sighs. 'I'm stoked for you. Really I am. I'm just worried about how we'll pay Phil back, worried about the extra work involved, worried that it will change us.'

'I can go along with the first two,' I tell him, 'but why would it change us?'

He shrugs. 'These things do.'

'Not if you don't let them.'

'I want to do everything I can to support you,' Olly says. 'I'll take on some extra work so that you can cut back on your shifts.'

I don't like to admit that I haven't quite worked out how

45

we'll pay Phil back yet. Maybe we can give him a bit each month and then pay off the lump when I land myself a fabulously creative and extravagantly paid job at the end of the course. It's something I need to discuss with him, but my boss is so excited that I'm going that he won't even deal with the nitty gritty of the finance.

'It's this little lady I'm concerned about,' Olly continues. 'What will we do with her?'

'I'm taking a course, Olly. At the local college,' I remind him. 'I haven't signed up for NASA's astronaut training programme. It'll be a breeze.' I think, famous last words, even as I say it.

'You're right. I'm probably overthinking it.'

'I want our daughter to be proud of us.'

'I know.'

At that moment Petal lifts her skirt above her head and bends over, displaying her rugby player's legs and spotty pants to the world.

Olly puts his head in his hands. 'She gets that from you.'

'Petal!' I call out. 'What are you doing?'

'I'm showing the ducks my bottom,' she shouts back.

Clearly, she's not quite so concerned about making *us* proud of *her*.

Chapter 11

Day one of my new life as an art student. I got up mega-early in order to leave myself hours of calm and collected preparation, so I can walk into my college in a Zen-like state ready to absorb knowledge like a sponge.

Petal sicking up in the bed is not a good start. 'I've got a poorly tummy,' my daughter complains.

I lift her and take her into her own room, wiping her down with a warm flannel, changing her sicky pyjamas for clean ones and settling her in her own bed. Then my daughter promptly throws up down herself again and I repeat the process once more. After that I go and chivvy Olly out of our bed.

'I'm not feeling that great myself,' he moans.

He does look a little peaky but I've no time to be sympathetic to man-illness now. Has he *actually* been sick? No. I'm afraid that Olly will just have to get on with it.

'Take her temperature regularly,' I instruct. 'If she doesn't look like she's getting any better by mid-morning, call the doctor.'

'You're still going into college?' he asks.

'Of course.' That shouldn't even be a question. What else can I do? I bite down my impatience. 'I have to, Olly. How can I miss my very first day?'

He groans and sways a bit. Now I think he's putting it on. 'How can you leave us?'

'I'll call Constance. She'll come up and sit with you for a couple of hours.'

'Don't worry,' he says. I swear he's putting that croak in his voice. 'We'll manage.'

'It's probably just a twenty-four-hour bug,' I assure him. I rack my brain to remember what we had for dinner last night and whether I've poisoned them both by giving them something to eat that was past its sell-by date. But we just had oven chips and fried eggs, so I think I'm in the clear.

Stripping the bed, I put on clean sheets while Olly has a shower. I grit my teeth as much groaning emanates from the bathroom. By rights, it's me who should be in there now. This was my master plan. Instead, I carry the sheets downstairs to put them in the washing machine, but when I eventually reach the kitchen, a bloodbath awaits me.

'Oh, no. Not today! Dude, what's happened?'

The dog bounces up and down, so pleased to see me and, therefore, puts more bloody footprints on the kitchen floor. On the work surface, the biscuit jar is up-ended and there seem to be more than a few missing. It seems that Dude's attempts to have a biscuit frenzy also led him to upset the knife block and judging by the blood trail, it looks as if he's cut his paw on one of the knives. Bending down to examine it, I get licked all over my face for my trouble.

'Oh, Dude. Look at you.' Manhandling my pooch, I manage to see that the cut doesn't look too bad in relation to the amount of blood he's managed to daub round the kitchen. More licking interspersed with whimpering.

With a new J cloth, I bathe his paw and conclude, thankfully, that it doesn't need stitches. A vet's bill on top of everything else would finish us off. I've had to spend a hundred and fifty quid on the list of required materials to take in with me to college – something I perhaps should have expected, but hadn't.

I tie Dude to the back door handle with his lead, while I set about mopping the floor with disinfectant and wiping down all the surfaces that have been customised with red paw prints. By now, according to Plan A, I should be sitting down to watch a relaxing ten minutes of *Daybreak* with my cup of tea and my bowl of Lidl muesli. Fat chance.

When I've finished cleaning the kitchen, I throw the dirty sheets and the two sicky pairs of Petal's pyjamas into the washing machine before realising that I ran out of washing powder yesterday. I'll have to pop out in my lunch hour to get some. I release Dude from the door handle and feed him, then I find a bandage in the first aid drawer, which is always well-stocked due to Petal's propensity for walking into things, falling over them, having them drop on her from a great height. I wind it round Dude's paw knowing full well that it will be chewed off in five minutes flat.

I quickly make a sandwich – no disasters there – so that I can cut costs by avoiding the student canteen. Then, with the frantic realisation that time is running out, I dash upstairs to run round the shower.

Olly is back in bed and Petal is beside him. 'We're going to stay here,' he tells me. 'Until we're better.'

Marvellous, I think uncharitably. Bloody marvellous.

In the shower, no hot water left. Typical. All thoughts of an impressive hairdo, a quirkily different outfit suitable for an art student and maybe even some slap, go completely out of the window. Instead, I pull back my hair into a ponytail, bite my lips a bit to make them red and then throw on whatever's to hand that looks clean.

I blow a kiss to Olly and Petal. If they have got something contagious I should try to keep my distance. 'Love you both,' I say. 'I'll phone when I can, to see how you are.'

Olly groans and Petal bursts into tears. 'Don't go, Mummy,' she sobs. 'Don't go.'

That's my heartstrings twanged to breaking point. I rush over to cuddle her, taking her in my arms and pressing her against my chest. I'm a terrible mother for even thinking of leaving her.

'Go,' Olly croaks. 'You're going to be late.'

So I am.

'I'll be back before you know it,' I promise Petal and she wails some more.

With the sound of my daughter's crying ringing in my ears, I belt out of the house, leg it down into town like a thing possessed and fly through the doors of the college at a speed that Usain Bolt would be proud of. But nothing can disguise the fact that I'm late, late, late. And on my first day, too. I could weep.

Without too much fuss I'm pointed towards my classroom

and dash in there, still out of breath and panting in the style of Dude. Everyone else is in there, sitting down, looking bright-eyed and attentive, ready for action. I already feel that my morning has seen enough action to be going on with. All eyes swing towards me.

An elderly, pinch-faced woman stands at the head of the class. She looks as if she feels that life has dealt her a mean hand. She's immaculately dressed, stylish but with an individual edge. She also doesn't have a hair out of place. The sharp glance at her watch tells me that my tardy arrival hasn't gone unnoticed.

'Good morning,' she says crisply. 'So glad that you were able to join us.'

Chapter 12

The rest of my week does not get any better. Nor the week after. Nor the week after that. I race home from college every night at five o'clock, say hello to Olly and Petal and then race out again to get to my shift at Live and Let Fry by six. By the time I finish at ten o'clock and the entire population of Hitchin is filled with chips, I am on my knees. Then I rush home to take over from Olly, while he goes off to do his night shift at the pizza factory. When he's not making high-end, boxed pizzas, he swaps his beloved sixties gear for a black T-shirt and ripped bondage trousers and sets off – hair gelled into mountainous, and possibly lethal, spikes – to do the punk gig that he bagged at a local bar. The brief peck on the cheek in the kitchen as we hand over the baton is the closest we get to a sex life.

During the short window of time after closing Live and Let Fry and before I collapse into bed with exhaustion next to my darling daughter, I'm also supposed to be wonderfully creative with artwork to take in for the next day. It's fair to say that my meals of late have been largely chip-based.

I'm so grateful that Olly and Petal did only have a quickie stomach bug and were both as right as rain again within a couple of days. Is it bad that I don't have time to either be ill myself or to have my family ailing?

It will get better, I keep telling myself. It has to. Because I can't really afford for it not to. Everything is riding on this and I'll let so many people down if I can't cut it – including myself.

Plus, it seems that my main course tutor, Ms Amelia Fallon, has taken an instant dislike to me. Every time she talks to me she curls her nose up and I wonder if it's because I am permanently surrounded by *eau de* fish and chips or if there's another reason for her distaste.

It could well be that I'm the only one on my course who's always late, always harried, always one step behind everyone else. But then Ms Amelia Fallon seems to have her own issues. She clearly thinks that in her day she should have been the next Vivienne Westwood or Nicole Farhi. I don't think she ever saw tutoring students at a local art college as her role in life, so I try not to think too many mean thoughts about her. Perhaps if she knew what was going on in my life she would be more sympathetic, cut me some slack.

In my defence, I have been out of formal education for so long, that I'm struggling to get back into it. The last time I was in a classroom was over fourteen years ago. I'm distinctly out of practise. And I wasn't that great at it, even when I was last at school.

It also feels like I'm a hundred years older than all of the other students, which doesn't help. They all look so young and carefree, so fresh-faced and impossibly trendy. They all look

53

like they have no commitments, no significant other, no demanding four-year-old, no dog, no evening job at the chip shop. They all look like their mums still do their washing and ironing. They sit around together sipping coffee and gossiping, probably exchanging ridiculously creative ideas and I do not. During all of my breaks, I ring Olly and check that he and Petal are still alive and coping without me. During my lunchtime, I shop for food, pay bills and do all the stuff that real grown-ups have to fit into their lives.

At the chip shop my home-made or vintage clothing makes me stand out as individual, kooky. Here I look as dated as my clothes and although I thought that art courses might attract individuals, all the other students look exactly the same. I know that I need to give myself a fresh image if I have any hope of blending in. But when? When am I actually going to fit this in along with everything else?

'Back in the room. Back in the room,' Phil says, clicking his fingers.

I laugh and jerk myself back into the present. 'I *was* away with the fairies then.'

'Tell me about it.'

Luckily for me, we have a brief lull in the steady stream of customers needing their chip fix tonight. 'Thinking about tomorrow's coursework,' I lie.

But now that I *do* think about tomorrow's coursework, I realise that I still have to do it when I get home.

'Is it all going OK?'

'Yeah, yeah.' How can I tell Phil anything else when he is helping me to fund this new venture? 'It's fine. Very exciting.'

And it is. In some ways. I've already learned so much – I can find my way round a decent camera now, I know the basics of screen printing, I can handle a glue gun and all kinds of other fun stuff. It would just be nice if I had a clone or two. One of me could then go to work and earn the money, one could look after the childcare and the dog's requirements, one could enjoy this course to the full, and the other one could produce fabulous, nutritionally balanced meals every night shortly before having wild sex with my other half. I am beginning to realise that one person can not hold all this stuff together. But how do I ever get out of this rut if I don't soldier on?

'Done the right thing?'

'Oh, God, absolutely.' This *is* the right thing. When I'm not worrying about my snotty tutor or how young and silly my fellow students are, I love every minute of it. I adore the things I'm learning and the fact that I feel like I'm bettering myself. If only I had more time, I feel like my creativity would explode out of me like a volcano. Then watch out, world!

Some more customers wander in and our conversation is curtailed, which I'm relieved about. I don't want Phil to think that I'm not enjoying it or that I'm not supremely grateful.

Half an hour later and we're shutting up the shop together.

'You would tell me if there was anything wrong, wouldn't you?' Phil says as he locks up and we stand outside on the pavement together in the cold night air.

'Yeah. Sure. Everything's fine.' It's just that I'm trying to cram a quart into a pint pot.

'Want a lift home?'

'Thanks, but I'll walk. I could do with five minutes of fresh air.'

I set off home, walking through the old part of Hitchin and past my favourite shop. In the window of Betty the Bag Lady, the handbags glint in the moonlight.

I have my foot in Betty's world now. One day I could be like her and be someone and do something. And nothing that happens is going to make me give up my dream.

Chapter 13

'Why doesn't Mummy ever come home any more?' Petal asked Olly.

'She does.'

'Does not.'

They were in the kitchen making cupcakes together. Their cakes were safely out of the oven, golden and brown. Baking on a regular basis with his daughter had certainly brought out his own inner Jamie Oliver. Petal was standing on her pink plastic box so that she could reach the kitchen surface and his heart squeezed every time he looked at her. Four years on the planet and he still couldn't believe this beautiful creature was his child. She was the one amazing thing he'd done in his life and he loved every hair on her head, every pout of her rosebud lips. A surge of joy went through him every time she called his name – except, of course, when it was three in the morning. Then he much preferred it if she wanted her mummy.

The cakes were cooling nicely on a wire rack. Now they were at the critical icing stage.

'Put this water into the icing sugar. Gently, gently.' He guided his daughter's hand as she gripped the spoon, ham-fisted. More than once they'd both been covered in a cloud of sweet white dust due to Petal's exuberance.

'I want her to be at home,' his daughter continued, trying out her extra-whiny voice.

'Well, Mummy's at college at the moment, sweet pea. She's learning how to be a famous artist.'

Judging by the scowl on Petal's face, it seemed that she wasn't overly impressed by this state of affairs. Though, if he was honest, three weeks into Nell's course and he was beginning to feel exactly the same as his daughter.

'Does she still love us?'

'Of course she does. And we're baking these cakes to show how much we love her too.'

Petal took a moment to digest that and dipped her finger in the bowl of icing sugar to aid concentration.

'We don't put our fingers in the bowls, Petal.'

'We do, Daddy,' she corrected. 'Yes, we do.' To prove it she scooped up another blob of icing and ate it with relish.

Ah, well. Kitchen hygiene was overrated anyway. A certain amount of germs were good for you. He was sure he'd seen Nigella doing the same thing on her TV show. That was prob-ably where Petal was picking up her bad habits from.

In his dark moments though, he did wonder where Nell's sudden desire to change their lives had come from. Wasn't Nell happy with him any more? The thing that he loved the most about her was that she never complained, never whined, she just always got on with whatever life threw at her. Had he misread her all these years and instead of being content, she'd been simmering away with unspoken dissatisfaction? They might not have money to burn, but they had a roof over their heads and food on the table – even though it was from the more bottom-end supermarket chains. Was that really a problem? Maybe that just wasn't enough for the modern woman.

He'd seen what ambition had done to his father. He'd been a builder out in all weathers, all hours of the day. When he did get home, he'd shut himself away in the office and do paperwork until the small hours. As a child, Olly had rarely seen him. When he did, he never smiled and was always stressed. His bark wasn't always worse than his bite and sometimes he'd have to move quickly to avoid a back-hander. Olly realised now that it was just due to the pressure he was constantly under, but he didn't ever want to be a dad like that to his child. Throughout his childhood, they'd lived in a decent sized house and his mum and dad both drove top-of-the-range Mercs. His dad had an ulcer by the time he was thirty. He'd died at the age of forty-six. Keeled over with a heart attack while he was mixing concrete.

Looking back, had his dad's desire to make money at all costs been the right thing to do? Wouldn't it have been better for him to have eased back, had a little less money, but enjoyed life and stayed with them for longer? His widowed mother had sold the big house within months and now lived in Spain and he hardly ever saw her. Olly didn't want that kind of future for himself or his family.

'What colour shall we make the icing?' he asked Petal.

'BLACK!'

'I have pink, yellow or blue.' Petal was clearly not bowled over by the feeble selection on offer.

'Blue,' she ventured, somewhat reluctantly. 'Let's do blue.'

'We also have sprinkles to put on top.'

'Yay!' she shouted. 'Sprinkles! Sprinkles! Sprinkles!'

Well, that had cheered her up considerably. If only grown-up ladies were so easily pleased.

Chapter 14

When I get home, Olly and Petal are both lying flat out on the sofa in the living room, sparko.

I tiptoe towards them, kneel down beside Olly and kiss him on the nose. It twitches in his sleep. 'Hey there, sleepyhead.' I stroke his arm gently and he rouses.

'What's the time?'

'Time you were at work and time this little one was in bed.'

Olly pushes himself up. He looks completely shattered. I think he would have been there for the whole night if I hadn't woken him up. I'm not the only one burning the candles at both ends.

'We both must have dropped off,' he says with a shake of his head and a stretch. 'The last thing I remember is watching *In the Night Garden*.'

Petal might be too old for it now, but it's still her favourite programme. Frankly, if they ever needed a stand-in for Igglepiggle or Upsy Bleeding Daisy, then I'm your man. I could recite every word off by heart.

'I'll take her upstairs,' I say.

We have made a rod for our own backs in that Petal always sleeps with me when Olly is working nights and that means, of course, that she won't settle in her own bed when he's not. I think she'll still be sleeping between us when she's twenty-five. I just hope she doesn't bring home too many boyfriends.

'I'll do it.' Olly yawns again.

He scoops our daughter into his arms. At least Petal is already in her pyjamas.

'Stick the kettle on, love.' Another yawn.

'Coffee?'

'Yeah. Nice and strong. Black.' He throws his head back and groans. 'Need something to keep me awake all night.'

I go through to the kitchen and make coffee. I'm going to need one myself if I'm going to have any hope of doing my work for tomorrow, rather than give in to the overwhelming urge to go and slip into bed next to my child. I feel as if I haven't seen her properly for weeks and I'm missing my Petal fix. But there's a dozen different things I need to get on top of, so I put two good spoonfuls of full-hit, instant coffee in the cups and hang the expense. The work to be handed in is stacking up and I feel as if I'm slipping behind. I can appreciate that there's a lot to be crammed into this short year, but I wish we'd started at a slightly more sedate speed so that I could ease myself into it. I wonder, does the pace let up at all as we get into the course or is it going to be flat out all the way?

It's clear that Olly and Petal have spent the afternoon baking and I get an unwanted and unfamiliar twinge of jealousy that Olly is spending much more quality time with our daughter than I am. I sample one of the cakes and conclude that they really are very good.

When Olly comes down, he's changed into his work clothes. A grey-that-was-once-white T-shirt with The Beatles on the front and jeans with no knees. The scruffier he is the more I love him. He adds some cold water to his cup and gulps down his coffee. 'Got to fly.'

'So soon?' I wind my arms round his waist and pull him close.

'Oh, what I wouldn't give to lie in these arms tonight.' He presses his face against my hair. 'At the weekend,' he says. 'We can snatch some time together at the weekend.'

'I'll hold you to it.'

He kisses me briefly and then leaves.

I wander round the house aimlessly for ten minutes while I sip my coffee and I would so love to switch on the television and just lie on the sofa and watch something mindless, but I have a project to do for tomorrow and I haven't even begun to think about it.

Clearing a space in the middle of Petal's toys, I settle on the floor and pull my bag with my college work in it towards me. My eyes are so heavy. I could just do with half an hour's sleep, but it's just not going to be possible. I must get this work done. It's for Amelia Fallon, my course tutor – she of the pinched face and the turned-up nose – and I know that it doesn't just have to be good, it has to be marvellous.

Dragging a cushion from the sofa, I plump it up and then stretch out on the floor, resting my head on it while I start some doodles. My eyes feel like lead weights. This level of tiredness surely isn't conducive to fabulous creativity. Coffee, coffee, I need more coffee. I shake myself awake and swallow the dregs from my cup. I'll just do half an hour on this and then I'll make myself another one.

What seems like a minute later and Olly is stroking my hair. I open my eyes. Oh, God, I must have fallen asleep when I really didn't mean to. 'What are you doing here?'

'I could ask you the same thing.'

I'm still lying on the floor, head on my cushion, work – untouched – spread out in front of me. I hear myself groan. Surely he hasn't come back from his night shift already? 'Please tell me that I haven't been here all night.'

'Sadly, you have been here all night.'

I haul myself up. Every bone in my body aches where I've been lying on the hard floor.

He sits down beside me and I lean against him and start to cry. 'I'm so tired,' I tell him. 'So very tired.'

'Don't go in today,' Olly suggests. 'Go to bed. Catch up on your sleep.'

'I have to go in today. I've got an assessment with that old harridan who's my course tutor.' She would just love it if I was absent for that. I'm sure she'd just love to mark up a *nul points* on my report card. 'I can't miss this.'

'You can barely keep your eyes open, Nell. Nothing is that important.'

'It is,' I sob. 'It's important to me.'

He studies me and his face assumes a resigned expression. 'Then go and have a shower while I make breakfast.'

I glance at my watch. No chance of churning out a fabulous project now. I'll just explain exactly what happened to Amelia Fallon and the difficulties of my situation. I'm sure she'll understand. Won't she?

Chapter 15

'It's not good enough, Nell,' Amelia Pinched-Face-Turned-up-Nose Fallon says. 'It's really not good enough.'

We're sitting at opposite sides of her desk and I feel like I am five years old again and in trouble with the head teacher. Needless to say, I was late and my interview/interrogation has not got off to a good start. Outside the door I can hear the noisy buzz of the college, students chattering, feet clattering. In here it is silent, and about as comfortable as a tomb.

I have just explained that I have not completed – not even begun – my latest project and to say that it has not gone down well, is something of an understatement.

After an awkward amount of time has passed, Amelia folds her arms and leans forward. Her face is close to mine and I resist the urge to back away. She lets out a weary sigh. I am all the troubles in her world personified. 'I'm going to have to ask you to leave the course.'

That hits me like a body blow. 'Leave?'

'I'm afraid so.'

She isn't afraid at all. I can tell that much. But whatever I had expected from today, this wasn't it. I thought she would complain, lecture, reprimand. I didn't think that she would simply truncate my dream. I'm struggling to hold my tears in check, but this woman will not make me cry. When I find my voice, I ask, 'But why?'

She purses those hideous lips. 'I'm not really sure that you're cut out for this. Your work is always late. *You're* always late. When you do deliver the required projects, they aren't really up to scratch.'

'I've been here a few weeks,' I plead. 'How can you tell yet? I've been out of full-time education for years. It may just be taking me longer to get into it than the other students.' I could be the tortoise to their hares. I can't be worse than any of those kids, I think. I can't. Really, I can't. 'On top of everything, I have a job to hold down and my daughter to look after.'

'This only makes me think that you won't be able to manage *at all* when the pressure is really on.'

I'm speechless.

'Do you think I should make allowances for you? When everyone else is coping quite nicely, you think you should be a special case?'

Yes, I want to say. Isn't that the point of your job? Aren't you here to help me when it's all going tits up? You should understand, more than anyone, that I'm trying my best and this is probably more important, more critical to me than any of the other youngsters who have much more of their lives left to make mistakes, to realise their ambitions.

'I can arrange for a refund for you for the rest of your fees,' she says without warmth. 'That's the best I can offer.'

'Don't I have the right to appeal?' What I mean is, can't *someone* in this college help me? I can't only be at the mercy of this woman who has clearly decided to get rid of me simply because she can. Because she's bitter and twisted. Because she has some point to prove.

'I'm afraid not.' My tutor closes the folder in front of her that bears my name.

I'm history. Just like that. She stands up. I'm to be dismissed.

'One day you'll thank me for this. I'm doing you a favour, Nell. Perhaps you need to rethink your plans. I simply think you aren't good enough to make it in this world.'

That cuts me to the quick. I am good enough. I'm sure that I am.

'I can prove that I am.'

'I don't think so.'

'Everyone deserves a second chance.'

But as she ushers me to the door, it seems that Amelia Fallon is unmoved.

Chapter 16

In a daze, I walk out of the college. For hours I wander about aimlessly trying to get my head straight and failing. My dreams, before they even got off the ground, have crashed and burned round my ears. Up by the busy library, I sit alone in the small and pretty Physic Garden that's right next door. I sometimes come to this place with Petal after we've collected new books for her to read. We both love it here. It's a quiet little oasis in the bustling town centre. I'm surrounded by plants that are supposed to heal or provide succour – lavender, chamomile, St John's wort. Today, they do nothing for me. I crush some lavender in my hand and breathe in the scent. Pretty, but my mind remains in turmoil. The wind whips up and I get so cold that my bones start to freeze and my brain goes numb. So I move on again.

I don't really know where I'm going, but I eventually find myself outside Live and Let Fry just as they are about to close up after lunchtime service, which is just as well as I don't want to go home while I'm in this state.

My eyes are raw from crying and I stumble inside. Constance is wiping down the tables and as soon as she sees me, she abandons her cloth and takes me in her arms.

'Nell, love,' she says, frowning. 'What on earth is the matter?'

'College,' I sob. 'I've been thrown off my course.'

'Oh my goodness,' she says, hand going to her heart. 'Is that all? I thought someone was hurt. Now dry those tears. Thrown off your course?' She tuts. 'That can be fixed.'

She leads me to a table and sits me down. Then she calls out. 'Phil! Phil! Our Nell is here and she needs tea!'

Phil and Jenny appear from the back of the chippy. My boss's face falls when he sees me. 'Nell, love.' He comes and slips into the seat next to me and puts his arm round my shoulder, which makes the tears that I just about had under control flow again. This place feels like my sanctuary, my home. I'm loved here, not out on a limb. They don't think I'm stupid, lazy, incapable. They don't tell me here that I'm not good enough.

Jen says, 'I'll make that tea.' She disappears into the back once more.

Constance hands me a napkin and I blow my nose into it.

'Now then,' Phil says softly. 'Tell us all about it.'

I launch into my tale of how I've struggled to keep up with the work, struggled to keep all of my balls in the air, struggled to make the one important person at the college like me, like my work.

'Oh, Nell,' Phil says after he hears me out. 'We could have helped you out. Why didn't you say? We thought you were eating it up for breakfast. None of us knew you were struggling. We're your friends, Nell.'

'I wanted to show you all that I could do it.' Look where that's left me. My eyes fill with tears again.

'Don't fret,' he says, patting my back. 'There are other courses.'

'She thought my work was rubbish, Phil.' She thought *I* was rubbish. 'What if I sign up for another course and they say the same thing?' Then all my dreams, my hopes will be truly crushed.

'They won't,' he assures me. 'You're wonderful. I've a good mind to go down to that college and drag that woman up here and make her look at what you've done. You were too good for them, that's the problem.'

I have to laugh at that. 'It's lovely to have friends who have such blind faith in me.'

'It's not blind,' Phil points out. 'We can see what your work has done. She's the one who can't.'

Jen brings the tea and some chocolate digestives and we all dig in, gratefully.

'She's probably just jealous,' is Jen's take on this. 'You're young and fit and have the whole of your life ahead of you. Well, most of it. She's a bitter old bag who probably hasn't had a decent shag in years.'

That makes us all laugh. If only life were so simple. But the long and the short of it is that, decent shag or not, she still had my future in her hands. And she decided that it was not going to be on her bloody course, come hell and high water.

I put my head in my hands.

'So what now?' Constance wants to know.

'Can I have my full-time job back, Phil? I'm going to be free at lunchtime now.' I try to make light of it but inside my heart is breaking.

'No,' Phil says. 'No. I'm not having you back here.'

He sounds fairly adamant.

'You're not giving up that easily, Nell McNamara. Oh, no.'

'I can't face starting another college course,' I tell him. 'Anywhere I went would be further away for one thing, and even more difficult to work round Petal.' Not to mention the fact that my already shaky confidence, my self-esteem, has been smashed into the weeds.

Constance holds my hands. 'Phil's right, love. Don't give up this easily. We need to come up with a Plan B.'

Plan B could just be to stay working in a chippy for the rest of my life with my good and well-meaning friends.

'Will you get any money back from the course?' Phil asks.

'Full refund,' I tell him. That offers some consolation. Phil's money hasn't been completely wasted. 'At least that's not lost. I'll give it straight back to you.' Otherwise I might be tempted to have a retail frenzy of the handbag nature to cheer myself up.

'That's not what I'm worried about,' he says. 'I want you to keep it and put it to good use.' He looks thoughtful as he chomps on his biscuit. Eventually, he declares, 'You have to set up on your own, then you can work hours to suit you. It's the only way.'

'I can't do that. I don't know the first thing about running a business.'

'I'll help you all I can,' Phil offers. 'You know that. The

money you get back from the college course can go towards start-up costs.'

Start-up costs? 'But what would I do?'

'What have you learned on your course so far?' Jenny wants to know.

'Not a lot, Jen,' I admit. I've only been there a scant month. 'A bit of the basics of screen printing. I know my way round a camera better than I did and I can handle a glue gun now.' All great stuff, which I've loved doing, but not that much practical to show for nearly a month of study.

'You could start up a company that revamps chippies,' Constance suggests.

'She did that for a bit of fun,' Jen says, 'and to help Phil out. What she really needs is to do something that she's got a passion for.'

They all turn to look at me, expectant.

'Handbags.' It's out of my mouth before it's gone through my brain. 'Handbags.' I blink at the revelation and they blink back. 'That's what I've got a passion for.'

'Brilliant,' Jen says, applauding. 'Handbags it is!'

'But I don't know anything about *making* handbags.'

'Get on that internet then, love,' Constance suggests. 'You can find out how to make anything on there, they must have a section on handbags.'

We all giggle again and I sigh with relief as the tension ebbs out of me.

'There are all kinds of grants for new businesses,' Phil says. 'Once you get your plan together, I'm sure you'll be eligible for something.'

Plan? Even the word terrifies me. 'Do you think?'

'You'll never know until you try, love,' Constance says. 'You've got to give it a go. You can't give up at the first hurdle.'

'What about if it all goes horribly wrong, like the college course?' I'm not sure my fragile ego could take another knock-out blow.

'Do you think Alan Sugar would have given up at the first hurdle?'

I shrug. 'I guess not.'

'You've got a lot to think about, Nell,' Phil says. 'But never forget that we're here to help you.' He squeezes my shoulder. 'We're your friends.'

'I don't know what I'd do without you guys,' I admit. 'Now,' I wipe my eyes on my sleeve, 'I'd better get home as I'm due back here *very* soon.' In less than an hour to be exact.

'I'll cover your shift tonight,' Constance says. 'You look exhausted.'

Normally, I'd protest and insist that I carry on and think about how much we need the money, but I feel completely wiped out and emotionally drained. Plus, Constance has her not-to-be-argued-with face on. 'I would quite like a night in with Olly and Petal.'

'Then that's what you should do.' She pats my knee.

'Thanks, Constance.' I kiss my friend gratefully. 'Thanks to you all.'

'Go home,' Jenny says. 'Or you'll have us all blubbing.'

So I gather myself together and leave them to finish tidying up.

I walk slowly towards my home and take my usual route past Betty the Bag Lady. Betty isn't in this afternoon, it's her assistant who's on duty, so I stand outside and stare at the bags in the window. All of my life I've loved them.

Could I do this? Can I skip the whole formal training thing and go straight into doing something like this? My friends seem to think that I can, but then their confidence in me could be entirely misplaced. After all, I have absolutely no confidence in myself.

Chapter 17

Olly and I lie on the sofa facing each other like bookends, feet entwined, enjoying the rare night in together. He still looks rather shell-shocked by my news. To be honest, I'm not much different. My thoughts are scattered all over the place like seeds in the wind. On the one hand, Amelia Fallon's nagging voice is in my head, filling my brain with negative vibes. On the other, it feels like a tiny little bud of something exciting might be blossoming in there too.

'I'll support you, whatever you want to do,' Olly says. 'But starting your own business? Wow.'

'I know. It's crazy.' But crazy actually feels quite good. 'I thought I could perhaps design and make handbags. Maybe sell a few in Betty's shop.'

'You're not going to become rich and famous selling a few in Betty's shop,' he quite rightly points out.

'It's a start, though.' I hug the cupcake cushion to me. 'I can fit it in round my shifts at the chippy and see if it takes off. Phil said I can hang on to the money he loaned us. He thought there might be some business grants available too. Do you think I should go for it?'

'Why not?' Olly says. 'If you do it part-time. As a sort of hobby.'

'Yeah.' Hobby, my arse. 'It won't be as mad as the last few weeks have been. I promise.' I keep quiet about my budding plans to give Lulu Guinness a run for her money.

'Petal has missed you,' he tells me. 'So have I.'

He shimmies up to my end of the sofa and we lie along the length of each other, settling into the contours that are now so familiar.

'Hmm,' Olly says. 'Remember when we used to do this as teenagers?'

'Oh, yes,' I murmur. 'I always had to watch where your hands were in case my mum or dad walked in.'

'Oh, happy days,' Olly says. His lips find mine and he holds me tightly.

Then the door opens and, instinctively, I check if my clothing is in place.

'When are you coming to bed?' Petal says, rubbing her eyes. 'I can't sleep without you.'

Olly rolls away from me. 'Petalmeister, what are you doing up? You should be in bed.'

'So should you,' our daughter says. 'Have you seen the time?'

Why is it that your children like to parrot back your own phrases to you?

'OK,' Olly says. 'We're coming now. Scoot up those stairs as quickly as you can, otherwise you're in your own bed.'

Petal leaves the room in a whirlwind.

Olly sighs. 'When did our lives become controlled by our child?'

'When she was born,' I remind him.

'Shall we go up? We're not going to get a minute's peace until we do.'

'You go up,' I tell him. 'I just want to do a few things. Maybe sketch out some ideas.' After the last few weeks of struggling to be creative on request, I suddenly find that I've got all kinds of things buzzing round my head.

'Don't be long, hun.'

'I won't.' He plants a lingering kiss on my head and goes out of the door.

I get my college bag and pull out my sketch pad. I settle back into the sofa with it propped up on my knees and push away the yawn that wants to come. It's no good. I'm way too comfortable. If I stay here, I'll only fall asleep.

I take my pad and climb the stairs. Dude lopes out of the kitchen and quietly follows at my heels. Trying not to disturb my family, I creep into the spare room and, surrounded on all sides by Olly's beloved records, open the wardrobe. The dog curls up in the corner.

My collection of handbags is neatly laid out in front of me. Frankly, it's about the only bit of the house that is neat.

Pulling out half a dozen, I lay them on the floor then tenderly slip each one out of its dust bag. There's a striking black-and-white canvas bucket bag with a screen print of Judy Garland on it – still one of my favourites. Next to it there's a bag with bamboo handles and a bright tropical print featuring parrots and palm trees studded with sequins and beads, which was fantastic to wear when Olly and I used to have holidays that didn't involve a cramped tent or a caravan. The tiny shimmery gold affair with cream vintage lace was bought for my cousin's wedding from a flea market and hardly ever gets an outing, even though it's gorgeous. I might take it with me to the chippy tomorrow just to give it some fresh air. There's also a pretty little cerise fabric one that looks like a flower and it has a big diamanté sparkle in the middle. I don't think I've used this since Petal was born either, as it's only big enough to hold a lipstick and a tissue and these days I can't go out without a suitcase full of emergency gear. On the more unusual side, I have a green leather bag in the shape of a watering can, one that's made from two old vinyl records and one that's a recycled number plate. One is a red patent leather radio complete with moving dials and there's a big yellow teapot too. Petal's favourite.

Finally, my top treasure. My one and only Lulu Guinness bag. Olly bought this for me when Petal was born, at great expense. It's a slim clutch in black with a picture of a London bus and a woman in a sharp fifties suit with a nipped-in waist embroidered on the front. It's my prize possession. If the house was burning down, I'd first rescue Petal, then the dog, then this handbag. I'm assuming Olly would be able to make his own escape.

An hour and one chewed pencil later, and I've roughed out two designs that give me a frisson of excitement all along the hairs on my neck. Dude snores away in the corner, paddling the air with his feet. In his dream he could well be chasing next

79

door's cat with whom he has a hate/hate relationship. The entire house is asleep but me. I know that I'm way too excited to settle tonight. Somehow I resist the urge to go into the bedroom and show these to Olly as I'm sure he wouldn't be very enthusiastic after having his precious beauty sleep interrupted.

I hold my designs out at arm's length and try to regard them with a critical eye. They're good. No matter what the dastardly Amelia Fallon might think, I know in my heart of hearts that they're good.

Chapter 18

I'm in the offices of Best of Business and, accordingly, I'm trying to look like a businesswoman. Phil was right. Even in these straitened times, there is still help to be had with setting up new businesses. I am classed as a micro-entrepreneur in Best of Business jargon and am to be the future of our country. Jolly glad about that.

I found out all about them from the library and when I called the helpline, I was offered an appointment for the next day. From there I was matched with my very own advisor to help me through the trials and tribulations of business start-up. An official hand-holder for the first year of my company's existence. Believe me; I feel that I need one as this all seems totally daunting. They've managed to hook me up with some-one, they say, who has experience that matches my business perfectly. I do hope so. Best of all, there's no charge for his services for the initial period of a year. Nothing. This is equally good as I'd never be able to afford it otherwise. Today, I'm due to meet him for the first time.

The offices are very posh – all glass, stainless steel and low lime-green sofas. I don't think I've ever been in a place like this before. Frankly, I'm feeling a bit wide-eyed and unworthy. I'm glad that I spruced myself up. Today, Ms Nell McNamara, micro-entrepreneur, is wearing a black dirndl skirt, red blouse and ballet flats. I'm also carrying my Judy Garland bag – primarily because it's the biggest one I possess and I'm anticipating taking away lots of pamphlets.

Sitting opposite me in an armchair that mirrors mine, is a man called Tod Urban who is to be my appointed mentor and it's fair to say that Mr Urban is very easy on the eye. I had expected a business mentor to be staid, soberly dressed in the style of a bank manager. But he isn't. This man's wearing slim black jeans, a white T-shirt and winklepicker shoes. His hair is showing some grey at the temples and it's worn long, swept back from his face. I think some men get better with age – you only need to look at George Clooney (something I try to do as often as possible) – and I think that Tod Urban is also one of them.

'No need to be nervous, Nell,' he says. His mouth curls into a warm smile. 'Just relax. Kick back.'

I fiddle with my handbag. Kicking back won't happen. Bolt upright is going to have to suffice.

'We're just going to have a chat,' he explains. 'Find out what makes each of us tick. See if we can work well together.'

I nod. Come on, voice, make a reappearance!

'Shall I start by telling you about myself? How I came to be an advisor for Best of Business?'

'Yes, please,' I squeak.

'Well, I've been in the fashion industry for longer than I care to remember. For the last fifteen years I was a buyer in the trade,' Tod tells me. 'Before that, I was a designer working with people like Brit Connection, Nikki Dahly, Made with Love.'

All big designer names. I'm impressed. And not a little over-awed.

'I'm semi-retired now,' he goes on.

I think he can only be late forties, early fifties at a push. Young to consider retiring.

'I wanted to get out of the rat race. You know how it is.'

I can only nod. I think I may actually be trying to get *into* the rat race.

'I have a house in the South of France that I like to spend time at, so I do some consultancy work now and I usually mentor one or two people here at Best of Business at any one time. We should all give something back, right?'

'Right,' I echo. But I think that first I would actually like to take something out.

'I like to think that I could help you to avoid making the mistakes that I did when I started out.'

That's music to my ears. I'm so naive that I don't even know what mistakes I can make.

Tod Urban spreads his hands expansively. 'So,' he says. 'I'm all yours.' His smile is very disarming and I think I'm getting a bit hot under the collar. 'How can I help?'

'I'm looking to start a business,' I tell him, 'and really have no idea where to begin.'

He glances at the folder on his lap. 'Designing handbags, it says on my notes.'

'That's right.'

'Any experience?'

I shake my head. 'Not in that line.'

'But you do work now?'

'In a chip shop.'

He roars with laughter. 'Quite a change then.'

'I guess so.'

'Well, I admire your ambition, Nell. If you want to know, I started out as a welder. It was the other blokes on the site who persuaded me to try something else. They could see that my heart wasn't in being on a building site for the rest of my life.'

'That's pretty much what the guys I work with in the chip shop have done with me,' I admit. 'I gave the shop a makeover and they all said that I should try something else. Something more creative.'

He makes a steeple of his hands and studies me over it. 'As well as being creative, you know that you're going to need a lot of grit and determination.'

'I think I have that.'

'Plus some cash to get you going.'

'That I don't really have,' I confess. I only want to tap into Phil's money as a very last resort. If I can give it back to him now, so much the better.

'Luckily, that's where I come in. I'll go through your business plan with you and see if we can't get you a grant or two as a kick-start. Times are tough but, if we look hard enough, there's money to be had.'

I risk a smile. Is it really that easy?

'You have your business plan with you?'

Oh, I've been a busy little bee in the last few days. There's a track worn from my house to the central library and back. The computer I've been using there is probably still smoking. Olly has been a trouper – as always – and has kept Petal entertained while I've put together my business plan. How grand does that sound! Business plan, eh?

The internet has been a godsend. What did we do before it? Sure enough, as Constance had predicted, I found that there were a million different sites all telling me how to not only buy handbags, but also how to make handbags, where to buy handbag supplies – in fact, everything I ever needed to know about handbags but was afraid to ask.

This morning, on eBay, I managed to find a man – only a few miles away from us – advertising a surplus of finished handbag frames for a sum that, even to me, seemed as cheap as chips. They look as if they might suit my purpose just fine. Currently there are no bids on them and there's a mobile phone number listed. I jotted it down with a view to calling him later to see if I can buy them outright.

As Tod waits patiently, I rummage in the depths of my voluminous bag and pull out the folder I've taken such care in preparing.

He takes it from me and scans the pages carefully. 'Looks good,' he says, a few minutes later. 'We'll go through this together carefully, step by step. But it certainly seems as if you're on the right track.' He tosses the folder with my name on it to one side. The second time that has happened to me in a week. But this has a very different feel to it. 'Now on to important things.' My new mentor slides his armchair next to mine and rubs his hands together. 'You have some designs with you?'

'Just a couple.' Nervously, I delve into my bag again and find my initial sketches. I feel sick at the thought that Tod might not like them, that he might tell me I'm rubbish, that I'm not good enough. Clearly, Amelia Fallon's barbs have got stuck under my skin.

I've sketched out a large, rigid-framed handbag with a diamanté clasp and detachable shoulder strap, something simple and something very like the ones I've found on the internet this morning. On the first one there's a drawing of a juicy piece of battered cod on one side and on the other some chips in a bit of newspaper.

Both bags are silver and have hot-pink satin lining and a Nell McNamara tag. I thought I'd finish both bags with little sparkles of diamanté. I pass the sketch to him.

Tod laughs again when he sees them, but in a good way. 'Fabulous,' he says. 'Really fabulous. This should give you a nice start.' He holds up the designs. 'Pop art meets commercial irony.' He nods his approval. 'I'm liking it.'

I have no idea what he means but, clearly, he thinks it's good.

My other idea is a different design on the same basic frame – already I have an eye on the costs. This one has a pink cupcake on one side with 'Eat Me!' written above it and on the flip side a blue beaker with 'Drink Me!'

'Fun,' Tod says. 'A lot of fun.' He puts the drawings down. 'I certainly think you're on the right track here.'

'You really think so?'

'Without doubt.' He rubs his chin. 'I think you're going places, Ms McNamara. Great name by the way. Are you planning to use that?'

'Yes,' I say uncertainly. 'I thought so.'

'Excellent. I'm thinking Anya Hindmarch, Loren Taylor, Orla Kiely. Nell McNamara is a name that says "designer handbags".'

It is?

His eyes rove over my outfit. 'The image is great too.'

I can't help but grin. Not only does he like my name but he seems to like everything about me. Up yours, Amelia Fallon!

'Now, let's have a proper look at this business plan and see if we can't get you some funding.'

So from art college reject to budding entrepreneur in one fell swoop. I think I like this mentor much better than the last one.

Chapter 19

Olly is already dressed in his punk gear ready to do his gig tonight and is wearing more eyeliner and mascara than I am. His face is pale, his lipstick red. Clearly, it's not only Petal who likes to play with my make-up bag. I'll be lucky if I get a look in soon. There's a ragged black wig on his head. He currently appears to be channelling Robert Smith of The Cure and, strangely, I quite like the style.

'What?' he asks.

I smile at him. 'I was just wondering if I could love a man who wears more lippy than me.'

'Needs must. As long as I don't start teaming it with a twin-set and pearls and calling myself Olive at the weekends, you'll be fine.'

'Thank you,' I say. 'Thank you for doing this.'

He shrugs. 'There are worse jobs. I'm just hoping that no one I know sees me.'

'Daddy, I like it when you look like a lady,' Petal pipes up.

'There you are,' Olly says. 'Seal of approval from the Petalmeister.'

I chew at my fingernail as he, Petal and I finish our plates of beans on toast. 'Promise you won't want to kill me' – Olly looks as if he doesn't want to commit himself – 'but I really want to go and get those handbag frames from the eBay man before someone else nabs them.'

The cheque for the refund from my college course came in today and it's already banked and in our joint account. I was planning on handing it straight back to Phil, but this is too good an opportunity to pass up and now the thought of it is burning a hole in my hot, little hand.

'They're a bargain,' I remind Olly, in case he's forgotten in the five minutes since I last told him. 'What if they've already gone?'

'We should wait until we know if you've got any kind of grant or funding,' Olly reasons. 'It's not a good idea to count your chickens before they've hatched.'

'Tod didn't seem to think it would be a problem at all.'

'But we don't know if *Tod*' – he mimics a girly voice. Not mine, I think! I might have mentioned Tod Urban quite a lot in the week since my excellent meeting with him, but I don't say his name like that – 'is talking about two hundred pounds or ten thousand. It makes a big difference to what we can do.'

That's true enough.

'We should wait,' Olly reiterates.

'Constance is coming to babysit.'

'I'm not a *baby*,' Petal complains. 'I'm *four*.'

'Eat your beans, Petalmeister.' Our daughter rolls her eyes at her father, but she pushes her fork into her baked beans.

'We've got an hour before we have to be at work.'

'I can't go looking like this.'

'You look fine,' I tell him. 'Sexy even.'

He's weakening. I can see it in his frown. 'Where do we have to go?'

'I'm not exactly sure. Shall I call him?'

'OK. Do it,' Olly says, resigned.

And sometimes I wonder where Petal has learned how to wheedle and whine from.

I find the piece of paper that bears his number and punch it into my phone. The man answers in three rings and I ask him about his handbag frames and how much they are and, moments later, the deal, it seems, is done.

'They're mine,' I tell Olly, hardly able to contain my excitement. Hurrah! My toe has been firmly dipped in the water of the fashion world. 'But we have to get them tonight. He's clearing out the warehouse tomorrow.'

Olly gives me a reluctant smile. 'You drive a hard bargain, woman. You'd better phone Constance and ask her if she minds coming round a bit earlier.'

I do just that and my friend is here in a flash, wearing gold satin leggings and a leopard print top for her babysitting duties. Constance admires Olly's new look and then we both kiss our sitter and our daughter goodbye, dash out of the door and pile onto the Vespa.

'Where exactly are we going?' Olly shouts out to me and I yell back the address. 'I hope this helmet doesn't ruin my hair.'

'I have that problem all the time.'

'I'll be more sympathetic in future!' he offers and, with that, we drive off into the night.

In less than fifteen minutes we find the small trading estate and pull up outside the equally small warehouse. There's a man outside loading a van and I'm guessing he's the person I've come to see. He looks in surprise at the scooter as we climb off. I slip off my helmet. When Olly takes off his helmet and reveals his Maybelline look, the man takes a further step back.

'I'm here about the bags,' I say.

'In there.' The man nods to the roll-up door behind him and with him still keeping one eye suspiciously on Olly, we both follow him inside.

On a rack at the side of the room the unfinished handbag shells are all lined up. They are the perfect shape. And there are lots of them. I feel myself gulp. 'All these?'

The man nods. 'Tell me you're not just on that scooter.'

'We're just on that scooter.'

He shakes his head. 'Good luck.'

I count out the cash into his hands. That has made a serious dent in my college refund and I get a pang of anxiety as I see him pocket it. The man returns to loading his van and leaves us to the rows of handbag frames.

Olly's eyes are wide. 'You're kidding me.'

'I brought black bin bags,' I tell him. 'I thought we could put them in there.'

'There's got to be six dozen handbags there.'

'A hundred,' I say. 'There should be a hundred.'

'This is going to take us at least three trips,' Olly warns. 'We can't pile them all on the scooter in one go. It'll just fall over.

But if we come backwards and forwards to get them in smaller batches then we'll never get to work on time.'

'We won't if we hang about yapping,' I say.

So with a quick glance at each other, we launch into filling the black bin bags with them. I had no idea that a hundred handbag frames was quite so many. Or how many black sacks they would fill. Neither have I any idea where I'm going to put them all when I get home.

It takes us ages to bag them all up and, as Olly rightly predicted, we are both going to be *so* late for work. Still, we eventually load up the first lot. I have a black sack full of bag frames in each hand and Olly piles another load in front of me so that they're sandwiched against his shoulders.

'We'll be back for the rest soon,' I tell the man.

He gives me a look that reads incredulous.

'Ready?' Olly asks.

'Yes.' I feel decidedly unsteady. 'Don't go too fast.'

'I just pray that we don't see a police car on the way home or we're dead meat.'

Olly kicks the Vespa into life. 'Try to look inconspicuous,' he shouts over his shoulder to me.

Impossible. I'm struggling to hold onto the bin bags and they're flying out like wings into the night. I should have 'wide load' stamped on my back.

'Woo hoo!' I shout.

'You're mad,' Olly yells. 'I love you.'

'I love you too!'

If this is what being a handbag designer feels like, then bring it on!

Chapter 20

'Woaw!' Olly says when he comes into the living room at the end of his late-night punk gig. 'It looks like a sweatshop in here.'

He's not far wrong. A week after we brought them home and the black bin bags filled with handbag shells are still stacked in the lounge awaiting a more permanent home, I'm not sure where. I have all my trimmings and diamanté bits and bobs spread out over the floor. My trusty glue gun is at hand.

The ever reliable Phil lent me his posh camera and a few days ago I took some photographs of a beautiful, battered cod and some very cheeky chips nestling in newspaper. Today I picked them up from the printer who has transferred the images onto cotton for me. Despite the hour, I just had to make a start on them.

'How did the gig go?' I ask.

'The landlord is still pissed off with me for being so late last week,' Olly says as he pulls off his wig and roughs up his own hair.

That'd be the day we collected the handbag shells.

'I'm trying to win him round again, but it's a bit of an uphill struggle.'

'I'm sorry,' I say. 'That was all my fault.'

'It had to be done.' Olly sighs, and then flops down on the sofa. 'I just wish there were more hours in the day.'

His lipstick is smeared, his mascara smudged. My heart squeezes for him. I wriggle along the floor with my work until I'm sitting with my back against the sofa where he's flaked out. 'It'll be worth it,' I promise him. 'You'll see. All this hard work won't last for ever.'

'We'll both be in an early grave if it does.' Like his dad, are the words that are left unspoken.

I know that the premature death of his father still sits heavy in Olly's heart and I can understand why he likes his life to be as laid-back and as stress-free as possible. But sometimes you have to let the past go and embrace the future, and I see a different future for us. I see one where I'm sitting in the front row at Paris Fashion Week sipping a champagne cocktail and watching a catwalk show featuring my latest, hugely successful, collection with an immaculately dressed Olly and an impeccably behaved Petal at my side.

'I could kill for a Pot Noodle,' Olly says, breaking into my fantasy. 'Any in the cupboard?'

'I'm sure there must be. Want me to look?'

'No. I'll move myself in a minute. I just need to work up the enthusiasm.'

Olly strokes my hair while I cut and trim and sew and glue.

'Look.' Ten minutes later, I hold up my first completed handbag. As it's made from a bought and already finished shell, there's no diamanté clasp, the lining material is silver rather than the hot-pink of my dreams and the name tag I'd envisaged in cool steel is a hand-stitched, padded star instead, but it's nearly there. The pukka article will have to come when we have some more cash behind us. 'Number one!'

'Wow.' Now he sits up. 'For real?'

'Yeah.' I think it looks good. Standing up, I parade the inaugural Nell McNamara signature Fish & Chip handbag round my front room. 'Think it will sell?'

'I'm no fashion expert,' Olly admits. 'But I think it should go like hot cakes.'

'I hope you're right.'

'Hmm.' He winds his arms round my thighs. 'I think such genius calls for a celebration.'

The look in his eyes says that he doesn't mean Pot Noodle for two.

He slides off the sofa and pulls me to the floor with him. We lie down amid my fabric and trimmings and sparkles. Olly finds a tiny feather from somewhere in the heap of the mess and starts to tickle my face and neck with it. Then he moves lower and lower and lower.

'If we make love here,' I warn him as my breath quickens, 'you might get a needle in your bottom.'

'I'll risk it,' Olly says. He kneels above me and peels off his God Save The Queen T-shirt.

Despite our advancing years, his body is still taut; his six-pack – honed through years of karate practice – is still in place even though he has zero time to exercise any more. Mine, in contrast, shows the signs of childbirth and too many chocolate bars.

'God, you're beautiful,' Olly says.

As he leans in to kiss me, I'm so glad that he never notices my flaws. Then, just as I'm reaching for the buckle of his belt, the living room door flies open.

'I'd like milk,' Petal announces. 'I'd like it now.' Then remembering that nothing is forthcoming in this house without the 'p' word she adds as an afterthought, 'Please.'

Olly groans before we both dissolve into fits of laughter.

'I don't know what's funny about that,' our daughter complains. 'You forgot to give it to me before I went to bed, Mummy.'

'I did not, Petal. Don't tell fibs or your nose will drop off.' My child looks terminally unconcerned that this tragedy might befall her. 'But if you go straight back to bed, you can have a *tiny* bit.'

'And a biscuit?'

'No. No biscuit. Or your teeth will fall out.'

Not bovvered about that either.

Olly hauls himself from the floor. 'I'll get it.'

Petal slides her hand into Olly's. 'I love you, Daddy,' she smoothes and I can hear his heart turning to mush.

I wonder if Petal is so determined to remain a cosseted only child that she hides behind doors all the time, just waiting for us to get down to it before she pounces. I don't suppose that we're the only celibate couple, but it certainly feels like it sometimes.

Passion thwarted once more, I turn my attention back to my handbags. Before this night is out, if I'm not going to get any hot sex, then I'm determined to have bags to sell!

Chapter 21

The next morning, I swing through the doors of Live and Let Fry for my shift, feeling as if I'm walking on air.

'I come bearing gifts,' I tell Phil, Constance and Jenny.

After they've all hugged me to death, I hold out my new Nell McNamara handbags complete with pink-and-white candy-stripe protective dust covers.

Jenny and Constance take them and pull out the bags inside.

'Oh, wow.' Jen's eyes are out on stalks. 'You seriously didn't make these?'

'I seriously did.'

'Nell, they're fantastic.'

Phil, as he so often does these days, looks a bit teary. 'Fish and chips.' He examines the handbag that Constance is holding. 'That's funny.'

'I didn't think that you'd want one for yourself.'

'Oh, I don't know. It might suit me.' He takes Jen's bag and models it. 'Aren't man-bags all the rage?'

'Thanks for being my inspiration.' I mean that sincerely.

Phil returns the bag to Jen. 'Well done, girl,' he says to me. 'Well done.'

'I've got to sell some yet, Phil. Tell me well done this time next year if I've made it.' I turn to Jen and Constance. 'In the meantime, ladies, you are my walking billboards. I want you to wear these as much as possible.'

'We can keep them?' they chorus.

'Absolutely.'

'Thanks, Nell,' Jen says. 'You're a star.'

The door opens and our first customer of the day comes in.

'I hate to bring you all back to reality,' Phil says, 'but aprons on.'

With some muttering, the girls reluctantly slide their handbags back into their protective covers and we all don our aprons and prepare for the lunchtime rush.

Four hours of dishing out fish and chips and I'm done. The apron is stripped off again and I dash out as quickly as I can as I have a meeting with Tod Urban. I can't wait to show him my finished product.

We're meeting this time in a coffee shop and when I push, breathless through the door, he's already waiting. As always, he looks cool, calm and collected as he sips his cappuccino. I plonk myself down in the seat opposite him.

'Sorry, I'm late,' I puff. 'The entire population of Hitchin wanted fish and chips today.' It took us ages to clean up afterwards and I could hardly just walk out and leave the others to it.

'You look tired,' he notes.

'Late night too.' I was cross-eyed from sticking diamanté sparkles on by two in the morning. Now I could actually put my head down on this table and fall fast asleep.

'Let me get you something,' Tod says and he lifts his tall, lean frame out of the bucket chair.

'Tea,' I say. 'Just tea will be fine.' What I could really do with is a double espresso, but I'm thinking it would just make me jittery and hyper. Cake would be good too. But Tod isn't the kind of guy that you want to stuff your face in front of.

While he queues at the counter, I try to gather my thoughts and get out the Fish & Chips handbag that I've brought to show him.

Tod hands over my tea when he comes back and I show him the bag.

'Impressive,' is his verdict as he turns it back and forth, examining every detail. 'You've done a good job.'

'Thanks.' I feel ridiculously pleased when I get praise from Tod. 'I thought I'd take it into Betty the Bag Lady this afternoon to see if she's interested in stocking them.'

'Great idea. I've found you a fantastic web designer for when you're ready to get that up and running. I'm sure you'll love his style and he's not too expensive.'

Always good to know.

Then Tod looks serious. 'Some bad news though. I've drawn a blank on the grants. Cutbacks, I'm afraid. You know how it is. Everyone has used up their funding for this year.'

'Oh.' What am I going to make stock with? How can I get a website up and running? I've spent all night making handbags. Now what am I going to do with them?

'It's not dead in the water,' he assures me. 'There is money to be had. But it's not worth applying again until next year.'

That's months and months away.

'This is business,' Tod tells me sagely as he sees my disappointment. 'You have to be prepared to take the knocks, Nell.'

'Yes, yes. Of course.' But my heart sinks nevertheless.

'I'll see you again soon.' He finishes his coffee and so I glug down my tea. 'Chin up. Rome wasn't built in a day.'

But I just want to make handbags, I think, not build Rome.

Chapter 22

I'm in Betty's and, once again, I pull out my new design. I feel like giving it a fanfare. A bit of ta-da! After all the years of rocking up in here like the poor relation, now I'm coming in here as a business colleague!

Betty looks at me. I thought she'd be grinning, perhaps even jumping up and down. But no. The expression on her face is puzzled, slightly put out even. She examines my handbag as if it's an unexploded bomb.

'Do you like it?' I ask, eager and nervous in equal measures.

'Wow,' she says. I don't think her voice says 'wow' though, it says something else. Something that I can't identify. 'It's very interesting.'

Interesting? Why is she making that sound like a bad thing?

'Amazing.' She purses her lips. 'I had no idea that this is what you wanted to do.'

'Neither did I until recently.' I'm trying not to bob about from foot to foot.

She stares at me. 'Yet you never said anything?'

'No.' That stops me bobbing. She *is* put out. Does she see me as a rival now? Did she like it better when I was just a hard up customer drooling at the altar of her bags? I wouldn't exactly call Betty a bosom friend, but I thought that we were more than acquaintances and had enough of a connection for her to be pleased for me. 'This place has been an inspiration to me,' I say. 'It's the hours I've spent in here that finally made me realise what I want to do with my life.'

'Really?' Her stare turns to my bag again. She hates it, I can tell.

'I'd love you to stock them.' I'm too excited to look at what's on offer today, but I know that my bags would sit perfectly among them. 'Perhaps just have the one, this one, to see how it goes.'

Betty looks shell-shocked. 'Let me give it some thought, Nell,' she says. 'Leave it with me.'

'Right,' I say. 'Right. I'll do that.'

'Call in again next week and we'll sort something out.' I'm here on almost a daily basis. Was that a warning to stay away?

'See you next week then,' I say and slink out.

I stand on the street, stunned. What now? I was absolutely sure that Betty would go mad for my bags. I hate to admit that I had a window display in mind. A great one that she'd keep for weeks and weeks to be admired and drooled over by the good folk of Hitchin. She knows me. She knows that I work in a chippy, that I have a small child dependent on me. Why would she not want to help me if she could, give me a leg up?

I wander aimlessly, trying to get my head round her reaction. The market's on today and it's bustling with life as usual.

Some of the stall holders have been here for as long as I can remember and feel like old friends. The vintage stall that I love is here too and I flick through the racks of once-loved clothes, but I'm not really paying attention to the feel of the fabrics, the cut of the dresses as I normally do. Today my head is elsewhere. If I can't afford a website yet and Betty isn't going to stock the handbags for me, where can I possibly sell them?

There's nothing in the house for tea and we need to eat quickly as I'm due back at Live and Let Fry before long, so I pick up three fresh homemade pasties from the stall adequately named, Mr Pasty. Then, as I'm shoving my purchase into my bag, it dawns on me. I could have a stall here too. If I can get one on Saturday, Olly could have Petal during the day and I can ask Jenny or Constance if they would swap the lunchtime stint with me. It's an idea. I haven't a clue how much it costs to get a market stall or what you have to do, but pretty soon I will.

Take that, Betty. I may just have hit upon another way to get my handbags out there!

Chapter 23

A week later and I have a market stall. My first day is this coming Saturday and, frankly, I'm bricking it. I told Olly before he went off to bed, but his response to my momentous decision was somewhat muted. He may have just been too tired to get excited. Or maybe he's just heard one too many momentous decisions from me recently. But I feel like I have no choice. I have to do something and it's a relatively modest outlay to display my goods and it will, hopefully, bring in some money for me to reinvest in the business.

Surrounded by handbags on my lounge floor, I'm thinking of calling Tod to tell him – hoping that he will be more enthusiastic and raise my flagging spirits – when the phone rings. 'Petal, can you pick that up please.' I'm up to my eyeballs in glue guns and sparkles. 'Answer nicely.'

'Hello, this is Mummy's phone,' she says politely. 'She is busy and she is still in her pyjamas.'

Quickly, I snatch the phone from her. 'Hello?'

'Pyjamas, hey?' Tod says with a laugh.

'I'm so sorry,' I tell him. 'My daughter is a receptionist of variable reliability.'

'She sounds delightful.'

'She is absolutely delightful. When she wants to be.' Then, to distract him, 'I was just thinking of you.'

'Same here.'

My awestruck heart does a little lurch. 'You were?'

The sound of his laughter again.

'I have some news.'

'I'd love to hear it but I can't talk now, Nell. This has to be a quick call. I'm just going into a meeting. I do, however, have a proposition for you.'

I'm infinitely open to propositions from Tod Urban, I think.

'I have a reception to go to tonight at Buckingham Palace and my date has let me down. Fancy it?'

'B . . . B . . . Buckingham Palace, did you say?'

'It's a promotion for The Prince's Trust. It would be a great way to meet some influential people, which certainly wouldn't hurt if we were to apply to them for some funding for you. What do you say?'

'Tonight?'

'I can pick you up about five.'

That would give me just an hour to get home from my shift at Live and Let Fry and change into my glad rags. I'd also need to find someone to cover my evening shift, which would mean that I'd struggle for a babysitter for Petal as Olly has his punk disco gig tonight. Oh, God. Oh, God. What to do?

'You can tell me your news on the way down in the car,' Tod continues. 'I have to fly. Are you up for it?'

Buckingham Palace! How can I possibly turn it down? 'Er—'

'I need an answer now, Nell.'

'Yes,' I blurt out. 'Of course, yes.'

'Great. See you at five.' He hangs up.

Now I'm in a flat spin. I instantly phone Constance who, of course, agrees to cover my shift, but that puts my chief babysitter out of action. My second call, Jenny, is also working. So I then phone every friend I've ever had to see if they would come round and look after Petal when Olly goes off to his gig. They are all busy with other things. It seems that I do not put enough into the babysitting circle to warrant taking anything out. Now what?

Finishing off a handbag, I add extra diamantés so that it will be ultra sparkly and ready for me to take to *the palace* tonight. No matter how many times I say that in my head, I can't convince myself that I'm actually going there. I race upstairs and fling open my wardrobe to see if I have any suitable outfits for palace-type events.

Petal plods in behind me and promptly goes to the wardrobe to help herself to my shoes.

'Mummy is going to Buckingham Palace tonight,' I tell her as I bounce round the room giving full reign to my excitement.

Her raised eyebrow indicates a modicum of interest. She clacks about in my heels.

'Will you meet the Queen?'

'I don't think so, but I might meet a Prince.'

'Will you kiss him?'

'I do hope not.' Has she *seen* Prince Charles?

My daughter looks disappointed by this turn of events and I wonder exactly what I'd have to do to impress her.

I pull out a vintage Audrey Hepburn-esque dress – black, sleeveless, full twirly skirt – and I can't even think when it last came out of the wardrobe. I hold it up against me and pose. The perfect accompaniment for a Fish & Chips handbag.

'Nice, Mummy. Can I come to the Palace too?'

That brings me down to earth with a bump. I sit down on the bed and pull my daughter into my arms and kiss her hair. 'No, sweet pea,' I say. 'It's just for grown-ups.'

'*Everything's* for grown-ups,' Petal complains.

'Before you and I know it, you will be a grown-up too.'

'I hope you're not telling me a fib,' she warns, 'or your nose will drop off.'

'I'm not,' I promise. 'One minute you'll be a little girl and the next you'll be a big lady with a life of your own.'

'So what will Daddy and me do while you're with the Prince?'

'I don't know, sweet pea.' But I'll have to sort something out pretty soon.

Chapter 24

'Of course, I'm pleased for you,' Olly shouts.

I'm fresh out of the shower and in the bedroom getting ready for my posh night out. 'You don't seem it,' I shout back.

Rubbing the towel over me briskly, I squirt myself liberally with Chanel No 5 – a very welcome Christmas present from my dear Dad every year, which I usually manage to eke out to last me the full twelve months. I'm hoping it will hide any residual chip aroma. I want to make a big impression tonight and I don't want to do it with a lingering scent of haddock.

'It would just have been handy to have had more notice.'

'That's the way the cookie crumbles,' I point out. 'The reception is tonight. Tod asked me to go this morning. What am I supposed to do?'

'More importantly, Nell, what am I supposed to do?' He lowers his voice, but the anger is still there. 'What am I going to do with Petal?'

'I don't know,' I admit. 'I tried everyone I could think of. No one was free to babysit.'

'Then maybe you should have said no to *Tod*.' He uses the whiny voice he does whenever he says Tod.

'Tod' – no whining – 'told me it was very important for me to be there. I happen to agree. This is a once-in-a-lifetime opportunity.'

The straighteners get a cursory tug through my hair before I twist it up into a chignon. I add a big black bow to the back. I can't ever remember seeing Olly so cross with me before and I don't understand what the issue is. I *have* to do this. Does he not see that?

'Phone in sick,' I say. 'It's the only thing to do.'

'How can I?' Olly asks. 'I'm hanging on there by a thread after being late the other week. I don't want to lose this gig and I can't let other people down at the last minute. It may not be the O2 arena, but a lot of people turn up on punk night.'

'This is *Buckingham Palace*, Olly. The Prince's Trust. If I get some funding from them, maybe you won't have to spend your evenings doing punk discos. Ever think of that?'

'I don't think punk and disco go in the same sentence, Nell,' he retorts before he continues with his rant. 'You just can't dump everything at the drop of a hat. Not when you have a family to consider.'

'It's the first time I've ever had to do this. Don't give me a hard time about it.' Goodness only knows I feel bad enough already. But this is business. Can you see entrepreneur Karren Brady or Ultimo bra lady, Michelle Mone, turning down an invitation to the Palace? But then I bet they both have nannies to fall back on and that their husbands don't have to do two-bit discos for the princely sum of fifty quid a night.

I pull on my dress and turn to offer the zip to Olly. He zips me up, but rather crisply. Slipping on black velvet gloves that were my mum's and black patent kitten heels at the same time, I check myself in the mirror.

Suddenly, Olly is still. All the fight goes out of him. 'You look sensational,' he says softly.

'Thanks.' Now I feel ashamed for shouting. For the first time in my life I'm torn between duty and ambition.

A car pulls up outside the house and I hear the hoot of a horn. This is more than likely my ride.

'Go on,' Olly says. 'Have a wonderful time.'

Perhaps it's also due to the fact that I'm driving off into the night with a rather fabulous man to a rather fabulous do. I'm sure I'd feel put out if the boot was on the other foot.

'What about Petal?'

'I'll sort something out,' he says. 'Don't you worry. Just go and knock them dead for the team.'

'I'll try to.' I go and kiss him. 'This *is* all for us, you know.'

'Sometimes I have to remind myself of that,' he says.

Petal comes in, the cartoon-on-television babysitter clearly having finished its shift. 'Were you shouting at Daddy?'

Ah. I'd hoped the noise of the telly might cover that. 'No,' I tell her. I flash a glance at Olly. 'We were just having a grown-up talk.'

'Well, you were making too much noise.'

I kneel in front of Petal. 'Mummy's going out now. Give me a kiss.' My daughter hugs me and I have the urge to never let her go.

'I don't know how late I'll be,' I say to Olly. This feels weird because I could count on one hand the amount of times I've been out in the evening without Olly in the last five years.

He comes and winds his arms round my waist. 'I'll be here,' Olly says. 'Whatever time it is. You know that.'

Tod toots his horn again. I pick up my handbag and blowing a kiss over my shoulder, I rush out of the door.

Chapter 25

We speed down to London in Tod's car. I don't think I've ever been in a vehicle so plush. I have no idea what it is, but the soft-leather seats mould around you and it whooshes when every other car I've ever been in rattles. There's some sort of soft jazzy music on the stereo, which isn't really my kind of thing, but tonight it hits the spot. If there was a drinks cabinet in here with a bottle of chilled white wine in it, I would be in seventh heaven. I sink back into my seat with a shuddering sigh.

'Nervous?' Tod asks.

'Terrified.' I've never been to anything like this before and don't know what to expect.

'No need to be. You'll be fine. The Prince's Trust has helped hundreds of businesses just like yours get off the ground. Plus, I hope we're going to make some important contacts tonight. All you need to do is be charming and keep your fingers crossed.' He casts a glance at me. 'Loving the look, by the way.'

'Thanks.'

Tod doesn't look too shabby himself. He's wearing a dinner jacket with a Nehru collar and it has a dragon embroidered in black thread on one side. Out of the blue, I think that we fit well together. Discomfited, I wonder where that thought came from.

'What was your news?'

'Oh.' In the excitement I'd forgotten all about that. 'I've organised myself a market stall. I start next week.' It hardly feels groundbreaking now that I've said it out loud.

'That *is* good news,' he says with a smile. 'Well done. Great initiative, Nell.'

I love the way that Tod is always so encouraging. I don't, however, tell him that I was spurred onto it because of the lack of enthusiasm from Betty.

'I'll give you any help that I can.'

It feels good to know that Tod has got my back.

Before long, we sweep up the broad expanse of The Mall and the magnificence of Buckingham Palace looms ahead of us. My knees start to tremble. Tod parks up in a side street and then, casually, takes my arm as we walk the short distance to the imposing gates of the palace.

We're stopped at the gates by armed policemen and Tod shows our invitation. We're waved in and we follow the rest of the guests heading towards the Grand Entrance. There are footmen in red and gold livery to show us the way. We enter a large quadrangle and make our way across and up the red-carpeted stairs and into the palace itself. My grip on Tod's arm tightens.

'OK?'

I take a deep breath. 'A bit wobbly.'

'You're doing fine.' He puts his hand on top of mine.

We're shown into an impressive hall decorated in white and gold with red carpet. This is quite the most sumptuous room that I've ever seen. It's thronging with people and is babbling with welcome noise. They all look like they know what they're doing, whereas I don't. When we're offered champagne by a liveried butler, I take one and try to sip it demurely while resisting the urge to knock it back in one. Tod, probably quite wisely, sips an orange juice.

There's a clap of hands. 'Ladies and gentlemen,' a man says. 'Please make your way to the ballroom.'

We're escorted up a stunning staircase decked with enormous, sparkling chandeliers and into a long gallery that has a high, glass ceiling and is lined with pictures of past royalty. The excitement inside me is rising to fever pitch and I don't know how I manage to keep myself walking beside Tod at a sedate pace. It opens into a vast ballroom hung with dazzling chandeliers. At one end is a canopy of red velvet drapes embroidered with gold, beneath which are the thrones for the Queen and Prince Philip. The walls are lined with tables, laden with trays of canapés and fabulous flower arrangements. Music wafts from the gallery at the other end, provided by a string quartet.

'This is the room where they hold the Investiture ceremonies,' Tod whispers to me.

I don't think I'm ever likely to get a knighthood so this may be my only ever chance to be in this room.

'Impressive, eh?'

Mind-numbing, speech-robbing, breathtaking. 'Oh, yes,' I finally manage.

I notice that Prince Charles is in the middle of the crowd and I've only ever seen him on the telly before. I've never even seen a member of the royal family in the flesh, let alone been in the same room as any of them. I get a star-struck head rush. 'Wow,' I breathe.

'Let's work the room,' Tod says. 'We'll see if we can get nearer to the Prince later.'

Still clinging to him, I trail in his wake as he approaches people we don't even know and introduces us.

As the night wears on and the champagne starts to loosen my tongue, I find myself talking to other people who are just like me and have been helped by The Prince's Trust to start their own business. I meet a woman who runs a small tea room, a young man with his own landscape gardening business and someone who designs funky stationery. I even find myself talking to the Ambassador for Nigeria about diamanté sparkles of all things.

Tod introduces me to a woman called Della, who I have a real laugh with as I tell her all about my business. She asks me to send her a sample handbag and slips me a business card. She's from a PR agency, but I've never heard of it. They are all suitably impressed with my handbag.

Just as the evening is drawing to a close and my jaw is aching from smiling and my head is spinning from too much champagne, one of the footmen approaches us and ushers us towards Prince Charles. We stand in a short line and then I'm presented to His Royal Highness. I have no idea what he says or what I say back, but I shake his hand and I think I curtsy, even though I'm not sure if I'm supposed to. Before I have the chance to do anything else, I'm whisked away again.

'Did that really happen?' I ask Tod.

'Feel good?'

'I feel fabulous,' I tell him. 'Thank you so much for bringing me.'

'My pleasure,' he says.

I leave the palace and the Prince behind me, walking on air.

Chapter 26

The small club where Olly did his punk gigs was painted primarily in black.

'It's dark in here, Daddy,' Petal said.

'Don't worry, sweet pea. I'll put the lights on.'

Against what every fibre of his being was telling him, he'd brought Petal along to his gig tonight. What else could he do?

Nell said that she'd trawled round their friends to try to find a babysitter and, just in case she'd missed anyone, he'd tried them all again. She was right.

He flicked on the lights that, to be quite honest, just made the place look seedier. His daughter wrinkled her perfect nose.

'It's only for a few hours until Daddy has finished work and then we can go home. Will you promise me that you'll be a good girl?'

Petal nodded, her butter-wouldn't-melt-in-her-mouth face firmly in place.

He had already dressed her in her favourite little pink pyjamas and she was swaddled against the night air in her

117

matching fluffy dressing gown. She'd sat quietly in the taxi he'd had to call. Unfortunately, Petal wasn't quite old enough yet to go on the back of the Vespa.

'I want you to sit under here and be really, really quiet.' Beneath the mixing desk was a large, vacant space. Just perfect for hiding a small child. He pushed away the thought that this was a really stupid idea. 'No one must know that you're here,' he whispered. 'It will be our special secret.'

'Mummy says that you shouldn't have secrets,' Petal expounded. 'It's naughty.'

'She's right,' Olly agreed. 'Absolutely right. Usually. But this is an extra special secret for one night only.'

His child didn't look convinced.

'We can tell Mummy,' he assured her. 'Just not anyone here.'

She looked moderately appeased.

'I want you to slide under here. I've brought Dude's bed.'

'But where will Dude sleep?'

'I've left him his cushion. He'll be fine. The minute we get home, Dude can have his bed back.' He placed it under the desk and hurried on. 'Your favourite blanky is in there and I want you to keep yourself nice and snuggly. Can you do that?'

Petal sucked her thumb and nodded.

'Good girl. That's great.' He kissed her smooth, warm cheek. 'You're Daddy's big girl.'

He could kill Nell for putting him in this position. If he'd have thought quite how awful this would be, he should have asked if Phil would have minded Petal being at the chip shop for a couple of hours. That would be better than this. As it was, Constance was on standby to come to the house in case Nell wasn't back in time for him to go on his night shift.

But it was too late to be thinking like that now – the place was about to open up and he was due to start in five minutes. No time to dash Petal off to Live and Let Fry before kick off.

It was unusual that he hadn't seen the owner, Jimmy, yet and he was thankful for small mercies. No doubt he'd be putting in an appearance soon. He normally opened up, cleared off into the back room for the duration of the evening, and then put his face out again at closing time. For someone who ran a music venue, he didn't seem all that keen on it.

'You need to settle in there now,' Olly said to Petal. 'People will be arriving in a minute.'

'Don't want to,' Petal said.

'Remember what we agreed?'

She nodded.

'It's just for a short while and you have to be as quiet as a mouse. It's like a little game.'

That brightened her face up considerably and he hated the fact that he was doing this. Petal slid under the desk and climbed into Dude's bed.

'Comfy?'

It was fair to say that his child didn't look impressed.

'I've brought these and when the music starts you must put them straight on.'

'I don't want to wear my ear muffins,' she complained.

'Ear muffs.'

'I had them when I was a baby.'

'The music will be very loud.' And some of the lyrics very ripe. 'They'll help to protect your ears.'

Petal put on the pink piggy ear muffs. God, she looked adorable enough to eat. Every time he looked at his child his heart contracted with love – though she was currently looking back at him with something bordering on contempt.

'I've brought some colouring books and pencils for you.' He handed them over. 'Happy?'

She shrugged her indifference.

'Daddy . . .'

'Yes, sweet pea?'

'I need a wee wee.'

'Not now, Petal,' he said. 'You went just before you came out.'

'I do need one. I can't hold it in.'

A sigh. 'All right, all right,' he said. 'Quick, quick. Come out.'

She clambered out from beneath the desk and he scooped her up and rushed her towards the loos. The gents was definitely a no-no and he just hoped that the ladies was considerably cleaner and with less lurid graffiti.

Thankfully, it was.

'Can you manage?'

'I'm not a *baby*,' Petal insisted. It was a recurrent complaint.

He waited outside the cubicle while his daughter seemed to take ages doing what she needed to do. 'Hurry up, Petal!'

'You can't hurry up wee wee, Daddy!' Voice indignant. 'It comes when it has to come.'

Why did women always take so long in toilets? It seemed that it started at a very young age.

'Finished!' she trumpeted eventually, and he rushed her back to the safety of the mixing desk.

He'd settled her with her books and piggy ear muffs just as Jimmy appeared. 'All right, Olly?'

'Yeah, mate. Good.'

'All set for tonight?'

'Yeah.' He was willing Petal to keep quiet and not pop her inquisitive little head out to see who it was.

'Let's get the punters in, then.' Jimmy wandered off to open the door.

Three hours. That's all he needed to get through. Just three hours. Then he and Petal would be home and dry.

Two hours in and all had been going quite well. Relatively. The dance floor had been jumping – or, more accurately, pogoing – with punk throwbacks enjoying tracks by Stiff Little Fingers, The Damned, Dead Kennedys and the obligatory Sex Pistols. If he played this stuff for long enough, he might even begin to like it – even though it couldn't compare to the likes of The Kinks, The Who and The almighty Beatles.

Petal had stayed in the hidey-hole, reading books and giving him an angelic smile every time he bent down to wave at her. She'd even kept her ear muffs in place and although she'd kept up a constant stream of chatter while she coloured in her books, it was completely inaudible above the rest of the noise. Now, unfortunately, she was getting restless.

As the club was getting warmer, she'd kicked off her

blanket and now the dressing gown had been tugged off too. It was difficult trying to keep a close eye on her as he mixed the tracks. He had hoped, in vain, that she might have been so tired by now that she'd have nodded off to sleep. No such luck.

'Daddy!' Petal tugged at his trouser leg. 'Da-dee!'

Olly crouched down. 'What, Petalmeister? Just be a good girl for a little bit longer.'

'But Daddy, I'm *bored*.' She rolled her eyes to prove just how bored she really was.

He couldn't help but smile. 'I'm nearly done. Then we can go home and you can have a lovely treat for being so good.'

'What?'

He racked his brains. 'Ice cream?'

'Play me a song.'

'Now? I can't do that, sweet pea.'

'*Glee*,' she said. 'I want *Glee*.' Her face said, I've listened to this crap all night; you'd better come up with it.

'I haven't got any *Glee*.' The song that was her very favourite was 'Don't Stop Believing'.

'It's in your box, Daddy,' his daughter informed him. 'I put it there.'

'Really?' His heart sank. How could a child of his loins possibly have such awful taste in music? He rummaged in his bag and, sure enough, Petal's favourite *Glee* CD was safely secreted in here. Petal smiled smugly at him. 'It won't work in here.'

Her expression said, liar.

'I can't, Petal.'

Now we'd moved on to, 'If you loved me . . .'

He could feel himself weakening. 'OK, OK,' he said to her, holding up his hands in resignation. 'Then you promise to be a good girl until we go home?'

'Yes.' The nod was adamant.

Olly sighed to himself. 'For one night only, a break with tradition. A little lady has specially requested this tune, so bear with me for three minutes.'

For better, for worse, he put on the cast of *Glee* singing 'Don't Stop Believing'. It seemed that most of the stunned audience couldn't *begin* to believe it. They began to jeer as Petal sang along happily under the desk. They were barely into the chorus when Jimmy burst through the door at the back.

'What the hell are you doing?' he demanded. It seemed that he did listen, after all.

'I'll take it off,' Olly promised.

'Are you taking the fucking piss?'

'Right now. It's off. It's off now.' And the cast of *Glee* screeched to a premature halt. The audience cheered.

It was then that Petal decided to pop her head out. 'Hello.'

Jimmy looked at her open-mouthed. 'Finish tonight,' he snapped. There was froth forming at the corners of his mouth. 'Don't come back. Ever. This isn't a bloody crèche.'

'He's not a nice man,' Petal observed as Jimmy stomped away.

'No,' Olly said.

But it was only fair to admit that he had a point.

Chapter 27

'We can't go straight home,' Tod says. 'The night is still young.'

Unfortunately, I'm not. Already I've gone from feeling like I could swing round all the lamp posts in the style of Gene Kelly to yawning my head off. This must be what it feels like to come down from a drug high. I'll swear I could lie down and sleep for a week.

We're still arm in arm walking back towards Tod's car.

'Let's go for a nightcap.'

'I don't want any more booze.' I hold up a hand. 'I have drunk deeply at the cup of the Prince's hospitality.'

'And why not?' Tod laughs. 'It's not every day you get the chance to do that.'

No. However, all I really want to do now is go straight home to Olly and Petal and tell them all about my evening and how I would have loved them to be there. But Tod has been so good that I don't want to put a dampener on his mood.

'Let's have coffee, then,' he suggests. 'I'll take you home, fit and sober.'

I can't argue with that. 'Sounds good.'

Tod finds a swish hotel nearby and we settle ourselves into the lounge as he orders coffee for both of us. Ordinarily, I would have been blown away by this place, but I've just come from Buckingham Palace and it would take an awful lot to beat that. I sink back into the plush sofa with a happy sigh. Tod sits next to me, close, and rests his arm across the back of the cushion.

'You did really well,' he says. 'You impressed an important contact tonight.'

'I did?' That yawn escapes again.

'The woman from Prestige PR,' he says. 'You've never heard of them?'

'No.'

'Della Jewel is a player. You've got her card?'

'Yes.' Safely in my handbag, along with a dozen others.

'Send her a sample bag *tomorrow*. Don't forget.'

I promise that I won't.

'You will not believe whose hands she can get them into. She's one well connected lady. You did well to charm her.'

'I just had a good laugh with her. She was a lot of fun.' If I'd known how important she was I'd probably have clammed up completely.

The coffee appears and as we drink it, my eyes grow heavier.

'You look like you should be tucked up in bed,' Tod says, and there's a twinkle in his eye.

I feel myself flush. Is he flirting with me? This is the first time in years that I've been alone with a man who isn't Olly and I'm suddenly very conscious of it.

'I should go home now,' I say.

'Drink up,' Tod instructs, with what may be a rueful smile. 'Your carriage awaits.'

A short while later and we're whizzing up the motorway. The traffic is much lighter on the journey home and soon we take the turn-off to Hitchin. Not much longer and we pull up outside my house. How very scruffy and small it looks after what I've seen tonight. I realise that I have a severe case of palace envy.

It's late but there's still a light on. Olly should be home from his punk gig and getting ready to go on his night shift. I'm glad that I've caught him before he leaves.

Tod and I sit there under the orange glow of the street light.

'Well,' Tod says. 'I'll wish you good night.'

'Good night. See you next week.' I gather my handbag to me. 'Thanks so much for everything. I've really enjoyed it.'

'Thanks for being the perfect guest.' Tod leans towards me. He tilts my chin with his finger and then softly kisses me on the lips.

And, at that, I bolt out of the car.

Chapter 28

On the Saturday after my trip to Buckingham Palace, I make my debut at Hitchin market. I'd like to say that it's much anticipated, and it is – but only by me. My hedonistic night out with Tod and member of our royal family is a fast receding memory. It was very, very pleasant but it doesn't actually feel like it happened to me any more.

The only part that is permanently seared in my brain is my kiss with Tod. Whatever happens, whatever future work events that we have to go to, that must never, ever be repeated again. I'm a woman in a long-term, committed relationship, for heaven's sake. A mother of one particularly exuberant four-year-old. What on earth was I thinking? But, in truth, I wasn't thinking. I was caught up in the moment and I wasn't thinking at all. That doesn't make me feel any less guilty though. Still, I have enough on my mind today to keep me occupied and stop me from dwelling on it.

It's pouring down with rain when we set up the market stall and it doesn't look like it will stop for the entire day. The sky is dark and sagging with grey, water-laden clouds. A cold wind swirls round my feet and even my faux-vintage army boots – twenty quid from Shoe Zone – can't keep it out. Forget fairy tale parties at palaces and softly stolen kisses. This is more like my version of reality.

Everyone else is unloading vans but as we don't have a car, Olly and I lugged our stock up here in bin bags first thing this morning – after his night shift and before he went to bed. Even Petal was loaded up. If we can train Dude to pull a sledge, then we might well do so.

'Good luck,' Olly says and gives me a peck on the cheek.

Things are a bit cool between us and I know that he blames me for losing his punk gig, which despite insisting he hated it, I think he quite misses. We both miss the money, that's for sure.

I've spent half of the night wide awake and making stock and now have about thirty handbags to display. There's a handful of Fish & Chips bags and some of the Eat Me/Drink Me ones. My new design features the Sindy doll in a silver frame with a view of Buckingham Palace behind her. I'm sure you can guess what inspired that one. But as I put them out, I realise that there probably isn't enough choice to fill a stall. I've got plenty of designs knocking around in my skull, but it's the time and the cash that I lack to bring them all to fruition. Hopefully today will give me some more money to play with.

I've done my best to dress the stall and have made candy-stripe curtains to brighten up the framework and I've hung some multi-coloured bunting across the front, which I spent half the night making. I've got big glass jars that I've filled with colourful sweets and there are swirly lollipops sticking out of the top. I've covered cardboard boxes of differing sizes with bright wrapping paper so that I can display the bags at a variety of heights.

Petal is currently eating my decorations, dipping her chubby fingers into the jars of sweets.

'No more,' I say. 'You'll be sick.'

'I won't,' she assures me.

'Well, no more or you won't eat your dinner.'

My child huffs. 'Mummy, that's *hours* away.'

I'm opposite a fruit and veg stall and the man is already bellowing at the top of his voice, despite there being a mere handful of shoppers braving the elements.

'POUND A BOWL, LADIES! POUND A BOWL! GET YOUR APPLES HERE. POUND A BOWL!'

My daughter studies him, open-mouthed.

The price labels on my handbags read sixty-five pounds and I wonder nervously if they are going to be too steep for my audience.

'HANDBAGS!' Petal shouts, making me jump. 'GET A HANDBAG!'

'Shush,' I say.

'*He's* shouting!' Petal points to the fruit and veg man with indignation.

So he is. 'I don't want you to shout. It's not what little girls do.'

Petal pulls her get-a-life face.

'Just be good, Petal. Mummy has to concentrate on work.'

'But nothing's happening.'

Which is also true. People are looking with interest at my handbags as they pass. One or two have even been brave enough to pick them up and examine them. They've taken my sweets. They've listened to my patter. They've all cooed over the bags and have told me how witty they are and how they're great fun and how someone they know would love one. But not a single soul has bought one.

By lunchtime, I'm completely demoralised and starving hungry. The shouting from the man on the fruit and veg stall has started to punch a hole in my brain and I'm still no nearer to making my fortune from handbags. At this rate, I'm not even going to cover the cost of my stall. My hunger is not helped by the fact that I'm just a few metres down from a stall selling Chinese takeaway and the delicious smell has been drifting towards me all morning.

'Want some Chinese food, Petal?'

My daughter nods her acquiescence. She's getting restless and cranky. My heart goes out to her. Normal mothers would be taking their daughters swimming or street dancing or putting them through stage school so that they can become the next *X Factor* fodder. My child has to hang round a market stall in the freezing cold getting told off.

'When can we go home?' she wants to know.

Now, I think to myself, but in all honesty, I know that I mustn't give up so easily.

'Later,' I say. 'First we'll have something to eat. That'll make us feel better. Mind the stall while I go and queue up.' I point at the takeaway food stall. 'I'll be right next door. Don't move. I can see you from where I'll be.'

I leave Petal behind our stall and go and get us two cartons of sweet and sour chicken and rice. When I return, Petal sits on the one stool we have and spoons the food gratefully into her mouth with a plastic fork. It's delicious and warms me up at least down to my knees. Beyond that, I have lost all feeling and may never get it back.

'Better?' I ask Petal.

She nods, smiling again.

Then a miraculous thing happens. A young, trendy woman moves down from the vintage clothes stall that I so often frequent and works her way towards me and, more importantly, my handbags.

'Wow,' she says as she sees them. 'They're totally gorgeous.'

'Thanks.'

'Would you like a sweetie?' Petal says. 'I'm not allowed one.'

'You can have one more,' I say to my child, who instantly helps herself and then offers the jar to the woman.

'I'd love a sweet,' she says, and takes one from Petal, 'and I'd love a bag too.'

I nearly fall over in a dead faint. 'Really?'

She laughs. 'Really.' She pulls her purse out of her handbag. Old, tatty. Not a patch on mine. I should ask her if she'd like to wear it now and I can bin that one for her, but I'm not bold enough to do so.

The woman counts out the cash for me.

I allow Petal to help me slide the bag into its protective cover and I hand it over. 'I hope you enjoy it.'

'I'm sure I will,' and she swings away, oblivious to the admiring stare from the fruit and veg man.

I feel like crying with joy. My daughter offers up her hand and I high-five her. 'Daddy will be so proud of us. We made our first sale, Petal!'

Chapter 29

It is, of course, our one and only sale of the day. All that cold, that standing around for a few pounds' profit. Can I put my daughter through that every weekend? Can I put myself through it?

Maybe I'm not cut out for business. I just thought I could set up in business easily, making great handbags and although I didn't expect the world to fall at my feet, I thought it would all go reasonably smoothly. I hadn't quite bargained on the relentless slog for precious little reward.

I'm in two minds whether to cancel my stall for next week and just stay at home licking my wounds. But when I have my now weekly coffee session with Tod, he urges me on. Later, I find myself sketching out new designs, in response to my realisation that I need a larger range to offer.

Then, a week after my fabulous trip to Buckingham Palace, the local papers hit the mat. I'm all over them. To my delight and surprise, I even make the front page on one of them. LOCAL GIRL MEETS PRINCE is one headline. FROM FISH AND CHIPS

TO THE PALACE is the other and there's a picture of me shaking hands with Prince Charles that I had no idea was taken. Tod is smiling serenely in the background.

'Look at Mummy!' Petal cries with delight. 'She's a famous lady like Cheryl Cole.'

Praise indeed.

Olly comes and peers over my shoulder. 'I'm impressed.'

'So you should be,' I tease. 'Not everyone's girlfriend rubs shoulders with royalty.'

'Great photo,' he says, taking the paper to read the write-up. 'Wish I could have been there.' There's something in his voice that I can't put my finger on – a touch of jealousy, sadness or even some resentment.

'This won't change me,' I assure him teasingly. 'I'll still be the same down-to-earth girl you met and fell in love with.'

'I know,' he says. But he doesn't sound like he means it.

'Sometimes I'll have to do things without you.'

'Yeah,' he says. 'I'll be the stay-at-home husband while you get all the glamour.'

One event, I think. That's all it's been, one event.

Olly stares up at me and frowns. 'I'm worried that you'll be up, up and away and you'll forget about us.'

'That's ridiculous. Why on earth would I do that?'

The phone starts to ring as other friends start to get their papers delivered and it's red hot for the rest of the day. I get dozens of emails from well-wishers and my spirits lift once more. The text messages never stop. Olly brings me tea, on the hour, every hour, and something to eat for dinner. I can't even remember what. I can't even remember eating it. And I don't get time to address the strained atmosphere with him and what it's really all about.

I rush out of my house with a brief kiss for Olly and a bear hug for Petal, and run down the road to the town centre so that I'm not late for my shift. When I reach Live and Let Fry, I see a familiar figure waiting outside.

Slowing down, I try to compose myself and fail. My mentor is waiting for me and as I approach, he drops his usual cool demeanour and, instead, he picks me up and twirls me round.

'Woo hoo! Well done, Nell,' he says breathlessly as he spins me back down to the ground. Somewhat reluctantly, it seems, he releases his tight hold on me.

This is the reaction that I'd hoped for from Olly.

'I've been out all day,' Tod explains. 'I didn't have a minute to call you. Fabulous coverage. You can't buy that sort of publicity.'

'Thanks to you,' I acknowledge. 'I'm so grateful that you asked me to go to the reception with you.'

'It turned out well,' he admits. 'I hoped that you might get some column inches, but front page? Wow.'

'So what now?'

'We try to capitalise on it. I'll put some ideas together this week.' He slips a bag from over his shoulder. 'In the meantime, you can borrow this.'

'A laptop?' At least that's what I think it is. I'm sure he just doesn't mean the bag, which I have to say is a somewhat utilitarian plastic one. Perhaps I could do a range of fab laptop bags.

'You can put some of your products on eBay while you're

waiting to start up your website. At least then you'll have an internet presence.'

'Absolutely.' I don't like to tell him that I'm clueless when it comes to computers. 'That's great. Thanks.'

'How did the market stall go?'

'Er . . . slow,' I tell him, thinking that's probably all he needs to know, otherwise it will sound like I'm whining. 'I guess it will take time.'

'Let's hope that business picks up for you this week.'

'I have to go,' I tell him with a nod towards the shop door. 'Or I'll be late for my shift.'

'I wanted to see where you worked.'

'Come in,' I offer. I'd love him to see how great the shop looks and show off my work. 'You can have some chips on the house.'

He laughs. 'I'm going out to dinner with friends.'

'Of course.' That makes me feel gauche. 'I didn't think.'

'It was a nice offer, Nell,' he says. 'I'm sorry I can't stay.'

A shrug. 'Another time.' All the while I'm thinking how stupid it was to offer someone like Tod free chips. I could cut out my own tongue.

I have no idea what Tod's personal life is like. Maybe there's a pretty little blonde waiting at home. I don't know. Maybe there are several of them. He's never mentioned anyone and, besides, it's none of my business. He's just a mentor, nothing more. We're not even friends. This is his job. He's looked after dozens of people like me. I wonder how many other people he asked to go to the Palace with him before he got to me?

I watch him walk away and when he gets to the end of the

alley, he turns and waves. I puff out a sigh and head for my night's work.

Swinging inside Live and Let Fry, I'm greeted by a loud cheer. Jenny, Constance and Phil are all holding balloons that say 'Congratulations!'

'Aw, guys!'

They come and hug me.

'Clever girl,' Phil says proudly. 'Clever girl.'

'I just had my photo taken with Prince Charles.' I think I'm blushing.

'Oh my word,' Constance says. 'Was it all lovely?'

'It was pretty impressive,' I admit.

'We always knew you were going to be brilliant,' Constance gushes.

'Yeah, remember us when you're rich and famous,' Jenny adds. I think she's teasing, but it worries me that she's not the first person to voice that sentiment.

'They gave a lovely mention of Live and Let Fry,' Phil says. There are carefully cut out copies of the article stuck on the newly painted wall above each table. 'There'll be no holding you back now. You won't be doing shifts here for much longer.'

I don't like to tell him that I lost money on the market stall and that Olly was kicked out of a nice little job due to my last-minute jaunt to the Palace. They all have such faith in my abilities that I want them to believe that everything is wonderful. And, as everything is resting on this, I want to believe it myself.

Chapter 30

The next morning, Petal and I are curled up in bed together. My daughter has been wriggling since the break of dawn and I'm hugging her close to me, which I hope she interprets as a sign of maternal love, when all I'm really trying to do is keep her still.

I hear the front door close quietly and the sound of Olly tip-toeing into the kitchen as he comes back from his night shift. Reaching for my phone, I text him: We R awake!

He texts back, T? xx

To which he receives a row of kisses in return. As we live in a terraced house and we're trying to encourage Petal not to shout, Olly and I spend a lot of time texting each other even though we're often in the next room.

Moments later he comes up the stairs and I rouse myself enough to take the mug of tea from him.

'Hi,' he says as he sits down next to me and kisses me.

'Good night?'

'Not that you'd notice,' Olly says. 'Sitting at a conveyor belt for eight hours putting mushrooms and peppers on pizza isn't the most exciting way to spend a night.' He raises his eyebrows at me. 'I can think of better ways.'

'I would like to spend a night eating candyfloss,' Petal pipes up.

'I'd like you to spend a night in your own bed,' I add.

'You, young lady, can go and get your breakfast,' Olly says. She pulls a face. 'You make it for me, Daddy.'

'I have. It's all set out on the table. I've poured your juice, and your cereal is already waiting in the bowl. All you have to do is put milk on it.'

'OK.'

She bounces out of the bed and I spread out into my rightful space. 'Ah, bliss.'

'I heard that, Mummy,' my child says.

'Pour the milk carefully,' Olly advises. 'Make sure it doesn't go via the floor.'

'What does "via" mean?'

'It means that the milk goes into the bowl, not on the floor or the table.'

'I'm not a *baby*,' she tuts before disappearing out of the door.

'Remind me,' I say, 'why are we thinking of having another one?'

'We are?' Olly queries as he lies down beside me. 'Chance would be a fine thing.'

'If you're very quick and very quiet, we could make a start now.' I try to look seductive even though I probably have a severe case of bed-head.

He shakes his head. 'Too tired,' he says, which is unusual as Olly tries never to miss an opportunity because we're never quite sure when our next one might be. 'Besides,' he continues, 'I've got something I'd like to ask you.'

'Oh.' I hope he's not going to grill me about my relationship with Tod. I don't want to start this fine and unsullied morning with an argument.

Olly rolls onto his tum and stares up at me. I can't read the expression on his face. He takes my hands in his. 'Nell McNamara,' he says, 'would you do me the very great honour of marrying me?'

It's a good job that I'm not drinking my tea, otherwise I would spit it out.

'Marry you?' I can't stop myself from blinking. 'Just like that?'

'It can't be so much of a surprise.'

'Olly, we've been together for ten years and you've never really mentioned it before.'

'Well,' he says, 'we've always been OK as we are before.'

'And we're not now?'

He shrugs. 'I just thought the time was right.'

I don't know why I suddenly feel so nervous. I've known Olly for ever. We were little more than children when we started going out together. I always hoped this day would come. Perhaps it's just that being together for so long has taken the edge off the excitement. Or maybe if Olly had whisked me away to Paris for the weekend to propose it would feel more special. But in our own bed when I'm barely awake? It's just so out of the blue and why now?

'What do you reckon?' Olly, while I'm musing, is waiting patiently for my answer.

'Yes,' I say. 'Of course.'

He comes and snuggles up next to me, taking me in his arms. 'Good.' He kisses me in a long and leisurely fashion and, finally, the excitement starts to rise in me.

Right on cue, Petal appears in the doorway. My child is the best contraception known to man. 'I've finished my breakfast.'

'Come here, Petalmeister,' Olly says, clearly feeling much more charitable than me. 'How do you fancy being a flower girl?'

'A flower girl?' She climbs onto the bed. 'What's that?'

'Mummy and Daddy are going to get married. You get to be the most important person on the day because you carry the flowers for us.'

'Yay!' she shouts and bounces up and down excitedly. 'Yay!'

Olly holds her hands as she jumps and they both chuckle with delight. 'Yay!'

'Yay!' I echo, but the bouncing up and down feeling doesn't quite come.

Chapter 31

After my shift at Live and Let Fry, I sit having a cup of tea with Phil, Jenny and Constance. The sign on the door reads 'closed' and we all heaved a sigh of relief after the lunchtime rush. The steady stream of customers beating a path to Phil's door after the makeover looks like it has no intention of returning to a trickle.

'You've been quiet today, Nell, love,' Constance notes. 'Everything OK?'

'Yeah.' I nurse my tea.

'Tired?'

I smile at my friend. 'Always.'

'But this is something more?'

'All is well in the world of big business, isn't it?' Phil looks anxious.

'It's fine,' I assure them. 'More than fine. One of the contacts I met at Buckingham Palace asked me to send her a sample handbag. I sent her the Fish & Chips one.' I can only sit and hope that Della Jewel likes it.

In the meantime, every spare moment this week has been spent making up my new designs. I'm particularly pleased with one that says Ms on one side and Mrs on the other, and is trimmed with lace. Perhaps that should have been an omen for what was about to come? I wonder if it was seeing them laying around that put the idea into Olly's head. 'Tod told me that she's really well connected, so keep your fingers crossed for me.' I take a deep breath and they all wait. I muster a smile. 'Oh, and Olly has asked me to marry him.'

'Oh, love,' Constance says, her face breaking into a wide grin, 'that's marvellous.'

'Lucky bitch,' Jenny says.

I flinch inside at the hard edge to Jenny's voice. It's unlike her.

'Jen!' Constance admonishes.

'Well,' Jen tuts, 'she is.'

But I don't have time to dwell on it as Phil pumps my hand heartily.

'Congratulations, Nell.' He crushes my fingers. 'Congratulations.'

Constance studies me. 'So why the sad face?'

'I don't know,' I admit.

Jen frowns. 'You have said yes?'

'Yes. Of course, I have. It's just that . . . ' I'm at a loss for words. Exactly what is my problem? Is it the timing of this that's all wrong? I want all my attention focused on building my business, but perhaps that's what Olly is worried about. Is this his idea of a distraction? Does he think that this is a way of pinning me down? Olly says that he's enthusiastic about my fledgling business, but is he really? Is it some sort of threat to his manhood that I want to be the high-flyer? Does he think that by marrying me, I'll be content to go back to being the little woman at home again?

'It's a big step,' Constance says, 'but you've already got a child together, Nell. There's no bigger commitment than that.'

'I know.' Petal loves that we're getting married. She'd already started to ask why we weren't. We gave her Olly's surname – Meyers – and it's sometimes complicated that I have a different name to her. The practicalities of getting married far outweigh the reasons not to.

'It's just a piece of paper,' Jen adds with an attempt at a careless shrug.

But it's a piece of paper that I know Jen desperately wants – so much more than I do, it seems.

'I'm being silly.' I shake my concerns away. 'It'll be wonderful.' If Olly is worried about business changing the status quo, I'm worried that marriage will do the same thing.

'We'd better all be invited,' Jen says.

'I'd love to get a new hat.' Constance pats her hair.

'I've got a suit that never gets an airing these days,' Phil adds.

'Get the kettle on again, Phil,' Jen says. 'We need a toast.'

'Righto.' Off Phil goes.

'Have you set a date yet?'

'Soon,' I tell Constance. 'Now that we've finally decided, Olly says there's no point in waiting.'

'It is *your* decision, too,' Constance points out.

'I know. And I am happy. Really, I am.'

144

'God,' Jenny mutters, 'listen to her. You'd think she'd been asked to a funeral, not a wedding! *I'll* have him if you're not interested.'

But I am interested. I don't know why I'm being like this. It will all be fine. Absolutely fine.

Chapter 32

When I do my stint the next Saturday at Hitchin market, the sun shines. The handbags sell like hot cakes. I thank my lucky stars for the coverage in the local paper, which is clearly what has brought the punters to my door – or to my stall, in this case.

Petal and I work flat out all day and it makes me smile when I listen to my daughter who is, one day into being a market trader's daughter, already developing her own line of patter and charming the customers.

After last week's let-down, I only brought twenty handbags with me – all I could carry single-handedly. Olly has a casual driving job today for a friend, so he's tied up. As well as the Fish & Chips style and the Eat Me/Drink Me bags, I tried out two more designs. The Ms & Mrs bag for brides was a big hit. So was the one with nothing but big red lips on it. By lunchtime they had all gone. Every single one. What a difference a day makes!

Counting out the money, I'm surprised by how much we've

taken. By any account, that's a handsome profit for the day. Next week, I'll bring much more stock – assuming that I can split myself in two in order to find the time to make it.

Flushed with success, I give myself and Petal the rest of the day off. From my takings, I treat her to a pretty hot-pink scrunchy from the haberdashery stall as a thank you for being a good girl. While I'm there, I pick up a few buttons and bits, determined to try out some more designs. I'll spend the rest of the afternoon making handbags and having a go at putting up a page on eBay now that I've got a laptop on loan from Tod.

But before I do all that, I buy piping hot pasties from the bakery stall for me and for Petal. We take them and sit at our favourite spot by the edge of the market on the steps that overlook the duck pond and St Mary's Church. We sit quietly together amid the hopeful ducks and Petal stifles a yawn, too tired today to chase after them. There's probably some law against having your child working at four – even if it is part-time – and I pull my daughter close and she rests her head on me. I don't even mind that she drops bits of flaky pastry down my coat as she eats. Petal has been an absolute treasure.

When we've eaten our lunch and the cold is starting to set in again, we walk towards home, hand in hand. I pop into the printers and collect some of the printed designs that he's been producing for me. After that, we swing past the library and I help Petal choose some new books to read as she gets through them at a rate of knots. Then, at home, we settle down for an afternoon of handbag production.

Switching on the telly, I find some rubbish for Petal to watch and then I get out Tod's borrowed laptop. I manage to create myself an eBay account and link it to PayPal – it's all new to me but it's not too complicated, even for a committed technophobe. With Phil's camera, I take a smart picture of the bags and without too much muttering, upload them, then I write a bit of blurb. Sorted. It feels good to finally have the bags up for sale on the internet but I do wonder if anyone will realise I'm actually there.

When I've done all that, I join Petal in front of the television and surround myself with bags and trimmings and sketches. Petal shuffles up next to me and I keep her amused with some scraps of fabric and her kiddy scissors. One day, I hope she'll be keen to help me properly. Nell McNamara and Petal Meyers, handbag providers to the stars! How nice would that be?

It's coming up to teatime and I haven't a clue what to cook, but it will be something quick. Pasta again, more than likely. I'm sure that I should have been born Italian. Or I may eventually turn into one with all the pizza and pasta we consume. I wonder what time Olly will be home. I'm not working at the chip shop tonight, so we can all settle down and watch whatever delights Saturday-night telly has to offer together as a family.

In companionable silence, Petal and I watch *What's New Scooby-Doo?* and a repeated episode of *Come Dine with Me*, which I've always said that Olly should apply to go on. Petal gets bored with that so we flick over and watch some sort of youth chat show. The first person is someone from one of those popular teen soaps that neither Petal nor I watch. JLS are on singing their new song, which I think my child enjoys far too much, and then we're back to the studio couch and some other minor celeb who's talking about nothing of particular interest.

One of my new designs features a big Jammie Dodger – my daughter's favourite biscuit. Another is taken from a colourful line of Russian dolls that my parents bought Petal for her last birthday. I cut and stick and glue and embellish like a thing possessed. Looking good. I also need to do some more Fish & Chips and Eat Me/Drink Me bags as I don't want to make the mistake of running out again next week.

On the television, a famous footballer's wife pops up. Chantelle Clarke – on here to promote her new 'young adult' novels – is all blonde hair and white teeth. I have one eye on the telly, one eye on my bags, so I'm not really paying full attention.

'Look, Mummy.' Petal points at the screen.

I look up, and as Chantelle twitters on about her books and how marvellous they are, I suddenly realise what I'm seeing.

'Oh, my goodness.'

Petal beams at me. 'It's your handbag.'

She's right. There on the sofa next to this high-end, celebrity WAG is my Fish & Chips handbag. In full view of the camera. My mouth drops open. Della Jewel, the PR woman I met at the Palace must have organised this. How else would someone like Chantelle have got hold of it? I could ask for no better endorsement for my handbags.

'It looks pretty, Mummy,' Petal says, clapping her hands together.

It does. And I hope that a lot of other people think so too.

Chapter 33

Well, of course, life then goes crazy. In this age of celebrity worship, every woman under the age of sixty seems to want what Chantelle Clarke has and I can't make stock quick enough to keep up with the orders.

I send flowers to Della Jewel at her PR agency to thank her for the exposure. I can't believe that she's been kind enough to do this for me when I hardly even know the woman. Her office calls and asks if there's been some mistake. I just tell them that I'm really grateful for her input and it's simply a small token of my thanks, but I wonder if Tod is really behind this. It's just like him not to take the credit for it.

Christmas came and went with minimal fuss. We stopped for a turkey dinner that Olly made and then I went straight back to making handbags while we watched the ninety-seventh showing of *Raiders of the Lost Ark* and *Mary Poppins* – now a firm favourite with Petal.

Within a few short weeks, the money starts rolling in and I soon have enough to commission a website. The web designer that Tod found for me puts it together really quickly so that I can sell directly from there as well as through eBay. As soon as I'm online, the orders ratchet up one more notch.

Amid a torrent of tears, I give up my shifts at Live and Let Fry, although I keep the market stall. It's too lucrative not to. I miss Phil and the gang terribly and try to pop into the chippy whenever I find myself in town. My phone never stops ringing. I don't even try to pause to answer it now or I'd never get anything finished. At midnight every night, I'm still packing up orders. At six every morning, I'm up and doing it again. As my name starts to spread, I give a dozen different press interviews in trade magazines and, after that, the phone rings even more. Several high-end boutiques call me and ask to stock my handbags. Betty the Bag Lady – who has never contacted me since the day I left my first handbag there – rings and texts constantly. Peevishly, I don't return her calls.

Then Chantelle Clarke is featured in *Heat* magazine with my bag over her shoulder and the pressure increases further.

Jen and Constance have been brilliant. When they've finished their shifts together at the chippy, they come straight to my house and get stuck into hand-finishing the handbags with me for a bit of extra cash. They both prove to be demons with the glue gun and the hot-fix diamanté applicator. But even that is failing to keep pace with demand and I realise that I'm going to have to take on more staff if I'm to have any hope of keeping my head above water.

Straight from his night shift, Olly has been on the phone all morning taking orders and he comes into the living room while all three of us are working. Petal is at pre-school now every morning, so that gives us some breathing space too.

'Woaw,' Olly says as he stands and surveys the wreckage around him. 'It looks like a small nuclear bomb has exploded in here.'

It's fair to say that our house is no longer our own. Every square inch of space is filled with boxes of handbags, fabric and trimmings. Cartons with orders ready to be dispatched are stacked in the hall. Even the kitchen table is covered with sketches. Family mealtimes are a distant memory. So is our sex life.

'Who's been on the phone?'

Olly reels off a lengthy list of the businesses he's dealt with this morning.

'You need to get onto Dodmans too' – the handbag frame supplier – 'and order some more stock. I need to have some more diamanté sparkles by the end of the week before we run out. Can you also give the printer a ring and see if the latest batch of designs is ready?' As I'm pausing for breath, Jenny looks up from her work.

'You look absolutely knackered, Olly,' she says softly.

'I am,' he admits, seemingly pleased that someone has actually noticed.

'We're both exhausted,' I butt in. This may be all my dreams come true, but there's certainly a nightmarish quality to it as well.

'Come here,' Jen says to my lover (a somewhat loose term now). 'Sit down for five minutes. Let me rub your shoulders. I have healing hands.'

Olly does as he's told and Jen stands behind him and starts to massage his back. My dearly beloved makes suitably appreciative noises. Just as I'm starting to get a tiny bit jealous, Jenny looks up at me. 'You next, lady,' she says. 'Neither of you can go on at this pace.'

Olly and I swap places and I have to say that Jen manages to find knots that I never knew I had.

'Let's stop for a break,' I say when some of the tension has been eased from my shoulders. 'I'll go and put the kettle on.'

Olly trails after me into the kitchen. 'Jen's right,' he says as I clatter about with the cups. 'We don't get a minute's peace now.'

'The business has to come first,' I tell him. 'Just while we're setting up. This is critical for me. All the publicity has been fantastic and I have to make sure I capitalise on that. Tod says—'

At that Olly rolls his eyes and so I let the sentence go unfinished. But what Tod does say is that this is probably the best possible chance I'll have to establish my brand in the public eye and I have to seize every opportunity before the media move on to someone else – as they inevitably will. I just don't understand why Olly can't see this. It seems as if he just wants me to knock out a few bags at Hitchin market every week and be content with that. But this is my big break. This could transform our future.

'What about the wedding?' Olly says.

The date that we've settled on is in less than a month and it's fair to say that I've done very little towards organising it. I simply haven't had the time.

'Maybe we should postpone it,' I suggest tentatively. We were being ridiculously optimistic about booking it for when we did. Things are quite strained between us at the moment and I'm not sure that it's the right time to be tripping down the aisle. 'We've waited this long. Can't we wait a little longer until things settle down here?'

'What if they never do?' Olly says. 'What if this craziness is how our life is going to be from now on?' He paces the floor. 'I saw what being obsessed by his business did to my dad. It completely destroyed him, Nell. Because of the strain, he died long before his time. I don't want that kind of stress for us.'

'I can understand that, but at some point we have to put in more effort to get a better life. Now is my opportunity.'

He doesn't look convinced.

'I want more than this, Olly.' I gesture at the shabby kitchen. 'I want our own home, not one where the landlord can chuck us out at any moment. I want a garden for Petal, somewhere for her to play that doesn't involve a ten-minute walk to the park. I'd like a car. We're too old to be riding round on a scooter now. It's ridiculous. You're a family man. You have responsibilities. I'm trying to do this for all of us. Don't you want more?'

'I want *you*,' he says. 'I want you and Petal and life as it was before. That's all. I'm frightened that you want more than I can ever be.'

'Oh, Olly. That's so not true.' All my rage dissipates and I go to him and we hold each other tightly.

'You do still want to get married?' he murmurs against my hair.

'Of course I do.'

There's only ever been Olly. He's been the one love of my life. I need to make time to do this. If only I could think how.

Chapter 34

We have a beautiful Norman church in the centre of Hitchin, set in its own grounds, but as we're not churchgoers, we opt instead for the register office in Stevenage, which is not beautiful and not Norman and is at the back of Matalan.

I did wonder whether we were actually going to make it to this day at all. It's been touch and go on several occasions, but somehow, in the midst of all the madness, we've managed it.

My plan to make my own dress seemed insane at three o'clock this morning when I was still hemming it. Pink is the theme – Petal would hear of nothing else – and so I've got a hot-pink shift with a vintage cream lace cape, a long string of cream pearls, and shoes that I had dyed to match. My bouquet is a handful of hot-pink and cream gerberas bound together with ribbon, the dark centres studded with diamanté. I top my outfit with my Ms & Mrs handbag. Just perfect.

Petal's tutu-style dress is fairy tale pretty – pale pink with hot-pink details and fairy wings to match. She's carrying a small pompom studded with daisies to complement mine. Olly is wearing a vintage sixties shirt in a pink paisley pattern with tailor-made mohair trousers and his favourite pointed Chelsea boots. He looks more handsome than I've ever seen him.

The wedding is small, which is probably just as well as it's the only way that I've coped with it. My rocks – Jenny, Constance and Phil – are here. The reception is our wedding present from Phil and it's going to be held back at Live and Let Fry, which he's closed up especially for the day.

This morning I went in and decorated it all with balloons and put bunches of brightly coloured gerberas in jam jars on the tables and the place is looking great. One of Constance's friends has made the cake for us and I put it out on one of the tables. It's iced in a pale cream colour and has three small tiers. Truly an extravagance with the size of the wedding party! But you can never have enough cake, can you? The bottom tier is decorated with chocolate and hot-pink hearts while the middle has matching stripes and the final tier is all spotty. A marabou feather confection stands on top. Glasses are out waiting for our return and I know that there's a stash of champagne chilling in the fridge that Phil bought from Costco.

Olly's mother, unsurprisingly, declined to come out of her sun-soaked retirement to attend and my parents are away on a three-month cruise. They won't mind missing it as they'll just be delighted that we've finally tied the knot. Olly and I will go to visit them as soon as we can when they're back. If I'm really honest, Phil, Constance and Jen feel more like family to us now so we won't feel as if we're missing out. We've got a few more of our friends dropping by to toast us later and Tod also said that he'll pop in afterwards.

Thankfully, with Nell McNamara Handbags being so busy, we do have some money to spend on a few luxuries to make the day more memorable. We've hired two pink-and-cream stretched mini-limousines to whisk us and our guests to our wedding.

'OK?' Olly asks as the posh minis pull up outside the register office. I nod in response. 'Sure?'

'Absolutely.' I lean against him. Despite the stresses and strains of the last few months, I'm glad that we have actually made it.

We sip chilled champagne on the journey – even Petal has a little taste – and I think I'm finally beginning to relax enough to enjoy it. Out of the other mini, Jen, Constance and Phil stumble, giggling. Looks as if they've been enjoying the in-car hospitality too. They all look great. Constance has toned her usual leopard print right down and is wearing a smart pink suit. I'm pleased to say that her trademark vertiginous heels are still firmly in place. Jenny is looking very comely in a Marilyn Monroe style silk number. And it looks like Phil has splashed out on a new grey suit for the occasion. As instructed, he's wearing a pink tie and has a gerbera buttonhole.

'You look fabulous,' I tell my old boss, straightening his tie as I do.

'So do you, Nell,' he says. His voice cracks with emotion. 'You're a stunner. Olly's a very lucky man.'

'That's what I keep telling him.' I link my arm through his. 'Come on, we'd better go in or we'll miss our slot.'

We all pile into the register office, which, thankfully, is much nicer on the inside than it is on the outside.

Olly and I take our places, flanked by our witnesses, Phil and Constance. I notice that Constance slips her hand into Phil's. Petal stands behind us, flowers in a death grip in her tiny hands, as she concentrates hard on 'being good' as instructed.

The registrar completes the formalities and then asks, 'Do you, Nell McNamara, take Oliver Meyers to be your lawful wedded husband?'

As I look at Olly, my lover, my friend, my soon-to-be husband, all doubts, all fears, fly out of my mind when I say, 'I do.'

Chapter 35

Back at Live and Let Fry the champagne corks pop. Some of our friends swing by to join us and swell the numbers. In his usual inimitable style, Phil serves us all fabulous fish and chips. The mood is high. I put disposable cameras on the tables and everyone is taking photographs – lovely mementos of our special day. We let sixties music rock out of the stereo system and I feel all the tension of the last few months melt away.

Looking over at Olly, I watch him tenderly wiping tomato ketchup from the front of Petal's dress, and smile.

'It does feel different,' I say as I sidle up next to him and link my arm in his, 'being Mrs Oliver Meyers.' Who would have thought so after all the years we've been together? But somehow it does feel like we're a proper family now. A tight-knit little unit. Us against the world.

'You think so?'

'Yeah.'

'Maybe I should have become Mr Nell McNamara if you're going to be the famous one?'

'I don't think so. I'm happy being Mrs Meyers.'

Tonight, Constance has offered to take Petal home with her for a sleepover so that Olly and I can have a one-night-at-home honeymoon. My husband (I like the sound of that!) thought that we should at least have a few days away somewhere, but how can we when I have so much to do at the moment? Our two-week extravaganza in an exclusive beach bungalow in Bali will more than likely have to wait until our tenth anniversary. It was more by good luck than good management that we've actually had the whole day off today. I can certainly manage one night of wedded bliss though!

'Happy?' Olly asks.

'Very.'

'Mummy and Daddy! You're being all squishy,' Petal complains.

'That's because we're very much in love,' I tell her.

Our child doesn't look very impressed by that, but Olly and I exchange a dreamy look nevertheless.

The afternoon wears on. Phil, jacket already thrown off, loosens his tie and spends an awful lot of time cosied up with Constance, which makes me smile. Everything about Jenny is getting looser due to the amount of champagne that she's necked. She comes up now and plants a wet kiss on my cheek.

'I bloody love you two,' she slurs. 'Bloody love ya.' She wraps her arms round Olly. 'And you,' she continues, 'have missed your big chance.' He gets a big fat smacker on his lips. It must be like being licked by an over exuberant puppy.

'Great,' Olly says. I can tell that he wants to wipe his mouth with the back of his hand and I grin at him. 'Shall we cut the cake now, Nell?'

'Excellent idea,' I agree, coming to his rescue.

We clear the decks a bit and we all gather round the rather grand cake. A battery of disposable cameras flash as we pose with the knife held precariously above the bottom tier. Just as we're about to make our first cut together, the door chime signals the arrival of a new addition to our party. I look up and see Tod coming through the door. Immediately, I abandon the cake-cutting and rush to greet him.

There's a hiatus while I say hello.

'Hi.' I feel flushed and overexcited, whereas Tod is as cool as always. 'Glad you could make it.'

'I wouldn't have missed it for the world,' he says, then he turns to Olly. 'May I kiss the bride?'

'You'd better ask the bride yourself,' Olly, quite wisely, answers.

Tod tilts his head, silently asking for approval, then he lifts my chin and for one fleeting moment I get a flashback to when we were in the car together. He kisses me softly on both cheeks. 'For the blushing bride.'

He's right, the bride *is* blushing now. My face probably matches the bright pink gerberas in my bouquet.

Tod proffers an exquisitely wrapped present, which looks like it might well be a bottle of fizz. 'Thank you.'

'I have one more surprise for you, if I may?' With that, he throws open the door again and lets in a photographer laden down with equipment.

'Oh?'

'What better backdrop to photograph your new Ms & Mrs handbag than this?'

I'd forgotten that I'd even told Tod about that. Fancy him remembering. 'Fantastic idea,' I gush. Some of it may be the copious champagne talking.

Tod waves airily at our guests. 'Don't let us interfere. Carry on with your cake-cutting, Nell. That will be just perfect.'

So, somewhat bemused, we return to pose with the knife. I notice that the expression on Olly's face has darkened somewhat.

As we cut the cake, the professional photographer clicks away, this way and that. I pose and preen with my handbag on full show and get Petal in on the act too, but I can't help but notice that Olly doesn't seem to share my enthusiasm.

The deed is done. Our friends clap. The photographer finally puts down his camera. I start to help Constance and Jenny dish out the cake to our friends.

'Can I steal you away for five minutes?' Tod asks. 'Kyle here would like to take some more shots of just you on your own with your handbag.'

'Oh, OK.' I put down the plate in my hands, lick my sticky fingers and wipe them on my dress.

Olly takes my arm and pulls me to one side. 'Nell,' he says. His teeth are gritted. 'This is not a good time.'

'It's only five minutes,' I say. 'No one minds.'

'*I* do,' he hisses. 'I mind. Not everything has to be turned into a publicity stunt.'

'But this is a great chance,' I counter. 'I don't know why I didn't think of it myself. Tod has been kind enough to organise a photographer.'

'I'm not happy, Nell.'

'It makes perfect sense. Tod's right. It's the ideal setting to launch the Ms & Mrs handbag.'

'We could have just staged a wedding if that's how you feel,' he snaps. 'Why go through the bother of all those tiresome vows?'

'I don't feel like that,' I snap back. 'It's just that I happen to think, in this instance, that Tod is right.'

'Tod, Tod, Tod,' my husband mutters.

'Come on,' I urge. 'Just have a couple of photographs of us taken together. For me.'

'No.' He pulls away. 'Leave me out of this. I'll have nothing to do with it.'

'Well, excuse me,' I say crisply, 'but I'm going to have my photograph taken.' I snatch up the handbag that's causing so much controversy. Olly stomps away.

Looks like we've had our first domestic as Mr and Mrs Meyers. That didn't take long. But surely Olly understands by now how important this is to me? Clearly he doesn't.

I sigh to myself. Looks like the one-night honeymoon isn't going to be much fun after this.

Chapter 36

Two weeks after the wedding, I'm sitting in my pyjamas watching *Lorraine*. Petal is sitting on my lap eating her breakfast and has just spilled her porridge all down me.

'Sorry, Mummy,' Petal says.

'Breakfast at the table tomorrow,' I say. That will teach me to encourage my child to have slovenly habits. Even though there are extenuating circumstances today.

Petal's got a sniffly cold and is red-eyed and runny-nosed. The nursery are hysterical if you send any children in with the slightest thing wrong, so I'm having to keep her at home for a couple of days until it clears up. She's not poorly enough to be confined to bed, but she's ill enough to be tired and whiny and tearful, which is a complete nightmare as I have so much to do.

In fact, I'm so tired that I didn't even jump up when the porridge ran down my jim-jams. I'm just looking at it with a sinking heart. More washing.

After the photograph of the Ms & Mrs handbag appeared

in the national press – all organised by Tod – the phone hasn't stopped ringing. Olly and I haven't had a moment to ourselves. The orders have gone completely crazy and every waking moment – and some sleeping ones – has been spent making handbags.

The house is a complete state. Every corner looks like a handbag factory. There's a small, clear track that winds its way through the middle like a maze but you have to move handbags from every seat before you can sit down. Already, before I got Petal up this morning, I've been making handbags for two hours.

My mobile rings again and I sigh. I can't even sit here in my porridge-covered state in peace for five minutes. From beneath the pile of soft toys and handbag trimmings, I locate the ringing and rescue the phone.

I know that it's a business call as no one else ever rings us these days. Our friends have long since given up asking us to go out as we're never available. Sure enough, the cut-glass tone on the other end tells me I wasn't mistaken.

'Karin Parks from *Fabulous* magazine,' the woman says. 'We want to run a feature on your handbags.'

I feel like falling to my knees and giving praise, but I am aware of dislodging my child and nicely congealed breakfast cereal by doing so. This is like someone phoning to tell you that you've won the lottery and that it's Christmas tomorrow.

'That's fantastic,' I manage to stammer.

I can hear the satisfied smile even down the line. 'We'd like to send a photographer to your offices today.'

Not so good.

'Offices,' I blurt. 'I work from home.'

'Even better,' she says. But I think maybe she is imagining some minimalist, penthouse loft apartment in the Docklands, not a tatty, terraced house in Hitchin.

Surveying the mess with dismay, I venture, 'Could you possibly make that tomorrow?'

'We're squeezing you into the next issue.' More crisply. 'I'd prefer today. I have a photographer free.'

'Today would be wonderful,' I say.

'He'll be with you at eleven,' she says. 'Can you email me your address details?'

Before I agree, she's already hung up. I look round the room again and my heart starts to pound with panic. 'Petal,' I say. 'Would you like to play a game with Mummy?'

'No,' my daughter says.

I'll take that as a 'yes'.

'We're going to play Tidy the Lounge,' I tell her. 'First we're, *you're*, going to put all your toys away.'

'I'm poorly,' Petal reminds me. 'You do it.'

'This will make you feel better,' I lie. 'We'll do it together.'

'I'm busy watching television and having a cold,' my daughter insists.

'A very important person is coming to visit us and we want the house to look all sparkly.'

She takes in the seemingly impossible task. 'I don't.'

'Let's just phone Auntie Constance and see if she'd like to help too.' When I call her, my dear, reliable and indispensable friend agrees to come round straight away. I quickly email my details to the magazine. That done, I reckon I have ten minutes before Constance arrives to get myself showered and dressed in clothes that make me look more like an up-and-coming handbag designer about to break onto the scene rather than a porridge-wearing slattern.

'Petal, start collecting your toys now,' I say. I try to sound as threatening as possible. 'Or they all go straight in the bin.'

My daughter rolls her eyes but, miracle upon miracle, she starts to round up her toys. It's all done, of course, at the slowest pace possible and she has a chat with each of them as she does. Leaving her to it, I make my escape and run into the shower.

I'm just downstairs again when Constance arrives. I hug her, give her the low-down and, without further ado, we set to. Petal also bucks up considerably now that Constance is here.

An hour later and my house still looks like a handbag factory, but it looks like a tidy-ish one. Trimmings are scooped into plastic cartons. Boxes are stacked. Bags are lined up for display. Sketches are piled neatly. Everything that can be hidden is hidden. We finish as the doorbell rings again.

Constance sighs with relief. 'I'll put the kettle on.'

I kiss her. 'I love you.'

'Do you love me too, Mummy?' Petal demands.

'Yes. You've been wonderful.' She gets a kiss too.

The photographer and her assistant sweep in. They are both unfeasibly slender and trendy. Black is the *mode du jour* and I feel clownish in my yellow, red and blue T-shirt dress and orange ballet pumps.

'Perfect,' the photographer coos. 'Workshop chic.'

Is that a compliment? Not for the first time, I'm embarrassed by my own house when previously I loved it so much. Its battered comfort suited us well as a family. Now I have the world's press trudging through it, I'm not so sure.

They both completely take over the living room with lights and equipment. I feel like a spare part. But, eventually, after rearranging all the furniture, they have me posing with the handbags. They also take some pictures of Petal as she's 'adorable', despite me having to continually wipe a slime trail of snot from her nose, and down as much tea as Constance can provide.

Three exhausting hours later and they sweep out again.

We all collapse onto the sofa. 'That was fun.' Like having your toenails pulled out or peeling off your own face with a spoon.

'I don't know how you do it, girl,' Constance says. 'I'm worn out just watching you.' She pats my knee. 'We miss you at the chippy.'

'I miss you all too,' I say honestly. 'I'll try to pop in more often.'

We all cuddle up together until Constance says, 'I'd better go now or I'll be late and Phil will give me what for.'

As if Phil ever gets cross with anyone.

'We'll walk you into town. Petal, get your shoes and coat on, some fresh air will do you good.' Because Constance is here, she pretends she's the model child and doesn't protest at all.

The day is crisp and bright. As we walk, my head whirrs as I think of all the things I need to do. We drop into the chip shop and get hugged to death by Jenny and Phil. Petal picks at some chips.

We leave the welcoming warmth of the shop and swing back out into the cold. I take Petal's hand in mine and she even manages to skip along beside me, clearly nowhere near as exhausted as I am by our photo shoot experience.

We make our way back home and as we do, we walk down through the Market Place to Church Yard. The shops in this row are all tiny, olde-worlde and are half-timbered, black and white. The shops here are always busy. Good footfall, I think the proper term is. My eye is drawn to the For Let sign above one of the doors. It's rare that one of these places becomes vacant. I stop abruptly and my daydreamy daughter walks straight into me.

That's what we need, I think. A shop. We have to move the business out of our home and into a shop where we can sell the bags and use it as our workshop too. Why didn't I think of it before? Because we didn't have the money before, of course. But surely there's enough cash-flow coming in now that we could consider it? I wonder how much this place would cost. Could we do it? One thing's for sure, this very afternoon, I'll be ringing up to find out. I make a note of the estate agent's name and number.

Standing back, I admire the shopfront. My name would look very nice hanging above the door in bold, bright letters. Very nice, indeed.

Chapter 37

'This terrifies me,' Olly says. He lugs another box out of the hired van and starts to climb the stairs.

'It'll be fine,' I assure him. 'It has to be.'

As it turns out, we have borrowed a stonking amount of money from the bank to fund this shop. It's a figure that has more noughts on the end than I'm happy with. But what can I do? I want the business to expand and this is the only way.

The rate we're paying back every month is pretty frightening, too. On the plus side, we've secured this gorgeous, period shop in a prime location that is, surely, going to give the business an immense boost. As a happy bonus, the shop comes with a flat above it, so we've given up our rented house and are moving in here.

Olly is crashing about, unhappily. I think the fact that we're moving in the pouring rain doesn't help. Everything looks better when the sun is shining, doesn't it? This is an old, old building, Tudor, I think, and I just hope he doesn't notice quite how wonky the floors are.

'Every floor in here is wonky,' he mutters.

My husband bangs down another box. A little cloud of dust floats up.

Frankly, it's not just the floors. Everything else is wonky too.

'But then everything is wonky,' Olly complains.

I decide to keep quiet.

The flat has been used for nothing but storage for years and it's in desperate need of a good clean. It's also filling up quickly. There's my handbag collection to accommodate and Olly's records. I've no idea, yet, where they'll all go. The downside of moving out of our house and into the flat is that it's much more cramped here. In my defence, it did look slightly bigger when it was empty. Things do, don't they? Now it's got all our detritus piled high in it, I do wonder how on earth we're going to fit.

'This is a dump,' Olly says, clearly picking up on my thoughts again. 'A small dump.'

'It'll be fine.' I have been saying this since eight o'clock this morning when we first opened our eyes and even *I'm* getting sick of hearing it. 'At least we can separate work and home a bit now.'

'How?' Olly asks. 'We live above the shop. Literally.'

'But we have a separate living space and all the handbag related stuff will be downstairs out of the way. You won't get a needle in your bottom every time you sit on the sofa.'

Olly looks sceptical.

'I promise.' Then, 'You have a nice little space to keep your scooter in the yard.' His *precious* bloody scooter. Olly

171

has already commandeered one of the small outhouses for that.

'Its one saving grace,' he concedes reluctantly.

I sigh. 'I know that it's daunting—'

'*Daunting*?' He laughs. 'That doesn't come close to describing how I'm feeling about this.' Olly looks round him. 'We might be a handbag-free zone in this poky flat, but the overheads have rocketed, Nell. The bills that are coming in are monster.'

'Don't you want me to succeed?'

'This is success?' He runs his hand through his hair. 'This just feels like debt and worry and stress. From where I stand, it feels as if we're in a worse position that we were before.'

I want to say that Tod is very supportive of this move, but every time I start a sentence with 'Tod', Olly just rolls his eyes and stops listening. A bit like Petal does when I tell her it's bedtime. Mr Urban's input into our lives has become something of an issue between us since the wedding/handbag/photo incident. I see Tod as someone who drives and encourages me. Olly sees him as meddling and interfering. But, to be honest, I don't know how I would have done any of this without him. Tod came to the bank with me to help me get the loan. He did the same at the solicitors when I signed the contracts. Olly just hates doing this kind of thing. And I don't think I could have managed it all alone.

'I've gone from working in a chippy to having my own shop, designing my own handbags, in a short space of time.'

'You've gone from having a decent paying job with no worries to being swamped with debt and up to your eyeballs in shit. You don't own the shop, Nell. The bank does. Everything we earn goes to paying them off. And it will do for the foreseeable future. Is that really what you want?'

'Yes,' I say softly. 'It won't always be like this. It's a means to an end.'

He shakes his head. 'I just can't see the fun in owning your own business.'

'But you're happy working in a pizza factory?'

'You were once happy working in a chip shop. Can't we get back to that?'

'No,' I say. 'I've seen what else is out there and I want more for us.'

'Do you really want it for us, Nell?' His face is bleak and I've never, ever, in all our time together seen him look so worried. 'Or do you want it for you?'

Chapter 38

Olly swung out of their new place. He didn't quite know what to call it: shop, flat, business premises? A combination of all three, he guessed. Whatever it was, it would be a long time before it felt like home. They'd been there for two weeks now and he still felt unsettled.

Hands in pockets, he walked towards the bus stop. Catching the last one got him to the pizza factory in the nick-iest-nick of time. Tonight, Hitchin was quiet. Not that it was particularly jumping any night of the week, he had to concede. Very few people were on the streets and the pubs were yet to turn out. It was a fine evening for some fresh air now that the nights were slightly warmer. Maybe things would get better soon. God, he hoped so. At the moment, all he could think of was that the numbers were racking up at an alarming rate and they all seemed to be going into the red column rather than the black one. If this was what business involved, then you could keep it.

As he turned into Market Place he nearly bumped into a

woman coming out of one of the shopping arcades in the centre.

'Sorry, love,' Olly said as he steered round her.

'Watch where you're going, plum,' the woman snapped.

When he looked up to apologise again, he saw that it was Jenny and that she was laughing at him.

'All right, Olly?' she said. 'You were in a world of your own, mate.'

'I was,' he admitted. 'Sorry.'

'No harm done. Off to work then?'

'Yeah. You?'

'Just finished,' Jen said. She flicked her head back towards the chippy. 'How are you getting on in your new place? It's just round the corner, isn't it?'

'You'll have to come by.'

'I've been meaning to,' Jen said. 'But you know how it is.'

'I'd better go,' Olly said. 'Got my bus to catch.'

'I'll walk down with you. If that's OK?'

Olly shrugged. Walking along with Jen might help take his mind off his troubles for ten minutes.

She linked her arm through his. 'How's married life suiting you?'

He could hardly tell his wife's friend that they'd never argued so much since they'd tied the knot. Nell was turning into a person he didn't know. Gone was the laid-back woman he'd spent the last decade with. She'd been replaced by someone who talked constantly about work, budgets, forecasts and flaming handbags. She didn't even seem to have as much time for Petal these days, let alone him. 'Oh, you know.'

Jen whacked his arm. 'Course I don't. Doh! I've never been hitched.'

He wanted to tell her that it was overrated, but that wasn't strictly true. It wasn't marriage itself that had him and Nell at each other's throats. It was much more complicated than that. 'It's fine,' he settled on. 'Fine.'

'You could sound a bit more bloody enthusiastic.'

'Give me a break, Jen,' he said. 'We've been together for ten years. We're not exactly in the first rush of love.'

They were at the bus stop now and the bus was due in a few minutes.

Jen turned and faced him. 'She's a lucky girl, that Nell. You tell her I said so. If she doesn't appreciate you, then there are plenty of others who will.'

He laughed. 'I'm not such a catch, Jen.'

'Go on with you.' She nudged him. 'I wouldn't kick you out of bed for farting.'

'I'll remember that.'

The bus came into view.

'At least I've put a smile on your face,' she said.

'Thanks.' Everything seemed to revolve round work and he wondered whether that's what they faced for the rest of their lives. He couldn't even remember the last time he and Nell had enjoyed a night out together, just the two of them. Their wedding night had been a disaster as they'd turned their backs on each other due to that stupid photograph debacle. Perhaps that was still in the back of both of their minds. 'I'm in need of a laugh.'

Jen was suddenly serious. 'Any time, Olly,' she said. 'I mean it. You only have to call me.'

Now he was embarrassed. 'Yeah. I'll remember that.'

'You do.'

Thankfully, the bus pulled up next to them. 'Bus,' Olly said, pointing at it.

'You're hysterical,' Jen chuckled. 'Catch you soon, Olly.'

'Yeah. Soon.' He jumped on the bus.

Jen stood on the pavement and waved at him as it pulled away.

She looked lonely, he thought. Vulnerable even. And, something else he hadn't noticed before, quite cute.

Chapter 39

It's late. Olly's just gone off to work. Petal has been fast asleep in bed, our bed, for hours. All attempts at keeping her in her own bed in the new flat have failed miserably. Other than that, she seems to have settled in quite well. More than I can say for Olly. He clearly hates it here and has done nothing but stomp round, muttering darkly since we moved in.

I'm in the shop now, despite the hour. I've switched on Petal's old baby monitor, although I'm sure I could hear her, anyway, if there was a problem. I'm not that far away and my child isn't generally known for the quietness of her voice.

We're due to be up and running for business next week, but everything is still utter chaos at the moment. The front is to be open to the general public but, to be honest, this is just as important for me to have as a showroom that will enable me to display my handbags properly for any agents or journalists who want to come and see us. The room at the back will serve as an office and workroom. All in all, we'll look more like a professional company than a seat-of-the-pants cottage industry.

They can't see how little is in my coffers. Right? What it does mean though is that I've given up the market stall on Saturdays and no longer have to subject my only child to hyperthermia every weekend. I suppose I could have paid someone else to stand there and freeze as it had turned into quite a lucrative pitch, but now that we've got a swanky shop, does having a market stall give out the right message for a woman who's going places? I need to try to tidy everything up so that, hopefully, Olly will start to see why this is a good move, in spite of the expense, and stop being grumpy.

I've freshened the whole place up with a coat of brilliant white emulsion and I've cut out some inspiring pop art pictures from glossy magazines and have hung them in cheap frames. I think it's starting to look more like it belongs to me. Earlier in the week, I revamped some shelves that I bought on eBay painting them in what's rapidly becoming my trademark pink. Now that they're dry, I can arrange a display of handbags on them and I'm taking the few hours I have on my own before I fall into bed to do that. I fiddle and fuss and then stand back, admiring my efforts. Deep in thought, I jump out of my skin when there's a knock on the window. Turning, I expect to give the finger to some drunks looking for a bit of amusement as they're wandering home. Instead, I'm surprised to see Tod's face pressed up against the glass, grinning. Smiling back, I go to open the door.

'Hey,' he says. 'I've just had dinner in town and I saw the light on.'

I don't ask who he had dinner with.

'You nearly gave me a heart attack,' I chide.

'Sorry.' He doesn't look chastised at all. 'I thought it would be a good opportunity to see how it's all going.'

'Yeah,' I say. 'It's OK.'

'More than OK, Nell,' he laughs. 'It must be fabulous to have your name above your own shop door. Glad to see that you didn't change it to Mrs Meyers when you got married.'

Actually, I did consider it. I know that Olly would like me to and so would Petal.

'You're a brand now,' Tod says. 'It would be the wrong thing to do. You are and always will be, Nell McNamara.'

A brand. Nell McNamara for ever. It's a sobering thought. I'm thinking that I won't even mention that to Olly.

I lead Tod deeper into the shop and show him my handiwork with a 'Ta-da!'

He gazes around.

'What do you think?'

'Looking good,' Tod says, voice full of admiration. 'Looking very good.'

'Through here will be the office and workroom.' He follows in my footsteps. 'I've got a couple of ladies coming in part-time to help me.'

'Next year, world domination,' he teases.

'Maybe the year after,' I counter.

He leans against the doorframe, looking way too cool for this small, untidy space filled with boxes that are still waiting to be unpacked. I can't wait to get this bit of the premises up and running too.

'I'm really pleased for you, Nell. I love a success story.'

'I'm not there yet,' I remind him. 'There's definitely a lot more cash going out than there is coming in.' Never a good situation to be in as my husband regularly points out. Frankly, I'm too frightened to look closely at the bank account.

'It won't be for long, I'm sure.'

I wish I had Tod's unwavering confidence.

'I was about to stop for some tea. Can I offer you something?'

From behind his back, Tod produces a bottle of champagne.

'You just happened to have that with you?'

'On the off chance,' he admits. 'I thought we should celebrate.'

'Shame Olly's not here.' Then I wonder if my mentor has deliberately waited until Olly was safely out at work. Why else would he be calling so late at night? Equally quickly, I dismiss the thought. I'm being silly. There's been no more unexpected intimacy between us since that brief kiss after our evening at the Palace and I put that down to nothing more than the mood, the madness and the moonlight.

'Come up to the flat,' I say. 'I must warn you though, that's looking distinctly less salubrious.'

We go up the creaky, wonky staircase to the creaky, wonky flat. Dude, from his bed, wags his tail, but clearly is too exhausted to get out and greet us. The dog, at least, has settled well into his new home. I move some boxes out of the way so that we can beat a path to the kitchen. We've managed to find the stereo, so I click it on. Very occasionally Olly and I make a nod towards modern music and the dulcet tones of Coldplay and 'Trouble' fills the small space.

'Champagne flutes may be beyond me,' I say, 'but I do have some pretty mugs in here somewhere.'

'Mugs are fine,' Tod assures me and, expertly, he pops the cork while I rummage in the cupboards to locate two of the best. He lets the bubbles foam into them and hands one to me.

'Cheers,' I say and go to knock my mug against his.

'We should toast like this . . .' He moves in towards me and links his arm through mine, pulling me close. 'That will enhance the experience.'

We drink and our faces are so close that they're almost touching. I'm not sure that this is enhancing my experience at all, but it is making me very hot and bothered. My hair falls forward and, before I can pull away, Tod lifts the strand and tucks it behind my ear. It's a movement so filled with tenderness that it takes my breath away.

'Nell,' he whispers.

The bedroom door crashes open.

'Bang-Bang is being very naughty,' Petal announces as if she's addressing the back of the stalls. Her favourite doll, the one with very little spiky hair – as a result of my child's lack of hairdressing skills – and no clothes, is thrust at me. 'You'd better come and sort her out, Mummy.'

Bang-Bang is given over to my tender loving care. I have no idea why the doll is called Bang-Bang. Nor why Petal's rather threadbare teddy is called Razzle Dazzle.

Tod, rather smoothly, steps away from me. 'Well, hello, little lady.'

Petal looks slightly disgruntled at being addressed thus. Normally, I'd be equally disgruntled that she had interrupted a rare romantic moment. In this case, I'm very glad that she did.

Chapter 40

As it turns out, the shop is a huge commitment. Bigger than anything that I've ever taken on before. Bigger than anything I could have ever envisaged for myself. Although it's proved to be a good separation of home and work space, the fact that work is just below me when I'm at home, means that I never really stop thinking about it.

Today I'm working on new sketches. These are retro designs of pop art-inspired and psychedelic images and, even if I do say so myself, they're coming along nicely. Ideally, I'd like to increase the range of products available to include coin purses, make-up bags and, perhaps, umbrellas – but that would involve a whole new world of expense in commissioning samples. Everything is made in China now, so I'd have to find a factory out there: a daunting prospect.

When the bag frames I bought on eBay ran out, we managed to find out who'd supplied them from a delivery note left inside one of them. We've been buying them direct from this warehouse ever since, but as my designs are getting more and more out there, I can't just keep customising existing bag frames. Now the time has come to get them made to my own specification, which involves more money and I can't even bring myself to raise that matter with Olly.

Petal is with me today playing, as usual, on the floor in the office. She probably spends way too much time in here when she should be playing out in the park or learning to swim or doing something entertaining or educational. But I keep telling myself that it is only a short time until she starts school and then my conscience will be in the clear. I try not to think of the precious quality time that I'm missing out on. It could be worse. How many mothers have to go out to work now and leave their children in the care of others simply to make ends meet? At least Petal is here with me, even though she's grubbing around on the floor while I try to concentrate on my designs.

The phone rings and at the end of the line, there's a very sexy male voice with a heavy, and inordinately attractive, French accent.

'I am Yves Simoneaux,' he explains. 'I am an agent based in Paris and I have heard very much about you. I would be interested in representing your designs if you do not have already your interests in France covered.'

I hope that he can't hear my heart thumping down the phone.

'No,' I say. 'We haven't got representation in France yet.' It hadn't even occurred to me. Despite joking with Tod about world domination, I'm paddling so fast to keep my head above water here, that I haven't even considered anything else. But Europe is a massive market. Just think how we could grow there.

'May I come to visit with you?'

'Yes. Yes, of course.' I look round at the showroom and am glad, at this moment, that we bit the bullet and moved here. How could I have had a sexy French agent come to my tatty old house?

'This afternoon?' he continues. 'I can be with you by two of the clock.'

'You know where we are?'

'Oh, yes,' Yves says. I can almost hear the shrug. 'I am very well organised. I can get a train to you from Kings Cross station, yes?'

'Yes. It takes just under an hour.'

'That is excellent.'

'I'll see you at two, then.'

'At two,' he agrees. And he hangs up.

I reward myself for my good fortune by jumping up and down on the spot. Petal abandons her crayoning and we jump together for a bit.

'Now,' I say. 'You must be a very good girl this afternoon as we have a very important visitor coming.'

'Another one?' She rolls her eyes.

'Yes.'

My child looks unimpressed by this. But then, of course, she doesn't realise that this could make the difference between her living in a flat above the shop for the rest of her formative years or moving into a four-bed detached place in one of the more posh areas of town, complete with her own swing and top-of-the-range trampoline.

Chapter 41

I fly round and tidy up, rearranging the bags time and time again, somewhat needlessly. An hour later and this place looks like a slick, professional operation or as near as, damn it. Only the somewhat surplus child detracts from it slightly. I think about trying to farm Petal out for the afternoon and call Olly, Constance and Jen, but I've once again left it way too late. They are all busy, busy, busy. So Petal stays and Mr Yves Simoneaux will have to take us as we are.

At the appointed time – by two of the clock – the bell chimes and the most handsome man I've ever seen swings in, ducking through the low doorway as he does. If this is Yves Simoneaux, then I have lost my heart and, more than likely, my senses are about to follow too. He's tall, slender, mid-thirties at a guess. His black suit hangs on his frame and he's wearing a white shirt with a black tie. A black leather man-bag is slung across his body and rests on his hip.

'*Bonjour*,' he says and his heavy eyebrows lift and a slow smile spreads across his face. His dark hair has a curl to it, but is swept back from his face and gelled into place. There's a fine line of designer stubble outlining his chin, a soul patch beneath his lip. He holds out his hand to me. 'I am Yves.'

When I take it, I notice his fingers are long, slender. Despite his hand being cool to the touch, it gives me palpitations. 'Nell.'

Petal clings to my leg and Yves kneels down in front of her. 'Who is this lovely little *mademoiselle*?'

My daughter has gone all silly too and I supply, 'This is Petal,' while she gapes at him open-mouthed and goggle-eyed. Looks as if Mr Simoneaux has the same effect on four-year-olds as he does on women of a certain age who should know better.

'Come in, please,' I say and hobble further into the show-room with Petal attached to my leg.

'This is a very beautiful space,' he says and looks round giving admiring nods.

'We've only just moved in,' I explain. 'So it's all a bit raw yet. My company is very new.'

'This I know,' he says. 'It is why I think that I can help you.'

'That would be fantastic.' But, because I'm all of a fluster, I'm forgetting my manners. 'Can I offer you a drink?' I should have gone out and got biscuits, posh ones, or something.

'In a moment,' he says, holding up a hand. 'First I would love for you to show me more of your designs.'

'Now, Petal.' I manage to dislodge my child and grip her by the shoulders as I speak, so I hope she knows that I mean business. 'Will you play nicely while I talk to Mr Simoneaux?'

'Yes,' Petal says with look as if to say she never does anything but play nicely all alone.

Obediently – thank God! – she trots off into the office.

'She is a very beautiful child,' Yves says. 'Like her mother.'

'Ha, ha, ha.' I laugh girlishly and flush and simper and generally don't behave like a rufty-tufty business woman who will stand no messing.

Yves smiles again. He is clearly well aware of the effect he has on women and has probably been milking it for years. There's no doubt he has this flirtation thing down to a fine art. This must be the legendary Gallic charm – or *garlic* charm, as Olly calls it.

'Now, to work,' he says and steers me towards the rows of carefully arranged handbags as he outlines the work of his company. He goes on to tell me about where he'd plan to place the products and how much commission they take from sales. I try to concentrate and not notice the coolness of his hand on the small of my back.

What has happened in recent weeks? I've never attracted this level of male attention before. Is it because I'm no longer seen as just a housewife and mother with a little (pat me on the head) part-time job? Or have I suddenly become a man-magnet because they think I'm someone who's going places? I haven't changed my perfume, so it's certainly not that.

Yves takes the handbags and runs his hands over them as if he's seducing a voluptuous woman. '*Beau. Très beau.*'

When he finally tires of making love to my handbags, I lead him through to the office.

'I'm just sketching out some new designs,' I say and pull the relevant papers to the top of my pile.

'They are wonderful,' he says, but his eyebrows pull together in a frown.

Maybe he doesn't like them at all. 'I've literally just been doodling this morning,' I rush in. 'Hot off the press. You're the first person that I've had the chance to show them to.'

One design is for a bag covered in candy-stripe fabric with hearts and stars sprinkled liberally across it. On one side it reads BAG, on the other LADY. Yves strokes his hand across the drawing. Another is covered in psychedelic hearts and flowers and says MAKE LOVE on one side and NOT WAR on the other. The last one has four pouting lips in Andy Warhol style on it and the back reads MY FIFTEEN MIN-UTES OF FAME.

Still no response.

'Perhaps they need more work.'

A shrug. 'Perhaps.' He takes off his man-bag and then rifles through the sketches again, but makes no further comment.

Before I can ask him any more, Petal appears. I hadn't actu-ally even registered that she wasn't in the office. How observant am I as a mother? She's bearing a pink tray, and two mugs and a teapot are balanced precariously on it. Her tongue is out and the concentration on her face is a sight to behold. For reasons best known to my daughter, she has also found her pink cycling helmet and is wearing it.

'I have maked tea,' she announces.

'Oh, lord.' I immediately swoop down and rescue the tray from Petal's shaky grip as the teapot starts a death slide. 'Sweet pea, you know you're not allowed near the kettle.'

'I didn't *go* near the kettle,' she informs me with a scowl.

189

'You didn't?'

'I'll pour,' she insists.

I touch the teapot and realise it is, in fact, stone-cold. Oh, dear.

'We can't have tea now, Petal. Mummy's busy.'

'You're never too busy for tea,' my child says imperiously. 'That's what you say.'

I do. Frequently. Even though I'm invariably wrong.

When, reluctantly, I put the tray down on the coffee table, my daughter manoeuvres herself between me and the teapot and sets about pouring.

'Sorry,' I mouth to Yves.

'It is fine,' he assures me.

The pot wobbles and we get a fair amount of Petal's tea sloshing about on the tray rather than in the cup. That gives me the chance to see that her 'tea' seems to involve half a dozen tea bags floating in cold water with the milk already added. She stands and, with every ounce of her being focused on delivering the results of her endeavour, hands the first cup to Yves.

'This is wonderful,' he says. 'This is exactly how we French like to take our tea.'

Petal beams, easily fallen under his Parisian spell.

Yves winks at me and, above and beyond the call of duty, sips his tea. '*Délicieux*.'

'Thank you,' I say as I take my cup too. 'You're a very clever girl.'

Somehow we manage to down Petal's cold tea and then Yves says, 'I am sorry to be rude, but I must rush away.'

'Of course. You must have lots more to do.'

His smile says that he has. 'We have a deal? Yes?'

I try not to look surprised. Or to leap into Yves' arms in excitement. I'd fully expected finding an agent to be a lot more complicated than this. Never in a million years did I think that one would just bowl up on my doorstep and take me on straight away. Wait until I tell Olly about this. He'll be pleased for me. Surely?

'We do,' I confirm gratefully. Yves and I shake hands again. '*Merveilleux*.'

'Again, I'm really sorry we've kept you here so long.'

He takes my hand and lifts it to his mouth, kissing it softly. 'The pleasure has been all mine.'

Once more, I go into a girly flat spin.

'Here is my card.'

I gaze at the business card he hands me, slightly goggle-eyed.

'We will speak,' Yves says as he slings his man-bag back across his body. 'Very soon.'

'That would be lovely.' I sound more breathless than I would have hoped.

'May I?' My daughter is waiting shyly behind me. He takes Petal's hand and kisses it. '*Au revoir, mademoiselle*. Thank you for my excellent cup of English tea.'

Petal is as bewitched as I am.

With us both safely under his spell, Yves leaves us and I watch as his rangy frame turns heads as he lopes away down the street. I don't think Hitchin has ever seen anyone as gorgeous.

'Now,' I say, still all of a flutter, 'better get back to work before the day slips away from me.'

'He was nice,' Petal observes.

'Yes,' I say, somewhat wistfully.

I go back into the office, settle Petal with her crayons once more and sit myself back at my desk. With a deep and rather shaky breath, I prepare myself to carry on with my new designs. But despite searching the desk high and low, I can't find them anywhere.

Chapter 42

The next few months go by in a blur of trade events – or fashion shows as I would have previously called them. Spring comes and goes and I hardly notice it. The daffodils bloom, carpeting the town with yellow. Petal adores them. I barely lift my head to acknowledge the changes. Then summer is upon us. A hot one, for once. Everyone melts in May but me. The blistering heat of 'flaming June' doesn't trouble me either as I spend most of my time indoors in deep-freeze air conditioning and darkness, listening to pounding music while staring at catwalks, being jostled by the crowds with nothing but a stale, mass-catered sandwich and some machine tea for sustenance.

Are the trade events useful? I think so. It gives me a chance to see what else is out there and who my competitors are. Besides, Tod tells me that I must attend them. So attend them, I do. I and, more importantly, my handbags grace the aisles of the Clothes Collective in Birmingham, Fashion Fusion in Manchester, Gladrags in Leeds and Sustainable Chic in Scotland. I'm networking my little backside off in the hope that it will all pay off one day.

The culmination of my chilled-to-the-bone travels is Designer Extravaganza in London, the most crucial show of the year where, with the help of a grant that finally materialised from The Prince's Trust, I've been able to secure myself a stand. This is the first time that I'll actually display my wares and the cost of doing so is truly staggering. We could buy a decent family car for the same price. The fact that it is the world's smallest stand is neither here nor there. It's a stand at a prestigious event and for the first time in my life, I'm going to be a presence in the big bad world of fashion. I'm so excited that I feel permanently sick.

I've had to draft in Jenny and Constance to help Olly look after Petal for the week I'm away. To say that my husband isn't best pleased is something of an understatement. He's sick of the amount of time that I've already spent away from home so far this year and finds every opportunity he can to tell me so. It's been the subject of countless rows. But what can I do? This is our livelihood. This is what the business demands.

Now, I'm running round the workroom like a headless chicken, getting last-minute things together for the stand.

'Dinner's ready.' Olly sticks his head round the door. His face falls as he sees the bags and boxes all over the floor. 'Aren't you done yet?'

I try not to bristle. He has no concept of how important this is for me, for all of us. Then I get a rush of guilt. He also has no idea quite how much this is costing us. I can only hope that it's worth it. All the promotions that I'm doing have certainly brought the orders in, but not necessarily the cold, hard cash. The cost of fulfilling them all seems to be spiralling out of control and that scares me. One day the income has to become more than the outgoings, otherwise we're in real trouble.

The preparation for this trade show has been staggering. I've had to think of everything from sending out press packs, getting business cards, ordering passes for me, Olly and the van, booking a hotel, writing blurb for the brochure, sending out invitations and designing everything from the lighting down to the electricity points on the stand. And let's not forget the stressing about the handbags themselves.

My idea for the space we've rented is to make it look like a candy shop and I've roughed out designs for decorating the walls. I can access the space two days early to give me time to paint it. There'll be display shelves round the walls and the handbags will be slotted in between jars of old-fashioned sweets. In the middle of the floor there'll be a big claw-foot bath (bought from my prop store and general saviour, eBay) overflowing with things like sherbet fountains, black jacks, flying saucers, giant swirly lollipops and candy canes, with my handbags in among them. I'm hoping there'll be a lot of sweet-toothed buyers at the show who will find it irresistible.

'Nearly,' I tell Olly. 'I'll have to come down here for a couple of hours afterwards.'

'Thought we might watch a movie tonight,' Olly says. 'Have some time together before you go away for the week.'

'That sounds lovely.' And it does. How long has it been since Olly and I just vegged out on the sofa together? 'I'll try,' I promise.

But in my heart of hearts, I know that I'll be burning the midnight oil so that I'm ready in time for tomorrow. This is my first show and it's important that I get it right. Once I'm on the stand, that's it. I can't pop back home if I happen to forget something. At first light, we need to set off for the city and I've hired a van so that Olly can drive all the stuff down with me. I try not to be hurt that Olly hasn't even asked me how things are going or whether he can help when Petal goes to bed.

'I'd better get back.' He flicks a thumb towards the kitchen. 'It'll be burning.'

'Five minutes,' I beg. 'Just keep it warm for me.'

His expression tells me that I might as well have asked him to cut up Petal and put her under the patio.

'Five,' he says, 'or your dinner will be in the dog.' He stomps his way back upstairs.

I sigh to myself. The other worry is that I haven't had any real news from Yves Simoneaux. I've called him several times but have only managed to speak to him once since his impromptu visit. Now that I've appointed him as my agent, he doesn't seem quite as keen. I don't know how long these things are supposed to take, but I'd hoped that after the initial rush of enthusiasm, he'd have secured us some contracts by now. But there's been nothing. I would also have thought that he'd be at Designer Extravaganza as it's such an important date on the fashion calendar but, despite emailing him, I haven't yet had a reply to tell me whether he'll be there or not.

I held fire on the pop art designs because he didn't seem that mad about them and now I'm wondering if that was the right thing to do. Perhaps I should have something new and exciting to show on my stand, but I haven't. The designs are still the same ones I started out with. I'm just hoping that the buyers, who probably won't know me from Adam, will see them as fresh and new.

Tod will be at the show for the entire week – not just helping me, but working as a consultant for other people too. I haven't told Olly that either. It seems that I keep a lot of secrets from my husband these days for the sake of peace and we've never had that in our relationship before.

Once more, I attempt to reconcile myself to this by thinking that it won't be for long, it won't be for ever. There has to be a breakthrough in the business and then, well, we'll be set for life. We'll live in a mansion and eat gold-plated Weetabix and have Porsches coming out of our ears. See what Olly has to stomp up and down about then.

Chapter 43

At six o'clock in the morning, Jen arrives, yawning and bleary-eyed. Olly and I already have the van loaded. I start to download a list of 'to-do's' for Jenny even though her charge is still fast asleep in bed and will no doubt be for some time yet.

She holds up a hand. 'Don't stress, Nell,' she says. 'Even I can manage to get Coco Pops in the kid and Chum in the dog. Everything beyond that is a bonus.'

'Thanks.' I let out a shaky breath. 'Thanks so much for doing this.'

She yawns again. Clearly wide awake babysitters are extra. 'Any time. No worries.'

'Ready?' I ask Olly. He downs the dregs of his coffee and nods.

I take a moment to creep into Petal's room just one more time and watch my daughter's slumbering form. This reminds me what all my hard work is for. Providing a better future for Petal is all that matters. I softly kiss her goodbye, wiping a tear from my eye when I think that I won't see my little sweet pea for a whole week.

Olly and I jump into the van and set off towards the big smoke. Needless to say, last night my dinner was a dried up mess by the time I'd finished stressing about what last-minute bits to take for the show. Olly and I never did get to smooch on the sofa watching that film. Instead, I fell into bed beside my husband at two in the morning and then anxiety kept me tossing and turning for the rest of the night and Olly added to it by tutting under his breath. At five, when I got up, I was just about ready to fall into a deep sleep.

It's fair to say that the atmosphere between us is still a little frosty this morning.

Two hours later and we're pulling up at the venue in London's Earl's Court. The enormous 'Designer Extravaganza' banner flutters overhead and I think, I'm part of this. I'm really part of this now. I pinch myself a couple of times to make sure that I really am.

Olly shows our pass which, thankfully, among one hundred and one other things, I remembered to print off, and we drive into the exhibition hall. We unload as quickly as we can, hauling the claw-foot bath between us. We're only allowed to park on-site for a miniscule amount of time as there are a million other identical vans all waiting for access.

'Wow,' Olly says when he sees inside the vast hall for the first time. 'This is the real deal.'

Already many of the stands are well on their way to being built and furnished. We have a lot to do. On a fraction of the budget that most of them seem to have. In direct line of sight, all I can see is recognisable and well established high street brands. Then there's little old me with my little old handbags. I can only hope that my stand design lives up to my expectations. It also worries me that the people on the stands are wafting about, all looking unfeasibly trendy whereas, at the moment, I look like the hired help. I'd better sharpen up for the start of the show.

'Can you see now why I've been so worried?' I ask him.

My husband takes me in his arms and holds me tight. 'You'll knock them dead,' he assures me.

For a moment the passion sparks between us again and then Olly says, 'I'd better go and move that van. You make a start and I'll be back just as soon as I can.'

So, I find the box with the various tins of paint in it and my overalls. I locate the brushes and, with the magic of emulsion, begin to transform our small, bland box into a sweetie/handbag wonderland. I've been painting for half an hour and Olly has just returned from parking the van and is busy admiring my handiwork, when Tod swings by.

'Didn't think that you'd be here today,' I tell him as I kiss him briefly on the cheek in greeting. I'm more self-conscious with him now after our close call in the kitchen.

'Thought you might need a hand,' he says. 'But I can see that you're ably assisted.' He and Olly exchange a wary glance. 'I'll catch you later.' He waves over his shoulder as he leaves the stand and is swallowed up by the crowds of workers already swarming in the aisles.

'I didn't know he was going to be here,' Olly notes as he watches him go.

'It's his job, Olly,' I point out. 'He's doing some consultancy work or something, too.'

My husband still scowls after him. I can't believe he's like this after all that Tod has done for me.

'Why? Is it a problem?'

Olly's face is dark. 'I always feel as if I'm on the outside of this, Nell,' he answers. 'I don't know what's going on half the time. You seem to deliberately keep me out of the loop.'

I don't like to tell him that if I keep him *in* the loop, all he does is complain. I'm well aware that he's hated me being away so much recently. But what can I do? This is business. I have to be here. I have no choice.

'I haven't even seen the design of the stand until now.'

'You didn't ask me about it,' I point out. 'I didn't think you were interested.'

'All you seem to want me to do is lift heavy things. You don't need my input on anything else.'

'That's not true. You know it's not true.' Although it is true that I keep things from him because I know he won't like them and I feel ashamed about that.

All the fight goes out of him. 'Why do we not seem able to talk about simple things any more?'

'I have no idea, Olly.' I wipe my hands on my overalls and prepare to thrash this out once and for all.

'I have to go,' my husband says abruptly. 'I'm on night-shift tonight and I need to catch a few winks. I didn't sleep much last night.'

That's my fault too.

'I hope you have a brilliant week, Nell. See you when you get back. Petal and I will be waiting.'

I take his hand. 'Don't leave like this. I need your support, Olly.'

'And I need my wife back. Petal needs her mum.'

With that, he leaves me and my paint, with all the shelves to put up and the boxes to unpack and I know that, despite paying a small fortune for a London hotel, I probably won't be getting to bed tonight either.

Chapter 44

Later that afternoon, when I'm just about ready to lie down on the floor of my stand and weep, Tod comes back. I have so much to do and, in the way of these things, so little time. Everyone else looks so much more organised than me. But then everyone else seems to have a team of people scurrying round and there's not just one person trying to do it all by their lonesome self.

Clearly sensing my despair, Tod strips off his jacket and rolls his sleeves up. He does not look like a man who is used to manual labour but, to my relieved surprise, he is. I show him what I want doing and he gets on with the job without complaint. Tod puts up shelves, drags the claw-foot bath into its rightful place centre stage, fills it with the sweets and generally helps to pull the stand together while I am busy doing the artistic bit and painting my designs on the walls. We're still there together, working in companionable silence, when the clock ticks eight.

Tod switches off the vacuum cleaner that he's blagged from

someone, which he's been using to such good effect. 'Time to call it a day,' he says.

'I can't stop yet.'

He comes and takes my paintbrush from my hand, which has cramped into shape around it. 'I know how these things work,' he insists. 'You're so tired that you'll start making mistakes. Stop now. We'll have a quick dinner, a glass of wine to unwind, sleep eight hours and come back fresh first thing in the morning to finish it.'

'Really?' This sounds like a very appealing option. 'What if I'm not ready in time?'

'You will be,' he assures me.

I gaze longingly at my one still-unpainted wall. 'Could I not just do this?'

'I am your mentor,' he reminds me. 'When have I ever misled you?'

'Never,' I concur.

'Then good Italian food and passable red wine it is,' Tod says. 'I know a little place nearby and I've taken the liberty of booking a table for nine o'clock. Think you can turn it round by then?'

I don't like to tell Tod that I can be ready in five minutes flat. That's what comes from usually having a four-year-old daughter in tow.

Together, we pack away the detritus on the stand and cover it with protective night sheets until the morning. I get a momentary pang and wish that it was Olly who was here with me to see my progress. But it isn't and I have to put that thought firmly to the back of my mind.

Tod and I are booked into the same hotel – and I haven't told Olly about that either. We hail a cab and I lay my head back on the seat while we work our way through the traffic to the conveniently located Scott Hotel.

The place is at the top end of my budget – probably beyond it, but I'd rather put more on my credit card and stay here with Tod than stay alone in some grotty fleapit or whatever in a dodgy backstreet. It's a five-minute drive from the exhibition centre and I now realise how valuable that it is too. We could probably even have walked it if I hadn't been so tired.

At the hotel, we're given our key cards with brisk efficiency. Tod checks my room number and finds that we're next door to each other. 'I'll knock for you in about half an hour?'

'That's fine.' All I really want to do is crawl into my bed and sleep, but that would be rude after all the help Tod has given me this afternoon. I have no idea what I would have done without him.

My room is unutterably stylish and I'm not used to such creature comforts. I have thirty minutes and I'm going to make the very most of it. Twenty seconds to apply lipstick. Two minutes forty to get dressed. Only one outfit brought for evening so no wasting time choosing that, which leaves exactly twenty-seven minutes to soak in a bubble bath. I hit the mini-bar and pour myself a glass of red wine while the water is running.

Closing my eyes, I lay back in the green tea scented foam – the rest of these complimentary toiletries are going in my bag! – and relish the fact that this is probably my only bath in four years that hasn't involved the background noise of Petal saying, 'Are you finished yet, Mummy? Are you finished yet, Mummy?' over and over.

The temptation to stay here for the rest of the night is very strong, but then I remember that I have a dinner date and I get a rush of something, a long-forgotten feeling, that I really don't want to have. This is a business dinner, I remind myself sternly, not a date. The word date shouldn't even have popped into my mind in this context. But as I reluctantly lever myself out of the bath and get ready to go out to dinner, I find my stomach fluttering with excitement.

Quickly, while I'm pulling on my dress, I telephone home and say good night to Petal. Olly is still crisp with me. A whole day is a long time for Olly to hold a grudge. He must be really mad with me this time. I feel resentful that he's putting me under extra pressure when, quite frankly, I already have enough to deal with.

On time, Tod knocks on my door. He's changed into a grey wool jacket and black jeans. His hair is damp from the shower. I don't really need to say that he looks great, do I? He offers me his arm. 'Shall we, madam?'

I take it. 'Indeed.'

The restaurant is just a short walk away and it's nice to be out in the warm night air instead of the air-conditioned chill of the exhibition hall. The place is intimate, buzzing and peopled with couples holding hands. I throw caution to the wind and order lots of things involving garlic, so I won't be tempted to kiss anyone. While we eat and drink too much, Tod laughs at all of my jokes and doles out kind words of encouragement. All the tension of the day seeps out of me and I find myself relaxing – a feeling that I've started to forget. We talk about fashion and handbags and music and I don't mention my child or my husband once.

Afterwards we walk back to the hotel, arm in arm, and when we get to my room door, we both stand there in the corridor. Me awkward, Tod considerably less so.

'You're a great lady,' he says softly.

'Thank you. I've had a lovely evening.'

'I've enjoyed your company.' He takes me in his arms and kisses me tenderly on the cheek. His lips, I think, linger too long.

If he asked if he could come into my room now, would I say no? Would I have the strength, the will, to turn him away? Even with a couple of glasses of red wine clouding my vision, I can see how easy it would be to say yes when, with all of my heart, I know that I should say no. It would be so simple to move my head, angle my body and our mouths would meet. A chaste kiss could, with so little effort, become something else entirely.

Tod releases me from his embrace. 'Get straight to bed, Nell,' he instructs. Is there a waver is his voice? The warmth of his hands, still on my arms, burns through the thin fabric of my dress. Were the same thoughts going through Tod's brain too? 'We've got an early start and a lot to do tomorrow.'

It seems that I'll never know.

As I let myself into my room and close the door behind me, I get a moment of wine-induced clarity when I realise that he sees me as just a woman to share a pleasant evening with, a business woman. But a woman, first and foremost. I'm not Petal's mummy. I'm not Olly's wife. I'm just me.

And it frightens me that I like this feeling a bit too much.

Chapter 45

'Thanks, Jenny,' Olly said. 'I don't know how we'd have managed without you this week.'

'We've had fun. Haven't we, Petal?' Jenny lifted his child out of the bath and helped her towel herself down while he leaned against the doorframe.

Petal nodded her agreement. 'We went to the swings. Jenny is good at pushing.'

'No finer compliment,' Olly said, impressed. 'You're competing with stiff competition, as I am the king of good swing-pushers. That right, Petalmeister?'

Petal high-fived him.

'Now bedtime, young lady.'

'Jenny said that I can have milk and *two* chocolate digestives.'

'Ah. No wonder she likes you so much.' Then to Petal, 'You have to be quick,' Olly said. 'No dillydallying.'

'I don't *dillydally*, Daddy,' Petal said, affronted by this assault on her blameless character.

His daughter had a whole range of tried and tested dilly-dallying techniques that he and Nell only just managed to keep ahead of. Actually, if he was honest, they usually lagged woefully behind.

They all trooped through to the kitchen and Jenny fulfilled her promise of milk and biscuits.

'I can make you something to eat, if you like,' Jenny said over her shoulder. 'I picked up a pizza in case you hadn't got anything in.'

He didn't like to remind her that every night of the week he worked making up pizzas and that it would normally be his last choice on the menu.

'Thanks, Jen,' he said. 'That's really thoughtful of you. I hadn't got anything planned.' Nell's friend was going to stay over tonight so that she could look after Petal while he was working. 'What time do you start work at the chippy?'

'I'm not on tonight,' she said. 'It's tomorrow the juggling starts.' Jen would do her shift and then come straight here in time for him to go off.

'Stay and have something to eat with me?'

'Stay! Stay! Stay!' Petal chanted.

Jenny grinned and shrugged. 'OK.'

'Bedtime for you, miss.'

'Can Jenny come and tell me a story?'

'If she wants to.'

'I'd like that,' she said.

He hung back as they all went through to Petal's tiny bedroom and whispered to Jenny, 'No funny voices. No dramatisation. Read it in a monotone voice. If you're too good, she'll only want more.'

Jenny looked at him from under her eyelashes and smiled.

In her room, Petal bounced onto her bed and, tenderly, he tucked her in.

He and Jen sat next to each other on the bed, backs against the wall, Petal curled up in a ball beside them while Jenny read out the story. Petal had picked *The Gruffalo* – a story she never tired of. Olly liked it because it was short and you could guarantee getting out of Petal's room before midnight. Unfortunately, that was the hour at which she usually came into their bed anyway.

As Petal dozed off, they both tiptoed out of the room. Olly closed the door. 'I'll just go and change the sheets on our bed. She'll probably want to come in with you in the night, if that's OK.'

'That's fine by me. Does she do that every night?'

'Yeah,' Olly admitted. 'Pretty much.'

'That must be difficult.'

'It's something we've just got into the habit of,' he said. 'But you're probably right; Petal should stay in her own bed by now.'

'You sit down while I throw this pizza in the oven. It'll take me five minutes to swap the sheets. Are they in the bedroom?'

'Yes. They're all out and ready.'

'You've had a busy day and you're going to be up all night. Have a little snooze in front of the telly.'

That suddenly sounded very appealing. 'Are you sure?'

'I like looking after people,' Jen said. 'Living on my own,

I don't get the chance to do it that often. You leave it all to me.'

So he did. Dozing off in front of a rerun of *Dragon's Den* until the delicious smell of cooking pizza woke him up. Maybe it was like most other things; pizzas always tasted better when someone else cooked them for you.

'Hey,' he said as Jenny brought a tray over for him. 'That smells great.'

'I did some garlic bread too. Can you have a beer?'

'Just the one,' Olly said.

Jenny snapped the top off a bottle and passed it to him. Then she brought her own tray and sat down next to him with it on her lap. 'This flat is lovely,' she said. 'Cosy. My place is a dump.'

'It costs us a fortune,' Olly replied. 'Especially with the shop downstairs too.'

'But Nell's doing well, isn't she?'

He shrugged. 'Hard to tell. The bags are selling all right, but the overheads are killers and getting people to pay up is another matter. There always seems to be more money going out than there is coming in.' He tucked into the pizza. 'This is good.'

'Thanks.'

'She seems to be away a lot,' Jenny remarked.

'Tell me about it.' Olly tore off some garlic bread. He seemed to have taken over the role of chief cook and bottle-washer at home. All Nell was interested in was handbags, handbags, handbags. He was rapidly becoming sick to death of living and breathing them.

Part of him really admired Nell for trying to do this and part of him just wanted his wife at home, them both pottering along in life like they used to. Like Jenny was content to do. Everything they did now involved stress and worry.

'If I had a hubby like you,' she said, 'I wouldn't be able to tear myself away.'

'Ah, well,' Olly said. 'You know that old saying "familiarity breeds contempt"? There's a lot of truth in that.'

Jenny lowered her eyes. 'I wouldn't think like that.'

Olly sighed. 'Fancy watching this film?' He held up the DVD of *Marley and Me*. 'It's a bit slushy for my taste but I thought Nell would like it. We never got round to watching it.'

'That'd be great. The perfect family night. Kid tucked up in bed. Good film. You can't beat a night in front of the telly with some good food and a beer.'

'Yeah,' he said with a smile. 'You're right.'

That was Olly's viewpoint exactly. He just knew it wasn't what Nell wanted any more.

Chapter 46

It's closing time on the last day of the show and I'm writing up my last Nell McNamara handbag order. I close the book and fight the urge to lie on the floor and sleep. Or to jump in the bath and let the remainder of the sweets close over me like water.

'Hey.' I turn and see Tod standing there. 'I came by twice today, but each time you were just swamped by people.'

'Next year I'll bring help,' I say. I didn't think to organise getting food delivered to my stand, so I haven't eaten since I shared breakfast with Tod in the hotel. Now I'm starving.

I feel completely exhausted after the busiest week of my life, but absolutely invigorated too. Every bone in my body aches, but my mind is whirling. The whole thing was absolutely brilliant. Well worth the ferocious expense. I'd do it again in a heartbeat. My stand was a big hit and I've picked up a dozen or more new stockists for Nell McNamara handbags. Plus my name is out there among the big boys, the players. I sigh to myself. Mission accomplished.

The downside is that I feel as if I've been away for months not a week. I've seen nothing of Olly or Petal, or any of my pals from the chippy, for aeons and I'm so looking forward to reconnecting with everyone.

'I'll give you a hand in breaking down the stand.'

I know there's a tight deadline in getting everyone out of the show tonight so that the next event can start to set up tomorrow. All around us is complete mayhem with people racing against the organiser's optimistic timescale.

'Have you got a van coming?'

'Olly's driving down now,' I tell him. At least I hope he is. I haven't yet had the chance to ring him to see if he's on his way.

'You've done brilliantly this week, Nell,' Tod says. 'I'm very proud of you.'

'Thanks.' I'm pretty proud of myself too.

'I'm going off to my house in France for a few weeks. We've got some time now before Paris Fashion Week. I'm taking a well-earned break. It's a shame that you couldn't come with me for a few days.'

I can't tell what's behind his eyes, but I'm assuming that he means me alone rather than *la famille Meyers en masse*.

'That wouldn't have been possible, Tod.' He knows that only too well. 'But thanks for the thought.'

For the rest of the week there have been no more untoward moments outside my hotel room – or inside it, for that matter – but it does hang in the air between us slightly. The unresolved kiss, I guess.

'Make sure that you take some time off, Nell. These trade

events really do take it out of you. Don't run down your batteries completely. You need time to recharge.'

It's not that easy though, is it? If I take my foot off the pedal, even for a minute, will all of my hard work go to waste? One thing that this week has taught me is just how cut-throat this business is.

'Want me to hang around and give you and Olly a hand loading the van?'

'No, no. You get off. Your work here is done.' It's probably not the best idea to let Olly see me with Tod as soon as he rocks up. Our phone calls have been somewhat strained and rushed this week, so I'm not sure what kind of atmosphere waits for me at home. 'Thanks so much again. Don't know what I'd do without you.' I risk a smile at him hoping that he doesn't misconstrue it.

In another time, another life, there may have been something between me and Tod, but I'm married. I'm Mrs Olly Meyers and I mustn't ever forget that. Besides, I've missed both Olly and Petal like mad this week and can't wait to get home.

'I'll be back from my break long before we go out to Paris. Want to travel there together?'

'I'd like that.'

So with a kiss, this time very brisk and business-like, Tod leaves me to pack up the stand and muse on the last few days.

I'm still packing handbags back into a big cardboard box when Olly turns up in the hired van.

'Hey,' he says. 'How's your week been?'

'Tiring,' I admit. 'But, hopefully, good for business.'

The show was great. Desperately hard work. And it's eaten up an inordinate amount of money. I don't even want to tot up the final numbers. But I'm sure it's worth it. A lot of buyers came and went, ate my sweets and made the right noises about my handbags. Now I just have to sit tight and wait and see whether it translates into mega-orders and, more critically, money in the bank for us. At the moment, I feel as if the business is teetering on a knife edge. One big order from one of the online fashion outlets like ASOS or Boohoo and we could go stratospheric. Fail to get that order and we could just as easily plummet into bankruptcy and I daren't even think about that as an option.

I want Olly to take me in his arms and hold me and, after a moment's hesitation, he does just that. I let myself melt into his embrace. Perhaps that's why things got a little too up close and personal with Tod; all week I've needed a hug, just someone to hold me.

'Everything OK?' I ask tentatively.

'Sure,' Olly says. 'Why shouldn't it be?'

I shrug. Looks like the crisis that was building may well have been averted. Perhaps my absence has made Olly's heart grow fonder. 'Has Petal missed me?'

'Like crazy.'

'Is Jenny looking after her?'

'Constance is on duty.' He fails to meet my eyes. 'Jen had something else on.' Olly picks up a box and busies himself.

'Did it work out all right with Jen looking after Petal?'

'Yeah,' he says. 'It was fine.'

But I know that there's something he's not saying. 'Sure?'

'Positive. She's a great girl.' Then, 'Come on, let's get all this loaded and get you home again.'

Home, I think with an internal sigh. Where I belong. With my husband and my daughter. And my dog. And my hand-bags.

Chapter 47

Olly and I didn't get back until late on Sunday night. It was such a rush to get everything off the stand again and I was so exhausted by the time we'd finished that there was no scintillating conversation between us on the way home. To be honest, we barely grunted at each other as we lobbed all the stuff in the van and shot off down the motorway, glad to be out of London. At home, we just collapsed into bed – but not before I'd been to look at my beautiful child who was fast asleep in Constance's care.

On the Monday after my return, I decide to keep the shop shut. The good folks of Hitchin can surely wait until tomorrow for their Nell McNamara handbag requirements to be filled. I'm trying to take Tod's advice and recharge my batteries – even if it's only for one day.

Olly and I walk Petal to her pre-school session in the morning. I have a moment of panic when I realise that Olly knows all the mums. He fits in seamlessly with them and I don't. Where has my ability to make kiddie small talk gone? Do I really think of nothing else but handbags now? Has work become my whole focus? I feel myself standing on the outside, not knowing any of them, feeling self-conscious that I'm over-dressed in a brightly printed dirndl skirt and ballet pumps and not the ubiquitous jeans and fleece that everyone else is sporting. Although they chat and call out to Olly, they look at me suspiciously, as if a woman going places is not to be trusted. It leaves me feeling unsettled. Did the school mums like me better when I was just working in the chippy? Do they feel threatened by my new career? I don't know. I feel that I don't fit in with the whole fashion crowd either – I'm not trendy and chic like they are – and yet I don't know my place here any more. So where exactly does that leave me? I should make more effort to do things at Petal's school, join committees and the like. But when would I find the time?

Olly slips his hand in mine and, Petal safely deposited for the next few hours, we wander into the town centre. Our plan is to do nothing but spend the morning drinking coffee together and catching up with the real world in the dog-eared newspapers provided by the shop. We have a proper talk about the show now that we're both more awake and receptive. For once, he seems genuinely enthusiastic. But then, I confess that I just tell him about the good bits and not how I spent much of the week with Tod, which he would definitely not view as a good bit.

It's a brilliant, sunny day so later, when we pick up Petal, we take her straight to Bancroft Gardens and we all run around the park like loons, swooping and chasing each other with aeroplane arms until we're sick with laughter. Then Petal plays on the see-saw with Olly and they run round and round the bandstand long after my energy has been exhausted. This is our favourite park to come to and it's been here since Olly and I were both kids. Petal loves it too. It has a bowling green, tennis courts, fantastic flower beds stuffed full of those plants that councils like so much – begonias, lobelia, chrysanthemums – all in gloriously clashing colours. I think it's nice that, after all these years, it still retains a quaint, old-fashioned air. There's always talk of redeveloping it, upgrading the facilities. But who knows if they ever will.

Probably the only addition to the park since I was a girl is a bench full of drunks who sit here day in, day out, and put the world to rights with their cans of Stella. We find a place on the grass away from them and eat our supermarket-made sandwiches while we listen to Petal's relentlessly cheerful stream of chatter. The sun beats down on me and I feel my heart ease. I've missed them both so much. It's good to be back and be normal again.

'I'm looking forward to staying at home tonight with you,' Olly says, arm slung round my shoulder. 'Quality time with my wifey.'

'Oh,' I say. 'I thought I'd pop in and see everyone from the chippy later. I wanted to see Jen and thank her for helping us out.'

'She's cool,' Olly says somewhat shiftily. 'I thanked her for us.'

I have to keep on the right side of Jen as, in the future, there'll be more and more of these shows to go to. The next one coming up is Paris Fashion Week, which I've arranged to go to with Tod, and I'll be begging for her help again then. 'I can go in late-afternoon instead. Catch them after the lunchtime rush. I haven't seen Phil or Constance properly for ages.' Apart from a two-minute handover last night on Constance's part. 'Do you mind?'

'No. It'll do you good to see them again.'

But his arm drops from my shoulders nevertheless.

At four o'clock, Olly takes Petal home and I swing into the arcade that houses Live and Let Fry. I throw open the door and, for a brief moment, have a rush of sensation that says 'I've come home.'

'Nell,' Constance cries out. 'Our Nell's here!' She completely abandons the customer who she was serving with his late lunch and comes to hug the life out of me. I don't remind her that she did the same thing to me just last night.

Phil also wipes his hands on his apron, peels it off and comes to wrap his arms round me. Only Jenny hangs back.

'Hey,' I say. 'I've missed you all.' I feel as guilty as hell that I've neglected these guys recently in my quest for fame and fortune. 'It's been weeks since I've seen you.'

'We're still here, Nell,' Phil says with a shrug. 'Nothing much changes.'

'Business good?'

'Booming,' he confirms. My handiwork still looks great, even though I say it myself.

'We've got someone to replace you,' Constance continues. 'Chloe. She's a darling. All the customers adore her.'

'Oh. Great.' But, for some reason, I feel piqued about that.

Chloe, eh? I've only been gone five minutes and, so soon, someone else has taken my place. I get the feeling that I'm disconnecting with my old life once more. I want to tell them all about my work, work that they helped me start, a career that without them cajoling me, I never would have had the courage to contemplate, but I feel that they wouldn't understand, that they wouldn't be all that interested. And who could blame them? But I've barely got my toe in the fashion world, so I've no one I can talk to there. Once again, it makes me wonder exactly where I do belong these days.

'We've heard from Jen that you've been here, there and everywhere. Haven't we, Jen?' Constance shoots her a look.

'Yeah.' Finally, Jen steps forward and hugs me. But there's a tightness about her body, a reluctance to touch me that I haven't felt before.

'You're my angel,' I tell her earnestly. Then to Phil and Constance, 'I honestly don't know what I'd have done without this woman.'

A slightly dark look passes between Phil and Constance. Fleeting, ever so fleeting, but I catch it anyway.

'Sit down. Sit down.' Phil clears one of the tables and we all slide into chairs.

I notice that Phil and Constance sit together and there's a growing closeness between them that's more than their usual familiar banter. I smile to myself. It would be nice to see them properly together as a couple. They've both been alone for too long. Perhaps it's nice that they're taking their time to edge closer together rather than rushing headlong into something that could spoil the relationship they've built up over many years. You need to be careful not to upset the status quo. Yeah. Look who's talking.

'Jen, love. Get that kettle on,' Phil says. 'Will you have some chips, Nell? Of course you will.'

'As if I'm going to refuse! I've been pining for your fries.' But I'm ashamed to say that in reality, I've hardly given my old mates a second thought in recent weeks. I have no excuse other than I've been ridiculously busy and that work occupies my every waking moment.

'Jen! Bring some chips too.'

'She's been brilliant,' I tell them both. 'Really. Petal adores her. I wouldn't be able to go away half as much if it wasn't for Jen helping out.' Suddenly, I feel as if I'm defending her, defending myself. Their faces are impassive. 'What?' I ask. 'What do you know that I don't?'

'Nothing,' Constance says.

Phil pats her leg and slides out of his seat. 'I'll just go and see how Jen's doing.'

That leaves me and Constance alone.

'Well?'

'It's nothing, love,' my friend says. 'Nothing at all. Nothing to worry about.'

'Now I am worried,' I tell her.

Constance's hand covers mine, which is always a bad sign. 'Just be careful,' she says.

'About what?'

'It's all very well running round the world with your new business but don't forget about your home, love.'

I bristle. 'I don't.'

Constance looks embarrassed.

'Has someone been saying something?' I ask. 'Has Olly complained?'

'No, no,' she assures me. 'It's just a silly old woman and her fears.' She pauses, clearly trying to choose her words carefully. 'Men like to be at the top of the list though, Nell. Not near the bottom.'

'All this is for Olly. And Petal.'

'*I* know that. *You* know that. But does everyone else?'

'Who?'

'Sometimes people are jealous of success, Nell,' she tells me. 'Don't take your eye off the ball, love, or someone might come in and steal it away from you.'

Phil comes back with a big plate of chips piled high, and Constance falls silent. Jen follows with a tray of cups and a big pot of tea.

Now I'm wishing that I hadn't called in at all. Clearly something isn't right and I'm the only one who's completely oblivious to it.

Jenny starts to pour out the tea. 'I'll be mum.'

The penny drops. Maybe that's what Jenny thinks she's going to be doing at my house! Maybe she thinks she's going to take over as mum there.

She sploshes the tea into the cups. 'Help yourself, Nell,' she says.

I wonder if she's been doing that too.

Oh, God. I feel sick. Have I missed any signs? Olly moans that I talk about Tod a lot, but he never says anything about Jen. I didn't even think he liked her all that much.

What to do? Perhaps I should confront her, confront Olly? But what would I say? I only have Constance's suspicions to go on.

Then a thought pulls me up short. I can't afford to upset Jenny. I can't afford to rock the boat. I need her to look after Petal while I'm away. My daughter loves her. That worries me even more. Jenny's the one who spends more time with her than me at the moment. But I've got Paris Fashion Week coming up. That's mega-important. I can't *not* go and yet it's too short notice to find someone else to look after Petal.

I grit my teeth. Jen had better watch it though. I'll be keeping a close eye on her from now on. I know that sacrifices have to be made for my career. But I don't intend my marriage to be one of them.

Chapter 48

Petal is puking up again. No one told me when I signed up for motherhood that part of the deal was regular and inappropriately timed bouts of vomiting. When I decided that I'd like to have a child, I really had no idea that they could produce that much sick. Now, after four years of practice, that I can deal with. What's more worrying is that Petal is also covered in livid red spots. She's not had those before.

'Chicken pox,' Doctor Olly pronounces as I wipe her down with a flannel.

'Is this a guess or are you sure?'

'Google,' Olly says. 'I'm pretty sure.'

'Oh, God.' I am due at the Eurostar terminal in less than an hour to catch a train to Paris. If I don't go soon, this minute, I won't make my connection. And this is Paris Fashion Week. This is a big deal. The *biggest* deal.

Olly must read the bleakness on my face. 'Go,' he says. 'You go. Jenny and I will look after her.'

I don't like the way that statement slips so easily from his tongue. *Jenny and I.* I'm still not sure if there's anything going on between them and, coward that I am, I haven't had the courage to ask.

'I can't leave my sick child,' I protest.

'Think how much this little jaunt is costing,' he says bluntly.

I ignore the fact that he calls my important business trip 'a little jaunt'.

'We can't afford to just lose that money. Petal will be fine. How long does chicken pox last? A week? Ten days?'

Better check with Google again. 'Suppose it's meningitis?' I know I'm probably fretting unnecessarily, but you hear so much about it now. And it always seems to be misdiagnosed.

'It isn't. I'll stake my life on it. This is a common childhood illness, Nell. She'll be over it by the time you get back. You see, she'll be better by then.'

That doesn't make *me* feel better.

Olly sighs with exasperation. 'What choice do we have?'

He's right. At vast expense my train tickets are booked and my hotel too. I'm not exhibiting out there, but it's a fantastic opportunity to network, to show that I can play with the big boys. I've only managed to secure a ticket, which are like gold dust, through Tod's contacts. And *he's* probably wondering where the hell I am right now. I'm supposed to be meeting him at St Pancras station and, knowing Tod, he'll be there already. He'll be sitting in a coffee bar looking immaculate and unflustered with newspaper in hand, enjoying a leisurely cappuccino. He won't be dealing with impromptu puke and a severe attack of guilt.

I can't not turn up today. It would certainly damage our working relationship if I left him in the lurch now. Tod, I'm absolutely sure, won't understand that I can't bear to leave my sick child. These are not considerations that he has in his life. How can I let him down at the very last minute? Particularly when he's pulled so many strings to get me a ticket. But in not letting Tod down, I'm letting Petal down. I feel as if I'm being ripped in two.

'If you don't go now, you'll have wasted the opportunity,' Olly says. 'Just go.'

He's right. I have to.

'I'll call you the minute I get there,' I say. 'Ring the doctor as soon as the surgery opens. Tell him you're worried it's meningitis.'

'But I'm not.'

'Then tell him *I* am. Keep her cool with flannels. If it is chicken pox, don't let her pick any of the scabs when they start to form or she'll get scars.'

I think of how my mum was when I had chicken pox – sitting with me all day long, spooning me homemade soup. That's the sort of mum I wanted to be. Not the sort who's halfway out the door with a suitcase, glibly throwing out not-picking-scabs advice.

Guilt-stricken, I go to kiss Petal but Olly holds up a hand. 'Don't kiss her,' he says. 'You don't want to spread this around the supermodels.'

'Mummy loves you,' I say. 'I'll be back soon.'

I look at Olly and his face is dark with concern. I don't want to leave him either.

'See you next weekend,' my husband says with a resigned shrug.

'I'll be thinking of you both every minute,' I promise.

His face says that he doubts it.

I fly out the door, picking up my case as I go. It's filled with sample handbags for me to show to people if I get the opportunity and it weighs a ton. By the time I get to the front door, I'm already out of puff and sweating. I run barefoot to the station, shoes in hand, coat streaming, fully loaded wheelie case banging along behind me.

Is this how women in business are supposed to behave? Can you see Anna Wintour doing this? She probably has a host of minions to live the boring bits of her life for her. She probably has chauffeur-driven cars and private jets. How does everyone else who runs a company manage to keep all of these balls in the air?

I make the Hitchin train by the skin of my teeth and then text Tod to tell him that I'm running late and that if I'm not there by the time he needs to clear security, then I'll meet him on the Eurostar. I hope.

Thankfully, my train is on time and a short while later, I'm racing through the concourse at St Pancras, red in the face and perspiring profusely. This is not the image I ever envisaged for myself.

The restaurants are brimming with people enjoying a leisurely breakfast, a chocolaty snack or a nice cup of tea. Oh, to be one of them! My stomach growls in protest to remind me that I haven't eaten at all this morning. But there's no time to stop now. I'll have to grab something extortionately priced on the train.

I'm held up at the security screening for the Eurostar as the guard wants to examine all of my handbags in minute detail as they've clearly shown up on the scanner as something highly suspicious. If a terrorist was going to make a bomb, would they really do it in the shape of a handbag? I don't voice this opinion just in case he decides to clap me in irons and throw me in jail. The clock ticks on relentlessly. When he finally deigns to let me through, I bolt to the gate. Upstairs on the concourse, people, even at this early hour, are sitting at the champagne bar enjoying a convivial glass or two of fizz. How do they do it? How does everyone else seem to run their lives better than I do?

As the guard is blowing the whistle, I throw myself on the train. Then, as it pulls away, I set about the task of finding my allocated seat. Three compartments along, I see Tod sitting there, reading the *Guardian*, sipping a latte in an oasis of calm. I throw myself into the seat opposite him, wheezing like an old steam train while the sleek, modern Eurostar slips silently towards France.

Tod looks up in surprise. 'Nell?' His face brightens and I'm so grateful for that. 'I didn't think you were going to make it.'

Me neither, I think. But what I puff out is, 'Can't speak. Can't speak.'

'Is everything all right?' Tod takes my hands in his.

Then I cry and cry and cry. I cry all the way through the Kent countryside. I cry as we whizz through the pitch blackness of the tunnel. And I cry until we emerge into the peace of the rural French countryside and we're well on our way to Paris.

Chapter 49

Tod and I take a taxi from the Gare du Nord terminal. Impressively, Tod rattles off where we're going in French to the driver. I've never been here before. I've never travelled much at all, unless you count a couple of weeks in Majorca every few years when the need for some sunshine became too desperate. And Olly and I haven't even been able to do that since Petal came along.

I'm glad that I'm here with Tod so that he can show me the ropes, as I might not have had the nerve to come on my own. I guess if he's got a house in France – he did tell me where, but it meant nothing to me – then he's probably been over here quite a lot.

The sun is shining and I know that Paris in the springtime is something special to write about, but summer doesn't seem too shabby either. It's an amazing city and I think that at any time of year, it would look absolutely stunning to me. We pass the Eiffel Tower and I gaze longingly at it. I don't know if I'll get the chance to visit it on this trip, but it's apparent that we have no time to linger now. So the sights of Paris whizz by the window and I can only press my nose against it.

As soon as we reach our destination, Tod and I throw our cases into the quaint, little backstreet hotel that he's booked for us. Oblivious to the cost of international calls, I phone home.

'How's Petal?'

'She's fine. She's stopped barfing now and is asleep.'

'Is she asleep or unconscious?' I want to know.

'Asleep, Nell. I've got it all under control. Stop panicking.'

Olly's calm reassurance does help turn down my stress levels down a notch. I know that he can manage without me and that should make me feel better than it does.

'I love you,' I say. 'I'll call later. Have to dash.'

I hang up. Then, without further ado, Tod and I jump into another taxi and rush headlong to the first event to which we've been invited. It's a trade reception for the up-and-coming designer, Freya, who's the daughter of well-known rock star, Tommy Blood, and has a huge budget behind her. I hate her already.

The reception is being held in the small and indecently trendy Galerie d'art Claude. Outside, bright young things in eye-catching clothing hang around just waiting for someone to take pity on them and slip them a spare invitation. To think that, but for Tod, I could have easily been one of them.

Inside the inner sanctum, it's all white and classy. A crush of beautiful people mingle, talking loudly, sipping cocktails. I recognise the rock star's daughter from across the room. Freya's laughing and being sparkling. A photographer is following her every move. Bet she didn't have to cope with a puking, chicken-poxed, borderline-meningitised child at dawn.

'OK?' Tod asks.

I want to tell him that I'm fine, that this is all old hat to me now – but he and I both know that this sort of thing doesn't come easily to me. I've discovered that I'm not a natural mingler. When I was working in the chippy, I was somehow able to be gregarious and knew all of the regular customers by name. That was fine. Perhaps I felt I was on a level with them. I have no idea. Here, I know no one and feel hideously out of my depth. They all seem to be so superior to me, so much wealthier, so much cooler. I wish I didn't have the tendency to turn into a wallflower, but I do. As usual, I attach myself to Tod like a limpet.

Ridiculously thin models, with hair piled high and eye make-up like carnival masques, work their way through the crowd, showing the designer's clothes, turning this way and that.

Across the room, much to my surprise, I see someone who I recognise instantly. He's leaning against the wall, foot up on the pristine white paintwork. He's dressed in a smooth grey suit and white shirt and looks every bit as handsome as I remember.

I tug at Tod's sleeve, just like Petal does to mine. 'It's Yves,' I whisper to him. 'Yves Simoneaux. The French agent I told you about.' The somewhat *elusive* French agent. I didn't know that he was going to be here, not just at this event, but at the show in general. But perhaps I should have guessed as it's on his home turf.

Tod rubs his chin. 'I don't know him,' he says. 'Not a face I've seen around. But there are dozens of agents out there and I'm a bit out of touch on that side.'

I realise that I didn't ask much about his background. Maybe I should have. Give me a fancy business card and I go all gaga.

'I'll ask around about him.'

'He seems nice,' I say somewhat lamely. 'I should go and say hello.'

'Of course you should,' Tod agrees.

'Come with me?'

'I'm just going to catch up with a few people I do know and then I'll follow you. I'll literally be five minutes.'

'OK.'

Sometimes I'll have to do things without hanging onto Tod, I guess. Nervously, I pick my way through the crush of people to where Yves is standing and then sidle up to him. He's holding court in a circle of chic hangers-on and when there's a gap in the conversation, I give a little cough.

Yves turns towards me and his eyes widen. 'Nell,' he says. 'How lovely. I did not expect that you would be here.'

I think that if perhaps he ever answered his phone calls or his emails, then he might have done so. Although, to be fair, I didn't contact him to say I'd be here. I thought that as an agent and designer we'd be more in touch than we are.

He takes my hand and kisses it. An impossibly slender woman with scarlet lips, her dark hair pulled back in a knot and wearing a long white dress, looks me up and down. Then he turns back to his circle and says, 'This is Nell McNamara.

Her handbags are *sensationnel*.' He and the woman in white exchange a glance that I can't read. Perhaps this is Mrs Simoneaux. If it is, then I'm not introduced. 'You are exhibiting here, *non*?'

'No,' I say. Surely I would have involved him if I was? The thought doesn't seem to cross his mind. 'I'm here with a friend who's in the trade, Tod Urban.' It's clear that Yves Simoneaux doesn't recognise his name either. I point out Tod across the room. 'Just looking this time. Seeing what the competition is like.'

'It is a good thing to do. We can meet up, perhaps. Make some good contacts.'

'I'd like that.'

Yves's entourage gradually start to drift away, the woman last of all, heading off to work the room until there are just the two of us left.

'Your friend?' Yves asks. 'He is a very good friend?'

'He's my business mentor,' I explain, wondering just what Yves is insinuating. 'He's been in the industry a long time.'

'Ah.' He narrows his eyes and, across the room, studies Tod some more. Then, 'How is your lovely little girl?'

'She's not very well,' I tell him. 'I felt terrible leaving her to come here.'

'Ah.' He shrugs. 'This is the way of the working mother, yes?'

'Yes,' I agree. 'I think it is. Do you have children?'

'No.' He laughs. 'I do not have a wife!' More laughing and those eyes tease me. 'I like living, how do you say, the single life?'

Yes, I'm sure you do, Monsieur Simoneaux. There are probably a string of broken-hearted *mesdemoiselles*, and possibly *mesdames*, across Paris pining for you.

'I must go now,' Yves says, checking his watch. 'Where are you staying? May I call at your hotel later?'

'Yes,' I say. 'Of course. I'd like to talk about the business with you.'

He smiles. 'I will tell you of my progress.'

Oh. There is some, then. Good. I like the sound of this.

I'd picked up some cards with the hotel address on from the desk in reception in case I got separated from Tod and wasn't able to make myself understood in a cab. I fish for one in my pocket and then hand it to Yves.

His eyes lock with mine. 'Until later.'

'Later,' I say and then my heart goes all fluttery and I know that I'm going to panic for the rest of the day.

Chapter 50

Tod and I spend all afternoon going to catwalk shows. One is for clothes by a designer called Isabel Green, the others are for accessories – hats, shoes – and one show is entirely devoted to handbags. I come away both inspired and terrified by the competition. These people seriously look like they know what they're doing. They don't look like they live hand-to-mouth in a flat above a shop in a small, middle-England market town. They look like they have bijou apartments overlooking Montmartre or somewhere fabulously ritzy, if that isn't.

Later, Tod and I grab a passable boeuf bourguignon and a glass of red wine from the *prix fixe* menu at a little brasserie near the hotel. If Tod was ever to be on *Mastermind*, I'm thinking his specialist subject could be Rather Romantic Restaurants of the World.

'Have you enjoyed your day?' he asks

'Amazing.' I try to stifle a yawn. I feel as if I've been awake for days.

'Grab an early night,' he instructs. 'Tomorrow will be just as busy.'

'I said I'd meet with Yves Simoneaux at the hotel. He's going to update me on his progress.'

'Want me to stay with you?'

I know that Tod really wants to go back to the evening show of someone he worked with years ago that's close by.

'No, no. I'll be fine. You go off to the show.'

'Are you sure?'

I nod.

'Just be careful,' Tod says. 'Remember you're an innocent abroad. Literally.'

'He seems OK,' I reassure him, but I wonder if there's some underlying jealousy there. Secretly – or perhaps not so secretly – I think Tod likes to be the expert in my life. 'I'll fill you in tomorrow.'

'Let's meet for breakfast at eight sharp,' he says. 'The first show is at ten.' He pays the bill and stands to leave. 'Sure you're OK?'

'Fine. Really.' When he leaves, to prove that I *am* OK, I order another glass of wine and stay in the bistro, drinking in the atmosphere and trying not to feel too self-conscious.

At eight o'clock, I make my way back to the hotel across the street. 'Has anyone called for me?'

'*Non, madam*,' the receptionist tells me.

'I'm expecting a Mr Yves Simoneaux.'

She shrugs her disinterest, so I take the open, wrought-iron and very rickety lift up to the third floor and let myself into my room. I wonder if everything in Paris is stylish as even on a budget, this has a certain charm.

The room is small, but has large French windows and a Juliet balcony, which looks out on to the bustling street below. The bed is big and the room is decorated in white with lime-green and lemon soft furnishings. In one corner is a wooden stepladder painted white in a designer-distressed way, which displays plants and pretty glass bottles. The original, claw-footed bath looks very appealing. But I daren't dive in, as I'd like to, because I don't know what time Yves will be arriving and I don't want him catching me in the nuddy – or whatever the French equivalent is.

Instead, I decide to give Olly a buzz again. As the phone rings, I'm thinking grumpily that my bill for calls home will amount to more than the entire cost of the trip. I'm even more disgruntled when Jenny answers my home phone with a chirpy, 'Hiya.'

'Hi, Jen,' I say. 'Everything OK?'

'Everything's lovely,' she replies.

'This is costing a fortune,' I remind her and myself. 'Can you put Olly on, please?'

'He's just popped out for a takeaway for us,' she says. 'He won't be long.'

A takeaway? I can feel my eyes narrowing. Why should that make me jealous? Because we have them on high-days and holidays when I'm at home, that's why. But I guess I can hardly complain when I'm sitting in a chic Parisian hotel, running up a phone bill the size of the national debt.

'Petal, then,' I try. 'Can I say good night to her?'

'In bed,' Jenny tells me. 'She was worn out, poor love.'

'But she is OK?'

'Don't worry yourself,' Jen assures me. 'Olly and I are managing just fine.'

There's something in her tone that niggles me.

'Can you let Olly know that I'll call tomorrow?'

'Will do,' she says brightly and then, before I know it, she hangs up.

I sit and stare blankly at the phone. I imagine her sitting on *my* sofa, in *my* living room, with *my* husband, eating takeaway off *my* plates while *my* child sleeps in the next room and I don't like what I'm picturing at all.

After the phone call, I can't settle. I try to tell myself that my stomach is churning because I've eaten too much but, if I'm truthful, it's other emotions that are making my tummy swirl. I trust Olly, of course I do. He would never do anything to hurt me. Or Petal. I'm sure of it. Absolutely sure. But I feel as if I'm handing him over on a plate to another woman and I'm not happy about that at all. Someone else is sliding into my life while I'm away and there's nothing I can do about it.

I mooch around the room and try the television, but I can't find anything on that's not in French. Funny that. I check my watch. Nine o'clock. Where is Yves?

Kicking off my shoes, I plump up the pillows and lie back on the bed. To distract myself, I pick up my pad and start to sketch. Perhaps I could do some Parisian-based designs and, as soon as I start, my head is buzzing with ideas. I rough out a fifties-illustrated poodle design, a bag shaped like the Eiffel Tower and one that would have a typical Parisian flower shop frontage with a corsage on the corner. Might as well use my current surroundings to inspire my creativity.

While I'm lost in my work, I hear a knock and it takes me a while to realise that it's at my door. When I check my watch, it's nearly midnight and any hope of an early night has long gone. I jump up, thinking that it must be Tod coming back from his show, but when I throw open the door, Yves Simoneaux is standing there.

'Hey,' he murmurs.

He's changed from when I saw him earlier today and is wearing a black leather jacket and jeans. His trademark white shirt is open at the neck. In his hand is a bottle of champagne and two glasses. He looks as if he may have been drinking already. 'I am late. I am sorry.'

'It *is* a bit late now,' I say and try to sound reproving. I'd like to hear what Yves has to say about the business, but it's a bit of a cheek turning up at this hour. I need my bed much more than I need champagne.

But he's past me and into the room before I can say otherwise.

The champagne cork is popped and the glasses full and I still haven't spoken. Yves hands me a glass. Reluctantly, I take it.

'My day has been very good,' he says. 'I have had many meetings about you.'

'Good.' I start to relax. It must be a very busy time for Yves and yet he's still made time to come and see me – a mere beginner, wet behind the ears. I must remember that, despite the lateness of the hour.

Yves sits on the bed. His presence seems to take up more of the room than it should. The air in the room is stifling and I throw open the French windows and let in the breeze and the sounds of the night from the street.

He flicks through my sketch pad. 'These are good.'

I shrug. 'I was just toying with a few ideas.'

'Come,' he says, 'sit with me.'

I notice a slight slur in his voice.

Yves pats the bed next to him and, suddenly, I feel tired and alone and I don't want to be drinking champagne in a strange bedroom with a strange man.

'You know,' I say. 'It's very, *very* late. I think you should simply bring me up to speed with what you've done to get me started in France and we'll call it a night.'

Yves does not look impressed by this idea. 'These things, they take time.' He spreads his hands. 'You are not a person who is known.'

I thought it was his job to *make* me known.

'Have you managed to get me in any outlets, any boutiques? Anything at all?'

'It will happen, Nell,' he says. 'Be patient.'

My patience is actually running quite thin. Tod would know what to do. He'd know if this man is just spinning me a line. But then, I think I've realised that myself. It isn't my fabulous charisma that's attracting all this attention. It seems that being a woman in business has you marked down as fair game. Well, not this one.

'In the meantime, we can have some fun, maybe.'

'Fun?' I laugh out loud and he looks taken aback. 'I don't want fun, Yves. I want a business. I want orders in Paris and Milan. So many of them that we can hardly cope. I want you

242

to do your job. If you're not doing that, then I need to find another agent.'

'Come on, baby,' he says, smarmy smile on his face. 'Loosen up.'

Baby? Did he really just have the gall to call me baby? I lean on the balcony rail and breathe in the coolness to try to calm me down. When I feel steadier, I turn to him, 'I'd like you to leave now.'

His face darkens. 'I do not think that you mean that.'

I march to the door and open it. 'I assure you, I do. Please leave now.'

At that, he stands up and knocks back his champagne. 'I am sorry that this is the way you feel, Nell. You make a big mistake.'

Then I panic that I've been too hasty. Perhaps he's just drunk and doesn't really realise what he's saying. Maybe he is a good agent. I don't know. I have nothing to compare him to. What if another agent won't take me on? What if this is my only chance of breaking into France? 'I'm sorry, Yves. It's late. We'll speak again. Let's meet up tomorrow.'

'Tomorrow, I am busy.'

I think this is it. I have to accept that Yves and I are going to part company. I had such high hopes, but it seems that my handbags won't be gracing the arms of the ladies of France after all.

'I will wish you good night,' Yves says crisply, 'and good luck for your future.' Without further ado, he leaves.

I lean against the door and sigh to myself. If it wasn't so late, I'd go and knock on Tod's room and tell him what happened. Instead, I slump into the one armchair and go over our last conversation in my mind again. I come to the decision that he really was out of order. It wasn't me.

As Yves has left his champagne behind, I pour myself another glass, even though I don't want it. I sit and sip it but, minutes after I do, my eyes start to grow heavy and I abandon it. What a waste. Still, tomorrow is another day and I'll have to see if I can repair the damage done. Perhaps Tod will know another agent I can approach.

Hauling myself out of the chair, I strip off my shirt. My head feels all swimmy and my limbs have suddenly gone heavy.

Then, through the haze, I notice that my sketch pad isn't on the bed any more. I force myself to stay awake and scour the floor. I look under the bed. I lift the pillows and check there. It's definitely missing. Then it strikes me. This has happened before. Didn't some of my designs go walk about when Yves came to my shop?

But, dizziness washes over me and sleep overwhelms me and it's too late for me to do anything about it.

Chapter 51

The next day, I meet Tod for breakfast in the tiny courtyard garden of the hotel. The birds are singing, the sun is shining, the smell of fresh croissants wafts out from the kitchen and I feel like shite.

Tod stands when he sees me. 'Wow,' he says. 'Heavy night?'

'No,' I say. 'Not really.'

That's the strange thing. I had two glasses of wine with dinner, then I had a glass of champagne with Yves and barely started one more after he left. I'm not exactly a big drinker, but does that constitute a heavy night? Does it warrant me feeling so truly terrible? I actually feel like I've been drugged. My head is banging and my mouth is as dry as dust. Then the thought goes through my fuggy brain – what if I have been drugged?

Should I voice my suspicions to Tod? What if Yves had slipped something in my drink? It isn't entirely beyond the realms of possibility, I think. It happens. At least, I've read about it happening to other people. Or am I just being ridiculously paranoid?

I have to ask myself what exactly was I doing letting someone I hardly know into my room at all. It also freaks me out to think that Yves might have helped himself to my designs. Not once, but twice. Though, perhaps, I should count my blessings that I gave him short shrift and that was all he was able to help himself to.

God, I feel so stupid.

Tod pulls out my chair for me and, gingerly, I sit down.

'Are you sure you're OK?'

'No.' I decide that honesty is the best policy. 'I'm not that great.' I might even want to be sick. Instead, I put my head in my hands and Tod pours me a glass of water. I gulp it down gratefully. 'Yves came to my room last night. Late. He brought champagne.'

Tod's face tells me that he doesn't like the way this is going. I can't say that I blame him.

'I don't know if it was drugged,' I confess. 'I certainly feel more awful than I should do after a few glasses of plonk.'

'Drugged?' Tod's face blanches. 'He didn't ... ?'

'No.' I shake my head. 'When it became clear he wasn't there primarily to talk about work, I told him to leave. He did.'

'Thank heavens for that.'

'Exactly.' I let out a shuddering breath. 'But I think he took some of my designs with him.'

Tod's face darkens.

'I don't think it's the first time. '

'Oh, Nell.'

Taking a deep breath, I plough on. Tod might as well know

everything. 'When he came to see me in Hitchin a few months ago, I'm pretty sure that he took some of my new sketches with him then.' I can't believe what a fool I've been. But I never expected anyone to do something like that? Why should I? 'I never suspected him at all at the time,' I admit. 'I just thought I'd misplaced them. Or Petal had binned them. Or something.'

'I think your nature may be too trusting for the cut and thrust of business.'

'I'm beginning to see that.'

'I asked around about him last night, Nell, but no one seemed to know who he was.'

I guess that shouldn't surprise me. 'I feel such a fool.'

Tod tuts. 'I should never have left you alone with him. This is my fault.'

'It's mine,' I counter. 'I should have made sure I checked him out more thoroughly.' And hadn't simply agreed to everything because I was blinded by his flattery. Stupid, stupid me.

The waitress brings us fresh coffee, so strong and black that it will either kill me or cure me. She also puts down a basket of croissants and a dish of creamy butter. My stomach rolls.

'Eat,' Tod instructs. 'We have a busy day ahead of us.'

I can hardly bear the thought of it. I want to go home. I want to run back to Olly and Petal. I want to be with people who love me and don't want to do bad things to me.

'We are going to track that man down,' Tod informs me as he tucks in. 'Whoever he is.'

'We are?'

He whips out his programme like it's a weapon of mass

destruction and, while I force myself to nibble at a croissant, he trawls through the listings.

'Right,' he announces eventually. 'I've got some shows marked down where he might be. Up for this, Nell?'

'Yes.'

Tod fixes me with a gaze. 'I don't want to find him only for you to go all nice on me.'

'No,' I agree. 'I can do not nice.'

'Excellent. Then let's go and get the bastard.'

Couldn't have put it better myself.

Chapter 52

I see the Louvre from another taxi window, and then Tod and I go to three different shows back-to-back on the hunt for *Monsieur* Yves Slippery Simoneaux. We see some nice stuff, but not the elusive trickster/agent. The last show of the morning is for a new accessories designer, Marie Monique, and Tod reckons that this might well be a good place for Yves to rock up. I sincerely hope so.

This venue looks like a disused factory and is called *Espace Blanc*. Inside, it's all industrial with concrete floors and exposed pipework. A central, galvanised steel staircase comes down from a gallery to join a runway that's flanked by rows of chairs. It's sparsely populated, at the moment, but filling up fast. Tod and I take the last remaining seats in the front row at the head of the runway. Despite the soothing music, a prickle of apprehension runs through me.

Sensing my discomfort, Tod says, 'OK?'

'Yeah,' I say. 'I don't know what's wrong. I just feel a bit funny.'

'Not sick?'

'No.' Something like a sixth sense. Yves will be here. I know it. I can feel it in my bones, in my water, in the hairs on the back of my neck.

Scanning the rows though, I can't see him anywhere.

Five minutes later and the music racks up several notches, announcing the start of the show. The chill-out sound of Groove Armada's mellow song 'At the River' fills the room. The models high-step down the staircase, a precarious move in canvas sandals with towering wedge heels. They're dressed only in white skimpy bikinis and floppy hats and wear brightly coloured beach bags in different styles slung across their bodies to sit low on their hips.

'Nice,' Tod whispers to me.

I can't argue with that. But I'm distracted and can't help but keep looking round in search of the elusive Mr Simoneaux.

The mood changes and a drum and bass version of 'Puttin' on the Ritz' pumps out. The models wear red playsuits and black stilettos. The handbags are glittering silver box shapes with red satin hearts attached. Cute.

The music changes tempo again and it's M People singing 'Itchycoo Park'. This time the models are dressed all in white with cropped T-shirts, pedal pushers and ballet flats. As they hit the runway in front of us, my heart stops, my limbs freeze and my eyes pop. I can't believe what I'm seeing. Or maybe I can.

The handbags that the models are wearing are as familiar as the freckles on my child's face. These are my handbags. The ones that I had sketched out when I was in my shop in

Hitchin. The ones with the pop art inspired, psychedelic designs. The ones that Yves Simoneaux had lifted, just as I suspected.

Tod turns to me instantly.

I nod. 'They're mine.'

'You don't need to tell me. I'd recognise them anywhere,' he says.

I knew that it was bad. But I had no idea quite how bad.

'That slimy French bastard has stolen your designs.'

He has. My God, he has. I don't know what I thought he was going to do with them, but I hadn't, in my worst nightmare, thought that he would do this.

Tod and I sit there mesmerised as my nicked handbag designs are paraded before our eyes. The applause is louder than for any other part of the collection and that's with two people not clapping at all.

'What can I do?' I whisper to Tod.

'This is a nightmare,' he hisses back. 'We can try to make a legal case against him, but it will be long and lengthy.'

Not to mention expensive, I suspect.

'How can you prove the designs were yours, Nell, if you don't have any record of them?'

Bloody hell. All I had was my original sketches. Yves knew exactly what he was doing, the sleazebag. He knew I was green and keen. It must have been like taking candy from a baby.

'But they're mine,' I say, sounding exactly like Petal would. 'They're mine.' The people are going crazy for them and they're mine.

'Don't worry,' Tod says, looking worried. 'We'll think of something.'

But we stay pinned in our seats, immobile and watch the models strut with goggle eyes.

The show finishes and still Tod and I don't move. At the end of the last catwalk run, as is customary, the models escort the designer to the front for them to take their bow from the audience. From the gallery above us, Marie Monique appears and I'd recognise her anywhere too. It's the woman in white who was at the gallery show yesterday – with Yves Simoneaux.

She's dressed all in white again today. A bodycon dress teamed with killer heels. Her hair is in a long, black plait. The woman who is passing off my handbags as her own designs struts up to just beside us. She's wearing one over her shoulder, dangling it in my face. She looks serene, sophisticated, a woman used to adulation. A battery of cameras flash. Striking a pose like a seasoned model, she takes her applause, basking in the praise and the cornucopia of cameras capture the moment.

My anger is boiling away inside me. A red rage is rising that I didn't know I was capable of. Marie Monique turns and smiles. She holds out her hands and from the side of the stage, at the back of the audience, Yves Simoneaux steps up onto the runway and takes her into his arms. They kiss each other warmly. The applause doubles. The cameras flash again.

Looks like they are rather well acquainted and are, more than likely, in this together.

'We'll grab him as soon as they're off that runway,' Tod says through gritted teeth. 'Though goodness only knows what we can do. I've a good mind to knock that slimy bastard to the floor.'

Something inside me cracks. Where there was rage there is now a cool calm. I'm out of my seat and on to the runway before I know what I'm doing.

'These are my handbags,' I say in a very loud, clear voice. 'They're my designs. And you've stolen them.'

The cameras flash. There's a collective gasp from the audience.

Marie's face blackens instantly. 'Go away,' she spits. 'Go away. I do not know who you are.'

'Maybe not,' I say. 'But he does.'

Yves has the grace to look panic-stricken.

'Nell,' he says in a placating tone. 'There is a mistake. We can sort this out.'

A reporter pushes a microphone close to us and more cameras move in.

'They're my bags,' I repeat more firmly and I hear it reverberate round the busy hall. I don't sound unhinged or hysterical. I simply sound like a woman who knows she's been wronged. 'You both know that they are.'

Marie pushes me. She pushes me in the chest. 'Get out of here,' she says. 'Get out of my show.'

She goes to turn away, to dismiss me as irrelevant, and the red mist descends on me once more.

I grab the bag on her shoulder and she pushes me again. As I snatch it from her, she swings round and tries to claw my face, spitting insults in French. She punches me in the eye, which hurts like hell, but still I hang on. Then, while she is screaming obscenities, I take aim and thwack her one back with my rescued handbag. It hits her with a resounding thud. A volley of camera flashes follow the action.

'This is my handbag,' I say again. 'I'm Nell McNamara and this is *my* handbag.'

Marie, not looking so serene or sophisticated now, makes a lunge for me, but I sidestep her and somehow grab her long, luxurious plait. It takes me back to the playground when I swing her round by it and, I have to say, it feels great. She topples off her stilettos and falls to the floor. Yves swoops in to help her. Marie lies cowering beneath him.

'You'll stop making those handbags right now,' I say, wagging my finger in her face. 'And you, you swindling bastard, you'll be hearing from my lawyer.' Said with the bravado of a woman who doesn't actually have a lawyer or the wherewithal to pay for one.

Then Tod is beside me leading me off the runway. Marie, still on floor, is swamped by reporters.

'Whoa!' Tod says as we move away from the commotion on stage.

'That wasn't "too nice", was it?'

Tod laughs. 'That wasn't nice at all. Let's hope she doesn't sue you for assault and battery with a handbag.'

'Let her try.'

Now all the cameras are focused on me. I'm breathing heavily, but I feel powerful, victorious. The journalists swarm towards me.

'It's my bag,' I say to no one in particular and I see a dozen pens scribble it down. 'Marie Monique has stolen my designs.' Just in case anyone didn't catch that.

'Your name?' someone shouts. 'What is your name?'

'Nell McNamara,' I reply.

Tod leads me outside. 'You'll be all over the trade papers,' he says.

'There's no such thing as bad publicity,' I remind him.

I can only hope that I'm right.

Chapter 53

Olly kissed Petal gently. 'It's late. You should be asleep, young lady.'

'I'm trying,' she replied. 'But it's not that easy, Daddy.'

Tucking her myriad toys around her, he said, 'Well, I'm going to work now, so you be a good girl for Jenny. Don't play up.'

He got her 'whatever' face in return for that. The minute he turned his back, she'd be up. That and the Pope being Catholic were two certainties in life.

Back in the living room, Jen was watching television. Her feet were up on the sofa. There was a glass of wine in front of her on the coffee table and she was watching some costume drama. She looked very at home.

When he closed the door to Petal's bedroom, she looked up at him and smiled. It was a very cosy routine that they'd fitted into. Jen was easy company. A bit like Petal in a way. So long as she was warm, fed and watered and there was a modicum of entertainment to amuse her, she wanted for little else. It was nice having her around. She made no demands on him. Didn't criticise his every move, question his every motive and he was quite worried that he felt like that.

'I'd better be off,' he said. It was so tempting to phone in sick – something he never did – and spend the night at home instead. That was all he wanted. A cosy home, someone to share it with. Instead his wife was off in Paris trying to make her fortune, turning their lives upside down, when really it had been quite pleasant as it was before.

Jenny pulled a little face. 'Gonna miss you,' she said.

'Yeah.' They'd fallen into a simple, domestic routine of bathing Petal and putting her to bed together, then Jenny would rustle them up some dinner. He'd expected not to see much of her due to her shifts at Live and Let Fry, but she'd taken the whole week off as holiday so that she could be around for them both. It was very touching. Surprisingly, he found out that they had a lot in common. They liked the same food, the same films, the same comedians. The only thing Jen didn't share was his love of all things sixties, but he was trying to educate her and she seemed to be a willing pupil. In fact, they'd laughed a lot across the dinner table and hadn't talked about handbags or business once. He couldn't remember the last time he and Nell had done that.

Olly sighed inwardly. Tonight, he'd rather have his own eyeballs grated than go and stand for eight hours making pizzas. He might insist to Nell that he was happy in his work, but it wasn't all true. He liked the people. The pay was reasonable. But no one in their right mind could truly say that they'd found satisfaction in doing something so crushingly boring for the rest of their lives.

Picking up his coat, he shrugged it on and then bent forward to peck Jen on the cheek. As he did, she turned her head away from the television and their lips met. He tried to pull back, but Jen took hold of the lapel of his jacket and held him firm. Her lips were warm and soft against his, full, inviting. The temptation to stay there and enjoy the sensation was overwhelming. The tip of her tongue slipped into his mouth and found his. It frightened him to think that he could easily stay here, throw off his coat, throw off his clothes, throw caution to the wind and make love to Jen. It would be so easy, so very easy.

Only the thought of Petal just down the hall prevented him from doing so. The thought of Petal. Not Nell. He pulled away.

'Sorry,' he said. 'I didn't mean for that to happen.'

The smile on Jen's face said that she, however, did.

'Got to go,' Olly said. His knees, his hands, his heart were shaky. 'I'll see you in the morning.'

Jen's smile didn't fade. 'See you tomorrow, Olly.' She blew him a kiss as he scurried out of the door.

He couldn't concentrate at work. After ten years with Nell and not a moment of unfaithfulness, not even a thought of it, he'd kissed another woman.

Tonight the line was churning out mushroom and pepperoni pizzas. Virtually the whole process was automated and it just took a handful of them to supervise the making of thousands of frozen pizzas. His role was to sit on a stool next to the conveyor belt and just re-sort any of the toppings that hadn't landed quite accurately on the pizza. A tiny human cog in a great, big, unstoppable machine. Already he knew he'd let several go by without even noticing them, as he was lost in a world of his own.

Thank goodness that Nell was coming back tomorrow, and then Jenny's services could be dispensed with. But what happened when his wife was off on her next business jaunt? What could he say? Could he really tell Nell that they shouldn't use Jen again? Not because she wasn't brilliant with Petal, but because he couldn't be trusted to be alone with her. Who would they get to come in and help then? Jen had been bloody marvellous – up until the unfortunate kissing incident – they couldn't have asked for someone more willing or helpful. Petal thought the sun shone out of her. He was pretty impressed himself, he had to admit. There was a gentle, easy-going domesticity to her that he hadn't noticed until she'd moved in. Until then, she'd just been Nell's slightly loud, borderline annoying, single friend. Nothing more. But there was a lot more to her than that. She was thoughtful, caring, easily pleased. She'd make someone a great wife. Olly wondered now whether there was an ulterior motive behind her willingness to take on him and Petal, seemingly out of the goodness of her heart. Perhaps Jen had seen herself slipping quietly into Nell's shoes. But maybe that was being unkind. Maybe this had all been done without thinking what was in it for her, and the kiss was just the heat of the moment, an overstepping of the mark. Who knows? He had always thought that he understood Nell, women in general. Now he realised that he really didn't have a clue.

The pizzas continued to slide by him on the conveyor belt.

259

Mindlessly, he fiddled with the mushrooms, the pepperoni, reorganising, rearranging. He could do this job in his sleep now. Other people counted sheep – he only needed to think about the regular hum of the conveyor belt, the soporific action of the pizzas sliding by and he'd be off in dreamland. Though sometimes in his dreams, he did find himself hand-decorating pizzas.

What was Nell doing now? he wondered. Was she having a fabulous, carefree time in Paris? Was she thinking of him and of Petal and what she'd left behind? Did they feature in her thoughts at all? Or was she glad to break away from the drudgery of the domestic routine? He knew that she was with Tod and that always rankled. Perhaps his wife would be better off with someone like that. Someone who was powerful, ambitious, driven. Someone who didn't work in a pizza factory.

'Meyers!' His supervisor's voice barking at him, snapped him out of his reverie. 'Is this your idea of a joke?'

Olly looked up as his red-faced supervisor slapped down a tray of pizzas on the stainless steel surface with a certain amount of venom.

'Every single one you've done tonight has been like this. Get your coat and don't come back. There are plenty of people who can do this job better than you. The whole run will have to be scrapped.'

When he got over his shock and looked at what was making his boss froth at the mouth, he saw that every pizza was bearing two pepperoni eyes and a sad, downturned mushroom mouth.

Chapter 54

I could cry with relief when I walk up to my shop, my flat. I've never been so happy to come back from anywhere. You can keep Paris as far as I'm concerned. For me there's no place quite like home. All I want is for Olly to take me in his arms and to see my darling daughter. I feel like lying on the floor and kissing the pavement. Which I probably would do if it wasn't raining and the pavement wasn't very wet.

Instead, I haul my wheelie case through the shop door, which chimes my arrival. In the workshop, I can see Olly sitting at the desk tapping away at the computer. At his feet, Petal is sitting on the floor with crayons and a pad. He looks up as I come in and his face lights up. My heart literally soars.

Petal looks up too. 'It's Mummy!' she shouts and abandons her drawing and runs through the shop to greet me. I pick her up and whirl her round, then I squeeze her to me as tightly as I can.

'Too tight, Mummy,' she gasps. 'Too tight!'

I laugh and lower her to the floor again. 'Are you better?'

I ask. Petal certainly looks a lot better than when I last saw her.

'Yes,' she says. 'And I didn't pick my spots.'

She could have picked them all – and probably has – and I wouldn't care. I'm just glad to see that she's well again.

Then, without speaking Olly and I fall into each other's arms. He kisses me deeply.

'Oooer,' Petal says and goes all silly and giggly. She dances round us singing, 'Mummy and Daddy are in love. Mummy and Daddy are in love.'

When I feel dizzy and need to come up for air, I pull away. Olly strokes my hair. 'It's good to see you.'

'I'm glad to be home,' I tell him earnestly. 'So glad.'

He stands back and looks at me, hands framing my face. 'What on earth happened to your eye?'

Ah. I'd forgotten about my nice, big, black-and-blue shiner.

'Did you walk into a door?'

I look sheepish. 'I got into a fight,' I explain.

'A fight?' Olly might well look surprised.

'Yeah.' I risk a smile. 'But you should have seen her.'

'I can't wait to hear about this.'

'Let's shut the shop for an hour,' I say. 'Go out and have some lunch together. Just the three of us.'

'If you're sure.' Olly knows that lunchtime is the busiest hour of the day in the shop.

'Let's do it. I'm in dire need of coffee.'

'You look exhausted, Nell,'

'I'm utterly jaded,' I confess. At this moment, I'm not sure how my legs are actually supporting me. It would be lovely just to lie down on the floor and sleep for a week. 'You won't believe what has happened while I've been away.'

'Then I'll buy you coffee while you tell me.'

I kiss him again. 'Sounds like a deal to me.'

We lock up the shop together and, arm in arm, stroll in the sunshine down to Halsey's Deli and Tearoom in the Market Place, our favourite lunch haunt whenever we have a few quid to spare.

The shop has been here in one form or another since Queen Victoria was on the throne and is one of the most popular spots in town. The food here is unbelievably delicious. It's tiny inside so, while we wait in line for a table to become vacant, Petal ogles the glorious homemade meringues in an array of pastel shades that are piled high in the window. While she's distracted, I take the opportunity to tell Olly all about my rather public altercation with *Monsieur* Yves Simoneaux and *Madame* Marie Monique.

'They stole my designs,' I explain.

'When? How?'

'Yves lifted them when he came to see me at the shop and there they were, bold as brass, parading them on the catwalk. I wanted to kill them both.' In fact, I have to admit that I gave it a good go. I sigh before I continue. 'I never thought that anyone would stoop so low. It's really shaken my confidence.'

Olly looks stunned. 'Do you think you'll be able to stop them from producing more?'

'I threatened them with legal action,' said with another weary sigh. Don't they say that sighing is the same as crying but without the tears? It certainly feels like that. 'But, in

263

reality, I couldn't afford to do that. *We* can't afford to do it. I just hope me whacking her round the head with the offending handbag is enough to make them think twice.' I don't tell him about the bit where Yves came to my room and made an attempt to seduce me – by fair means or maybe by foul. 'It will be all over the trade magazines, so her reputation will be sullied and I can only hope the coverage does me some good.' If it has anything to do with me I'll make sure that both of their names are dragged through the mud. Perhaps that will have to be revenge enough. 'Maybe that will be enough to stop them doing it again. Whatever happens, I'm certainly going to keep a close watch on both Marie Monique and *Monsieur* Simoneaux from now on.'

At that point, we're at the front of the queue. All the tables are cheek-by-jowl in the small café area and we're shoehorned in at the back corner. The walls are cheerfully bright with local artworks. This is Petal's favourite eatery and she realises what a rare treat it is to come here, so she always behaves impeccably. Olly knows what to order for us without even asking. He and Petal always have the fish finger sandwiches and I never fail to be lured by the special cheese on toast, which is much lauded locally. I also get my long-overdue caffeine hit.

'So the trip wasn't as successful as you hoped?' he asks.

'I just wanted to be at home all the time,' I confess. 'The shows were good. Very interesting. But the competition out there is terrifying. Maybe you were right. I should have done this on a small scale. Stuck to my market stall. I don't know if I'm cut out for the harsh reality of business.'

Olly puts his hand over mine. 'You're doing great,' he says. 'This is just a small setback. Next time you'll be wiser, savvier.'

'I don't know if I want there to be a "next time",' I admit.

'You're overtired, emotional,' Olly says. 'Understandably so. When you've had time to stand back and think about this, it won't seem so bad. It's all part of the learning curve.'

Our lunch arrives and, as we all tuck in, Olly says, 'Why don't we go away? Take a week, rent a cottage somewhere.'

'That's a bit out of the blue.'

He shrugs. 'It might be, but think about it. When did we last have a holiday?'

I can't remember back that far.

'Give yourself a break, Nell,' he pleads. 'You've been so hard on yourself these last months. This is just what we need.'

It certainly does sound very appealing. My soul is saying that this would be a very good idea. My pocket, however, is more practical. 'Can we afford it?'

'Let's find the money. Whatever it costs.'

'What about your shifts at the pizza factory?'

Olly stares at one of the paintings on the wall in a manner that's a bit too determined. 'They'll give me some time off.'

'Are you sure?'

'Yeah. Yeah. It'll be cool.'

'Are we going on holiday, Mummy?'

I wipe the ring of mayo from round her mouth with a napkin. 'Would you like that?'

She nods vigorously. 'Can we go to the seaside?'

I smile across at Olly, my handsome, thoughtful husband. 'I don't see why not.'

'Yay!'

Clearly, a holiday gets my daughter's vote. I can feel the grin spread across my face too. 'Let's do it. Let's go somewhere fabulous and get away from it all.' At the moment, I can't face seeing another bloody handbag. A break will do us all good. I need to hide away and lick my wounds and I can't think of a better way to do it. 'Give me a couple of days to tie up some loose ends, but there's nothing much to stop us going straight away.'

'I'll go into the library this afternoon.' Olly is all excited now. 'I'll see what I can book for us.'

'Now,' I say. 'You've heard all my news. I want to hear about all that's happened while I've been away.'

For some reason, Olly fails to meet my eyes when he replies, 'Oh, nothing. Nothing much at all.'

Chapter 55

So we hire a little car and *en masse*, Dude included, troop down to Cornwall. Olly has hired us a quaint cottage overlooking the beach at Poltallan Bay. The village is tiny, hardly touristy at all, and a world away from the hustle and bustle of nearby Newquay. It's the perfect place to recharge your batteries. There's an old-fashioned pub, a couple of shops and a smattering of holiday rental homes. Not much else. But that suits us down to the ground.

The cottage is small, homely. The ceilings low. Even I feel like I have to duck and I'm a little shortie. Olly has already whacked his head a dozen times. It has just two bedrooms, a steep wooden staircase and an open-plan living room. In the kitchen, there's a sturdy, family-sized table in front of the window, which looks out over a small courtyard garden. It will be nice to make our home here for the week. I can actually feel the tension seeping out of my bones as I unpack.

Unusually for a British beach holiday, the weather is sublime. Even though it's late in the summer, the temperature pushes up to the seventies every day and the sun is a big, yellow disk in the cloudless sky. All Petal wants to do is play on the beach, morning, noon and night. We buy her a bucket and spade – she insists on the pink set – and we all keep ourselves entertained by making sandcastles and digging trenches that lead to the sea. Dude gets more walks than he knows what to do with. He's not sure about the sea; he's absolutely desperate to go in it, but then runs away terrified when the waves rush towards him. Instead, Dude's consoling himself by barking at the seagulls. Olly rents a body board and tries his hand at surfing. I'm thinking that he wouldn't necessarily be classed as a natural, but he loves every minute. I rifle through the books left in the cottage and find myself a trashy romantic comedy to read while stretched out on a blanket. This is idyllic. Truly.

We all get on brilliantly. All the niggling between Olly and me has gone, vanished in the sea air. Petal doesn't have one single tantrum. I remember that this is how we used to be as a family and I wonder how we've managed to get so far away from this. Olly is right. Business isn't everything and I vow that I'll strive to achieve more of a work/life balance when we get home.

'Happy?' Olly says as he comes to lie down beside me.

'This is the life,' I say. 'You can keep your yachts in the South of France. This works for me.'

He traces his finger over my thigh. 'I do love you.'

'And I love you.'

'Let's never forget that.'

We twine our fingers together. 'Never,' I agree.

*

Already it's Wednesday night. We put Petal to bed early, mainly because she was struggling to keep her eyes open while she was eating her tea. All this fresh air is great for knocking her out. I wish I could bottle it and take it back with us. She's even stayed in her own bed every night so far and hasn't woken until nine. Bliss! I'm hoping this continues when we get home, but that may be too much to ask for.

The fact that she hasn't been wedged between Olly and me like an octopus on speed has meant that we've been able to rekindle our love life. Yay, us! We still have it and Olly has been particularly amorous. And I'm not complaining.

We've also had long, grown-up dinners, just the two of us, complete with candles and a bottle of cheap wine bought from the pub. Instead of snatching at meals that involve fish fingers, pizza and ready-made whatever, we've just finished a courgette and red pepper lasagne that I made from scratch, along with a bottle of sparkling pink something. I don't have time to cook, but occasionally I like to surprise myself with a reminder that I can actually do it given the right opportunity. Across the table, Olly smiles at me in the candlelight.

'What do you want to do this evening, Nell?'

There's no telly here, so we've been availing ourselves of the pack of cards and the board games that are here. I'm not sure that Olly wants to be thoroughly thrashed at Scrabble once again.

'I could whoop your arse at Boggle,' I suggest.

'You think so?' Olly says, raising his eyebrows.

'Loser washes up.'

Olly takes the plates and moves them to the work surface. 'I was thinking of a different game.'

'Oh, really?'

And with that he comes to me and kisses me long and hard. His hands slide over my body. Within seconds, we're tugging at each other's clothes. He moves the candle from the table and, when I'm naked, lays me back on it. He takes the bottle of pink fizz, dribbles it over my body, and laps it off me. There's a level of passion that rises inside me that's been sadly missing for a long time. I urge Olly into me and we make love on the big table and then, because we can, we do it all over again.

Afterwards we curl up on the sofa together, pulling a handy throw over our hot, naked bodies.

'I think *I'd* better do the washing up after that,' I tease.

'I think so too,' Olly agrees. He beats his chest. 'Man need rest.'

'Oh, worn yourself out, have you?'

'Hmm. Not entirely.'

'Oh, really?' I shift against him. It's true: he's not that tired. Hurrah!

He pulls me down towards him. 'I do love you,' he says and starts to kiss me again. *Again!* Clearly, all this sea air hasn't knocked my husband out like it has Petal. It seems to have put the wind in his sails.

When did we last have a mad, crazy sex session like this? Good grief, I think I was about nineteen! Our bodies slide together again and we throw off the blanket, letting the cool night air from the open window caress our heated skin.

Then, as Olly moves above me, my mobile phone starts to ring.

'Don't answer it,' he gasps. 'Don't answer it.'

'What if it's an emergency?'

'It won't be.'

But the moment is broken and, with a defeated sigh, Olly rolls off me. I lunge for the phone.

The voice on the other end says, 'Hi, Nell. It's Tod.'

I pull the throw back over me and Olly pads out to the kitchen with a tut.

'Hi,' I say.

'Is this a bad time?'

'No,' I lie. 'Not at all. It's fine.'

'I think you need to come back,' Tod says. 'Right away.' Then he proceeds to tell me why.

Chapter 56

We drive home in silence. The tension in the air is palpable. Olly has the steering wheel in a death grip. His knuckles are white. His face black.

'It's only a day early,' I point out.

'Two,' Olly counters. 'I don't understand why this couldn't have waited until Monday.'

'I can't afford to miss this opportunity.'

'If it's on the table today, then I'm sure it will still be there next week.'

I'm not so certain about that. Tod explained to me how these things work. Unless you jump, and high, then they move on to the next person.

The call that unfortunately interrupted our bouncy cuddles was from Tod telling me that Home Mall – one of those *huge* American shopping channels – wants to feature my handbags. It's by far and away the biggest opportunity to come my way. By miles. Nell McNamara designs would get a full half-hour coverage on prime time television, repeated every two hours for an entire day. All of this broadcast right across the United States. If I can secure this, then my bags will go global, stratospheric. We will be made for life! The numbers they are talking about are truly enormous. And, of course, as is always the way with these things, they need an answer yesterday.

So you can see that I *had* to take the terrible decision to cut short the family holiday. Olly, needless to say, doesn't see it like that at all. But I feel that I had no choice. I have to get back to work on this. The logistics of such large production numbers are frightening and I needed to get back to the office, pronto, to try to get my head round it.

We stayed until Friday instead of coming back on Sunday. So I think that was a fair compromise. I don't believe that two more days would have made much difference to our holiday. We'd done all the relaxing that we needed to do. Anyway, the forecast was for rain and storms. I just didn't expect the storm to be in the car on the way home.

I have so much to do. The sort of numbers they're talking about will mean that I'll have to go to China and source a manufacturer out there. This is way, way beyond what I can do with a few part-time workers.

Tod also said on the phone that Home Mall would need all the handbags in their warehouse ready to be shipped the same day – so there's not the comfort of getting all the orders in and then making the bags to correspond. I'd have to commit to produce the stock up front. Scary. It will require some more money from the bank. And I just can't think of all these things while I'm on a beach.

'Tod says that chances like this don't come along every day.'

Olly rolls his eyes whenever I quote my mentor. 'I just think that this sounds too good to be true.'

Here we are again, back to Olly being negative about everything and anything.

'Perhaps I'm finally getting some luck,' I say crisply. 'Perhaps things will finally start going my way.'

Olly doesn't look convinced.

I try very hard to see his viewpoint, but he just seems to want to keep us all pinned to the earth. Is it so wrong to want to fly?

'This is for us.'

'That's a refrain that's wearing very thin,' he says. 'How can dragging Petal away from her one proper holiday in years be "for us"?'

Our child is fast asleep in the back seat of the car, unused as she is to such luxurious travel. There's no doubt that she was really enjoying herself.

'I feel mean,' I say. 'Very mean. But how do you think I'd feel if I'd sat on the beach for the next two days watching this slip through my fingers?'

'You've decided now. We're on our way home. It doesn't matter what I say.'

With that, it's clear that the conversation is closed. Olly turns up the radio and focuses on the road. It's going to be a very long drive home.

How can I not do this? But it seems such a shame that after enjoying a few lovely days together we're now warring again. He's not going to forgive me easily for this one. Now it's up to me to prove that I'm right.

Chapter 57

I'm up bright and early the next morning. Well, I'm not exactly bright, but it is early. I didn't sleep much at all last night. My mind was whirring with figures and ideas. Now I'm glad to be up and about so that I can crack on with my plans.

I'm meeting Tod for breakfast in town. One of the cafés does an excellent full-English for three quid and we're going to avail ourselves of it while we talk about my business plan. I thought it was better for him to not come to the shop as it would only antagonise Olly. We're not exactly giving each other the silent treatment, but we're not exactly love's young dream either. I crept out of bed without waking him. Now I tiptoe out of the flat and into the coolness of the morning air.

Tod is already waiting for me when I bowl up at the café five minutes later. We order our breakfast and I tell him about our lovely holiday as we eat, leaving out the sex on the kitchen table part and the subsequent row after he'd telephoned while we were at it again. Sigh.

When we've eaten and the waitress has cleared the table, we

spread out the notes I've already made in front of us. When I got home from Cornwall yesterday, the contract from the shopping channel, Home Mall, had already been emailed to me. These guys certainly don't hang around.

I went online and checked out their website. It's filled with clips of the show and the type of products they sell. There's anything from books to blouses, floor mops to furniture, shoes to kitchen scales. It looks like a tightly run outfit. On a par with the other big shopping channels that are broadcast. The presenters are slick – if slightly inane – and flog the heart out of everything they pick up. The studio is a pastel-hued affair complete with fake French doors, beyond which is a mural of a bright blue sea and a big yellow sun. The doors are flanked by two potted palm trees. Miami in microcosm. Frankly, I could give this a funkier makeover. I wish I could watch the programme on air – it must be put out on one of those high number channels – but our meagre budget won't run to Sky telly, so we can't get any of them. The Meyers household is strictly terrestrial.

'I haven't heard of this outfit before, but their website looks very professional. If the others are anything to go by, it'll be massive,' Tod reiterates as he looks at my scribblings. 'They move thousands of units in each session. Thousands.'

Just how many they anticipate selling is listed on the email in front of me. It's a mind-boggling number.

'I need to go to the bank on Monday and see if they'll extend my borrowing.' I've already made an appointment with my business manager who, so far, has been quite amenable to loading up my overdraft.

'If you have this contract to show him, then it shouldn't be a problem.'

The worst thing is having to pay for everything up front, but that's apparently the way these things work. All of the shopping channels pride themselves on getting the stock customers have bought through their programmes out to them very quickly. That means that vast numbers of my handbags have to be ready and waiting in their warehouse. I simply don't have the time to rush to manufacture the handbags after the orders have been received.

'Do you know anyone who's done this before?'

'No.' Tod shakes his head. 'I asked around the office. You're the first we know of. It looks like the Nell McNamara brand is getting out there. Well done.'

'There is one thing on the contract that worries me immensely,' I confess. 'I have to pay over twenty thousand pounds to book the slot.' Apparently, this ensures that I'm serious about it. The money goes towards the cost of warehousing, shipping, the telephone ordering service and the actual filming of the products. When the programme has been aired and the orders roll in, then I get all of that money back – as long as the orders cover it. For Home Mall, it seems like a win/win situation, but they're calling the shots and I guess that's how the cookie crumbles.

'It's a huge sum,' Tod agrees. 'I ran it by the legal team at Best of Business and they seem to think it's all above board. This clause isn't unusual in this sort of situation.'

I feel naive to have even raised the question. These people are used to dealing with far greater sums of money than I ever have and probably think nothing of it. Me, I can't help my knees shaking when I think of the money involved. Money that, of course, I don't have.

'It does mean, though, that all the risk is with you, not them,' he points out. 'Are you sure that you want to take that on?'

I nod. At some time you have to bite the bullet and go for it. I think this is my moment.

'You'll have to go out to China to find a manufacturer,' Tod tells me.

'I've already thought about that.' I toy with my spoon, stirring my coffee. 'Don't fancy coming with me, do you?' Frankly, I'm terrified of flying out there and trying to sort it all out by myself.

'I'd love to,' he says and, for a moment, my spirits lift. 'But there's no way that I could justify the expense. Best of Business would never cover it.' They sink again.

Briefly, I consider offering to pay to take Tod with me. If I'm borrowing such ginormous sums then a couple more thousand is neither here nor there, surely?

Then I see sense and think that I must do this alone. If I'm ever going to consider myself a rufty-tufty, international business woman, then I must learn to do these things by myself. But the thought of getting on a plane to China terrifies me.

'If there's anything else I can do, you know that I'm here to help. You can always call on me.'

'Thanks, Tod. You've done so much for me already.'

'I really hope this flies for you, Nell. You put so much into this; you really deserve to have success.'

'Thanks.' But no one hopes for it more than me.

278

Chapter 58

That afternoon, while Olly takes Petal out to feed the ducks in the town centre, I check what time it is in Miami, the home of the shopping channel. I take a deep breath and with her email in front of me, I call Lola Cody, Chief Executive of Home Mall. A woman with a warm, motherly voice answers the phone.

I introduce myself and she bowls me over when she replies, 'Oh, honey, we just love your handbags here. We think they are just what Home Mall customers will go crazy for.'

Relief floods through me. She sounds like a normal person – just like me or you – and not some scary, high-powered, anorexic, workaholic in a pinstriped suit.

'We are going to make you famous,' she gushes on. 'Everyone will soon know the name, Nell McNamara.'

I'm liking the sound of this more and more.

'You don't know how good that makes me feel,' I tell her. 'I was so worried about this.'

'No need to be, honey.' Her sing-song American accent soothes me.

'How did you hear about my handbags?'

'I've seen you in the English media and now I think the *world* should know about you!'

'We're a *very* small business,' I stress. I'm not sure I need to go into details about *quite* how small. 'This is a huge deal for us. Plus, I recently had some of my designs ripped off, so it's made me very nervous about trusting people.'

'You're in safe hands now,' she assures me. 'You just send us your lovely handbags and we take care of everything else. There's nothing at all to worry about. Here at Home Mall we simply love to launch new designers.'

'I've had such knock-backs,' I confide. 'That really is music to my ears.'

The door of the shop flings open and Olly and Petal are back from their outing to the ducks. My daughter runs into the office, arms wide, shouting, 'Mummy!' before barrelling into me.

'Sssh, Petal. Mummy's on the telephone to an important lady.'

'Hello, important lady!' my child shouts into the phone.

'So sorry,' I say to Lola. 'As you can probably tell, my daughter has just come in.' That's my peace shattered.

'She sounds adorable.'

That is always the first impression of Petal.

'She's my life,' I tell her. 'All this is being done purely to give her a better future.'

At that I see Olly scowl.

'That is so lovely of you,' Lola coos. 'I have two children of my own and I know just how you feel. Everything I do is for them.'

This lady is my new best friend. She understands exactly what it is to be a woman in business, a mother.

'What's she called?'

'Petal. She's just four.'

'Well, then we need to sell lots and lots of your lovely handbags for this little lady.'

'I'm putting everything in place now,' I go on. 'This is a huge order for me. My manufacturing base here' – aka me, Jenny and Constance – 'just isn't big enough to cope. I'm going out to China next week to set up there.'

'You come back to me just as soon as you can,' she says soothingly. 'We want to run with this while it's fresh.'

I take that to mean that if I don't get a move on then someone else will be snapping at my heels.

'You know that you need to send me a fully refundable deposit to confirm your slot?'

'Yes, I read that in the contract.' It's thirty thousand dollars. Roughly twenty grand. *Twenty thousand of our English pounds!* I feel the gulp travel down my throat, even as I think it. That's a lot of money simply to prove that I'm serious about this. And here I am discussing it like it's two and sixpence.

'As soon as we have that,' Lola continues, 'we can book a mutually suitable date and we're good to go.'

My heart beats faster. It's as simple as that.

'I'm really grateful for this opportunity,' I say. I want to tell her how much I have struggled and how we can hardly make ends meet and how this will save us. But I think I will just come across as too pathetically grateful. 'You don't know what it means to us. It will, literally, turn our lives around.'

'We'll look after you here at Home Mall. We're like one big happy family.'

I wish I could say the same about the Meyers household, I think as I look over at Olly, who doesn't look very happy at all.

Chapter 59

First thing on Monday morning I organise my flight to China. There are a few factories for me to visit, all conveniently based close together in Guangzhou in the Guangdong Province. I can fly direct into Guangzhou Baiyun International Airport, a place I've never previously heard of. I book my return ticket online, which makes me feel sick with nerves. This is how confident I am that the bank will say yes to loaning me the money. With this opportunity in front of them in black and white, how could they turn me down?

That done, I rush straight to the bank for my appointment. I'm ushered into a plush office that I've never been in before and am even given a cup of tea while I explain what it is that I want. This is me in the big league!

Thank the heavens and all that is good, my allocated Small Business Relationship Manager, Simon North, instantly agrees to lend me the staggering amount of money I'm going to need to put these handbags into production and also the sum for the deposit to book my television slot. I throw in an extra bit for sundry expenses and the total climbs to a dizzying forty thousand pounds.

Simon barely flicks through the contract from Home Mall. He doesn't even hesitate. I, however, do. By any standards the interest he is charging me is extortionate. Quickly, I do my sums and work out that, even at this rate, it's still viable and if all goes to plan, will still give us an enormous return on investment. At least when I get my deposit back from Home Mall I can pay off some of the money I owe the bank, which will bring the sum owed down from a puke-inflicting amount to merely nausea-inducing.

I know that businesses do this sort of thing every day and that if I'm going to make it big, then I have to get used to dealing with these kinds of numbers. Although I can rationalise it perfectly, it's terrifying nevertheless. Simon North must lend out millions of pounds every single day without breaking sweat. My underarms, on the other hand, are damp with perspiration. I sign a form and he shakes my hand. The deal is done. Simon North offers me congratulations. He is smiling widely. I don't think I am.

I come out of the bank shaking and clutching my loan agreement. The money will be in my bank by this afternoon. I am truly on my way now.

Immediately, I call Tod to tell him my good news. He is delighted for me, as I knew he would be. It pains me that I don't feel able to call Olly and guarantee the same reaction. So instead of sharing my news with my husband, I head into town to do a few more chores. I buy a few bits for my impending trip to China, then I have a quick celebratory coffee all by myself before I have to go home and organise my entry visa.

When I do, eventually, arrive back at the flat, Olly is sitting on the floor in the living room playing Jenga with Petal. It smells as if they've just had their lunch and there are a couple of dirty plates on the work surface, a pan in the sink. Beans on toast would be my guess. I sit down next to them both just as the wooden tower topples over and, in tandem, they tut at me, even though it wasn't my fault.

'It was the wonky floor in here,' I protest. 'Not me.'

But neither of them looks convinced.

'How did it go at the bank?' Olly asks, though the question lacks any great enthusiasm.

'Good,' I reply, although I can't bring myself to tell him exactly how much we're in hock for now. He'd pass out. Or have a heart attack. It's giving me palpitations and I'm the one who really wants all this to happen. 'We're all set to go.'

'*You're* all set to go,' he corrects.

'You could come with me,' I suggest. The thought perks me up. I'm *so* not looking forward to making this trip alone. If I'm honest, I don't even like getting the train down to London by myself. This is a whole new level of sheer terror. 'If you want to. Come out to China. I could book you a flight. Do you think you could get another week off work?'

At that, Olly lowers his head.

'What?'

'Petal,' he says. 'Can you please go and read a book in your room while I talk about grown-up things to Mummy?'

'I hope you're not going to shout,' she replies.

'We're not going to shout.'

'You always say that,' she reminds him, 'but then you do.' With that parting shot, she stomps off anyway.

I wait expectantly. Then, '*Are* we going to shout?'

Eventually, Olly responds. 'I haven't got a job at the pizza factory any more.'

It takes me a while to process this and I stare at him, open-mouthed, as I do. *No job?* 'What? Why not?'

'I was sacked while you were in Paris,' Olly admits.

'Why?'

'I put sad faces on all of the mushroom and pepperoni pizzas.'

If this wasn't such a tragedy, I'd laugh. A lot.

'Sad faces? They can't sack you for that.'

'They can,' Olly says. 'They have. Virtually the whole run had to be scrapped.'

'And your excuse for this?'

He shrugs. 'I had stuff on my mind. I wasn't concentrating.'

He had stuff on his mind!

'Can't you ask them for your job back?'

He sighs now. 'To be honest, Nell, I'm not sure that I want it back.'

'But that was our main source of income.' It's not a case of *want*, the way I see it. We *need* that money to pay our bills.

'I'll find something else,' he says. 'In the meantime, at least, I'm at home to look after Petal while you go gadding off round the world.'

'I'm not "gadding off"; I'm finding a factory in China that will make my handbags. I'm not going to be lying on a sunlounger with a colourful drink with a bloody umbrella in it.' I'm trying to keep my temper under control, but I've had enough of Olly trying to undermine my attempts at growing this business. 'Jenny could look after Petal for us again. Or Constance.'

'You can't keep dumping your kid on everyone else,' he snaps. 'She's your responsibility.'

'I'm well aware of my responsibilities,' I bite back. 'Are you aware of yours? I'm not the one who's lost my job for making sad faces.'

Olly stands up. 'I can't do this any more. I'm sorry, Nell. I just can't. You've changed. Nothing is the same. I don't even know who you are.'

I stand up too. 'Now you're being ridiculous.'

'You have no time for me. Or for Petal.'

'We've just had a great week in Cornwall together.'

'Did we? All I remember is having to come back early because of your stupid business.'

'Is that really all that you remember?' I raise my eyebrow at him. 'Because I can remember us getting on *particularly* well!'

'If you're talking about our one night of passion, which was interrupted by a phone call from "Tod Urban"' – that mocking tone again – 'then you're deluded. There's no romance between us now, Nell. Is a few days of sun, sand, sea and sex in Cornwall supposed to sustain us for the rest of the year? Before then, when did we last sleep together?'

'It wasn't for the want of trying,' I remind him. 'Relationships aren't all about sex, anyway.'

'They aren't all about work either.' He shakes his head.

'That's *all* it's about now. Work. *Your* work. There's nothing else left.'

'I didn't know you felt like that.'

'Well, now you do,' he says and with that, he snatches up his jacket and thuds down the stairs, banging the door as he leaves.

Chapter 60

Olly walked round and round in circles for hours. He had no idea where he had been or where he was going. The afternoon was morphing into the evening and he knew that he should go back home and face Nell. But he just didn't want to, just couldn't.

Instead, he headed to the pub.

The Lord Dodgersley was one of the least salubrious establishments in the town centre. More commonly known as The Dodgy Arms, its floorboards were bare, the walls painted a deeply unattractive shade of matt black, the once bright-red sofas jaded and stained. But it was always busy and had a great atmosphere – until the fights started. Its main attraction was probably down to the fact that it sold cheap beer and vodka shots. Always popular with the young crowd. And also the cause of most of the closing-time brawls, of course. At night there were always people spilling out onto the pavement even in the depths of winter. Now, on a hot, end of summer evening, the place was heaving. There was a courtyard with patio umbrellas that was filled with business types who looked like they'd sloped out of work an hour early. They were all in high spirits and chatted loudly, all trying to outdo each other. Olly knew that if he sat out here, they would very soon get on his nerves. All he wanted was to blend in with the crowd and drink himself into oblivion.

He ordered a pint of beer from the barman, then found himself a corner in which to hide and settled in for the evening. Let Nell wonder where he was. Let her stew. She'd texted him a dozen times, but he'd let them all go unanswered. It was childish, but that was just how he felt. He wanted her to worry about him, to not know what he was doing or who with.

A couple of hours in and he was several beers up. The world was feeling fuzzy round the edges. He ordered lasagne and chips and more beer and wondered if Nell had made any dinner for him and if it was dried up by now.

When he'd eaten, a brash group of girls came barrelling into the pub. They were skimpily dressed, out for a night on the town and you could hear them cackling even over the noise of the music, which wasn't exactly set at an ambient volume. The hardcore evening crowd was arriving and that meant it was probably time to go home, even though his head still wasn't straight. He'd tried to think this afternoon, think about his relationship with Nell, what was happening to them, why they constantly seemed to be at odds with each other when, previously, they'd been perfectly happy. But his brain was just a swirling mass of unconnected thoughts and no progress had been made.

Olly downed his drink and stood up, ready to fight his way to the door. Not literally, he hoped. It was then that he realised he was a bit more unsteady on his feet than he'd thought.

'Hey.'

Looking up, he saw that Jenny was standing in front of him. He hadn't seen her since the week she'd looked after Petal. The week that they'd shared a kiss. If Jenny was thinking about that, then she didn't show it.

'Hi there,' he said. Did it come out slurry?

'What are you doing here, drinking by yourself?'

'Just needed a bit of a binge,' he confessed. 'Off home now.'

'Don't rush away,' Jenny said, her voice urgent. 'Not now I've just got here.'

'Looks as if you're up for a big night out.'

'Nah.' She laughed. 'Just a few bevvies with the girls. Got to blow off steam sometimes.'

'Yeah,' Olly said. 'Tell me about it.'

'Come and meet them,' she said. 'They're a great bunch.'

'Not really in the mood, Jen. I need to get back.'

She slipped her arm through his. 'The night is young, Olly Meyers, and so are you. Live a little.'

He felt as if he had already lived far too much.

'One drink,' she cajoled. 'Just stay for one drink.'

Knowing when he was defeated, he held up his hands. 'Just the one,' he said. 'I'll buy.'

'Don't be silly, there are six of us. I'll stand you a round.'

She pulled him over to her friends. Except for Jen, they all looked more orange than was good for a woman. They also looked as if they'd walked through an explosion in a Rimmel factory before they'd arrived. It was clear that the natural look wasn't what they were aiming for.

Jen introduced him to them all and he instantly forgot all of their names. It had been a long session. Longer really than he'd intended. Before he knew it, a line of vodka shots appeared in front of them.

'Down in one,' Jen said with a giggle.

This was a bad idea as he'd already lost count of the amount of beer he'd drunk. He knocked it back anyway. Another row materialised. Then another. And possibly another.

The noise got louder, so did the music. Someone was telling bad jokes to the accompaniment of women laughing raucously. Then he realised it was him. Definitely time to go.

He downed whatever drink was in front of him. 'Outta here,' he said to Jen.

'Nooo.' She pulled him to one side, away from her friends. Before she'd had time to bat her false lashes, she was pressing up against him, his back against the wall. Jen, it was obvious, had quickly caught up in the drunken stakes. 'Don't go,' she pleaded. 'Stay.'

'Can't,' he said. 'Can't.'

Then her lips found his. 'We could leave now,' she offered. 'Together.'

Her mouth was warm, soft, tempting. He could feel himself drowning in the sensation.

'We could go back to my place,' she whispered in his ear. 'Now.'

Jen's fingers roved over his chest, toyed with the buttons on his shirt. He opened his eyes and the seedy pub swam into view. Was this what he wanted from his life? To be drunk and snogging someone other than his wife? Someone who may be desperate for his body but, then again, could just be desperate for *anyone*?

'Stay the night with me, Olly,' she cajoled. 'You know you want to.'

But did he? Did he really want to?

'Nell would never need to know.'

But *he* would know. *He* would know that while his wife was at home worrying about him, while his child was sleeping soundly, he would know what he was doing. *He* would know that he was having loveless sex with someone he barely knew. In that moment, clarity hit home. This wasn't the answer. This wasn't the answer to anything.

'No.' He eased Jenny away from him. 'I need to go home. To Nell.'

Jen's face fell, then her soft, sensual mouth hardened. 'She doesn't love you like I would, Olly. She takes you for granted.'

Nell did take him for granted. He couldn't argue with that. But he took her for granted too. Wasn't that what you were supposed to do when you were married? Weren't you supposed to take it for granted that the other person would always be there for you whatever you did?

If Nell could see him now, she'd be devastated. What on earth was he thinking of? What a stupid fucker he was. How could he let a few drinks, an ill-judged kiss, put his family, his future, at risk?

'You're a great girl, Jen,' he said, extracting himself from her embrace.

But not as great as the one he had waiting for him at home.

Chapter 61

I went to bed at eleven o'clock, but Olly still wasn't home. If you'd have asked me, I'd have said that I lay awake all night, fretting. In reality, it seems I didn't. I must have dropped off at some time, though I'm sure I saw three tick by. I woke up at seven o'clock, Petal beside me and no Olly. I leave my daughter sleeping – miracle – and head into the living room.

He is, however, on the sofa fast asleep.

My heart goes out to him. He's all scrunched up underneath a blanket. His hair is like Jedward's on a bad day. Arm thrown above his head, he's snoring like a hibernating hedgehog. Dude, lying happily by his feet, opens his eyes and sets up a tentative wag of his tail. Tenderly, I stroke the stubble of Olly's chin, but it fails to rouse him. You won't believe how much I missed him last night.

I pad to the kitchen and make tea. Dude follows me, so I give him his breakfast. When the tea's ready, I sit on the edge of the sofa and watch Olly sleeping some more.

'Hey,' he says as, eventually, I gently shake him awake. I proffer a steaming mug.

'Hey, yourself. Late night?'

Looking shame-faced, he nods. 'I didn't want to wake you.'

Then, at the risk of starting an argument, 'Where did you get to?'

'Pub,' he says as he takes the tea and nurses it to him. 'The Dodgy Arms.'

'Ooo.' One of the divier dives in Hitchin.

'It was a bad move.'

'Yes,' I say. 'It was.'

Olly grins, despite the drink-induced pallor of his face. 'I'm sorry,' he says. 'I'm such an arse.'

I smile back. 'Yes,' I agree. 'You are.'

'Forgive me?'

I nudge him up and curl in next to him on the sofa. 'Don't do that again, Olly.'

'No.' I can't read the expression when he says, 'I did a lot of thinking last night, in the wee small hours. I want to be more supportive. I want to be involved in your business—'

'It's not *my* business. It's *ours*,' I interject.

'I know. I know that. I'm proud of you and what you're trying to do. It just frightens me, Nell. The money involved, the pressure. It scares me.' He shakes his head. 'But what scares me more is the thought that I might lose you.'

'That's never going to happen,' I promise. 'But if we're going to survive this, and I know it's stressful' – I give a small internal shudder as I think of the loan I've just taken on – 'then we need to talk. It's no good running away from problems. Or going to get pissed.'

Petal comes in rubbing her eyes. 'What's pissed?'

'It means getting drunk,' I say. 'And it's not a very nice, grown-up word. So I don't want to hear it from you.'

'Then you shouldn't say it, Mummy,' she advises.

'I'll try to remember that.'

'Come and give me a cuddle,' Olly says, and my daughter clambers across the dog, then my lap, and lands on top of Olly who gives out an 'ouff.'

Hah. Learn this, husband: no time for a hangover when you've got a four-year-old.

'Daddy had a little bit too much beer,' Olly admits to our daughter. 'Be gentle.'

So she bounces up and down on his stomach. Nice one, Petal.

'I'll go and start breakfast,' I say, and leave Petal to torture him.

Then, from the kitchen, 'Was The Dodgy busy last night? We haven't been there in years.'

'Rammed,' he replies. 'As always.'

'Jenny often drinks in there.'

'Really?'

'Yeah. God knows why.' A bit of toast is probably all that Olly can manage this morning. I crack open the Coco Pops for Petal. 'There are better places to go – unless you're drowning your sorrows.'

'Touché,' Olly acknowledges.

'Did you bump into anyone we know last night at The Dodgy?'

'No,' Olly says. 'No one at all.'

Chapter 62

Heathrow Airport. Ten-thirty on Thursday night. Petal is crying. I'm on the verge of tears too.

'Don't go, Mummy,' she wails.

Heartstrings. Twang!

'See you next week,' Olly says. He strokes my cheek. 'Come back safely.'

This is hell. Sheer hell.

Taking Petal in my arms, I hold her tightly. As it's late, she's already dressed in her snuggly pyjamas so that she'll sleep in the car on the way back. I was going to travel down to the airport by train, but Olly insisted that he drive me and borrowed a clapped out Corsa from his mate, Tom, so that he could do so.

I wanted to leave Petal with Constance, but Olly insisted that she come with us. Now I'm still thinking it was a bad idea as I can hardly bear to be parted from her. With very little persuasion, I would turn round, go home, and not get on this flight at all. Why on earth am I going to China? I don't even like rice. Or noodles.

The thought of going somewhere as far away and as foreign as China, completely alone, is making me feel sick to my stomach. It also seems as if I'm going for six months rather than a week.

Since Olly's bender, he's been very solicitous and much more supportive. Now I wonder why I'm going away at all.

'I can't do this,' I say.

'You can.' He kisses me. 'I'll look after everything at home. Don't worry about anything. You just do what you've got to do.'

As Olly's still not working, we haven't had to draft in Jenny or Constance to help out and he'll be around full-time to look after the Petalmeister. Every cloud has a silver lining, I guess, although I hope that he gets a job as soon as I come back as money is getting very thin on the ground and my credit card is maxed.

My bag is already checked in and it's time for me to go through to the departure lounge so I'm not rushing to find my gate. I'm convinced that I'll get on the wrong plane and end up in Timbuktu or somewhere.

'I love you, sweet pea.' I hug Petal again and then hand her back to Olly. 'I love you too,' I tell my husband.

'Love you. Ring me as soon as you get there,' he says.

'I will.'

We hug as a family and I tear myself away from them and head to passport control. They stand and wave to me for as long as they possibly can before I disappear out of view.

It's a long twelve-hour flight to the People's Republic of China. I'm squashed into the back of the plane and my in-flight entertainment doesn't work. No movies for me, which, of course, gives me plenty of time to stress. I'm missing Petal and Olly like mad already and I feel alone and vulnerable.

Eventually, when I've gone through all the rigmarole involved in air travel these days, I emerge into Guangzhou Baiyun International Airport. It's late and I've never seen anywhere so crowded in my entire life and, despite not being a statuesque woman, I feel as if I'm head and shoulders taller than anyone else. I am also, it seems, the only blonde.

Just as I'm starting to panic – a lone stranger in a strange land – a man rushes forward. He has my name on a sign but, clearly, has had no trouble spotting me. This, I'm assuming, is the representative from the Golden Bamboo Accessories Company who they've very kindly sent to collect me.

Mr Wu, whose English and manners are impeccable, escorts me to his car and then whisks me towards my hotel.

Guangzhou is a huge city, lit with an excess of neon. It sparkles in the darkness. We wind our way on the busy roads through a rash of skyscrapers that Manhattan would be proud of. I've booked the Vacation Inn, which is a modern, anonymous box that overlooks the Pearl River. Mr Wu leaves me there. Tomorrow afternoon, he tells me, he'll collect me and take me out to see the first factory I've arranged to visit.

My room is beige and I could be anywhere in the world. I'm jet-lagged, feel dirty and my body has no idea whether I'm tired or hungry or what. I've accomplished my first long-haul flight alone and the relief is palpable. I'm here. I've made it.

As I'm not sure what else to do now, I sit down on the bed and cry.

Chapter 63

As soon as I've stopped snivelling, I ring Olly to let him know that I got here safely. He's pleased to hear from me, but he sounds so far away that it makes me feel even lonelier.

It's approaching dawn here, but it's bedtime back at home.

'You'll be OK,' he tells me as I sniffle a bit more down the line. 'Don't worry.'

But I do worry. A few short months ago I was still serving fish and chips. Now I've somehow become an international business woman on the verge of negotiating a contract more enormous than I ever could have imaged. Frankly, I'm terrified. And with very good reason.

When Olly hangs up, I shower and crawl into bed where sleep consumes me.

It's lunchtime when I wake and I ring room service and order from the menu, which seems to involve more burgers than noodles. Nowhere in the world is immune from the American influence, it appears.

Mr Wu rings me to tell me that he's on his way and I rush

to get ready for my first meeting. But as I brush my teeth, a wave of nausea washes over me and I'm sick in the loo. Maybe my stomach hasn't recovered from the flight and a hamburger wasn't the best idea.

By the time I get downstairs, Mr Wu is already waiting for me in the lobby. We jump into his car and he drives me away from the plush downtown area and takes me out to the industrial area of the city where all the factories are situated. There are plenty of them. I'm staggered by the number as we pass by. Vast, hangar-sized buildings that go on for miles and miles. Mr Wu tells me that in China they have entire cities dedicated to the manufacture of zips or buttons or cushions. No wonder everything these days seems to be made in China. In among the factories are fields and fields of rice, buffalo up to their haunches in water, ancient workers in bamboo coolie hats driving carts down the highway. It's a stark contrast of the endearingly old and the horribly new.

Although I speak no Cantonese and the factory sales manager speaks very little English, Mr Wu does an excellent job of translating for us. I look at the factory, marvelling at the sheer scale and efficiency of the operation. I smile at the workers, but they put their heads down and don't look at me. I take some jasmine tea, which is drunk from tiny cups, turn down the kind offer of dinner due to my delicate stomach, and get a pleasingly reasonable price for my order. Mr Wu takes me back to the hotel and I thank him profusely and say goodbye. Tomorrow, another representative will collect me and take me to another factory and I'll repeat the process all over again. Whenever I used to hear about people travelling for their work, I was always really jealous, thinking how glamorous it must be to have a life like that. The reality of it is that I'd much rather be at home with my husband and my baby.

The next day, I'm still feeling sickly even though I pass on the burger and eat nothing at all for dinner. I throw up again. Perhaps it's the change of water or maybe I'm dehydrated. Perhaps I'm just not cut out to be an international jet-setter. What I'd like to do is crawl back into bed and sleep, but the show must go on.

I'm driven out to the Golden Lion Company – this time by an impeccably dressed and polite Mr Li – shuffling our way through the clogged traffic to the same area as yesterday. I take a tour of what the Golden Lion Company has to offer and note that the set-up is very much the same as the first factory. I have jasmine tea again and that traditional Chinese delight, a plate of Pringles.

That night I sit in the hotel and look out over the beckoning lights of Guangzhou and wonder what is out there. I should go out to a restaurant, take in a Chinese opera, see what's out there amid the twinkling neon. How can I come all the way to China and see nothing of it but the inside of three factories? There's no fun in travelling the world if you can't do it with the one you love and I vow that, in the future, when I have cause to go abroad with work then I'll try to take Olly and Petal with me as much as I can. This would be a very different trip if they were here.

So instead of tripping the light fantastic in Guangzhou, I stay put. Again. I read the *Cosmopolitan* magazine that I picked up at the airport. And as there doesn't seem to be much choice, I order a hamburger from the room service menu. Again.

I wake up early and lie as still as possible until the nausea has abated. It might just be the quality of air here, which feels so much more polluted than at home. The final factory in Shiling Town is the Very Good Handbag Manufacturer. I'm not sure anyone could argue with that. Mr Chu is a charming man and after three visits to three different places, I'm totally confused and my head is spinning. But the Very Good Handbag Manufacturer seems to offer me excellent terms, can turn the handbags round quickly and, having no one else to bounce my thoughts off, I decide to sign up there and then.

I wish Olly was with me, or Tod, or simply someone to tell me that I'm doing the right thing, that these are the people I should trust to make my handbags. But there's no one. I have to make this call by myself and follow my instinct. Because I'm a new and unknown client, I have to pay for all this up front. Gulp.

I take a deep breath, sign the contract, commit a vast amount of the bank's money to the deal, and walk out with shaky knees.

Chapter 64

'Muuuummeeee!' Petal races across the concourse towards me and joy surges through my heart.

Dropping my case, I scoop her up into my arms as she careers into me and twirl her round. I breathe in her scent. She smells of fish fingers, jam sandwiches and Matey bubble bath. She is what gives my life meaning.

'I've been a very good girl while you've been gone,' she says.

I lower her to the ground. 'I'm sure you have.' I root in my handbag and find the doll that I bought for her in a gift shop at the airport. Something else for my child to boss about.

I'm back home, safely on English soil once more. I sigh with relief and fall into Olly's arms. We hold each other tightly.

'Missed you,' he whispers in my ear.

'Not as much as I've missed you,' I tell him.

I'm so glad that he and Petal have collected me from the airport. I couldn't wait to see them both and I don't think I could have faced taking the train now. I'm exhausted and elated in equal measures.

Petal falls asleep in the borrowed car on the way home. The next thing must be to get some decent wheels of our own. As soon as the money starts to roll in from Home Mall, it will be top of the list. I also struggle to keep my eyes open, but Olly and I hold hands all the way back, even as he changes gear. We catch the end of rush hour, so the roads are still busy.

'Did you get everything sorted out?' he asks as we hit the M25.

'Yes,' I say. 'We will very soon be the proud owners of several thousand Nell McNamara handbags.'

'Wow.'

Well, more accurately, we have paid an enormous amount for handbags that we will most likely never catch a glimpse of. Apart from a dozen for quality control, the rest will be shipped direct to the warehouse of Home Mall in Florida. But, on the global stage, that's how business works now.

'It went OK?'

'Better than I could have expected,' I admit. 'But I can't wait to get home.'

Olly squeezes my hand.

There's no doubt that it was a steep learning curve for me but having done it, the process would hold no fear for me again. I am woman, hear me roar!

'Hey, sleepyhead,' Olly says as he shakes my arm. 'Home, sweet home.'

'We're back? Already?'

He laughs. 'It wasn't that quick.'

I glance at my watch. Thanks to the traffic, it's taken nearly two hours to travel home. I must have dropped off as I don't remember half of the journey.

We've pulled up outside the shop. Olly lifts a still-sleeping Petal out of the back seat and carries her to the door, while I lug my case out of the boot and then along the pavement behind them.

As Olly unlocks the door and climbs up the stairs, I pause at the shop window. The handbags are lit up with little spotlights and shimmer in the dusk of the evening. It brings a tear to my eye. This is my work. All my work. One day, hopefully very soon, it will be worth all the hard slog.

With a smile in my heart, I follow them both into the flat. Even the dreary pokiness of it can't make a dent in my contentment. Olly takes Petal straight through to her room. I abandon my wheelie case in the middle of the living room and sigh to myself. It may not be much, but it is home.

Dude is ecstatic to see me and leaps up and down, pounding everything in sight with his tail. 'Good boy.' I ruffle his ears and pat his head. 'I've missed you too.'

'Go and sit with her for a minute,' Olly says as he emerges from Petal's room. 'I'll run you a bath.'

'That would be lovely.'

'I have another surprise in store,' he says with a wink.

'Oh, really?' I raise an eyebrow.

'Yes, but you'll have to wait until I've taken the Corsa back to Tom.'

'I'm a patient woman,' I tell him.

'Yeah, right,' he says with a laugh. He kisses me. 'I won't be long.'

Kicking off my shoes with a grateful groan – my ankles are like a pair of pumpkins after the long flight – I pad through to Petal's room enjoying the feel of the rough carpet on my weary feet.

My daughter is fast asleep, amid a pile of soft toys, arm thrown above her head. She looks so peaceful. I stand and watch her in the glow of her little night light and my heart squeezes with love for her. I want to give her a life of ease, a life that doesn't involve worry or pain. Isn't that what all parents want for their children? I want her to be happy, whatever that means for her.

Nudging her up, I lie down beside her. She mutters something incomprehensible. If our roles were reversed, Petal would be sticking in sharp elbows and knees to make sure she got more than her fair share of the duvet. As it is, I balance on the edge of the bed, just content to be next to her. In the bathroom, I can hear Olly running my bath. My eyes grow heavy just thinking about it.

Just as I'm dozing off, he swings open the door softly. 'Bath's ready, madam.'

'Thank you.'

'You look too comfortable there.'

'Hmm,' I murmur. It wouldn't be hard to stay here for the rest of the night. 'A bath is a good idea though.' I haul my weary bones from Petal's bed and go through to the bathroom.

Olly has filled the room with candles and the bath is full,

steaming and overflowing with wonderfully scented foam. On the mirror, in the steam, he's written I LOVE YOU, NELL MCNAMARA! And there are lots of kisses.

Smiling, I strip off my crumpled clothes and slide into the welcoming hot water with a heartfelt 'Ahhhhh.'

Lying back, I relax and let the bubbles envelop me. Olly must have really missed me as I couldn't have hoped for a lovelier homecoming.

I doze again in the water and a few minutes later I hear the front door bang to signal his return. I can hear him clattering about in the kitchen, so I step out of the bath and dry myself. Towelling my hair, I slip on my dressing gown and go to find out what he's cooking up.

In the living room the table is set, the candles are out in force again. Olly is dishing out Chinese takeaway and he turns when I start to laugh.

'You said that all you'd eaten was hamburgers,' he points out. 'I thought this might be a nice finale to your trip.'

I wind my arms round his waist. 'It's a lovely idea.'

He piles our plates high with sweet and sour chicken, egg fried rice and spare ribs from Hong Kong Garden, our favourite takeaway in town. The remains go onto the table, still in their cartons. A mountain of prawn crackers fills a handy Pyrex bowl.

Olly cracks open a couple of the Tsingtao beers that he's bought and he clinks his bottle against mine. 'A toast to China.'

'To China!' I echo, then I chew anxiously at my lip. 'I hope I've done the right thing.'

'Of course you have,' he says. 'I know I've been a pain in the arse, Nell, but I do trust you. If you say this is right for us, then I believe you.'

'Thanks,' I say. 'That means a lot to me.'

Then, before our Chinese meal gets cold and before I let my doubts swamp me, we tuck in.

Chapter 65

The next day, I'm trying to get my jet-lagged head together by staring blankly at my computer screen, when Lola Cody from Home Mall calls me.

'Hi, Nell, honey,' she coos in her lilting southern accent. 'How's it going?'

'Fine,' I say. 'Just back from China. The shipment is ordered.' I give her the expected date for delivery.

'That's *so* wonderful,' my new best friend says. She sounds almost as excited as I am. 'Things are moving along just great. We can now go ahead and reserve the slot.' Lola clears her throat. 'There's just the small matter of the deposit. You know that's fully refundable providing the orders are worth more and, honey, I have no doubt that they will be.'

Thank goodness for that.

'I can get onto it today, right now,' I assure her. 'The money's in our bank. All I have to do is arrange for it to be transferred.'

'Then you'll need our details.'

Lola reels off her account number and bank details while I scribble them down on my pad. I notice that my hands shake. It's a lot of money. An *awful* lot of money. This is the final step. After I pay the deposit, I hand everything over to Home Mall to work their magic.

'We're all set to go,' she says.

'I can't wait,' I tell her. 'I'm really looking forward to it.'

'Maybe you and Olly and little Petal can come out one day and visit with us,' she says. 'That sure would be nice.'

'It sounds great,' I admit. Miami always looks fabulous on the television. Although I'm thinking that I've only ever seen it on crime shows. I'd love to go there and this would give us the perfect excuse for a family holiday. But, first, we have to get the money in. Can't do anything without that.

'I'll talk to you soon,' Lola says. 'Bye for now.'

'Bye. And thanks again,' I say and I hang up.

Sitting back in my chair, I stare at the screen again. I tap at the keys and locate the slick Home Mall website. Clips of pearly toothed, glossy-haired presenters selling their hearts out pass before my eyes. In a few short weeks this will be me. It will be *my* handbags on prime time USA television. This is it. My launch pad. Time for my big break. My stomach heaves majestically and I rush to the loo and am promptly sick. Do you reckon that Lord Sugar does this when he's just sealed a big deal? Does Donald Trump like a good business barf? Somehow I don't think so. I'm going to have to toughen up as the figures are getting bigger and bigger.

I wash my face, pour a glass of water and plod back out to the office. I'm sorry to have parted company with last night's

Chinese as Olly and I had such a lovely time together. We didn't quite get down to it on the table like we did in Cornwall, but we certainly had a very romantic evening. Petal, for once, stayed in her own bed and we made the springs in ours bounce. I really think that things between us are getting back to how they were. Hallelujah!

After calming my breathing, I pick up the phone and call the bank to speak to Simon North, my business manager. We exchange pleasantries and then I ask him to make the transfer. Moments later, he tells me it's done. My money – the bank's money – is now winging its way across cyberspace to the United States of America and, more importantly, the coffers of the Home Mall Shopping Channel. Soon my consignment of handbags will be following it. Hey! *Consignment*! Did I think I'd ever be throwing that word into conversation as a fish and chip lady, eh?

When the deed is done, I collapse back and sip my water. Then a wave of euphoria crashes over me, sweeping away my dread and nausea.

That's it. I'm on my way. Perhaps Olly and I can have a sandwich together at lunchtime and toast our good fortune with a frothy cappuccino. Maybe I'll pop into the chippy this afternoon and see how everyone is. The doorbell of the shop door chimes and breaks into my musing. With my grin still firmly in place, I go to see who it is.

I'm surprised to see Tod standing there.

'Hey,' I say. 'Good timing. I was just going to break out the kettle for a cup of celebratory tea.'

Then I notice that the expression on his face is grim.

'What's wrong?'

His dull eyes meet mine when he says, 'You may not be cel-ebrating when you hear what I've got to tell you.' He holds up a rumpled newspaper and shakes his head.

'This is not good news, is it?'

'No.'

And my heart sinks right into my boots.

Chapter 66

'You'd better sit down, Nell,' Tod says.

Without protest, I go back to my computer chair and drop into it. My mentor pulls up another chair and sits opposite me.

'No tea?'

Tod shakes his head. 'We'll need some in a minute.'

His face says that I actually may need more than tea. Much more.

He spreads out the newspaper on the desk in front of me. 'I bought this first thing this morning, but I've only just had the chance to read it. I came straight round here as soon as I saw it.'

The column is tucked away on the left-hand side of page fifteen. The small, insignificant headline reads 'Shopping Channel Scam' and I know that in my heart of hearts, before I need to read another single word, that I've been had. Royally, truly, had.

Tears fill my eyes and I struggle to read the piece through the blur. Fat, wet droplets splash onto the type. Tod reaches out and takes my hand and squeezes it tightly.

Sure enough the perpetrator of this fraud is the one, the only, Home Mall. There's a blurry picture of Lola Cody and she's not the slick, sharp-suited business woman with a killer manicure and GHD hairdo that I'd imagined. She's fat, robed in grubby sweats and a shapeless, tent-sized T-shirt. Next to her is an equally waddly man in a Hawaiian shirt with a bad combover; Mr Benito Cody, the newspaper informs me – if those are even their real names. Not only Lola's partner in crime, but her husband, I presume.

The article goes on to say that Home Mall have been operating this scam for several months now. A dozen or more businesses have been taken down by them. The deposits are sent, the stock delivered and both mysteriously disappear without trace. I feel vomit rising to my mouth, but I force it down.

'I'm sorry,' Tod says. 'This is the first time I've heard about it. There's been nothing in the trade papers, nothing from the Department of Trade and Industry. Usually, we'd hear *something* on the grapevine. Apparently, they're such professional operators that no one has suspected anything until now.'

Tell me about it. I was totally taken in by Lola Cody's easy charm and friendliness. She even invited me to go there on holiday with Olly and Petal, for heaven's sake! She knew that this meant the world to me, that it was going to mean a new start for our family. She knew that in order to scam me, she'd be taking food out of my child's mouth. She knew all this! The woman can have no heart, no soul, and certainly no conscience. I was stupid to be seduced by the fact that out of all the handbags in the world, she wanted mine. Olly said that it sounded too good to be true – and he was right. I should have listened to him. I should have listened to his doubts, but I didn't and the deed has been done. Have I learned nothing from having my designs ripped off by *Monsieur* Yves Simoneaux? Though his nasty little trick looks like amateur hour compared to the set-up of Home Mall.

'I know this was your dream.'

Was. Already past tense.

Still staring at the newspaper page, I let the tears fall. The editor may feel that this story only warrants a small column, a tiny headline, but with it a vacuum has just opened up and swallowed my life.

'I was so sure,' Tod frets. 'So sure. The contract looked above board. The website was professional. Everything seemed fine. So believable.'

I never suspected that someone would create something so elaborate, that they would go to so much trouble to perpetrate a fraud. It's beyond my imagination. Still is. However hard I find it to believe, the golden goose, it seems, was nothing more than a mirage. Something created with smoke and mirrors to lure in the susceptible.

'It looks like she's done this several times before.' He sighs heavily. 'Pull out now,' Tod says. 'It's not too late.'

Looking up, I realise that Tod doesn't know how far this has gone. He knew I was going to China, but I've not yet had the chance to update him since I've been back. He doesn't realise that the money has already been transferred to Lola Cody's bank account, which could be in the Cayman Islands for all I know.

'It *is* too late,' I tell him.

He looks at me blankly.

'The bags are ordered and have been paid for up front.' An inordinate amount of money. 'I transferred the deposit to Home Mall not half an hour ago.' Thirty thousand dollars. The best part of twenty thousand pounds. My head swims and I clutch the desk with my free hand. 'I'd just put the phone down to my bank manager when you came in.'

Tod recoils. 'Stop it,' he says. 'You must be able to stop it. Get onto the bank right away.'

I slip my hand from Tod's and with trembling fingers and the dead weight of fear dragging down my hope, I punch in the bank's number again.

Chapter 67

I feel the blood drain from my face and I hang up. 'Gone,' I say. 'Once the button has been pushed at this end, there's nothing I can do.'

'*Nothing*?' Tod questions.

'The business manager at the bank said that although it will take three or four days to clear into Lola Cody's account, there's nothing I can do to block the transfer. Once it's gone, it's gone.'

'That can't be right.'

'Apparently it is.'

'But that's ridiculous.'

Ridiculous. Unfair. Downright cruel. All of those things. I could rant all day, but nothing I could say would change bank policy. Simon North at least had the good grace to be embarrassed. Somewhere my money is whirling around in the banking system heading to a crook and there's not a single thing I can do to stop it. If they can push a button to send it, why isn't there another one to stop it? Particularly when we're all aware now that the transaction is fraudulent? In this day and age of high technology, you wouldn't think it was that difficult, would you?

'He said that all that I can do is start legal action,' I offer. 'Assuming that we can find Lola Cody, that this isn't all false and there's no one of that name at all.' But I have to say that Simon North didn't sound very hopeful. Frankly, he didn't sound like he cared that much at all. Whatever happens, *he'll* get his money back. I'll be paying off the loan for the rest of my natural life, but you can bet your bottom dollar that the bank won't be the losers in this.

Taking legal action seems very unlikely. Besides, how much will it cost to pursue? We don't have any more money to engage in an expensive legal battle. That could cost us thousands. Thousands that we now don't have thanks to Lola Cody and her husband. I shake my head. 'I don't think I'll be seeing that money again, Tod.'

My brain reels at the statement. I sound so matter-of-fact. Shouldn't I be lying on the floor and screaming, renting my hair asunder?

'Surely there's something we can do?'

'My only hope now is to stop the handbags. If the factory won't cancel the order, then I hope I can stop them being shipped to the USA and can divert the handbags to come here.' It will leave me with an enormous amount of stock and I'll have to pay to warehouse them but at least I'll have them in my hot, sweaty hands and they won't be in Lola Cody's.

'I should call her.' Give her a piece of my mind. And not a nice piece.

Tod nods. 'Want that tea before you do?'

'Yes. Please. You know where everything is?'

'I'll find it.' He squeezes my shoulder as he passes. 'I feel I've let you down, Nell. I'm your business mentor. I should have advised you against this.'

'It sounded perfect. We both thought so.'

'I should have been more cautious or realised that there was something not right about it.'

'How? They've gone to a lot of trouble to make this look professional and above board.' But then they stood to make a lot of money. 'It's not your fault, Tod.' If it's anyone's fault it's mine for rushing headlong into this deal without taking a step back. 'It's just bloody awful timing.'

'We'll sort this out,' he says. 'Don't worry.'

But I don't think we'll sort it out and I am worried.

While I pick up the phone, Tod goes up to the flat to make some tea. The number that I have for Lola Cody and the Home Mall goes straight to a voicemail message.

'This number has not been recognised,' it says. 'Please dial again.' I hold the phone to my ear while it repeats it over and over again. 'This number has not been recognised. Please dial again.'

I thought it was only good news that travelled fast? Seems as if bad news does too. Lola must already have got wind that her scam had been exposed. I wonder whether she knew when I spoke to her earlier and if she thought she'd just give it one last go at taking in another gullible sucker? If only I hadn't been so quick to set the ball rolling. If only I'd sat back and taken time to do this. If only I hadn't been so trusting. If only I hadn't been so blindly ambitious. If only. If only. If only.

Chapter 68

When Tod finally leaves – even though he was reluctant to go – I turn my face to the sky and howl. The floodgates open and I let a torrent of tears flow.

I have lost everything. *Everything*. How can I possibly carry on?

By the time Olly returns with Petal, I have managed to get myself under control again. Where there was rage and anger, a dull numbness has settled in.

'What?' Olly says when he sees my puffy face and red-rimmed eyes. 'Who's died?'

'My business,' I tell him flatly. 'Everything I've worked for, gone.'

He recoils slightly at that, but says, 'Gone? You can't mean that.'

'I'm afraid that I do.' My voice doesn't even falter.

Petal comes to sit on my lap. 'Don't cry, Mummy,' she says. 'Daddy will fix it.'

I pass Olly the newspaper that Tod brought for me to read and, face darkening, he sits and studies it in silence.

'Shit,' he says when he puts it down again.

'Daddy!' Petal admonishes. 'That's a very bad word.'

'Sometimes bad words are the only words that will do, Petalmeister,' he tells her. 'But you can only use them when you're eighteen.'

'Oh,' she says, clearly not taken in. She'll be saying 'shit' to everyone in the playground tomorrow and we'll get a complaint from the nursery. Another one.

Like I could care less at the moment if my daughter is a potty-mouth; very soon she could be homeless.

Olly looks up at me, eyes questioning.

'The money's gone. I've already checked with the bank. There's nothing we can do to get it back.'

'Shit,' Petal says.

That, at least, raises a glimmer of a smile between us.

'Want to go and see Auntie Constance?' Olly asks our daughter.

'Yay!' She's down off my lap in the blink of an eye.

'It will give us some time to talk,' Olly says. He drops his voice to a whisper. 'And we can use bad words at will. Lots of them.'

We lock up the shop and walk the few hundred yards down to the town centre in the sunshine to Live and Let Fry. Of course we're welcomed like the Prodigal Son. Constance throws her arms round us, as does Phil. Jenny is cooler and there's a look that goes between her and Olly that's distinctly shifty, but I don't have time to concern myself with that now.

There are bigger problems on my plate than my friend having a crush on my husband, if that's what this is.

'It's so lovely to see you,' Constance says. 'We do miss you.'

Phil is still pumping Olly's hand.

These are good people. Their straightforward friendship almost has me undone again. 'Everything OK?'

'Not really,' I admit. 'Olly and I need an hour to ourselves. Could you keep an eye on Petal if we leave her here?'

'Of course,' Constance says. She doesn't even need to check with Phil. His chip shop has been used as an emergency crèche on more than one occasion. They're just opening up for lunchtime service and, outside, a queue is already forming. Business here isn't suffering then. Perhaps I should have just opened a chip shop. It seems so uncomplicated in comparison to the hard-nosed world of fashion.

'Be a good girl,' I say to Petal. 'Mummy and Daddy won't be long.'

Take all day, her face says as she knows she'll be fed a constant stream of hot chips and there'll be as much Coke as she can drink. For a bit of peace now, she'll be bouncing off the walls later.

Olly and I link arms and walk out through the town and, eventually, along Hermitage Road where the steep and striking slope of Windmill Hill faces us. Without talking, we climb the hill side by side. Then, when we're both out of breath, we find a bench and sit at the top, taking in the breathtaking view over the rest of Hitchin town and far out to the verdant fields and rolling hills beyond. The rumble of traffic from the streets below and the faint hum of jets taking off from nearby Luton

Airport compete with the birdsong. But by all accounts, this is still an idyllic summer's day. Yet even the cloudless sky can't shake my blues.

We sit together in silence, until I ask, 'Don't you want to shout?'

Olly tucks my hand into his. 'No,' he says. 'What's done is done.'

'But I've lost all the money,' I reiterate. 'You'd be quite entitled to shout.'

'What good would it do?'

'We've got nothing,' I point out as if Olly doesn't realise this.

He shrugs. 'We had nothing before.'

In truth, we haven't got nothing; we've got less than that. Nothing would be a bonus. In reality what we have is an enormous debt hanging over us now.

'I'd like to go out to Miami and kill Lola Cody and her husband with my bare hands,' he says.

'It sounds like there'll be a queue of people wanting to do that.'

'She'll get her comeuppance. People like that always do.'

But do they? I think. People like that normally seem to get away scot-free if you ask me. It's people like us, straightforward people who always try to do the right thing, pay their way, don't cheat on their taxes, we're the ones that pay.

Olly puts his head against mine. 'We'll get through this,' he assures me. 'You and me. Your handbags are still fab.'

He nudges me, but I can't summon the required smile as a

response. At this moment, I don't care whether I design another handbag for the rest of my days.

'No one can take that away from you, Nell McNamara. You just need to carry on.'

But can I? Can I simply pick myself up, one more time, and carry on?

Chapter 69

We go back to the chip shop to collect Petal. Olly and I stayed in the park for a while, not talking much, but just sitting and watching the world go by. It sounds like it was restful, but it wasn't as my brain was still going ninety to the dozen.

Now it's late evening and the lunchtime rush has died down and the early teatime people haven't quite arrived yet. At one of the tables, our daughter is holding court. Somewhat tunelessly, she's singing a song, 'Rainbow Connection' from the *The Muppet Movie*, her current favourite. For some reason her tolerant audience, Constance and Phil, are wearing napkins on their heads.

We slide into the seats opposite them and wait for the song to finish. It seems to go on for a long time. I'm sure Petal makes up a few verses.

Eventually, she stops.

Phil, removing his napkin, asks, 'Everything all right?'

I shake my head. 'Not really, Phil,' I say and then proceed to explain to him all that has happened.

With shuddering breaths, I tell Phil all about my designs being stolen by team Simoneaux-Monique. Then I move on to the scam that Lola Cody of the fictitious Home Mall was running. I tell him how I fell for it hook, line and sinker. I tell him how I have lost all of our money. He sits there, face like stone, as he listens patiently. Constance's eyes well up with tears.

'Don't cry,' I warn her. 'You'll start me off again.' I've already cried a river and crying isn't going to do anything to stop Lola Cody or the likes of her.

'Is there anything we can do?' Phil asks. 'Anything? Just ask.'

'Give me my old job back?'

'No,' he says. 'Anything but that. You don't need a job here, you've already got one.'

I don't remind Phil that I've got a job that is not only bringing in no money, but is actually sinking us deeper into debt.

'You'll make it as a designer,' he continues. 'You'll get over this and make it big.'

'Yes,' I say. 'Of course I will.' But, in my heart, I know it's not the case.

To a chorus of sympathetic noises and good wishes, Olly, Petal and I leave. We walk the short distance home, Olly and me quiet, Petal chattering away to herself.

'I'll find something,' Olly says. 'I heard that Tesco are looking for delivery drivers. I might give that a go.'

'Fine,' I say. It comes out more like 'whatever' than I'd intended.

He sighs. 'We're in this together, Nell. I'm not expecting you to pick up the pieces by yourself.'

'Thanks.'

But at the end of the day, it's my bad. Mine alone.

'I'll make dinner tonight,' he says. 'Had you got anything planned?'

'No,' I admit. Food is the last thing on my mind.

'I'll throw some pasta in a tin of tomatoes, sprinkle some cheddar on it and call it Italian.'

'Sounds good.' To be honest I'd eat anything as long as it doesn't involve me going near the kitchen.

'Why don't you go into the office and do some sketches? That always takes your mind off things.'

So does lying on the sofa watching crap telly. But I suppose I ought to show willing. Olly has been really good about this. Would I have been so magnanimous if the boot had been on the other foot? I'd like to think so, but I'm not so sure.

'The Petalmeister will help me, won't you?'

My child's face says that she'd like to be watching crap telly too.

'Yes, Daddy.' She must be able to tell by the sombre atmosphere that it's probably best not to rock the boat.

So Petal and Olly climb up the stairs to the flat while I stay downstairs in the shop. I stand and stare blankly at my handbags all beautifully displayed and, for the first time, can take no joy in them.

I go through to the office and sit and stare blankly at the computer screen. What's the point of me designing anything when we now have no money to even commission a sample of it to be made? Plus, if I can manage to get all my handbags back from China, then we'll have more than enough to sell. In fact, I can't really imagine how we'll get rid of them without some massive television campaign.

Not knowing what else to do, I log onto the Home Mall website and watch the bright and bubbly clips that Lola Cody has posted on there, looking, searching, for some clues that I might have missed, something to tell me that all was not well. But even watching them with eyes that have had the scales peeled from them, I can see nothing amiss. The pastel-coloured studio looks perfectly respectable, the presenters are professional. I wonder if they even knew what they were involved in or whether the glossy, smiling women were a part of it too.

I've done nothing remotely useful, other than brood, when Olly calls down to say that supper is ready.

Petal is already sitting at the table. Quite wisely, she has a tiny bowl in front of her as I'm sure she's been snaffling chips all afternoon. Olly gives us both bigger bowls, but I toy with mine, not really hungry. I'll save what's left and ping it tomorrow. We'll have to be eating a lot more tinned tomatoes and pasta until Olly finds a job. I'll need to find one too, despite Phil's confidence in me.

When we've eaten, Olly insists on washing up and I watch *In the Night Garden* with Petal and my eyes, rather than hers, grow heavy.

'Come on, miss,' Olly says. 'Time for bed.'

'Aw, Daddy. Not yet!'

'It's late.'

'You know,' I say. 'I might go too.'

'It's half-past seven,' Olly points out.

Late for one age group is not necessarily the same for another.

'Jet lag,' I say. 'I'm absolutely bushed.'

'I'll stay up and watch a film or something. I can't go to bed now.' He kisses my forehead. 'You have a good night's sleep, then you'll feel better.'

Petal and I crawl under the duvet together in our double bed. I bet Olly ends up sleeping in her single.

Within seconds, my daughter has claimed two thirds of the bed. I have an elbow in my back, a knee where I don't want a knee and I'm struggling to keep hold of my share of the cover. I can hear Olly watching something loud involving copious car chases through the thin walls.

I'm still awake when the film has finished and I hear my husband pad through to Petal's room and settle down for the night. I should go and tell him that I'm not asleep, that he could come to bed with me and not disturb me. We could lift Petal into her own bed and snuggle down together. But I don't.

Instead, I stare at the ceiling until dawn and, in the morning, feel worse than ever.

Chapter 70

Two weeks go by and instead of getting better and coming to terms with what's happened, I'm struggling to function at all. I can't eat. I can't sleep. I see no point in carrying on. I must have lost a tonne of weight as all my clothes are hanging off me.

'You need to go to the doctor,' Olly says as I push away the toast that's in front of me. I feel constantly sick and just can't face it. His tone is slightly exasperated. 'You can't go on like this.'

'There's nothing wrong.'

'There is, Nell. He could perhaps give you some tablets,' Olly suggests. 'Just to get you back on your feet.'

'Pills?' I look up. 'You think a pill will get our money back?'

'It's *you* that I'm worried about.'

'I'm fine,' I insist. But even I know that I'm not.

I'm sitting on the sofa watching *Daybreak*, something I've taken to doing. In fact, I'm watching a lot of daytime television these days. I can't face going into the shop, the office.

Everything glares at me, accusing. The phone is silent. No one is ringing to order handbags any more. The glossy magazines have all stopped calling. So soon, they've moved on to the next new thing. Already, I've dropped off the radar. Another insignificant blip to be overlooked.

Only Tod is texting every day, but I don't reply. What have I to say to him? Nothing that he'll want to hear. Nothing good. Nothing positive. Nothing that will bring our money back. Nothing that will undo this terrible cock-up.

Olly has been doing his best. I can't fault him for that. He has phoned and phoned the police, who aren't the slightest bit interested in our story. He's phoned and phoned the bank. The response is much the same. He's pleaded with the business manager, reasoned with *his* manager, argued with the bank's Company Fraud Department and has threatened them with exposing the story on *Watchdog*. But they remain unmoved by our plight. They have hearts of stone. The only thing he has learned is that the Cody's bank account, as soon as our transfer had cleared, has been stripped of all cash. Somewhere, on the other side of the world, they have their hands on our money. As easy as that. Under the bank's averted gaze, they have got away with this audacious theft scot-free.

The only thing I've done since the bombshell dropped is phone the factory in China. They wouldn't cancel the contract, and who could blame them? It's a lot of money to forgo. But they have agreed to delay production and they'll deliver all the handbags here for me. Twenty grand's worth of them. What do you suppose I'm going to do with that lot, eh? We'll have to find storage for them, but I don't have to think about that for now. It'll be another few weeks before they rock up on our doorstep. At least we've rescued something out of the disaster, is Olly's viewpoint. But, frankly, I'm not jumping round the room doing a happy dance.

'Mummy, we need to see the ducks today,' Petal says. 'They'll be hungry without us.'

'Not today, Petal,' I say. Olly has been looking after our daughter. I don't know why but, at the moment, I'm just finding her chatter too bright, too relentless. I simply want to be quiet, to be by myself.

'We should go out,' Olly suggests. 'Take a walk. Get some fresh air. You haven't been out of the flat for days.'

Haven't I? I guess not. I look around me. The place is untidy, toys everywhere. Most days the bed goes unmade and I'm not the slightest bit bothered. No one else is concerned about anything, so why should I be? Nearly every day Olly has been going out for interviews, but nothing is forthcoming. At this rate we'll be on skid row sooner than we think. I wonder if we'll even be able to hang onto this place. I wonder if I even care.

'It's sunny out there.'

But it's raining in my heart.

'Let's take Dude for a stroll.'

At that, the dog wags his tail. Someone's keen, at least.

'OK.'

Olly looks relieved. Then, as I go to get up, tiredness overwhelms me. 'On second thoughts,' I say. 'You go. Take Petal and Dude. I'll just stay here.'

He sighs. 'You can't "just stay here", Nell. This is doing you no good.'

What's *this* exactly?

'Petal, go and put your shoes on.' She skips out of the room and my husband comes to kneel down beside me. He strokes my leg as if I'm injured, then he sighs before he says, 'I know you've been hurt, Nell. It's a terrible blow. But life goes on.'

Does it?

'It isn't the end of the world.' His tone is soft, cajoling. He toys with my fingers and I want to shake him off. His touch, for the first time ever, is irritating.

It *is* the end of my world, I think. How can he not see that?

'No one is ill.' He looks anxiously at me. 'No one has died.'

Something *inside* me has died, I want to say. I'm empty. A shell. But no words will come.

'You don't understand,' I tell him.

'I'm trying to, Nell.'

I round on him. 'You never wanted this business to succeed. Secretly, I think that you hoped I would fail all along.'

There's a stunned expression on his face. 'Where did that come from?'

'You know it's true,' I say bitterly. 'This was never what you longed for.'

'Nell,' he says, 'I admit, in the beginning, I was scared about it. But I've changed. Surely you must see that?'

'You don't care,' I hiss at him. 'No one cares.'

Petal comes back into the room. She has on her shoes. I wonder if she's going somewhere.

'I don't believe that you mean that, Nell,' Olly says sadly. He stands up and the pain on his face is unbearable, so I turn my eyes away. 'Petal and I will go out for a while. When we're gone try to decide what you want, what you need. Do something to help yourself.'

Help myself? I don't know how to do that. I want to say something good, something that will stop Olly looking at me like that, but still my fogged brain won't let anything go to my mouth.

I hear Olly and Petal walk heavily down the stairs. Then the front door slams and I'm left alone.

Chapter 71

Olly skirts round me for the rest of the day. He keeps Petal out of my way too.

I sit in my pyjamas and watch *The Jeremy Kyle Show*, which reduces me to tears. Then it's *Homes Under the Hammer*, *60 Minute Makeover* and five episodes of *Coach Trip* back to back. I can't remember what else. The mindless programmes, chewing gum for the mind, nearly manage to block out the flashback images of the villainous Yves Simoneaux, the duplicitous Marie Monique and the devious Lola Cody that are playing on a constant loop in my head. Nearly, but not quite. Food comes and goes. I think I eat some of it.

Eventually, Petal, bathed and in her pyjamas, is presented to me. Is it her bedtime already? How long have I been welded to this sofa? All day? Surely not? Only Dude, curled into my side like a limpet, is appreciative of the amount of time I'm spending on the sofa. If I could move, I would, but my legs have no strength and my mind even less.

My daughter's face is scrubbed and shiny. She smells of

strawberries. She climbs up on my lap and her tiny body moulds to mine.

'I love you, Mummy,' she says. 'Don't be sad.'

I hold her tightly and a chink of light shines through the darkness. She is my world. Not handbags. Not shopping channels. Not factories in China.

'I love you too,' I say.

'Daddy will make everything right,' she assures me.

But I think that Petal's optimism might be misplaced. No one can make this right. It's a disaster of my own making and I have to somehow learn to live with the consequences.

'Come on, Petalmeister.' Olly peels her away from me and carries her off to her bedroom.

When he comes back, he budges Dude out of the way and sits next to me on the sofa. We both stare blankly at whatever is passing across the screen.

I take hold of Olly's hand. 'I'm sorry,' I tell him. 'I'll try to do better.'

'Oh, Nell.' He sighs at me.

'I love you. I do.'

'I love you too,' he says. Olly gazes deep into my eyes as if he's trying to fathom what's going on behind them. I would help him out if I could, but I don't know myself. 'Whatever happens. I love you.'

We go to bed and lie very still in each other's arms. I stare at the ceiling, but for once I don't feel despair crushing down on me. At some time in the dark hours, I must fall asleep.

When I wake up, Olly is gone.

His side of the bed has clearly been abandoned several

hours earlier. I listen for sounds of him pottering about, making breakfast, as he always does, but the flat is silent. Dude is still slumbering on the floor, so he's not out walking the dog. A feeling of dread grips me. In my heart, I know that this is bad.

In a stupor, I climb out of bed and search the flat for him. I check all the rooms, which doesn't take long. He's not in the shower, or in the office. When, eventually, I check in the yard, I discover that his precious Vespa has gone. I call his mobile, but he's not picking up. One of the big holdalls is missing and his wardrobe is half-empty. I press one of his shirts – my favourite – against my face and inhale his scent. There's no doubt about it. Olly has definitely gone.

I slump onto the bed. Who can blame him? I've done nothing but push him away recently. Everything has been at the top of the list but him. Well, now it seems that he's had enough. Didn't Constance warn me as much? I should have listened to her. My eyes burn with tears. What have I done? What will I do without him? He has always been my rock, my best friend, my lover, my life. Until bloody handbags came and got in the way.

Petal will be distraught. He's a fantastic father and she adores him. I could see how he would leave me – goodness only knows I've tested him enough – but I can't believe that he would simply walk out on her.

I call his mobile again. Not answering. I check the flat again. I thought, at least, that he would leave me a note, say something. But there's nothing. The Olly I know would talk this through, he wouldn't just up and leave us. Petal is still asleep. I look down at her face, untroubled, peaceful. I don't want anything in her life to cause her pain. Particularly nothing that I've done, that I could have prevented. I have to find Olly and talk to him. We have to sort this out.

Just when I thought that my life couldn't possibly get any worse, it has. But, in some ways, it also feels as if I've woken from a terrible nightmare. Unfortunately, the reality is just as painful. The shock has jolted me out of my catatonic state. If Olly *has* left me and Petal alone, then I have to cope, I have to get on with my life. I can't sit watching daytime television and feeling sorry for myself. I have to get a grip.

First of all, I need to find my husband. But where would he go? What would he do? I can't think that he'd go very far as he'd want to stay as near to Petal as possible.

Think, Nell, I urge myself. Think. Where would Olly go?

It hits me like a body blow. I know someone who would take him in like a shot.

Chapter 72

Olly sat outside the shop on his scooter waiting for it to open. He knew the owner of Vroom very well by now. He and Ben had been at school together. They'd bought their first scooters at pretty much the same time. They'd done numerous runs down to Brighton on them. When Ben eventually set up his own business, Olly had been one of his most regular customers. He'd continued to support him over the years. Maybe he'd not been the highest-spending client he'd ever had, but whenever he'd needed work done on the Vespa this is where he'd brought it. He hoped that loyalty and a long-term friendship would count for something.

Olly checked his watch again. Ben would be here before long. He sat back on the scooter and tried to relax. It was shaping up to be a perfect day. For the weather, at least. The sun was already climbing in the sky, the clouds were wispy, insubstantial. He saw the jet trail of a plane streaked across the sky and wondered where it was heading. Despite the warmth, there was a chill in the pit of his stomach. He wasn't looking forward to doing what he had to do. Who would? Yet it had to be done. He could see no way round it.

When Nell woke, she'd be furious that he'd left without telling her. But, if he'd told her what he had planned, she would have tried to talk him out of it. Probably quite rightly.

Still, he wouldn't be going anywhere, if he couldn't get some cash – and fast.

A few minutes later and Ben pulled up in front of him on his own scooter – a 1960s Lambretta SX200 that had been lovingly restored from a rusting shell.

Ben took off his helmet. 'Hey, mate. Early for you.' He stuck out his hand and shook Olly's firmly. 'Have you been here since sun up?'

Olly shrugged. 'Something like that.'

'What's the problem?' He opened up the shop as he talked. Olly followed him inside.

'I need to sell the Vespa.'

'No way.'

'Times are hard,' Olly said.

'Thought you'd sell the missus rather than part with the old Vespa Rally.'

'Ha, ha.' The laugh sounded as forced as it was.

Ben stopped in his tracks. 'You're serious, aren't you?'

'Yeah. Deadly.'

'Fuck me,' Ben said. 'I never thought I'd see the day.'

'Me neither.'

'Everything all right?'

Olly shook his head. 'Not really.' He took a deep breath. 'Can you take it off my hands? I need the money like yesterday.'

Ben rubbed his chin and puffed out a breath. 'I'm not really into buying at the moment, mate. Times are hard here too. Tell me where they aren't.'

'I know. But I'm desperate.'

'I can see that.'

'You know its history.' Ben had more than likely done everything on it that had ever needed doing. 'You know that it's been treated like a baby.'

'Never known a more pampered pet.'

'Then you know what this is costing me.'

Ben pursed his lips. 'Let me lend you the cash.'

'I couldn't be sure to repay it. The scooter has to go.'

Ben sighed and spread his hands. 'OK,' he said. 'If you're sure.'

'I'm sure.'

'I'll give you fifteen hundred quid for it. That's all I can manage.'

It was lower than the market value, but beggars couldn't be choosers.

'Done.' Olly stuck out his hand and they shook again.

Fifteen hundred quid should just about be enough money. It would have to be.

Chapter 73

'I want *Daddy* to take me to nursery,' Petal says.

I do believe she stamps her little foot.

'That won't do you any good, miss. Daddy has had to go out,' I explain. 'He's busy today.'

Busy making a new life without us.

My daughter pouts. She has woken up scratchy and all my attempts to cuddle and mollycoddle her have been rebuffed. Perhaps she senses something unpleasant is in the air. *Unpleasant?* That's an understatement. Her world will be rocked when she finds out that Olly has walked out.

I can't be the one to tell her. He will have to face that himself.

When she's finished her breakfast, each mouthful a battle, I wrestle my moody child into her cardigan. God help her teachers today.

She drags her toes along the pavement all the way to nursery, ruining her shoes, and I don't have the strength to tell her off. Is this the sort of thing that Olly and I will have battles about in the future? Will the buying of school shoes become a matter of strife between us? I drop her off in the playground and, gratefully, hand her over to a teaching assistant. Some of the other mothers are there, but they all stare at me and no one speaks, so I hurry off.

I steel myself to walk to my next port of call.

Ten minutes later and I'm standing outside Jenny's flat. It's a tired council block on the other side of town to where we are. I wonder if we'll soon, by force of circumstances, become neighbours.

As I knock on the door, I feel that I should have some sort of speech rehearsed. My heart is in my mouth. If Olly is here, if he has come to her, then I have no idea what I'll do. Should I rant, rave? Should I calmly accept my culpability in this?

When there's no answer, I knock again. Perhaps they're in there together and simply won't answer. Opening the letter-box, I peer in. I can see right into the living room, but there's no sign of life. Olly's holdall isn't by the sofa. Maybe I should be grateful for that. I try his mobile again. If I can hear it ringing inside Jenny's flat then I shall just fall to the floor and die on the spot. It doesn't. Wherever he is, it's clear that my husband isn't here.

Thwarted, I walk back into town and, inevitably, find myself rocking up at Live and Let Fry. The shop is already open and, inside, I can see that Phil is gearing up for the day ahead. As yet, there are no customers.

'Hey,' I say as I go in.

'Hello, Nell, love,' he says. 'What brings you in so early? Come and give me a hug.'

I let myself sink into Phil's arms.

He pats my back as if I'm a small child. 'How's the big bad world of designer handbags?'

Tears spring to my eyes. 'Very big and very bad.'

He holds me away from him and can obviously read the bleakness on my face. 'Oh, no,' he says. 'What's happened now?'

'Have you got five minutes to spare?'

'Nell,' he says with a sigh. 'I have all the time in the world for you, love.'

Constance comes out of the back carrying a tray loaded with salt and pepper pots. 'Hello, Nell.' Then she sees my expression. 'You look like a lady in need of tea.'

'And sympathy,' I add.

Her eyes crinkle with kindness. 'I'll put the kettle on.'

Phil and I go and sit together. How many times have these café tables served as my therapy couch, my confessional over the last year? How much emergency tea have they provided? What would I do without Phil and Constance? Well, I hope I never find out as I'm certainly going to need them now.

When Constance joins us and we're all furnished with restorative cups of tea, I go on to explain that, this morning, on top of everything else that has happened in such a short space of time, Olly has left me.

Constance shakes her head. 'Not Olly,' she says.

'I thought that too, but there's no sign of him. No note. He's not answering his mobile.' I take a deep breath. 'I went round to Jen's. Before I came here. I thought that he might be there.'

'No,' Constance says. 'I'm sure he wouldn't have done that.'

'But you knew that they were getting close, didn't you?'

'I had my suspicions,' she admits. 'Jen is very impressionable and Olly's a lovely man, but I don't think it went very far.'

'Very far?'

'Anywhere at all,' she corrects.

'I don't know what to do. I've been feeling' – How can I explain that I've been unable to function properly since all this happened? That I've been neglecting Olly, Petal, myself? – 'poorly,' I conclude.

Constance slides her arm round me. 'You don't have to cope with this alone,' she tells me. 'We'll help you all we can. Won't we, Phil?'

'It goes without saying.'

'Thank you,' I whisper. 'Thank you so much.'

'We'll help you get Olly back.' She nudges her boss. 'Won't we, Phil?'

'Oh, yes,' he says. 'Don't you worry.'

That's all I want. I just want Olly back. But I'm really not sure how they can help me achieve that.

Chapter 74

The plane was about to touch down at Miami International Airport. And not a moment too soon as far as Olly was concerned. He'd been getting more and more het up about his mission the closer he got to his destination.

After selling the Vespa to Ben, he'd headed straight to the ticket desk at Heathrow Airport and handed over eight hundred pounds for a one-way ticket to Miami, Florida. Hopefully, he would be coming back.

He looked at the flight ticket in his hand and, even now, it seemed to have a surreal quality about it. Had Nell realised yet that his passport had gone from his bedside drawer? He hoped not. She'd called him a dozen times already before he'd even boarded the plane. More. It had been getting harder and harder to resist answering. He wanted nothing more than to hear the sound of her voice. As the doubts set in, he wanted her to tell him that he was doing the right thing. But what if she told him he wasn't? What if she begged him to abandon his plan and to fly straight home again? Then what?

It was too late now. He was set on this course and he'd have to see it through no matter what. The Vespa had gone and the remainder of the money would be used for a motel and rental car and, God willing, his return flight home. If this didn't work, then they'd simply have even less money than they did now.

His flight had left England at half-past nine yesterday evening. Now he was due to arrive in Miami shortly. He wondered what Nell was doing now and hoped that she wasn't too worried about him. Had she spent the night tossing and turning, fretting about where he was? More than likely. He'd tried to write her a note but nothing would come and in the end he'd just left without explanation. The worst thing was he hated putting her through this, but it was for the best. In the end she would come to realise that. For now, the least she knew about what he was planning, the better.

It was eleven o'clock on a fine Miami morning when he touched down. Olly thought the temperature must be well into the eighties as he hit the street outside the airport. The heat was searing and, instantly, sweat poured from him. He hailed a taxi to take him the ten minutes to the Wrecks For Rent car hire place and there he handed over twenty-eight dollars a day for the use of a Chevrolet Aveo that certainly wasn't the worst vehicle he'd ever been in.

It was the first time he'd driven overseas and terror gripped him as he swung out into the weight of traffic, while every bone in his body was telling him he was on the wrong side of the road. He gripped the steering wheel, hot with perspiration as the air conditioning struggled to chill the baking interior of the car. The highway was wide, anonymous. To make up for its lack of charm, the sky above it was ridiculously blue. A blue so sharp and pure that it hurt his eyes to look at it. Even in the height of summer in Hitchin it never even approached that stupendous hue.

Heading north in the traffic, the swanky art deco hotels of South Beach were way over to his right, as was the sparkling Atlantic Ocean. Holidaymakers were probably getting ready to have their lunch by the beach, sunbathing by the pool, perhaps enjoying an early cocktail to sharpen the day, but he wasn't here for the fun and sun. And where he was going definitely wasn't the playground of rich tourists. He was going to the darker side of Miami. The place where all the guidebooks said to avoid.

He'd managed to find out where the Home Mall shopping channel headquarters were situated from the internet. A few hours or so of poking around and he'd slowly been able to peel back the layers of their company to find out where they were based. At least he hoped he was right. Home Mall, it seemed, was located in a scruffy industrial unit in a run-down area in Dade County. The sort of area that should have made them deeply suspicious, if only they had checked more carefully. A look on Google Street View had allowed him to pinpoint exactly where the building was. He only hoped that the Codys hadn't already done a runner and that this wasn't a heinously expensive wild goose chase. He had to take the chance though. What else could he do? He only had to look at Nell, how crushed she was, how broken, and know that he couldn't sit back and do nothing. He wanted his wife back and if that meant getting their money back, then he had no choice but to do this.

Olly turned off Highway 95 and into the area of Opaville.

Perhaps Lola and Benito Cody thought if they scammed companies on the other side of the world no one would come looking for them in Miami.

How wrong they were.

Chapter 75

On the internet, most people seemed to say that this was the worst area in South Florida. Olly thought that he wouldn't really like to argue with that description. He couldn't think of anywhere in England that he'd consider quite so scary.

He'd come off the drab, traffic-clogged highway and was now working his way along Main Avenue in Opaville, moving slowly in his hire car. The vehicle might be a perfectly inconspicuous shade of beige, but he still felt like he stuck out like a sore thumb. Might as well paint a target on his forehead, really. This was an area that could, politely, be called 'depressed'. He could also think of a lot of far less polite words for it.

The broad street was characterised by broken windows, buildings sprayed with graffiti, burnt out cars. The internet had also informed him that it was a notorious area for drug gangs and shoot-outs. He thought it was probably true. Groups of bored youths sat on crumbling porches. They glared at him sullenly as he drove by. Feral dogs roamed the roads. Rap music at decibels high enough to make your ears bleed pumped out of a few of the houses. It looked like once, many years ago, it might have been a nice place to live. But not now. There were green areas, neglected and overgrown, that were probably, at one time, attractive parks. A few grand buildings still struggled to maintain some sort of dignity despite their decades of decay. Its heyday, if it ever had one, was long gone.

Main Avenue was where the 'studio' was supposed to be situated. He crawled along, looking for the right address. Clearly, doing this at night would be out of the question in this neighbourhood, as it might well be misconstrued. Alone and vulnerable, he felt terrified. How he would love to call Nell and hear her voice, but he didn't want anything to cause him to bottle out now. As he drove deeper into the decay, he locked the car doors and made sure the windows were firmly rolled up.

The derelict houses gave way to a smattering of scruffy shops. Some were boarded up; a few looked as if they had been permanently shuttered. Only the brave continued to trade and they mostly seemed to be second-hand shops or liquor stores. Olly pressed on.

Eventually, he reached the right part of the long street. A glance at the address he had on his piece of paper confirmed that he was close. Small industrial units sprang up now, most of them long since abandoned.

Moments later, Olly turned off into a side street. The squat building in front of him didn't look like the home of a television studio, but he was sure this was the right place.

There was no sign declaring its ownership. The outside was

covered in graffiti and there were no windows. The front door was covered with a metal shutter, also sprayed with colourful words. Olly pulled up in the Chevrolet and sat and stared at it. Clearly, there was no one home.

He parked and got out of the car. Across the street, there was a scruffy auto repair shop – DIEGO'S AUTO STOP it said above the door – and the two heavily tattooed mechanics watched his every move as he did. He hoped that they weren't eyeing up his vehicle for potential spares.

Was this really the right place? He guessed there was only one way he was going to find out.

There was no point in knocking at the door of the Home Mall shopping channel, so he walked round the side of the building. Rubbish was piled high in the alley and a scabby dog rummaged through it. There was one of those big commercial dumpsters and, above it, a broken window. Olly checked the rest of the building. This, as far as he could tell, would be the only way of him gaining access. Glancing around him to make sure that no one was watching, he levered himself up onto the dumpster and towards the window. He pulled out a few of the sharper-looking shards of glass and tossed them into the alley, then he elbowed in the rest so that there was a space big enough for him to ease himself through.

He dropped down into the room below and brushed himself off, thankfully unharmed. This was some sort of storeroom, but there was currently not very much being stored. There were some empty boxes, a bit of scattered paperwork, not much more. Gingerly, he opened the door, but there was no need as, obviously, there was no one here.

Olly walked into the corridor and checked a couple of other doors. Deserted offices. All shabby. Wastepaper baskets overturned. At the back, he opened a door and stepped straight into the studio he recognised from the Home Mall website that he and Nell had checked out. It was like entering another world. The fake French doors, the sunshine mural, the potted palm trees – they were all here. This space was pristine, painted in sugary candy colours and it looked Disneyesque in among the overwhelming grime surrounding it. Unfortunately, it was also completely empty

So this was the right place. He wasn't sure whether he felt good or bad about that.

The smartest office was at the very front of the building. It contained two desks, a computer on top of each. Both turned off. Next to one computer was a half-drunk takeaway cup of coffee. It was stone-cold. It could have been here for two days or two weeks. There was a bank of slightly beaten up filing cabinets just inside the front door. At the end of them, nearest to Olly, stood a baseball bat – always a useful addition to office equipment. Olly wondered what that was for. Perhaps Lola's husband had an interesting way of doing business. He'd have to be careful of that. In the corner there was a hefty safe. He wondered if Nell's money was currently residing inside it.

One thing about it though, a funny feeling in his stomach made him think that this part of the building didn't look as if it had been completely abandoned. Perhaps Lola Cody would be back here.

In the meantime, he could at least do something to stall their efforts, to help prevent this happening to others. He took up the baseball bat, which weighed heavily in his hand, then he went back through to the studio.

After a few practice swings, he smashed the potted palms, then he took out the fake French doors and punched a hole in the sunshine mural. Everything else that stood in his path in this phony set up bought it. He splintered it all into a thousand little pieces. Olly stood there breathing heavily, bat still clutched in his hand. Thanks to him, at least no more fraudulent DVDs would be made in this studio. It may not be sophisticated, it certainly wasn't legal, but it did feel very good.

Chapter 76

I've just collected Petal from nursery and she's now sitting at the table eating a sandwich and chatting about her day. I'm trying to concentrate on what she's saying, but my mind keeps drifting. All I can think of is Olly and where he might be. I'm forcing myself not to constantly ring his mobile as it's clear that he's not interested in talking to me for whatever reason. I thought that he would have called to speak to Petal by now. It must be killing him to be apart from her, if not from me.

I flick on the television and find some cartoons for Petal to watch when she's finished eating. Is this how life will be from now on? Just the two of us together? I never imagined it this way. I'm aware that I'm still going through the motions of being a mother, but I have to force myself to click back into real-life mode soon as I can't go on like this.

As I'm clearing away Petal's plate, there's a knock on the door. I'm not expecting anyone and, for a moment, my heart stops beating. Is every unexpected telephone call or ring on the doorbell going to strike dread into me?

I trail down the stairs and open it. Standing there is Jenny.

'Hi,' she says. Her voice wobbles. 'Can I come in?'

For a moment, I consider saying no. I'm not sure that I want to deal with whatever it is she might have to say.

'I don't know where Olly is,' she tells me flatly. 'Constance said you thought he might be with me. But he's not.'

Standing aside, I say, 'You'd better come up.'

Jen trips up the stairs and into the living room and I trudge behind.

Instantly, Petal is out of her seat and rushing across to her. 'Auntie Jenny!' she cries and my daughter is lifted high in the air.

'Hey,' Jen says, crushing Petal against her. 'How's my big girl? I've missed you.'

'I've missed you too. I'm going to watch cartoons,' Petal tells her. 'Want to watch them with me?'

Jen glances at me. 'Mummy and I need to have a little talk, then I'll watch cartoons.' She waits for my reaction, but I don't think I give her one as she adds, 'Maybe.'

Putting Petal down, she walks over to the table and takes a seat. When my daughter is out of earshot and safely ensconced in front of *Shaun the Sheep*, she says, 'Have you heard from him?'

As I don't know how else to handle this, I sit down opposite her. 'Not a thing.'

'He didn't tell me anything, Nell. No matter what you believe. I had no idea that he was thinking of leaving.'

'Neither did I.'

'He'll be back,' Jenny assures me. 'Wherever he is, he won't stay away.'

'How can you be so sure?'

'Olly loves you,' she says. 'He *adores* you. Petal is his life.'

I trail my finger through the crumbs on the table. There seem to be a lot of them. Did I give Petal her tea yet? I'm sure I did. 'I thought you wanted my life.'

Jen takes a deep breath. 'I did,' she admits. 'I'm jealous of you, Nell. Jealous as fuck. You have a perfect husband, perfect daughter; you're doing exciting things, making something of yourself. I wanted that too.'

'And now?'

'Now, I just want to be your friend again.' Jen sighs. 'I'm no threat to you or your family, Nell. I'm just a sad, desperate, lonely cow. I've no bloke, no kid of my own, no career, no plan. I'm just stuck at the chippy and probably will be for ever.'

'My perfect husband isn't here now,' I point out and I'm not sure that even I would class Petal as a 'perfect' daughter. But she's mine and I love her more than anything else in the world and I don't want anyone else taking her away from me.

'But he'll be back,' she reiterates. 'It might be today. It might be tomorrow. It might be next week. But we need to get you back on track by then, Nell. Don't let him come home to this.' Her voice trails away and her gaze travels round the room. 'It's a bit messy.'

Is it?

Now I look round too. A proper look. There are dishes piled high in the sink, clothes everywhere. When did this happen?

'When did you last spruce yourself up?'

I try to think, but nothing comes. It might have been in Paris or was it my wedding day? 'I don't know.' And that makes me want to cry.

'Why don't you go and have a lovely long bath? It'll cheer you up no end. I'll keep an eye on Petal while I have a bit of a tidy up in here.'

That makes me want to cry more. 'You'd do that for me?'

'That's what friends are for, Nell.' Jen gets up and comes round the table to give me a hug. 'You've just had some bad knocks, love. We'll all help to get you sorted. There's no need to struggle on by yourself.'

Tears splash onto the table and I think they're mine. 'I'd like that bath.'

'You go on, then. Leave everything to me.'

In the mirror, a haggard-looking woman with dark circles round her eyes stares back at me. She has the hair of a harridan. I'm quite taken aback when I realise that it's me. No wonder the other mothers in the playground gaped at me. I look terrible. Truly terrible. No wonder Olly has cleared off. I would have done the same in his situation.

Snivelling, I run myself a bath and sink into it. While I lay there, eyes closed, letting the water soothe me, I can hear Jen clinking the dishes, running the hoover round, all the time keeping up a stream of chatter with Petal.

Whatever she and Olly have done – and I don't think that I want to know – she's trying to be a good friend to me now and I'm so grateful for that. My copy book isn't blotless, let's face it; I have kissed Tod. I had lustful thoughts about Yves

Simoneaux. There are little dark spots on my soul. Sometimes, in the heat of the moment, the right opportunity presents itself and it's so hard to resist. We're only human, after all.

I wonder will I feel so philosophical about things if it turns out that Olly has run off with some nubile, nineteen-year-old. But, if he hasn't done that, what exactly *is* he doing? Why doesn't he just come home?

Getting out of the bath, I dry my hair and put on some make-up, then I find my favourite pink cardigan and cream vintage dress that I love and get dressed. I risk facing the mirror again and, this time, a human being stares back at me. Quite a hot one. I smile and, suddenly, I look even better. The smile might not reach my heart, but pinning it on my lips makes my spirit lift.

In the living room, Jenny is plumping my cushions. 'Wow,' she says when I walk in. 'Someone's scrubbed up well.'

'Thanks.' My lounge now looks like something out of *House & Home*. The dishes that were piling up in the sink have all been washed, dried and put away. Petal's toys are all tidy. The clothes that were gracing the floor and the sofa have disappeared. 'You've done a great job here too.'

Jen shrugs. 'It's the least I can do.' She straightens up and rubs her back. 'Feeling a bit better?'

'Yes.' I'm still not exactly ready to sing from the rooftops, but I don't feel quite as bleak as I did earlier. I can manage, I think. With the help of my friends, I can get through this.

Chapter 77

Olly sat outside the office of Home Mall for the rest of the day. It was only when night started to fall that he realised this wasn't the neighbourhood he should be hanging around in after dark in a hire car. Besides, no one had been back here all day and it was doubtful whether they'd turn up at night.

Jet-lag was now catching up with him and he was in danger of falling asleep in the car if he didn't move. A rap against the passenger window made him jump. His head spun round. Standing there was a young woman, a girl, dressed in something that looked like it might have come from the local sex shop.

'Hey, honey,' she said.

Olly groaned inside. He should have known that once dusk descended he'd be a sitting duck for the ladies of the night. At least the windows were up and the doors locked.

'Want to taste some sugar?'

He wasn't entirely sure what that meant, but he knew he didn't want to.

'Just leaving, miss,' he said. She was maybe only seventeen or eighteen. Her face was hard but he could tell that she had once been pretty. He wondered how long she'd been doing this.

'Aw, don't go.' He noticed that she weaved a little more than was necessary. 'Stay a while.'

'Sorry.' He held up his hand and then fired the ignition.

'Another time?'

'No, thank you,' he answered politely.

'Fuck you,' she said, sweetness suddenly disappearing. Her fist banged against the window.

Heart pounding, he pulled forward and then swung the car round. She was still shouting abuse at him as he drove away. Tomorrow he would leave the area a little earlier. All he wanted to do was find the Codys, not wind up in a body bag somewhere or in the boot of his own rental car.

Olly had booked a motel on his mobile earlier that afternoon and he now went in search of his bed for the night.

Just off the Palmetto Expressway was the Eezee Motel. It had cost him the princely sum of forty-four dollars a night including taxes. As he swung into the forecourt, he could see why.

A burly, bored desk clerk with one eye and a livid scar down one side of his face checked him in and handed over a key. Olly drove down the car park and pulled up outside his room door, which was right on the pavement. Not the best for security. It was a double-storey building notable only for its total lack of charm. There was a tiny swimming pool, also in the car park, but the water was an interesting shade of green.

It was the sort of place that any self-respecting serial killer would feel right at home in.

Inside the room things didn't improve much. It looked like it had last been decorated in the 1980s and that was also possibly the last time it had been cleaned. On the carpet there was a stain that could well have been blood. There was a king-size bed with a rough brown cover and a bedside table that may once have been varnished. In the bathroom, the shower was straight out of *Psycho*. With the sole aim of keeping costs down, this cockroach-ridden dump was to be his home for the next few days. Hopefully, he could do what he'd come to do quickly and get home to Nell and Petal just as soon as he could.

Throwing down his bag, somewhat reluctantly, Olly lay on the bed. His stomach rumbled and he remembered that he hadn't eaten since he'd arrived. There was no way he was going to go out again tonight. This was the sort of neighbourhood where they took pot shots at tourists just for fun. Hunger was the least of his worries. Now he just needed to sleep, for tomorrow he had to stay sharp. He wished that he could call Nell, just hear the sound of her voice. But, if he talked to her, his resolve might well crack and he needed to stay focused on the task in hand. Instead, he flicked through the photos of his wife and his daughter on his mobile phone and went to sleep with them close to his heart.

The next morning, he risked the *Psycho* shower and, thankfully, didn't get stabbed through the curtain. He didn't get any hot water either, but he didn't fancy complaining to the desk clerk who looked like he might want to rip his head off given half the chance.

Back in the beige Chevrolet and he headed once more towards Opaville and the offices of Home Mall. On the way, he pulled in at a scruffy burger outlet and bought a breakfast treat of synthetic bun, plastic egg and dubious hamburger. But at least it was food. It didn't taste of anything but it filled a hole and he did briefly consider eating the paper bag it had arrived in for extra calories. He would have hardly noticed the difference. The coffee he washed it down with could easily have been used as paint stripper.

Fortified – in a manner of speaking – Olly made his way to his stakeout point.

When he arrived, the two mechanics that he'd seen yesterday were still working in front of the beaten up garage on a beaten up car, albeit a different one this time. This one looked like it had bullet holes all down the side. He felt an unwelcome gulp travel down his throat. Olly held up a hand and waved in a cheery manner. Both of the mechanics glared at him and, heads down, returned to their work.

Surely it wouldn't hurt to ask them if they knew anything about the owners of Home Mall. What choice did he have? There was no one else to ask anything round here.

Reluctant to leave the air-conditioned car, he stepped into the alley and walked across to them. In for a penny, in for a pound.

As he approached, both of the mechanics looked up. He noticed that one picked up a monkey wrench and gripped it tightly. Not necessarily a good sign.

'Hello, guys,' he said, his English accent morphing into Julie Andrews' territory. 'Just wanted to ask a question.'

They didn't look impressed by that idea either. They both wore ripped sweats, grimy wifebeater vests and bandanas. They were both as wide as they were high. Each sported tattooed sleeves. It looked like they worked out. A lot.

'The offices over there' – Olly, as casually as he could, flicked a thumb backwards – 'does anyone ever come and go?'

'Depends who's asking.' The man holding the monkey wrench stood and squared up to him.

Olly's heart pumped erratically. But at least it was still pumping.

'My name's Olly Meyers. I'm here from England,' he said, perhaps unnecessarily. 'The guys who own this place took me and my family for over thirty thousand dollars.'

Now he had their attention. The other man, still crouched by the wing of the car he was working on, whistled low through his teeth. '*Thirty thousand*? That's a lotta dough, man.'

'All the money we had.' And more. 'They cleaned us out completely. I'm here to get it back.'

The man moved the toothpick he was chewing to the other side of his mouth. 'You're one brave mother to hang round here.'

'I have no choice,' Olly said. 'I've spent a lot of money and have come a long way to make this wrong right.'

They both nodded at that.

'I'm Diego,' the beefier of the two said. Obviously, the owner of the place. 'This is Andrés.' He glanced up at his friend and gave a barely perceptible nod.

Though he was the smaller of the two – it was a relative

term – Olly was relieved to see Andrés relax his grip on the wrench.

'There's a big, fat safe in there,' Olly said, nodding towards the shabby offices. 'I'd certainly like to take a look inside it.'

Diego raised his eyebrows at that. 'A safe?' He pursed his lips, chewed it over in his mind as he chewed on his toothpick. 'Sometimes someone comes along, opens up,' the man continued. He stood up and leaned on the bonnet, hood, of the car. 'Maybe two, three times a week. They don't stay round long.'

'You don't know who they are?'

'This ain't the hood to be asking questions in, bro.'

'I don't know what else to do.'

'They haven't been in a day or so. Maybe you'll get lucky today.'

Unless the Codys had already scarpered with their ill-gotten gains.

But what else was he to do? Any phone numbers that he'd found on the internet were all now dead. 'That's my only plan,' Olly admitted.

The mechanics exchanged another glance. 'I'll ask some of the guys,' Diego said. 'See what we can find out.'

'Thanks,' he said gratefully. 'I'd really appreciate that.

Diego smiled. One of his front teeth was gold. 'I like that you "appreciate" it.'

Were they laughing at him or were they really planning to help? How would he know? They could think he was some naive jerk fresh off the boat and way out of his depth. Quite probably, they were right. Still, there was nothing more he could do.

'Thanks again,' Olly said. He didn't want to push his luck too much. 'I'll leave you in peace.'

'I'd like to take a trip to England,' Andrés said. 'See Buckingham Palace and shit.'

'It's nice,' Olly said. 'You'd like it. If you ever come over you should contact me.' He would probably run a mile if they did.

They both turned back to their work, conversation closed.

He left well alone and went back to his hire car. Settling himself outside the offices, he hoped that Lola Cody or someone, anyone, would turn up and answer some questions for him. He wished he'd bought a newspaper or a book to read. It was going to be a long, hot day. The temperature was already climbing high and it would probably hit ninety or more before it was done. How did anyone survive summers like this? Give him good old temperamental English weather any day of the week. Switching on the radio, Olly fiddled with the buttons until he eventually found a station that wasn't hip hop. *Miami Beach FM* kicked out easy listening tunes.

Olly risked winding down the window, but the air outside was hotter and more sticky than it had been in the car. He felt like he was in *The Wire* or *The Sopranos* or some other gritty, late-night American cop drama. But this was real life and the future of his family was at stake.

Then The Beach Boys came on the radio. 'California Girls' pumped out and, for a few minutes, he pretended that he was in Miami on holiday, kicked back, and just enjoyed the tune. There'd be time enough for trouble later.

Chapter 78

Jen stays over. She sleeps in Petal's single bed while my knobbly-kneed daughter and I curl up together in mine.

'When does Daddy come back?' Petal demands. 'He keeps me warmer than you.'

'Soon,' I say. 'He'll be back very soon.'

The bed just seems so empty without Olly in it. I lie there awake while my child wriggles incessantly and I wonder where he is. Where is he sleeping? Is he sleeping alone? Maybe he wants to come home but can't get back. Perhaps he's hurt? Is someone holding him against his will?

Then I remember that he's taken his Vespa with him and has gone off on his own accord. His treasured record collection is still here, so I'm assuming he'll be back for that at the very least.

Despite the fact that my husband's not here, I manage to grab a few hours of sleep and I feel significantly better when I wake the next morning. Petal's nowhere in sight, but I can hear her voice coming from the kitchen. I check my phone but there's no message, no text from Olly. Nothing.

When I pad through, Jen is already up and about. She's in my dressing gown, so I'm wearing Olly's and the scent of it threatens to make me feel sad again. I wrap it round me tightly. Petal is sitting expectantly at the table and there's porridge on the go. Last night Jen rustled up dinner for us out of nothing.

'Morning,' I say with a stifled yawn. 'Good grief, you're organised.'

'You need to eat something.'

I don't tell her that eating in the morning is now beyond my limited capabilities.

'Sleep well?' my friend asks.

'Not too bad. How did you fare on the sofa?'

'It was fine,' she says. 'I can stay here until Olly comes back. If you want.'

Does she sense my hesitation? as she adds, 'You could do with an extra pair of hands, Nell.'

I think she just wants to keep an eye on me and, you know, I rather like the sound of someone keeping an eye on me.

'OK. That's very kind of you.'

'Want me to walk Petal to nursery? Then I'll go home and get some stuff?'

'Why don't we walk Petal to the nursery together? I could do with the fresh air.' To be honest, I still feel too shaky to face the mothers of the playground by myself again. 'We can take Dude.'

I think even the dog has been pining for Olly as he's been off his food like me.

'Yay! Yay! Yay!' That's Petal. Dude wags his tail enthusiastically. If only humans could be so easily pleased.

'Cool,' Jen says.

We all fight for the bathroom and, eventually, we're all dressed and head out together. We drop Petal off at nursery and then Jen and I walk back into town. She links her arm through mine and the simple contact soothes my frayed nerves.

'I'll see you later,' Jen says when we reach the place where we need to part ways. 'If you need me, just text me.'

'I'm fine. Really.' Then, 'You've been great, Jen. Thanks.'

'No worries.' She hugs me and I feel small against her. 'I'm just glad that we're mates again. Laters.'

I watch her walk away, before I say, 'Come on, Dude.'

Turning down Market Place, the dog and I walk back towards home. On our way we pass Betty the Bag Lady. No more lingering to look in the window for me. Instead, I cast a furtive glance to see what's displayed in the window. Betty still texts me regularly asking me to call her, but I have never done so.

The window, as always, looks stunning. I feel so sad that we couldn't have remained friends. It would be nice to feel that I had an ally in the business and didn't seem to just constantly accumulate enemies. Still, it wasn't to be. I quicken my pace and, as I do so, the shop door swings open. Coming out is Betty. I don't know who's more shocked – me or her. We both stop dead in our tracks.

Betty is the first to speak. 'Nell,' she says.

'Hi.'

Her face breaks into a smile. 'Good to see you.'

'Oh.' Is it? 'Good to see you, too.'

'I've been trying to contact you for ages.'

'I know.' Now I feel shifty. I study the pavement. 'I'm sorry I've not returned your calls. I've been so busy.'

'I know! It's amazing.'

I shrug. 'It was all after Chantelle Clarke appeared on the television with one of my bags. Everything went crazy.'

'I was so pleased to see that.'

'A big PR agency in London organised it for me.'

Betty looks taken aback by that. Is it so pathetic of me to want to brag about it? I feel that it is. I've no need to.

'That was me,' Betty says softly. 'Chantelle is a friend of mine. I passed on the handbag you gave me.'

Now it's my turn to be taken aback. 'It was you?'

'Yes.'

'I ... I ... didn't know.' I was aware that Betty had some celebrity friends, but I had absolutely no idea Chantelle Clarke was among them.

'That's why I was trying to call you. She desperately wanted another design. She adores your handbags.'

'I'm sorry,' I say. 'I didn't know.'

Now she looks at me closely. 'Is everything OK with you, Nell?' I realise that Betty looks her usual immaculate self and that I quite probably don't.

'I'm fine,' I lie. 'Everything's fine. Couldn't be better.'

'I'd love to put in an order,' Betty says. 'Everyone's been asking for your handbags in my shop.'

'They have?'

'Yes. Of course. They're great.'

'I thought you didn't like them.'

'Really? Why would you think that? I loved them. If I'm honest, I just couldn't believe you'd created them without saying a word to me. I was just stunned. You've such a talent. I thought of Chantelle straight away.'

'Oh.' How could I have read this all so wrong?

'You weren't mad at me for doing that, were you? I did worry that I'd offended you somehow.'

'No, no,' I stammer. 'I just didn't realise it was you.'

'Thank goodness,' she says. 'I thought we'd fallen out!' Betty glances at her watch. 'I just have to shoot out, Nell, but now that we've made contact again, I'd love to stock the bags. Would you let me?'

That is music to my ears. Not that it's going to get us out of our current mess, but at least it shows that someone has some faith in me.

'Yes. God, yes.' I'll give her the biggest discount I possibly can.

'I'll call you later,' she says. 'Promise me this time you'll return it.'

'I will,' I say sincerely. 'Of course I will. And thanks.'

'No worries,' Betty says. She touches my arm tentatively. 'Lovely to see you again, Nell.' Her concerned gaze roves over me. 'Take care of yourself. Don't work too hard. I'll catch you later.'

She waves at me and I watch, dumbfounded, as she trips off down the street.

What can I do to make it right with Betty? What can I possibly do to thank her? I have been holding a grudge against her completely without foundation. She could have thought

I'd turned into some stuck-up bitch who believed herself to be too good to return her calls. Who could have blamed her? I haven't behaved well towards her. I have blanked this woman thinking that she'd spurned me, when all along it was her who orchestrated my big break.

So much for Della Jewel. Looks like I did send flowers to the wrong bloody woman after all.

Chapter 79

In a daze of confusion, I wander back to my own shop. Outside, I stand and stare at the window. Even though I say it myself, the display looks so appealing. It still doesn't seem possible that my name is above the door. I sigh sadly. Pretty soon it may not be. I may be very grateful for Betty's order.

I don't even know if we've got enough money in the bank account to cover this month's rent and I can't bring myself to look. I don't even know if we have money for food, and we can't eat naffing handbags.

I let myself in, make a coffee and then go and sit in the office. Now that I'm alone, I try Olly's number, but there's no reply. He must still have his voicemail turned off.

What should I do? I stare at the computer and the pile of post that's mounting up on my desk. The letters all look like they're bills and I know that I don't have the means to pay any of them. I could do some sketches, think of some new designs, but what's the point? I don't even know if I'll have a business beyond the next few weeks. I could be dependent on a few bags in Betty's window rather than my own. I could be back on the market stall. I could be back in the chip shop.

Sipping my coffee, I shuffle papers aimlessly. The doorbell chimes and I look up, heart in mouth.

But it's not Olly. It's Phil.

'All right, love?' he says.

I nod. 'Bearing up.'

'We were worried. Constance and me.' He holds out a big, round tin. When I look inside, there's some sort of pie topped with golden puff pastry. 'Chicken and mushroom. She baked it for you, so that you'd have something in for your tea.'

'She's an angel. Tell her thanks.'

'She was worried, love. You didn't look like yourself at all yesterday.'

'Jen's been here,' I tell him. 'She's been a diamond.'

'I know. She said she was coming round. Wasn't sure how you'd feel about that. All things considered.'

'I'm fine. *We're* fine. She's coming to stay with me for a couple of days.' I'm just hoping that, by then, Olly will have made contact. 'Time for a coffee?'

'No thanks, Nell.' Phil pulls up a seat and lowers himself into it. 'I wanted to see how you are,' he says, 'but I also wanted to talk business with you.'

'I'm not turning out to be the greatest businesswoman of all time, am I?'

'It's a steep learning curve,' Phil admits, 'and you've had more than your fair share of bad luck.'

Is it just bad luck or am I guilty of being too naive, too gullible?

'I want to lend you the money, Nell,' he says. 'I can get my hands on twenty grand. Is that enough to get you out of this hole?'

Shaking my head, I say, 'I can't take that from you, Phil. We already owe you enough.'

'I'm not bothered about that, love. You know that.' He shifts uncomfortably in his chair and I think how much I love this man. He's been so good to me. Like a father. If Olly never comes home I am truly blessed by the other people I have in my life. 'It's just that I feel responsible for encouraging you to go out on your own. It's a big step and maybe I pushed you too much.'

'Oh, Phil Preston. Don't even think that. None of this is down to you.'

'I don't want to see you go under. Not when I can help.'

'The truth of the matter is that I don't know if I'm going to carry on, Phil.'

He recoils in shock. 'But you must. You can't give up so easily, Nell. You never know what's just round the corner. Something big could be on the horizon.'

Or there could be someone else out there waiting to rip me off, rob me of my hard-earned cash, undermine my family, and destroy my self-confidence. I sigh to myself.

'Don't give up, Nell. Promise me that. At least don't do anything until you've heard from Olly.'

'I promise.' What if he doesn't come back for weeks? Months? Or not at all? I don't voice my misgivings.

'Better go,' he says.

'At least your business is thriving.'

376

'Couldn't be better, Nell. Don't think that I've forgotten the role you played in turning it around.'

'I slapped a bit of paint about, Phil.'

'You gave it a new lease of life. And me.'

Standing up, I kiss him. 'You're a lovely man.'

'You've got a good one too, Nell. Whatever's going on in Olly's mind at the moment, don't forget that he's a good man.'

'I won't.' I walk Phil to the door and he gives me a peck on the cheek. 'Catch you later. Thank Constance for my dinner.'

He winks at me. 'I've got a good one there, too. I'm not going to let her go easily.'

'Too right,' I say. 'I'm hoping I'll be coming to *your* wedding one day soon.'

'You never know, Nell,' he replies. 'You never know.'

That, at least, puts a smile on my face. It would be lovely if Phil and Constance could find happiness together. Doesn't that prove that, despite everything, I'm still an old romantic at heart?

Then, as I lift the tin with my home-baked chicken and mushroom pie inside it from my desk to take it safely upstairs, my phone beeps. I have a text message.

It's from Olly.

Miss u, it says.

All I type is, Come home.

Chapter 80

Olly had cracked and had texted Nell. He just needed something to connect him to home as he felt as his life had turned into a bad movie, and reality was something that was steadily slipping away.

Now three days had passed and Nell had continued to text him regularly. He'd kept all the messages stored and read them over and over, but hadn't replied. He wondered what she'd say to him when he eventually did go home. It depended on what happened next, he assumed.

For three whole days he'd done nothing but sit outside the run-down offices of Home Mall. For three whole days nothing at all had occurred. For three long, hot, sweaty, sweltering, Miami days, he'd stewed in his rental car, eyes fixed on the door ahead of him. He'd talked everyday to Diego and Andrés who'd certainly become less wary of him, if not exactly friendly. But, so far, they'd been unable to find out anything more about the Codys than he already knew.

Olly had taken to bringing sandwiches, fruit and soft drinks to keep him going through the day. But they were all warm and wilting long before noon. An ice-cold beer featured heavily in his daydreams. At night he returned to the serial killer motel and, when his wide-eyed wakefulness finally gave way to sleep, it was punctuated by nightmares about their home being repossessed and him fighting big dragons or snakes, or him running through forests that snatched at his clothes with Petal clutched tightly to his chest. It was fair to say that none of it was leaving him feeling rested.

This morning, he'd been sitting there for three hours already. His shirt was melted to him and perspiration ran down his face. His hair was stuck flat to his forehead. He wondered just how much more of this he could take. Frustration was building up inside of him. This was necessary, absolutely necessary, but it felt so futile too. Before he thought he might give in to screaming hysteria, he got out and walked further down the alley to calm his nerves.

'Hey, buddy,' Diego called out to him. 'Wanna cold soda?'

'Please,' Olly said. 'That's very kind of you.'

Diego and Andrés exchanged a laugh. '"Very kind".'

From somewhere in the back of the garage, Diego produced an ice-cold Dr Pepper. Olly snapped the can opened and gulped at it gratefully.

'My God, that's good.'

'Hot work waiting there every day?'

'Yes.'

'How long you meaning to sit it out, man?'

'Not much longer,' Olly said. 'I'll have to go home soon. I just didn't want to go without my money.'

'That'd be a tough break.'

Perhaps neither of them realised quite how tough it would be.

'I'm missing my little girl.' Olly's voice cracked. 'I just want to get back to her. She'll be wondering where her daddy is.'

'You have a girl?' Diego said. From his back pocket he produced a creased and grimy photograph of a pretty Latino girl with long black hair. 'I have a baby girl, too. She's called Sophia.'

Olly reached for his wallet and produced his much loved picture of Petal. 'This is Petal. She's four.'

'Same age as Sophia. She's daddy's angel. Your kid is a very beautiful little lady.'

'I know,' Olly said proudly. 'Just like her mother.'

The men exchanged a grin.

'Sophia's mother is a bitch. Left me for another man.'

'Oh,' Olly said. 'I'm sorry to hear that.'

Diego shrugged. 'Sophia is my life. Best thing that ever happened to me.' He put the photo away. 'I don't often get to see her. One day I'll make enough money to take her away from here.' He glanced ruefully at his ramshackle garage. 'We'll go somewhere real nice.'

'Petal's my life, too. I'm doing all this for her,' Olly admitted. With one last look, he also put his picture away. 'That's why I need to get our money back. I don't want those bastards stealing her future.'

'You're right, my friend. Family is everything. We must never forget that.'

It was a lesson that Olly felt he'd already learned. All he

wanted now was to get on a plane and fly back to his wife, his child, to his old, safe life.

Diego clapped him on the back. 'Now I must work.'

'Thanks.' Olly crushed his empty can and threw it in the nearby rubbish bin. 'I'll catch you later.'

Diego held up a hand in farewell.

Olly walked back to his car and slid inside the baking tin again. Another long wait stretched ahead of him. He listened to the radio. He read about all the shootings in the local paper. It was as hot as hell in here. Despite himself, his eyes grew heavy. Eventually, he let his head sink back against his seat. On top of everything else, the bed in the Miami branch of the Bates Motel was lumpy and he could feel springs poking in his back. He didn't like to think who'd slept in it before him.

Chapter 81

He hadn't realised that he'd fallen asleep until he heard the purring of the engine of another vehicle slowly coming up the alley behind him. Olly blinked his eyes open as a Mercedes sports car passed by his parked car. It wasn't a shiny, new Merc. It was sort of battered and creaking. Suddenly he was wide awake. He had a feeling in his gut about this and his insides turned to water.

The car pulled up at the side of the Home Mall offices and his heart started to race. His palms, already sweating in the heat, grew slick with sweat.

Someone clambered out of the passenger seat of the car. The bulky frame, the moon-face; they were familiar to him now. This was, indeed, the woman he knew from the newspapers as Lola Cody.

He watched, eyes narrowed, as she waddled to the door of Home Mall. She wore white crops, a voluminous floral smock, flip flops and, of all the cheek, had one of Nell's handbags over her shoulder. Probably the original sample that Nell sent her after the initial contact. That racked up Olly's rage quota another notch. He watched while she unlocked the shutter and waited as it slowly rolled up.

A moment later and her husband and partner in crime, Benito Cody, joined her. His bad Hawaiian shirt was barely buttoned across the ample circumference of his stomach. Clashing shorts in what must have been XXXL size skimmed his knees. Neither of them looked like they'd stinted on the pizza and burgers. He could take on these two. No trouble.

They both heaved their lumbering bodies into the office. A second later, and before he had time to think better of it, Olly was out of the car and following them. The door was just about to swing closed when he stuck his foot in it. Lola Cody and her husband had entered the front office just ahead of him. He pushed inside and quietly dropped in behind them.

'Hello,' he said before they had a chance to get settled.

Both of them spun round, open-mouthed with shock.

Olly stared at them. They didn't look like slick con artists; they looked like greasy no-hopers and he wondered how they'd managed to trick so many people. He felt stupid that he and Nell had believed their tissue of lies and had been taken in by them. If only they'd thought to come out and meet them, see their operation, before they agreed to part with any cash, then they would have seen them for what they were. Still, there was no time for what-ifs now. He was here and he wanted his money back and wouldn't be going anywhere until he got it.

'There's nothing here,' Lola Cody said. Her voice was loud, brassy, and she was chewing gum. 'We have nothing.'

Clearly, they thought they were about to be robbed. In some ways, they were.

'I think you do,' Olly said. 'In fact, you have something that's mine.'

The couple backed away into the corner of the room, up against one of the dented filing cabinets that lined it.

'We don't know who you are, man,' her husband whined.

'The name Nell McNamara mean anything to you?'

Their mouths dropped a little wider.

'I've come to get our money back.'

'We don't have it,' Lola said, but her eyes travelled shiftily to the safe tucked away in the corner.

Just as he'd hoped. It looked like their cash was kept here.

'Open the safe,' Olly snapped. 'I want our money back and I won't leave until I've got it.'

Lola's husband lurched across the room, his bloated bulk swayed and wobbled and Olly knew instantly what he was targeting.

From behind his back, Olly produced the baseball bat that had previously lived there. He was glad now that he'd decided to take it and keep it in his car as a precaution, as insurance. 'This what you're looking for?'

Benito Cody blanched.

Olly casually tapped the baseball bat against his palm. 'Now perhaps you'll talk sensibly to me.' Lola Cody was rooted to the spot. 'Open the safe. Get out my money. All of it. Thirty thousand dollars. When you've done that, I'll leave you in peace.'

Neither Lola nor her husband moved.

Olly slammed the baseball bat down on top of the desk. The wood splintered.

'Do it!' he shouted. 'My patience is wearing very thin.'

The Codys both jumped and cowered away from him.

Olly shocked even himself. He did the baseball bat thing because that's what he'd seen happen in the movies. The worrying fact was that, as adrenalin coursed through him, he realised that he wanted Nell's money back more than anything in the world and nothing, and certainly not these two fat, badly dressed crooks, would stop him. He had no idea that, inside, he was quite so scary. He wondered if he should adopt an outlandish karate stance but was afraid that it was a step too far, particularly when he was so rusty.

'OK, OK,' Lola Cody said. She sighed and, cursing under her breath, waddled towards the safe.

'You,' he said to her husband, 'hands in the air where I can see them.'

With a gargantuan effort, Lola bent down and knelt before the heavy metal door. Huffing and puffing, she turned the dial, this way and that. A moment later the safe sprang open.

Now it was Olly's turn to stare, open-mouthed. The safe was stuffed full of money. Piles and piles of dollars bundled together spilled out. There must be hundreds of thousands in there. All in readys. His eyes bulged as he tried to take it all in. Clearly in Lola Cody's world, crime *did* pay. And really rather well, it seemed.

'Thirty thousand dollars,' Olly said. 'That's what you owe me. Count it out.'

At a ponderous pace, Lola Cody pulled the bundles from

the safe and let them fall to the floor. Olly now wished that he'd thought to bring his holdall with him. He hadn't realised quite how big thirty thousand dollars was in cash. There was an empty cardboard box on the floor and he kicked it towards her.

'In there,' he instructed. 'Quickly.'

The woman pulled the box to her side.

'Count it out,' Olly barked.

'One thousand, two thousand, three thousand,' she spat out as she placed the money into it. Her husband, hands aloft, watched her unmoving. It looked like Lola Cody was the brains behind the operation. He was just a useless pile of lard.

'Faster,' Olly said. 'I haven't got all day.'

The speed picked up a bit. The minute the box was filled, he was going straight to the motel to collect his stuff, and then his next port of call would be Miami International Airport and back home on the first flight he could get.

'Put an extra three thousand in there,' he instructed. 'That'll cover the expenses I've incurred having to come out here and collect it.'

Lola Cody curled her lip at that but silently complied. It made him feel better to think that she'd be picking up the bill for the skanky motel. If he'd been certain of the outcome, he might well have stayed somewhere nicer.

Eventually, the box was full of money.

'Done,' she said flatly.

'It had better all be there,' Olly said. 'The minute I leave, I'll be counting it and you don't want me to come back.'

'It's all there,' Lola Cody said. 'Now get out.'

Still sparky.

Olly wanted to hurt them, to make them pay for all the pain that they'd put him and Nell through, but that would just reduce him to their level. Getting their cash back would be enough.

'This is justice,' he said. 'If it was my call, you'd be going to jail. For a long time. Be thankful that I'm only taking back what's rightfully mine.'

With that, he picked up the cardboard box. Thirty thousand dollars was quite a heavy load, but it felt good to have it in his arms at last. He'd keep the baseball bat for the moment. Just in case.

'You're finished,' he said to Lola Cody. Whereas he felt like a phoenix rising from the ashes.

He backed out of the office and into the Miami sunshine.

Chapter 82

Olly walked briskly across to his car, conscious that he had a cardboard box overflowing with bundles of cash. His heartbeat was starting to return to a more normal pace. So far, so good.

'Hey, buddy!' Diego shouted across to him. 'Get what you came for?'

'Yes! Thank you!' he called back. Olly could only hope that they now didn't decide to mug him for his thirty grand. But Diego seemed like a solid bloke.

Sure enough, both he and Andrés simply waved to him and appeared to be staying where they were. If he'd had a hand free, Olly would have waved back.

'Look after that little girl of yours,' Diego called.

'I will do!'

Opening the boot, Olly tossed the baseball bat inside. He sighed with relief, glad that he hadn't had to use that. When all was said and done, he wasn't one for violence. Lola Cody might not feel quite the same, but he was pleased that this had been handled swiftly and smoothly. It had, in the grand scheme of things, been quite a painless operation. Like taking candy from a baby. He had got what he'd come for. Olly allowed himself a smile. Wait until he told Nell. She'd be beside herself with joy. He took one last look at the money he'd just recovered, *their* money, then he started to lower in the box.

As he did, the door of the Home Mall offices burst open and Benito and Lola Cody launched themselves out of it. They barrelled over to where he was and both pounced on him. The cardboard box fell on the ground and the bundles of money spilled out into the dust.

Benito Cody grabbed his arms, while Lola Cody pulled his hair and clawed at his face with her manicured nails. It was like wrestling with two vast marshmallow mountains. Within minutes, they'd pulled him to the ground and Lola Cody sat on him. His breath was squashed out of him instantly.

While she had Olly pinned to the floor, her husband scrabbled on the ground to retrieve the money. This was all going horribly wrong and he could see Nell's money slipping away from him.

'Help,' Olly gasped out. 'Help me.' He didn't want to die in a dirty Miami alley being squashed by an extraordinarily fat woman. That wasn't how it was supposed to end.

Then he heard the pounding of feet heading his way and Diego and Andrés appeared at the back of the car. They both grabbed Lola Cody and hauled her to her feet. Olly breathed again, gasping at the hot air. She was shrieking like a banshee and struggling against the grip of the strong mechanics.

As his lungs were working again, Olly jumped to his feet and went to tackle the husband. Benito barged into him with his huge bulk and sent Olly flying. He was tempted to grab the baseball bat again from the car boot but, that way, danger lay.

Benito Cody waddled away, picking up surprising speed and dodged back into the Home Mall offices.

'Get the money and get in the car,' Diego shouted. 'We'll hang onto her.'

Olly didn't have to be told twice. 'Thanks,' he said, still panting. His chest hurt where Lola Cody had crushed his ribs. 'Thanks so much.'

He scooped the money up and dropped it back into the cardboard box and then into the boot of the car. Splitting one of the bundles, he gave Diego a wedge of money for them both. It could have been as much as five hundred dollars but, frankly, it was worth it for their help in getting out of this pickle. Who knew that these two fat felons would decide to bite back!

'Have a drink on me,' Olly said. 'I appreciate your help.'

'No need, man,' Diego replied. 'But thanks.'

Lola Cody, still restrained, spat at him.

'Nice,' Olly said.

She spat again.

'That safe in there is stuffed full of money, guys. Fill your boots!' Then, hurriedly, he slipped into the car.

'Give my love to the Queen,' Andrés said.

Olly turned the car in the alley and then started to pull away. In the rear-view mirror he could see the two guys still holding Lola Cody firmly and she seemed to be spouting venomous abuse in his direction. Well, she could shout all she liked; he now had the money safely in the boot of his car.

Then he saw that Benito Cody had reappeared from somewhere. The man was staggering towards the car, a deranged look in his eye. His arms were up, pointing forwards and, to his horror, Olly saw that Benito had a gun clasped in his hands.

Instinctively, he ducked as the shot hit the back window of the rental car and shattered it into oblivion. He felt the bullet whistle past his ear. He touched his face. There was blood on it. In shock, he slowed down.

'Go, go, go,' Diego shouted at Olly through the car window. 'Don't stop! Go! Get out of here.'

Another shot rang out and Olly flinched, but it didn't seem to connect with anything.

Andrés let go of Lola Cody and Olly saw a monkey wrench travel through the air and knock the gun spinning from the hand of her husband. It skittered across the ground and Benito lunged for it. But Andrés was way too fast for him and kicked it out of harm's reach. The mechanic was on top of Benito before Olly hit the end of the alley.

His mind whirled. Should he stop, help them? But then he wasn't really sure he wanted to know what happened next. Christ, he was out of his depth here in this mean neighbourhood. It had turned violent so quickly. He'd had no idea that Benito Cody might produce a gun. His hands were shaking as he gripped the wheel, his knuckles white.

'Go!' Diego shouted again. 'We'll take care of it.'

So that's what Olly did. He floored the accelerator of his rental car and went.

Chapter 83

I've heard nothing more from Olly since his one text message. I've tried his phone over and over again, texted him and have even thrown words out into the universe. As yet, I've heard nothing back.

Petal is at nursery. Jen, who continues to be an unfaltering support, took her there this morning. The idea was that I would have some peace and quiet in which to work. All I've done is drink coffee and stare at my screen in a trance. I can think of nothing but Olly and where he might be now. Until he comes back I am in complete limbo.

Mid-morning and the doorbell on the shop door chimes. Tod shakes the raindrops from his hair as he comes in.

'Is it raining?' I say in the way that we British do.

'Summer shower,' he says. 'It felt quite nice.'

I wonder if it's raining where Olly is. 'Come up to the flat and I'll make some coffee.'

'I don't want to disturb you.'

I sigh. 'Believe me, Tod, I'm not doing anything but staring into space.'

'Hard, eh?'

Like I couldn't have begun to imagine. Where did my previous life go when I had a happy boyfriend, a job that involved dolling out chips and smiling, and no worries? Tod probably doesn't even know that Olly has gone AWOL.

'Not working on any new designs?'

I don't like to tell him that I think my creativity has gone the same way as my money – down the pan.

'Let's take a ten-minute tea break.' Turning the closed sign on the door, I lead the way upstairs to the flat. My footsteps sound leaden. Tod wanders around the living room as I bang about with the kettle and cups. I even find the teapot.

Thanks to Jen, we have an exciting supply of biscuits, and milk, and coffee, and sugar, and even nutritious vegetables in the fridge. What would I have done without her? Petal and I could well have starved.

Putting some of the chocolate chip cookies my friend bought on a plate, I take a tray over to Tod. I sit on the sofa and he flops down next to me.

'I've texted and texted you.'

'I know. I'm sorry I didn't reply.' I sigh. 'I was in a bad place.'

'I just wanted to come round and say that I'm sorry.'

'You already apologised, Tod, and I told you then that none of this is your doing.' I pour us both tea and Tod takes a biscuit. Nursing my tea to me, I enjoy the feel of the cup burning against my hands. To feel something is better than feeling nothing.

'I still feel that I let you down,' he says. 'I should have

advised you better about the shopping channel contract. I had no idea it might be a scam.'

'Me neither,' I say.

'I think I just got caught up in the moment. I so wanted it to happen for you that maybe my normal rationalisation went out of the window.'

The same way that mine did. 'I don't blame you at all.' This is, undoubtedly, all my own fault.

'You don't know what it means to me to hear you say that, Nell.'

Who'd have thought that Tod Urban would ever need my approval?

'I thought you were blanking me out of your life.'

'No,' I say. 'I've just been having some ... troubles.'

He brightens. 'So you're happy to continue working with me? There are still things we can do to turn this round.'

I shrug. 'The way things are going, I'm not sure I'm going to be able to continue to work at all.' How do I explain to him that I care about nothing but getting Olly to come home? 'I'm thinking of asking Phil to take me back in the chip shop.'

'He won't do that,' Tod says. 'He knows how much you have to offer.'

I don't tell him that Phil has already knocked me back on that front. Nor do I tell him that he's offered me the money to pay off the bank.

'You can still do great things, Nell. Don't lose that belief in yourself.'

Do I confide that actually remembering to breathe in and out is all that I can cope with at the moment?

'Is Olly OK with it?' He purses his lips. 'I don't like to pry, but are things all right at home?'

The fact that my husband is currently absent makes me think not. I would say that pretty much shows that they're not all right at all. I can keep this all to myself and pretend that Olly and I are fine, but what would that achieve? I decide to come clean. 'Olly's not around at the moment,' I say. 'I don't know where he is.'

'But you need him here.'

'Yes, I do.' Can't argue with that assessment.

'Has he left you?'

Tears burn behind my eyes. I didn't want to get into this with Tod, but my emotions are raw, rubbed open, and I haven't the strength to hide them. Just pretending to Petal that everything is fine is taking all my energy. 'I don't know.'

He takes my hand. 'I'm sorry to hear that, Nell. I had no idea that things were so bad.'

'That makes two of us.'

'Did he give you any reason?'

I shake my head, unsure of my voice. Then, 'I haven't heard from him in days.'

'What will you do if he doesn't come back?'

'Wait.'

My mentor looks as if he doesn't think this is the best plan, but I can't think what else to do.

'If there's anything I can do to help, you must let me know.' Tod clears his throat. 'This may well be inappropriate timing, but you know that I care more about you than simply being your mentor.'

'You're right,' I say softly. 'This probably isn't the time.' At any other time, any other place, with any other woman, Tod would be one hell of a catch. But I'm not interested in anyone else but my husband.

'I wanted you to know that you're not alone in this. All you have to do is say the word and I can be here for you.'

'That's nice to know, Tod. You're very kind.'

'And you're still very much in love with Olly.'

'Yes,' I say. That just about sums it up for me.

Chapter 84

Olly drove back to the motel. Once inside, he locked the door and leaned against it, breathing heavily. The cardboard box full of money was in his hands, clasped against his chest.

Blood dripped down the side of his neck and he put the box down on the bed and went straight into the bathroom before he added to the blood-stain count already in the room.

In the mirror, the one with the dim strip light above it, he examined his wound. It looked like the bullet had just grazed his ear and it had bled profusely. He pulled some toilet paper from the holder and dampened it in the cracked sink, then used it to wipe away the blood. Once it was cleaned up, it didn't look nearly so bad. A little nick; that was all it was. But if the bullet had travelled just an inch to the left, he might not be here to tell the tale. He might never have seen Nell or Petal ever again. The very thought of it made him shaky.

He rinsed his face and dragged his fingers through his hair, hoping that it would make him look better. It didn't.

Back in the bedroom and he changed his shirt, which was soaked with perspiration and dirty with his own blood. He threw it in the bin and then he tipped the rest of his possessions out of his holdall onto the bed. Suddenly he was grateful that he wouldn't have to spend another night in this room. He was going home. He was going home to his girls. The thought nearly had him undone.

He upended the cardboard box and the money spilled out. Quickly, he counted the bundles, putting each of them into the bottom of his holdall as he did so. The money was all there, present and correct. Perhaps Diego and Andrés had gone in after they'd dealt with Lola Cody and her husband and had helped themselves to a bit of their cash – goodness only knows there was enough of it stashed in the Codys' safe for them not to miss some. Olly wouldn't have blamed them if they had. In fact, part of him hoped that was exactly what his two saviours had done. He hoped that Diego had taken enough to start a new and better life with his darling daughter somewhere away from the hell hole of Opaville.

The money just about fitted into his bag with room for a few toiletries and his dirty laundry on top. He zipped it up tight. No one was going to get this baby out of his hands.

He looked round the room. If he never had to see another place like this in his entire life, then it would be too soon.

Outside, he jumped back into the car – the car with no back window and shattered glass all over the rear seat. How was he going to explain this to the rental company? For now, that was the least of his problems.

*

Six hours later and his plane was ready to taxi down the runway. Later tonight he would be in Heathrow and it couldn't come a moment sooner. It had cost him another bundle of dollars to book his ticket, but it was well worth the money. All he wanted to do now was leave this wretched place and get back on home turf. Get back to the ones he loved. The ones who loved him.

The rental company had kept his deposit but it seemed a small price to pay for the damage inflicted on the car. He'd had to fill in a report too but, perhaps unsurprisingly, they didn't seem unduly fazed by the return of a shot-up car. Maybe it was more common here than it was in Hertfordshire.

On the plane, the air steward had insisted in prising the holdall filled with cash out of his fingers and putting it in the overhead locker for take-off. Reluctantly, he'd parted with it. There was no way he wanted it out of his sight for a second. It was his – his and Nell's – and no one was going to take it from them again.

Thankfully, he'd got this far without Benito or Lola Cody chasing him, which had to be a good thing. He'd spent an anxious afternoon in the airport expecting them to come crashing through into the departure lounge at any moment, guns blazing – but they hadn't. Thankfully.

Olly had checked the in-flight entertainment. The films were all high-action thrillers, shoot 'em up stories that were way too strong for the current state of his stomach. He'd opt for the Cartoon Channel instead and, with a restorative brandy, would look forward to nine hours of some of Petal's favourites – *Monsters Inc*, *Finding Nemo* and *Toy Story III*. That should help relax him.

The plane hurtled down the runway and lifted into the air. It swooped away over the sparkling sea, the golden beaches, and the art deco hotels of Miami. None of which he'd seen. Perhaps one day he'd come back here with Nell and Petal for a family holiday. But, then again, perhaps not.

Chapter 85

Jen's phone beeps and she stops doing the Cinderella jigsaw with Petal and glances at the text which has just come in. We're all sitting on the floor of the living room and Petal is already bathed and ready for bed.

'Wow.' Jen looks up, surprised. 'I've got an offer of a date tonight.'

Now I tear my attention away from the cherry blossom tree that I'm puzzling over. 'Good for you.'

The picture is of Cinders and her prince dancing together in an enchanted garden, bluebirds flitting round their heads, his magical, ten-bedroom castle in the background. Just like real life, eh?

'It's only someone who's been coming into the pub for a while.' She shrugs as if it's of no consequence, but I can tell that she's excited. 'No big deal.' Avoiding my eyes, she fiddles with the piece of unfeasibly blue sky in her hand. 'Thing is, I'm not sure I want to leave you.'

To prove that I'm perfectly fine, I give a little laugh. 'You've been fantastic, Jen,' I tell her. 'I don't know how I'd have managed without you. But I'm a big girl. I have to cope on my own some time.'

'I'm a big girl, too,' Petal pipes up.

'You are, and we both think that Auntie Jen should go on her date, right?'

'Yay!' Petal shouts. Then, 'Can I come too?'

'Maybe another time,' Jenny says. She turns to me. 'Are you sure, Nell? I don't have to go.'

'Of course you do,' I insist. 'You should spend your night off doing something more interesting than Disney jigsaws.'

Petal's face says that she can't imagine *anything* more interesting than Disney jigsaws.

'Besides, I can't keep you prisoner here for ever. Much as I'd like to.' The house has run like clockwork since my friend swooped in and took over. It's given me just the break that I needed, but now I ought to step back into my own life and do it myself again. I'm certainly going to miss Jen though. We've never enjoyed so many home-cooked meals – half of them from Jen, the other half from Constance. Mind you, I think I've put more than a few pounds back on because of it. The house will certainly seem quieter without Jen, and Petal adores her. I can see why Olly might have ... well ... let's just leave it at that.

My thoughts wander again to my absent husband – not that he's ever far from them. If he doesn't come back to me, will I find myself going out on date nights with Jen? It doesn't bear thinking about.

Jenny texts her date back to find out when and where

they're to meet. 'I should go home and get myself ready,' she says.

'You've got Cinderella to finish first,' Petal points out.

She kisses my daughter. 'I'll have to do that tomorrow, darling.'

Petal tuts. Now is not the time to point out that one day men will be a lot more important to her than her Cinderella jigsaws. But I hope that it's a day that's a long time coming. Instead, I content myself with, 'It's your bedtime now, little lady. Kiss Jenny good night.'

Without protest, she does, then I kiss Jenny too and she shrugs on her jacket. 'Text me and let me know how you get on.'

'Wish me luck,' she says.

'You don't need it,' I assure her. 'You'll be fabulous.'

As I watch her go, I do hope that Jenny finds herself a nice man. It's clear that all she wants is a home, a family of her own. That's not a lot to ask for, is it?

'Bedtime,' I remind Petal. 'Now.'

My chubby-legged child pads through to my bedroom and climbs onto the bed. 'You could have your own room tonight,' I point out. 'Jenny's staying at her own house tonight.'

'I like your bed,' she says.

I sigh. 'OK.' But to be truthful, it's nicer having Petal here rather than sleeping alone.

She snuggles in under the duvet and demands, 'Story.'

'A *short* one.' I slide in beside her and read from a book called *Fussy Freya*, which we got out of the library last week.

'When is Daddy coming home?' she asks sleepily.

'I don't know, sweet pea.'

'Doesn't he love us any more?'

'He adores you.' See what I did there? That neat deflection? I have no idea if he adores Mummy any more is what I really mean.

'Then I wish he'd come back. I can only have *The Gruffalo* when he's here. Daddy's better at it than you.'

He is. I can't argue with that. He's an excellent father. None better. That's why his continued absence is all the more confusing. As Petal slips her thumb into her mouth and sinks into sleep, I think I might join her myself. The night is young, but I'm not. I give in to a glorious yawn. I could force myself to stay awake and sit on the sofa watching rubbish television by myself, but what's the point? Might as well have an early night.

I'm curled up next to Petal, drifting in and out of sleep, when I hear a key in the front door. Dude barks and bounds out of the bedroom wagging his tail like a loon.

Rousing myself, I glance at the clock. Not yet midnight. I thought Jenny wouldn't be back this evening. Perhaps her date didn't go as planned and she doesn't fancy spending the night alone. Slipping out of bed, I pull on my dressing gown. We can have a cuppa and a data download together about her evening before she goes to bed. Hopefully, that will make her feel better.

In the living room, I flick on the light and then jump out of my skin. It isn't Jenny. It isn't Jenny at all.

At the top of the stairs, there's a man standing there and,

probably because I'm disorientated with sleepiness, it takes me a minute to realise that it's Olly.

'Hi,' he says and the familiarity of his voice makes my heart contract.

He drops the holdall he's carrying on the floor and, seconds later, we're in each other's arms. I hold him tightly, feeling that if I let go for even a moment, he might just disappear again.

'Where have you been?' I ask as I smother him with kisses.

'Miami,' he says as he smothers me back.

That makes me pull away. 'Miami? What on earth have you been doing there?'

Olly sighs. 'It's a long story,' he says.

Chapter 86

Olly whips open the holdall on the floor. He pulls out the dirty shirts and pants and socks, tossing them onto the carpet with abandon. Underneath it all is a whacking great pile of cash.

I gasp out loud. 'Have you robbed a bank?'

'This is straight from Lola Cody's safe.'

More gasping. 'It's *our* money?!'

'All of it,' he says.

Throwing my arms round him, I hug him again. 'You did that? For us?'

'I couldn't let them get away with it, Nell. I couldn't have lived with myself, so I sold the Vespa, bought a ticket with the money, and went to stake out the offices of Home Mall.'

He's *sold* the Vespa. Good grief, I know how much that scooter meant to him. I never thought he'd consider parting with it. Pulling my dressing gown round me, I cuddle up next to him. For the next few days, I think I'm going to be glued to his side – as I'm sure Petal will be too.

'But why didn't you tell me? Why didn't you let me know where you were?'

'Because you would have told me it was a bad idea. You would have wanted me to come straight back.'

He does have a point.

'Say you understand,' Olly urges. 'I needed to do it without any distractions.'

I don't like to tell him that in doing it this way he's driven *me* to distraction. 'I've been out of my mind with worry.'

'Now you don't have to worry any more,' he says.

While we both sit on the floor and stare at the money, Olly fills me in on the details: the dreadful serial killer motel, the long days sitting in the rental car, the dodgy neighbourhood, the scuffle as he tried to leave, the two burly mechanics who came to his aid.

I'm just so filled with emotion that he would think to do this for us and I could also kill him for putting me through the agony of thinking that he'd run off with another woman. But as I look at him I can see the hollows round his eyes, the tiredness there. His clothes are rumpled and he smells like a skunk. It doesn't look like he's been eating properly either. There's a bad cut on his ear and I wonder if the unexpected fight as he left was more difficult than he's letting on.

'We could have done it together, Olly,' I say.

'We couldn't. I had to do this alone. If it had gone wrong . . . ' Suddenly, his voice cracks and his words are thick with emotion. 'If something had happened, I couldn't have lived with myself.'

I wrap my arms round him tightly once more. 'But it

didn't,' I say. 'You've come home safely to me. We're a family again.'

'That's all that matters, isn't it?' Olly strokes.

I nod, uncertain of my own voice. 'I'm so pleased you got the money back,' I whisper. 'Delighted. Thrilled.' I let my fingers trace the contours of his face. 'But all I really wanted back was you.'

His lips find mine and there is nothing that has ever tasted sweeter. If I'm kissing these lips for the rest of my life then I'll die a happy woman.

Olly's body presses against mine and together we lie down on the carpet. He undoes the belt of my dressing gown and I shrug it off so that it becomes a blanket for us.

In my haste to get my husband naked, my fingers fumble with the buttons of his shirt. I give up and help him to tug it over his head. His ribs are black with bruises and I trace the outline of them, wondering how these were caused.

Olly stills my hand with his. 'Explanations later,' he murmurs. He sinks on top of me once again.

The door crashes open.

'Daddy!' Petal cries. 'I thought I heard you.' She launches herself across the room and barrels into him.

He lets out an 'ouff' as she crashes into his ribs. Olly envelops her in a bear hug. 'Have you missed me, Petalmeister?'

'Yes,' she says. 'Mummy isn't a very good daddy. You're much better at it.'

Olly looks over at me and smiles. 'I'm glad to hear it.'

I can see tears filling my husband's eyes as he holds our daughter close.

'You look completely worn out,' I say, squeezing his arm.

'I am,' he admits.

'Then let's go to bed.'

He raises a questioning eyebrow.

'All three of us,' I confirm. There's no way that we'd get Petal back into her own room now that Olly has just returned home.

So, with a wince, Olly picks Petal up and carries her through to our bedroom. We all slide under the duvet. Me on one side. Olly on the other. Petal slap bang in the middle. Dude slinks in and settles at the foot of the bed.

'Now go to sleep, Daddy,' Petal instructs. 'Or you'll be tired in the morning.'

'Night, night. Sleep tight, Petalmeister.' Tenderly, he tucks the duvet around her.

Our daughter knees us both into position until she's comfortable.

He winks at me over her head and mouths, 'I love you.'

Looks as if the passionate reunion will have to be put on hold. I grin to myself. But we will get it.

Chapter 87

I'm panicking, panicking, panicking.

'Calm down,' Olly says. He puts his hands on my shoulders and massages them. 'Everything will be fine.'

I try to breathe so that I don't hyperventilate.

'Have I remembered everything?' I ask.

'It's too late now,' Olly says. 'It's all about to kick off. Are you ready?'

'Just need to slip on my dress.'

'Better get a wiggle on, Mrs McNamara.'

Turning to face him, I give him a long, lingering kiss.

'Hmm,' Olly says. 'What was that for?'

'For making this possible,' I say. 'For rescuing me from the depths of despair.'

'Isn't that the duty of a husband?'

I smile at him. 'Then you execute your duties very well.'

This is my first show. *My first proper show!* I've just taken a quick break from the madness to get myself ready. We've managed to secure a small dressing room backstage, which, frankly, is little more than a cupboard but at least it's away from the main fray.

Three months have gone by since Olly returned from Miami with all of our money, safe and sound. Now we're at the massive Fashion Frenzy design show in the heart of London. With some of the money that Olly got back from Lola Cody, I splashed out and organised a catwalk show to feature my handbags. I have a warehouse full of Nell McNamara bags that arrived from China several weeks ago and this is the start of our big push towards moving them. The handbags came out better than I could even have hoped and I'm just praying that we get enough interest for it to be the first order of many.

I also took some of the money and bought back Olly's cherished scooter without him knowing – which was, miraculously, still in the showroom window of Vroom. Ben sold it back to me for the price he'd given Olly. I think he was just glad to see it returned to its rightful owner. Olly, it goes without saying, was beside himself with joy. I think it's the least I could do after what he did to get our money back.

The rest of the cash, of course, went straight to paying off the bank, to help cut my loan repayments. I tried to give some money back to Phil too, but he wouldn't hear of it. So that's where we stand now. We're still in debt, but not cripplingly so.

What else can I tell you? Oh, we had an order from a high-end French department store for our handbags. They'd seen the scandal about Yves Simoneaux and Marie Monique in the trade magazines and fell in love with the products and decided to give them a trial. It's not a massive order, but it's a start, and I'm thrilled that something good has finally come of that whole episode. Of Yves or Marie, I've heard or seen nothing since. Thank goodness. I'd give her another good whacking if I did. And him. Seems as if they've disappeared off the face of the earth, or at least crawled back into the hole that they came out of. Result!

Also, Olly has managed to secure a couple of regular gigs in pubs in town, three nights a week, playing his beloved music, which will help to ease our cash flow situation as he'll be bringing in some regular money. I wouldn't say that we're exactly solvent, but we can, at least occasionally, veer out of the 'own brand' aisle in the supermarket now. Tod also helped me secure some funding from The Arts Council to go towards the costs, so, whereas to come to this show would normally have cost me an arm and a leg, it's just costing me an arm.

You might have gathered from all my excitement that I've finally found my mojo again. It might have taken a long time, but with Olly safely at home and things firmly back on track between us once more, my confidence gradually returned too.

Following Tod's advice, we've taken on a PR agency and they've managed to get some of the bags to A-list celebrities who we're hoping will be papped while wearing them. The money that we've spent on the agency already seems to be paying dividends. Today alone, I've done a dozen press and television interviews that they fixed up for me. They've also arranged for the editors of some of the biggest fashion magazines to be here in the audience today. One of the big, glossy lifestyle magazines has offered me a double-page spread, featuring me in their 'entrepreneur and mother' feature. *Me!*

This is a brand new collection that we're showing today and I'm just head over heels in love with it and I hope that everyone else will be too. I've gone retro Britpop, mod-inspired in a big way and the handbags are going to feature the Union Jack, the London Underground map, traditional red buses, and the iconic telephone box.

The models will all be sporting sixties-style clothes, plus some original vintage pieces I've sourced from the market at home – our forte, I think – and Olly has dug deep into his record collection to take charge of the music for the event. If it's a success, we're planning to take the concept over to the New York, New Designers show next spring.

Petal's with us and because of the electric atmosphere, she's as hyper as if she'd had two dozen bags of Haribo Starmix, and is racing round the room, bouncing off the walls and the ceiling. I've given her a little role in the catwalk show and I'm hoping that this is a good idea.

'Petalmeister,' Olly says. 'Chill.'

'But I'm too upcited, Daddy!'

'Come and sit on my knee for five minutes to calm down. You need to be ready for your big moment.'

Our daughter sighs her resignation to this plan and clambers onto Olly's knee where he grips her in a bear hug, which does look somewhat like a police-approved restraint hold. I smile to myself. What will we do when she's fifteen?

Then, just as I think I really must get changed, there's a knock on the door and Tod pops his head round it. 'We've all just come to say good luck. Have you got time?'

'Yes, of course.'

For my big day all the chip shop crew are here – the indispensible Jen, Constance and, of course, Phil. I wave them into the cramped space.

Whatever happens in my life, I'll always have time for the most important people in my life. Without them, none of this would have been possible.

'Nell, love,' Phil hugs me. 'It all looks great out there.'

'Good. You lot seem as nervous as kittens.' They're also all done up in their Sunday best.

'Tod's been doing a great job keeping us all well topped up with champagne,' Jen tells me. 'Soon we'll be feeling no pain.'

I laugh. 'Just don't drink so much that you nod off in the show. I want you wide awake and cheering loudly.'

'You can rely on us for that,' Phil assures me.

'Good luck, Nell, love. I've got butterflies for you,' Constance admits. Her hands flutter anxiously to her chest.

'Hey,' I say, catching sight of the big sparkler on her finger. 'What's all this?'

My friend flushes and glances over at Phil. 'We were going to tell you later, after the show.'

'You're engaged?'

'Yes.' They giggle in unison.

'Yesterday,' Phil says. 'We came up to London early and I proposed.'

'You dark horse!'

He grins shyly. 'Let's just say I'd been planning it for a while. We didn't want a fuss though.'

'A fuss you will have,' I warn them. 'You must tell me all

about it.' I throw my arms around Constance and then Phil. 'I'm delighted for you both.'

'Nearly ready?' Tod asks.

I take a steadying breath. 'Just about.' This is turning out to be quite a day.

'One more thing,' Tod says. His grin says that's he's left the best until last. 'I've just had a text from the office.' He pauses to increase the suspense.

'You're killing me,' I tell him. 'Just spit it out.'

'Lola and Benito Cody have been arrested for fraud. Looks like there's going to be a court case. The other businesses that lost their money now have a chance of getting it back and Mr and Mrs Cody could be looking at a custodial sentence.'

I want to slump to the floor with relief. 'Did you hear that, Olly?'

My husband nods his head. 'I did, but I'm not sure that I believe it.'

'Me neither,' Tod says. 'Let's cross our fingers and hope that those guys get what's coming to them.'

Overjoyed, I hug Olly and then I hug Tod. I know that, in the background, Tod has been working away to bring this to fruition. Seems like his hard work may well have paid off.

A woman with a clipboard and headphones puts her head round the door. 'Ten minutes, Ms McNamara.' She disappears again.

'I have to get ready,' I say to Tod. My models will be waiting for me to give the last-minute once-over to their outfits before the show kicks off. 'But I'm going to make damn sure that I have a glass or two of champagne to celebrate that later.'

'We'll leave you in peace,' Tod says, despite the mayhem that's about to break out around us.

'Thanks, Tod.' I touch his arm and I hope that Olly doesn't see the fleeting look that travels between us. We have been through so much together and I have a lot to be grateful to this man for. He was right when he said that there's more between us than just mentor and student. We have a shared respect, a shared affection. Tod is a great bloke, no doubt, but he's not the man for me. I already have one of the best.

'Look after these guys for me,' I tell Tod.

'You don't have to ask.' He kisses my cheek and there's more hugging from Constance, Phil and Jen. 'See you later. Break a leg.'

When they're all gone, I slip my outfit from its hanger. I'm just about to undress, ready to put it on, when there's a tentative knock on the door.

'Shall I get them to see you after the show?' Olly says.

I shrug. 'Depends who it is, I guess.'

Olly opens the door for me and, standing there, is a glamorous woman. She says, 'Could I please have a word with Ms McNamara?'

'Time is tight,' Olly says. 'The show's about to start in a few minutes.'

'I know.' The woman sounds apologetic. 'But I have to leave straight afterwards and I wanted to catch Nell before the hordes descend. I'm an agent,' she says. 'I work for all the big stores – Harvey Nichols, Harrods. I'd like to represent Nell. My name's Sheryl Hallaway.'

'Come in! Come in!' I shout. Sheryl Hallaway is such a big

noise in the fashion world that even I've heard of her. This is someone that I definitely want on board.

The immaculately groomed Sheryl Hallaway squeezes into my cupboard.

'Sorry about the surroundings,' I say.

'Hello,' Petal says. 'You're a pretty lady.'

Sheryl laughs, kneels in front of my daughter, and says, 'So are you, darling. What's your name?'

'Petal.'

'She's adorable.' Sheryl stands up and then to me, 'I'm sorry to barge in on you when you're in a hurry, but I simply had to talk to you.' She holds out a business card for me. 'Call me. I've followed your work in the press and I'd love to be involved in taking it to a whole new level. In fact, I'd like to take you right to the top.'

'Wow.' Sheryl Hallaway wants me. 'I'll call you tomorrow.'

'Good. Enjoy the show, Nell. It'll be the first of many.' She shakes my hand, then Olly's, and leaves.

'Pinch me, Olly,' I say.

He wraps his arms around me. 'You're not dreaming,' he assures me. 'It's just the start of your dreams coming true.'

Chapter 88

The woman with the clipboard appears again. 'Five minutes, Ms McNamara.'

Now I'm really, really panicking. I grab my dress from its hanger. 'Can you give me a hand into it please, Olly?'

'Sure.'

Olly holds it out and I wriggle into it. My outfit is very sixties; a sleeveless, Peter Pan-collared shift dress in block colours – red, white and blue, naturally. I've teamed it with white tights, navy flats and one of my Union Jack handbags. It's a dress I've had for quite a while, but it's one that's perfect for the occasion. A big navy bow and some original, chunky Bakelite bangles complete the outfit.

Petal is, thankfully, already dressed. She's wearing a similar pink shift with a white PVC sixties-style cap covering her crazy hair. I've made her a miniature handbag with the same Union Jack design on the front, but in pink and white. It also has extra sparkles on it as demanded by my darling daughter. Now she's parading up and down in the small space we have, practising the moves that I've shown her.

'My goodness, this is a bit tight.' I only tried this dress on a couple of weeks ago and it fitted perfectly. But whereas it previously skimmed my hips, it now has them in a vice-like grip. What's happened? Now I come to think of it, my boobs feel bigger too, and there's a definite bump where my flat tum used to be.

Oh.

Suddenly the penny drops. Perhaps all the sickness in China wasn't down to the change of water, the food, the jet lag, after all. Perhaps it was more to do with the wild night of passion that Olly and I had in the cottage in Cornwall. I can't even think when I last had a period. With everything else that's been going on, I haven't had time to notice.

I could very well be pregnant. My hands go to my tummy. Yep. Distinctly rounded. This isn't all down to Constance's home-made pies. How far gone must I be? Can it be as much as four months?

'Everything OK?' Olly asks.

'Yes. I think so.' I smile to myself. Now isn't the time to tell him. I'll break it to him when we're alone, just me and Olly. I'm sure he'll be thrilled.

My husband struggles with the zip, but finally I'm in the snug-fitting dress. I try not to let him see my contented smile.

'You look fantastic,' he says.

'Thanks.'

Goodness only knows how we'll fit a new baby into our manic work schedule but we'll manage. Somehow we've coped with everything else that's been thrown at us. I can't see why a little addition to our family would be any different.

The woman with the clipboard comes back one more time. 'One minute, Ms McNamara.'

I take a deep breath. I'm done. I'm as ready as I'll ever be. 'Let's go and see how those models are getting on.'

Backstage is manic. Racks of clothes are ready for the quick changes. I'm relieved to see that the models are all dressed and that no one is squabbling. All the girls are in classic sixties dresses that have been individually made to reflect the handbag collection. They're all wearing sharply cut, bobbed wigs and heavy black eyeliner. I go along the first row of girls and check that their handbags are all in order. Each one is modelling a different Union Jack design. Looking good.

Petal is, for once, speechless. Her mouth and eyes form wide circles as she takes everything in.

Taking a peek out round the side of the black curtains, I can see that every chair in the place is full and I breathe a sigh of relief. Jen, Constance, Phil and Tod have prime seats in the front row. Right next to them are the fashion editors who could make or break my career. Betty is there, sipping from a glass of fizz and she's brought Chantelle Clarke with her whose presence is creating quite a stir. They both have my new Union Jack handbag and I'm hoping that Chantelle's makes the newspapers tomorrow. More than that, I'm pleased that Betty and I are now firm friends again. Needless to say my handbags have pride of place in her shop window.

Alongside Betty are students from the fashion and textiles course at my old college – the one I was at so briefly. I thought it would be nice to encourage some of the youngsters, give them a taste of what it's really like, and sent along a bunch of free tickets. I'd like to say that my old course tutor, Amelia Fallon, was here and that she now bitterly regrets how mean she was to me and she can see now that I was a unique talent and how she feels it was her 'turning down The Beatles' moment. But, unfortunately, she didn't even have the courtesy to reply to my invitation. Seems as if she holds a grudge longer than I do.

Close to my side, Olly slips his arms round my waist and asks, 'Ready, Nell?'

I turn and kiss him. 'Yes,' I say. 'I am.'

Looking at the backstage manager, I give her the thumbs up.

The lights go down. The music starts to pump out. 'The Self-Preservation Society' song from the fabulous film *The Italian Job* fills the auditorium. How appropriate.

My heart pounds as the show begins. The models do me proud. They prance, preen and pout down the catwalk to rapturous applause. The quick changes go perfectly. For the second part of the show, the mellow sounds of 'Waterloo Sunset' by The Kinks wash over the audience and the girls slink on in monochrome outfits, all with white knee-high boots.

For the finale, the girls switch into colourful psychedelic mini dresses and dance to The Rolling Stones and 'She's Like a Rainbow'. When the models have finished, they come to stand at the back of the stage. Even above the clapping, I can hear Phil, Constance and Jenny cheering. Always my staunchest supporters. But I'm also pleased to see that the fashion editors, smiling broadly as they applaud, seem to like it too.

This is my moment. In time-honoured tradition, the designer takes to the runway at the end of the show. The curtains part and I'm facing my audience. As one, they rise from their seats and give me a standing ovation.

'Listen to that, Nell,' Olly says. 'They love you.'

'I never expected this,' I tell him.

He squeezes my waist. 'Nothing more than you deserve.'

'Let's say thank you.' Tears in my eyes, I grab his hand and we walk down the catwalk, revelling in the applause.

Then, as we stand together, the curtains open again and one of my favourite songs, The Monkees and 'Daydream Believer' kicks out. This should be my theme tune. Olly couldn't have chosen better songs for us. The crowd cheer their approval as Petal, all kitted out in her sixties dress, wearing her miniature handbag at a jaunty angle, struts down the catwalk towards us.

My daughter, hamming it up terribly, milks the moment for all it's worth. With her short chubby legs, she mimics the models' walks and then strikes a pose at the end of the runway. More cheering. She's positively glowing. Olly and I exchange a glance and laugh. Our child is definitely a diva.

Hand in hand, Olly and I join her. Judging by the response of the audience, Nell McNamara handbags are now firmly on the map. Believing in my daydreams has taken me down a rocky road. There have been incredible highs and terrible lows. But together, Petal, Olly and I have got through them.

Despite all the tears, the trauma, the pain, I now know that I wouldn't have missed this crazy ride for anything. I look at my friends in the audience, my family beside me, and I know that it's all been worth it.

Acknowledgements

A big thanks to Helen and Julian who allowed me a little glimpse into their world so that I could write this book. Much appreciated!

What happens next?

Will Phil and Constance be together for ever?
Is Jenny going to find the man of her dreams?
Can everyone get their happy-ever-after?

Find out for FREE in an
EXCLUSIVE short story from Carole!

Simply visit www.carolematthews.com,
sign up to her newsletter and you'll receive details
on how to claim your FREE story via email.

Carole Matthews

In conversation with Carole Matthews and Helen Rochfort

Carole: People always ask me where I find inspiration for my books. Well, this one started a few years ago when we met on Facebook. Remember?

Helen: Oh, my goodness. I do remember that.

C: Your status photo was of Barbara Cartland in all her shocking pink glory and I felt sure that you must be a romance writer. But when I looked at your page I then saw that, in fact, you were a designer of delicious handbags and sent you a note to say how much I liked them.

H: I went straight out and bought one of your books. It was *With or Without You* and I was instantly hooked on your novels. We started chatting regularly on Facebook from there, didn't we? Then I designed some exclusive handbags as promotional prizes for *The Chocolate Lovers' Club* and we became friends in real life not just on the internet.

C: The bags were gorgeous! Mine still gets an airing when I'm going somewhere glam. But it was only after I'd known you for a while that I found out how you started on your career. Lady, you have such a tale to tell!

H: I love our long, chatty lunches. We can both talk for England.

C: Once we'd dispensed with our usual gossiping, you started to tell me how hard you'd worked to get to where you are now. I thought that it was just such an amazing story that I felt it would make a fabulous backdrop to a novel – plus I just love handbags so that was a great excuse too. In five years you've started out from nothing with your business and now have your handbags in stores worldwide.

H: Oh, yes. It's been an amazing journey. I still have to pinch myself when I'm at the Paris and London Fashion shows or see well-known celebrities with the handbags splashed across the pages of fashion magazines. I then go home and go back to being a mum. Like anyone else, I enjoy all the glamour of washing, changing nappies, doing the school run and drawing imaginary monsters, reading *The Enchanted Wood* and dancing to The Who with the girls. I wouldn't change that for anything though.

C: I love the way that you've strived to grow and manage your business while bringing up two adorable daughters. It's so hard. I don't know how you do it. That was my initial inspiration for Nell in the book. There's definitely a lot of you in Nell and I think she's a great character. She's warm, funny and always tries her best for her family. I think it's very tough for women to make their way in business – especially in something like the fashion industry. It's a juggling act and can involve so much guilt. You have to wear so many hats. I think you do a fantastic job. In *Summer Daydreams* I've made Nell a strong and determined woman, who is really fighting against the odds to make her dreams become a reality. She goes all out to get what she wants, which is essentially a better life for her and her family.

H: I really like the fact that you deal with issues that are affecting contemporary women in your novels, but you do it in such a funny, light-hearted way. I often find myself laughing out loud one minute and then crying the next.

C: I always like it when people write to me and say that they've been through what I've written about. I try to use real life situations as much as I can. I think a lot of modern women will empathise with Nell.

H: The other characters in *Summer Daydreams* are so warm and friendly. How do you create those?

C: I wanted people who would help Nell on her journey. If you want to be successful at anything, then it's very difficult to do it in isolation. Everyone needs people around them who encourage them to be better. I also think it's essential to have a strong network of friends when you're trying to bring up young children and, for various reasons, Nell and Olly's parents aren't around to help. That's tough. Her friends in the chip shop – Phil, Constance and Jen – really rally round for Nell. They adore her and want the best for her. Tod Urban really tries to help her with her business and sometimes crosses the line into something else!

H: Petal made me laugh out loud. I could just imagine my own daughter doing those things.

C: With Nell's daughter, Petal, I could have a lot of fun with her. She's such a little madam and provides a lot of the funny moments in the book. I like children with a bit of spark to them. She doesn't let Nell or Olly get away with anything and can wrap them both round her little finger. I think a lot of parents will identify with that too!

H: Olly is a lovely romantic hero too. He reminds me very much of my husband, Julian!

C: Ha, ha. I'm sure he'd be happy to hear that. I like my heroes to be 'real' men. The sort of person that you'd bump into in the street or meet at work. I'm not one for these big, alpha male types who are arrogant or treat their women with disdain. I like my heroes to be very down-to-earth, sometimes flawed but always well-intentioned.

H: But you like your bad boys too! What about Yves Simoneux?

C: Ah, I think most women have been secretly attracted to the bad boy at some time in their life! And Nell does have her moments with this man, as you know. Women in business always have to deal with a total sleazebag at some point! I think it's compulsory that every company has one. I hope that dealing with Yves makes Nell realise that Olly is a really great bloke.

H: The bizarre thing is that I actually met someone rather *too* like Mr Simoneux when I was away on business recently. So that did make me smile.

C: Sometimes fact is very much stranger than fiction!

H: I absolutely adored *Summer Daydreams*. It's a great book, Carole. You're such a talented writer. Every book I read just gets better. There's such a lovely, hopeful feel to this one. It left me on a real high and I didn't want it to end. Everyone deserves to find their dream and I'm happy that Nell was able to chase hers. I was so glad that I could help with the story and be such an inspiration. I'm flattered.

A Beginner's Guide to Designing a Handbag
by Helen Rochfort

How to get your Design Inspiration

I have always believed in going with your instinct, what you love, what you feel inspired by, what excites you, digging deep to evoke all senses.

Initial ideas can come from absolutely anywhere: film, art, nature, music, different eras, a piece of vintage fabric, a sweet shop, a vintage boutique, even a scent or taste of your favourite chocolate or cupcake.

Carrying a little notebook or sketchbook in your handbag is a great idea. If you see something you love when you are out and about you can simply jot it down or do a quick sketch. I find using my camera on my mobile phone is extremely useful. If I see anything that's inspiring, a quick snap and it's captured! Images I often take when I am out and about (often with my daughters in tow) include carousels, ice cream vans, jars of sweets, candyfloss stalls, vintage toys and ornaments. Anything that catches my eye.

I will often watch old films to evoke ideas, a great source of inspiration. My favourite films being *Willy Wonka and the Chocolate Factory* – sorry, Johnny Depp but the 1970s version is my favourite! – *Mary Poppins* and *The Wizard of Oz*. Old classic books and fairytales including *Alice in Wonderland*, *Little Red Riding Hood* and *Cinderella* are also great.

Sometimes just walking around your local town and getting some fresh air is a good way to evoke those creative sparks and juices. Look at the window displays in your local deli, cake shop or boutique. In my home town of Hitchin the fantastic deli and tearooms Halsey's has beautiful cupcakes and meringues in the window, independent boutique Rubarb has fabulous dresses and vintage shop Jolly Brown has an eclectic mix of everything vintage.

Visiting art galleries and museums is another amazing source for inspiration. I love wandering around with the family then going for tea and cake at the café, then onto the gift shop to stock up on more postcards, anything from Pop Art to pre-Raphaelite.

Your Handbag Design

When you feel you have enough ideas, make yourself a cup of tea and grab a couple of chocolate biscuits, then you can begin to look through everything you have been collecting.

Making an inspiration board is helpful and lots of fun. Add images from magazines, sparkling buttons, ribbons, textured and patterned fabric pieces, sweet wrappers, feathers and even poems. Using a large cork board is a great idea as you can add and take off any bits and pieces very easily, and when you have finished with that particular design you can reuse it for your next fabulous creation.

I find it useful to just take your time and digest all of the images and notes until your ideas start to flow. There is no right or wrong way to do this so just sketch what you think feels good – try different shapes, patterns and textures. Ask the questions: who is the handbag intended for? Is it just for you so that you'll have a handbag that's totally unique or are you making it for someone else? If it's for another person what age group is the design intended for? What type of woman? Fashionista, urban, street, vintage, chic, classic, quirky or a mixture? What time of year is the handbag going to be used – is this a fresh spring/summer design, a sumptuous autumn/winter handbag or an all-year-round design? What type of handbag is it going to be – an evening bag, a shopper, a tote, a clutch?

When I am creating new designs, ideas and concepts, I often ask my friends, husband and sometimes even my eldest daughter on what they think (my youngest daughter is only one, so her feedback is wiping jammy fingers all over the designs!). Feedback is important as it gives you other perspectives and sometimes a better development of an idea.

Creating your design into a sample 'real life handbag' is another design process in itself, as ideas on paper may or may not translate or work on an actual working handbag. I am fortunate that we have a fantastic team in the sample rooms at the factory, where they translate my designs, sketches, ideas and working scaled drawings into the handbags that have been whirring around in my head. To create your 'real life' handbag from your sketches, www.josyrose.com is very good for fabrics, buttons, ribbons, handles, clasps, diamantes, motifs and zips. Everything you need to create your very own hand-bag masterpiece!

Whatever you do, just have fun and enjoy it. Happy creating! To see my own handbag designs pop along to www.helen rochfort.com and take a peek.

Helen Rochfort
xxxxx

If you enjoyed *Summer Daydreams*,
you only have to wait until October 2012
for Carole's next bestseller,

With Love at Christmas

Meet Juliet, Rick and their family
as they get ready for a heartwarming Christmas

EXCLUSIVE!
Read on to enjoy the first three chapters!

Chapter One

You can tell that Christmas is just around the corner. Slade's 'Merry Christmas Everybody' is belting out of the speakers filling the busy supermarket aisles with festive cheer. That's a pension fund song if ever there was one and it never fails to get me humming along. I ask you, what would Christmas be without the dulcet tones of Noddy Holder?

I love this time of year. Even something as mundane as the weekly food shop is transformed into a magical experience. I'm at the bread counter in Tesco, squeezing the loaves to check their freshness. Cheery Santas hang above my head. Silver tinsel and colour coordinated balls spiral down from the ceiling. I wish it could look this jolly all year round. Someone at head office has put a lot of effort into planning this. Perhaps I could borrow their theme and refresh my decorations this year. My husband, Rick, would have a fit. He's considerably more 'bah humbug' than I am when it comes to Christmas – the original Scrooge. Every year the expense of it all nearly gives him a heart attack. Every year I vow to cut back. And every year, I don't. Maybe, for the sake of marital harmony, I'd better just get out the 'old faithfuls' one more time.

I'm happy to say for the record that I'm the complete opposite of my husband. My name is Juliet Joyce. I'm a forty-five-year-old woman with one gorgeous grandchild, two troublesome, supposedly grown-up children, an annoying mother, a gay father, a very grumbly husband and a rather stinky dog. I am also a shameless Christmas addict. And I'm not the slightest bit interested in a twelve-step plan to cure me of it.

Slade slides seamlessly into Wizzard and 'I Wish It Could Be Christmas Everyday'. I heartily agree with that. We all need a bit of escapism from the daily grind of life, don't we? Jesus picked a lovely time of year to be born into the world as it really cheers up the long winter months. It just wouldn't be the same if he'd been born in, say, July.

Skipping down the seasonal produce aisle, I slip a Christmas pudding into my trolley, rapidly followed by some mince pies and a panettone, which has somehow become a festive must-have. None of the family are that keen on it really but, like brussel sprouts, Christmas just isn't Christmas without it. I put in an extra box of mince pies – just in case. You can never have too many mince pies, can you? I don't like to be caught out without some nibbles in case people drop in. I'd better get some dates and assorted nuts too.

I'd like to tell you that I make my own pudding, Christmas cake and all that – but I don't. I'm working full-time now in the office of a busy estate agents and with that and the demands of my family, I hardly get time to breathe let alone anything else. I aspire to be able to produce a completely homemade Christmas, but every year it seems to slip further beyond my reach. I love the thought of creating a decadent Nigella-style celebration with a bit of Kirsty Allsop thrown in for good measure but, at this rate, that will have to wait – possibly until I retire. Even for a modest Tesco-based affair, like my own, you have to start early. That's the key. I was very organised and bought my Christmas cards in the January sales. What's the point in paying full price when you don' t have to? I picked up a couple of great presents at craft fairs in the summer. It's nice to find the perfect present, isn't it? And, of course, you never do when you're looking hard. Like middle age, perfect presents just sneak up on you. The festive napkins were safely secured in August, as were the crackers for the table. The only thing I have to do now is find the 'safe place' where I can put them all. It will mean a trip into the loft for Rick, which he'll be cross about.

Since the first week of September I've been putting a few seasonal bits of food in the back of the cupboard but now, at the beginning of December, the Christmas food shopping must start in earnest. I've got a few things in here for Dad and his partner, Samuel, too just to help out as I know how busy they are. Queuing at the checkout, I close my eyes and listen to the sounds of 'Do They Know It's Christmas?'. In front of me a harassed-looking woman is berating her child who's whining for sweets.

'I've no money for naffing sweets, Beyoncé,' she shrieks as she shakes her little girl by the arm more roughly than is right. 'If you don't start bloody behaving right now, Santa won't come to visit. He'll throw your Wii out of the sleigh and it will break into a million pieces. Then what will you do?'

The child screams. I think I would too. I should step in and remind them both about the true message of Christmas but, before I can, she's through the till and out, dragging the sweet-less and still screaming Beyoncé behind her.

Would they both think I was mad if I'd have told them that at Beyoncé's age I was given one of my dad's old knitted socks – washed, I hope – filled with an orange and some nuts? That was it. Sum and total of festive present exchange. I couldn't eat the nuts because mum could never find the ancient pair of nutcrackers needed to go with them and the orange went straight back into the fruit bowl where it had come from. I couldn't ever buy presents myself because I was never given pocket money. But I was given some paper, glitter and some glue with which to make Christmas cards. Times were differ-ent then. We had so little. Our family Christmases were always cheerless, meagre affairs. We never had visitors to call. My mother put the moth-eaten tree up for a short a period as pos-sible. Sometimes it didn't appear until Christmas Eve, late in the afternoon when I was almost beside myself with longing, and then with much sighing. It was usually gone again shortly after Boxing Day. My dad used to do his best to liven it up. He'd laugh too heartily at the Christmas shows – *Morecambe and Wise* being his favourite. Tears would roll down his cheeks and I used to find that funnier than the programme. But Mum was never a Christmas person. To her, it was absolute torture every year and, consequently, we all had to suffer. Perhaps that's why I like to make Christmas so special now. I like my home filled with laughter and love, overflowing with presents and food. If you can't go completely over-the-top at Christmas when can you?

'One hundred and forty-seven pounds and thirty-two pence,' the checkout girl says when she's rung through my shopping. Even I wince as I hand over the money. It's going to be yet another bill that I hide from Rick.

Outside the sky is white and heavy. A few flakes of snow are starting to fall, drifting, drifting down into the car park. The first this year. I smile inside. I love snow. Though I realise that I'm in the minority as everyone else grumbles about how difficult it is to get around. And, it's fair to say that the country does usually grind to a halt once there's anything more than a sprinkling on the ground. Me, I'd be happy to be trapped indoors and let it cascade down until it was three feet deep. Holding out my hands, I let the flakes settle. They're delicate, lacy and land on my upturned palms like filigree butterflies before instantly melting away. I shake it from my short, brown bob and think that I need to remember to wear my hat. It would be lovely if we had a white Christmas this year. A bit of snow makes everything look so much better, so much more festive.

Someone honks their car horn in a bad-tempered manner. I glance up from the joy of snow on my hands. The car park is heaving now and it looks like there's a dispute over a parking space. One driver winds down his window. Christmas carols blare out. '*Peace on earth, goodwill to all men*'.

'Oi, arsehole,' he shouts at the other man. 'I was here first.'

The other driver who has a sticker stating that 'Santa does it with reindeers' in his back window, clearly doesn't agree with his opinion and shouts back. 'Fuck off. This space is mine.'

I push my heavily laden trolley, which wants to go in the other direction, towards my trusty little Corsa. Heaving out the bags, I load them into the boot.

Both drivers jump out of their cars and shake their fists at each other. One has an aerial with a star and some tinsel on it. The other driver snaps it off and stamps it into the sprinkling of snow.

I sigh to myself. Not everyone, it seems, enjoys Christmas as much as me.

Chapter Two

I pull into the drive of number ten Chadwick Close and kill the engine. What I need now is a restorative cup of tea and perhaps my first mince pie of the season. They're possibly my most favourite festive food. I know that the shops start selling them in earnest in July now but I like to put off the moment for as long as humanly possible so that I can really savour it. This year I have excelled myself in holding out for so long. I hope it also means that I won't have to spend as long on a diet after Christmas as I usually do.

My family and I live in a lovely part of Stony Stratford, a pretty market town in the heart of Buckinghamshire, a stone's throw away from the ever-encroaching city of Milton Keynes. We've been here for years and have brought up our two children in this solid 1970s home. I suspect this is where we'll see out our days.

Rick is up the ladder, busy draping the front of the house with Christmas lights. That's good. I like to have them up nice and early to make the most of them. The one area where all my husband's abhorrence of Christmas disappears is when it comes to decorating the house with lights. It's a job that he relishes. Every year Rick likes to adorn the place until it looks like Santa's grotto. It's the one trip of the year that he doesn't mind taking up to the loft. He disappears in there for hours, searching and sorting, and then he lifts down the lights gently like treasured children.

We currently have LED icicles dangling down from the rafters with changing patterns. We have a string of coloured bulbs across the garage that flash on and off at regular intervals. The front of the house has a sleigh and reindeer in white above the porch. The big cherry blossom in the front garden has its own string of lanterns. On the lawn we have a wire reindeer covered in tiny lights. The rest of our neighbours don't bother much at all. Though number two do, on alternate years, throw a sparkling net of lights over their cotoneaster bush. We're the one and only house in the close that attempts to create a Christmassy spectacle. I don't quite know when or why this started, but I'm glad that Rick enters into the spirit at least in this one small area.

I climb out of the car. Rick comes down the ladder. My husband is one of those men who's grown more attractive as he's aged, I think. At least he has to me and I guess that's all that matters. His long, lean frame is all knees and elbows – always has been. We seem to have so little quality time together now and, somehow, it seems even harder to find time for ourselves once the Christmas frenzy is upon us. Every year I vow that it will be different and every year it isn't. I smile as he comes towards me, but he seems to be in a hurry and somewhat red in the face.

'Have you seen that?' he rages without preamble. A finger shoots out and points in an accusatory fashion at the house opposite.

Chadwick Close is a very staid neighbourhood, quiet. There's never any excitement to be had. That's why we like it here. Any scandal that there has been in the past has mostly emanated from the Joyce household anyway.

'Look,' he reiterates.

So I look.

Across the close, directly opposite our house is the sight that's offending him so much. Our good friend, Stacey Lovejoy, used to live at number five but last summer she moved out. Now she's in Gran Canaria living the high-life with Rick's old boss, Hal, and they're both having a lovely time according to the intermittent email updates she sends. The new people weren't here last Christmas, so Rick would hardly have expected to see this.

Our new neighbours, it seems, also like Christmas lights on their house. There's no one in sight, but it's clear that, like Rick, Neil Harrison has been very busy this morning. They have a display that far outshines ours.

'How nice,' I say. 'It's lovely.'

'*Lovely?*' Rick has gone quite purple in the face now.

'What's the matter?'

'*We're* the house that has lights up,' he points out.

I shrug. 'Now we're *one* of the houses that has lights up. I think it's looks pretty.'

'Typical female response,' he snorts. Rick runs a hand through his hair mussing it into his customary Stan Laurel hairdo. He's never been able to tame his hair and now it's sticking out all over the place. I know that's the fashion for seventeen-year-old boys, but in a gentleman of a certain age it just looks like mad hair.

'I don't think you should view it as a challenge to your supremacy.' Clearly Rick thinks that this is Neil banging his chest and roaring in his face. 'Maybe Neil just likes Christmas lights.'

Further snorting from Rick. 'I'll have to get some more,' he mutters. 'I want ours to be the *best* house.' He casts an envious glance at the giant-sized blow-up Santa complete with his own chimney that's fixed to Neil's roof.

'Ours look great, Rick. Especially with a little bit of snow on them. Very festive. Already I feel quite in the Christmas mood.'

My husband tuts. I'm disappointed that all this pointless willy-waving has soured his mood.

'Come on,' I say. 'Help me in with the shopping and I'll make you a cuppa and you can have a mince pie with it.'

With an exaggerated sigh, Rick puts down his screwdriver. I flick open the boot.

'Good God, woman!' He recoils in horror. 'What the hell have you got in here? It's not the feeding of the five thousand, you know.'

'It's Christmas,' I say. 'We have to have a little bit extra in. Just in case.'

'Just in case what?' Rick looks perplexed. 'You've got enough for the Joyce clan to survive a nuclear holocaust. The shops barely shut for ten minutes these days. We can always run out and get a loaf if we're stuck.'

'Oh, Rick,' I chide. 'You know that you always enjoy it.'

'You know that I always want to go away to the Bahamas, just the two of us, and ignore the whole bloody thing.' He heaves two carrier bags out of the boot, making a big show of how heavy they are. 'Instead we'll stay at home, suffer your mother, the Queen's speech and eat too much and drink nowhere near enough to ease the pain.'

'It's not that bad.'

Again he casts a dark glance at our neighbour's festive display. 'Putting up the lights was the only pleasure I had,' he complains. 'Now even that's been taken away from me.'

'You could go down to Homebase and buy a few more bits if you want to,' I suggest. 'They've got some very pretty things in.'

Rick rubs his chin. 'I need something with more impact,' he says under his breath. 'Much more impact.'

With that, he brightens up considerably.

Chapter Three

My mother, Rita Britten, is sitting in the kitchen when Rick and I struggle in with the shopping. She's wearing a cardigan that's buttoned up all wrong, and it doesn't look as if she's combed her hair since getting up.

'Get the kettle on, Rita, love,' Ricks says.

She looks at him, perplexed. 'Why would I want to do that?'

'We'll all have a cup of tea, Mum.'

'Oh.'

'Here, you're done up all higgledy-piggledy.' I go to her and she tries to stare me down while I rebutton her cardigan.

'You do *fuss*, Juliet.'

'That's better.' I resist the urge to untangle her hair.

Rick rolls his eyes at me and I shrug back. My mum's not herself. I blame her trip to Australia. She's never been quite the same since. When she turned seventy, she dumped my true and faithful father, who had stood by her stoically despite her being a fairly miserable and demanding wife. She moved in with me and Rick, uninvited. My husband was not impressed, but what could I do? She had to live somewhere and no matter how we tried to cajole her, she wouldn't go home to Dad. Then, to make matters worse, she took up with a pensioner toy boy, Arnold. We had to endure weeks of them 'doing it' in our back bedroom, which our daughter had been required to vacate to accommodate her. It was horrendous. The only way I could get any sleep was to clamp a pillow over my head. They'd only been together for five minutes when she and Arnold decided that they wanted to see the world. At the age of seventy, I ask you. Before you could say hip replacement they went out, booked two tickets to Australia, rented a camper van and set off touring in the outback.

I was beside myself. She'd never even been abroad before; now she was going to Australia for the foreseeable future with a man she barely knew. I thought it was children who were supposed to give their parents problems! Isn't that the way it happens? Rick was delighted, as he thought we'd seen the back of her for good. He was sure that in Australia, being the continent with the most venomous and lethal animals, she'd come to some great harm. No such luck. He hadn't reckoned on my mother's tenacity. After six months she was back, bronzed and broke, and poor Arnold had disappeared into the wilderness never to be seen again. I am distraught that Arnold, an elderly and rather pleasant gentleman, is missing in a strange land. My mother, however, doesn't seem too bothered by this turn of events. Rick thinks that the hapless Arnold most likely threw himself to a pack of wild dingos in an attempt to get away from my mother. He has a point. After spending six months in a glorified caravan with her, I'm sure anyone would feel the same.

Rick is rooting through the carrier bags. 'Panettone?' he says. 'What is it?'

'It's like a cake or bread. A bit of both. You've had it before.'

'Really? I don't remember.'

'We all like it,' I assure him.

'I don't,' my mum adds helpfully.

'Dad does.'

'Your father has gone all foreign,' she counters.

Which, I have to say, is partly true. Frank Britten was, until my mother abandoned him, the most unadventurous man on the planet. His comfort zone was never more than a foot away from his armchair. My dad, a man who, until he was seventy-two, thought that anything other than a half of bitter was for 'nancy boys', decided he'd been gay all along. Then he met Samuel, a charming bookseller who is younger than both myself and Rick, who has made his life infinitely more colourful. No one was more surprised than me when they moved in together. Well, except perhaps for my mother. I'm still not sure that she fully grasps the nature of their relationship. Anyway, now that Dad is a fully paid-up and enthusiastic member of the 'nancy boys' club, thanks to Samuel, his tastes have become distinctly more adventurous – and not just in 'that' department. He loves foreign food, foreign travel, enjoys good wine, speaks a smattering of several languages, plays chess, knocks up meals from Jamie Oliver and Nigel Slater cookbooks and is generally very lovely to be around. It's taken him a long time to discover domestic bliss, but I'm so pleased that he has.

'Your dad phoned to say that he's coming round later with Samuel,' Rick says.

'Oh, that's nice. There are some bits for them in one of the other carrier bags. They can take them home with them.'

'I thought they were coming here for Christmas?'

'They are.'

'So why are you buying them Christmas food?'

'Christmas isn't just one day, Rick.'

'No,' he mutters. 'It's from bloody August onwards.' He stamps out to get the other bags.

'Are we having a cup of tea, or what?' Mum asks.

I sigh to myself. Now Mum is back for good, she is currently ensconced in Chloe's bedroom once again, much to the consternation of my daughter. Chloe had moved out when she accidentally fell pregnant with her first child and was renting a flat in the town with her partner, Mitch – the father of baby Jaden and a man she barely knew. Not surprisingly, they've now split up and she's also back at home with Jaden in tow. But I can hardly wag my finger at her as, all those years ago, Rick and I tied the knot rather hastily when I fell pregnant with Chloe.

Chloe won't ever really say what went wrong in their relationship. I guess it comes from having a baby with someone whose favourite drink, film and holiday destination are a total mystery to you. The pressure on them both was enormous. Right from the start she was coming home every two weeks over some row or other. Rick said we should have turned her round and sent her straight back to deal with it, but I couldn't. That's what my mother would have done to me, and I couldn't watch Chloe suffer. I know she found it hard that Mitch was working long hours and, instead of being out partying, she was sitting at home every night with a baby. Then last month, with no justifiable explanation, she flounced home, supposedly for good. Mitch appeared on the doorstep every night for two weeks begging her to go back to him, but she wouldn't listen.

She's just had difficulty adjusting to being a responsible adult with a young child to care for. The fact that responsibility has been thrust on her rather than it being of her choosing must have something to do with it too, a case of too much too soon. Chloe has always been selfish, and still tends to think only of what she wants. Mitch, on the other hand, seems saintly. I know it's different when you live with someone – you see all their little foibles in sharp relief. But I don't know what else she could want in a man. Yet only Chloe can decide that. I can only be here for her, help her and hope that one day she'll realise what she might lose and she'll grow up, and sooner rather than later.